CUT AND SHUT

CUT AND SHUT

JONATHAN PEACE

This edition produced in Great Britain in 2023

by Hobeck Books Limited, Unit 14, Sugnall Business Centre, Sugnall, Stafford, Staffordshire, ST21 6NF

www.hobeck.net

A CIP catalogue for this book is available from the British Library.

ISBN 978-1-915-817-02-0 (pbk)

ISBN 978-1-915-817-01-3 (ebook)

Cover design by Jayne Mapp Design

Printed and bound in Great Britain

ARE YOU A THRILLER SEEKER?

Hobeck Books is an independent publisher of crime, thrillers and suspense fiction and we have one aim – to bring you the books you want to read.

For more details about our books, our authors and our plans, plus the chance to download free novellas, sign up for our newsletter at **www.hobeck.net**.

You can also find us on Twitter **@hobeckbooks** or on Facebook **www.facebook.com/hobeckbooks10**.

PRAISE FOR JONATHAN PEACE

DIRTY LITTLE SECRET

'A masterfully told thriller which mines the darkest corners of the 1980s as an experimental police unit race to save a young life from a sadistic killer.' *Graham Bartlett*

'My goodness what a novel!! This story was absolutely full of suspense, mystery, strong female characters, misogynistic males in roles of power and thrills. Honestly I devoured it as quickly as I could, I couldn't put it down!' *Bex Books and Stuff*

'This was well written, pacey, the plot was solid and the ending left you quite stunned and ready for more.' *Hanny May Reviews*

'Jonathan Peace did a fantastic job of expertly weaving story lines like spider's webs, interweaving them until you were so wrapped up, you forgot all notion of time.' *Books With Gina*

'Altogether an addictive and immersive read.' *Sharon Beyond The Books*

'There is a tautness to the storytelling, especially until the climax block, that keeps us hooked.' *Surjit Book Blog*

FROM SORROW'S HOLD

'Easy five stars for me.' *Donna Morfett*

'One to look out for.' *Pete Fleming*

'Although I enjoyed the first book, I enjoyed this one more ... An enthralling read throughout.' *ThrillerMan*

'I would like to applaud Peace for handling the delicate issue of teen suicide, anxiety and depression. I think he handled it very well.' *Monika Armet*

'Compelling read from a writer who knows his trade and boldly handles the subject matter.' *Avid Reader*

CUT AND SHUT

'Take a bow, Jonathan, you have created another brilliant book ... an amazing thriller, full of suspense and mystery that will blow your mind.' Surjit Parekh

'Cracking read ... definitely one to be adding to your reading list.' Peter Fleming

'Thoroughly enjoyed this book.' Sarah Leck

'Another excellent book by Jonathan Peace.' Carole Gourlay

'A humdinger of a book!' Sarah Blackburn

To those who leave reviews, authors the world over love ya!

JUNE, 1989

Women are the twin halves of men.
The Prophet of Islam

PROLOGUE

SATURDAY, 24TH

She could hear him mumbling to himself somewhere in the darkness.

His words were lost within the ringing that pulsed in her ears; the place he had struck her throbbed painfully, and when she focused on it, the pain only intensified. Thoughts rolled around in her head, jumbled together. The rally, people pushing close. Shouting, and then strong hands grabbing her. Something hard hitting her head. Blackness that closed all around her. The screams and the shouts drifting away as she floated in the darkness.

Something crashed, a metallic clash that echoed through her head with the stabbing pulse of hot needles.

He cried out, the words a low murmur of angry whispers.

She could feel four hot lines on her face where she had been slapped into silence when she had been taken.

The fog in her head lifted slightly and her stomach rolled. If she hadn't been bound to the table with thick straps of leather she would have turned to the side to vomit. Four of them; two across her legs, another two across her chest. Each one was secured in the centre with a silver buckle, it too secured with a small gold padlock, the kind she used on her locker back at the office. Not that that had stopped them from getting inside. Leaving her 'jokey' messages and gifts.

She thought about calling out, but knew it would only signal that she was awake once more. If she had any chance of getting away, it would be now, when he was preoccupied.

Her wrists wiggled just enough that she could move her hand fractionally. The straps covered her forearms, the sleeves of her jacket bunched up beneath the elbow to reveal the soft skin of her arms. Several long cuts ran across in jagged streams, the blood already hardened into a crisp shell, the result of the scuffle in the marketplace.

It was starting to come back as the fog lifted; the BNP protest in Dewsbury town centre that she'd attended. The lines of police with their batons and their shields. The cries for white justice. And then it all went to shit and everyone was being pushed back. The call came and they all fled back towards Savile Town.

The fog fell again, drifting across her mind to the pulsing beat of her headache. Still, she fought on, fought to stay awake for fear that if she closed her eyes, she would never open them again.

She could move her arms from side to side. Maybe only a couple of inches, but it was enough to give her hope. If she moved enough times, perhaps she could loosen the straps and slip her arms out one strap at a time.

She tried to look down and then realised she couldn't move her head further than a slight nod. Another strap crossed her forehead, her hair pulled back tightly beneath her head like a purple pillow.

Another crash came from the darkness, followed by the heavy tread of footsteps on a metal floor. Two sets of them, judging by the delayed echo, she thought.

So, there were definitely two people. Not one.

'You've not given us much time,' a voice said with a Yorkshire accent so thick it was almost clichéd. 'Going to have to work fast.'

She flinched as a sudden bright light exploded all around her. She closed her eyes under the harsh glare.

'She's awake.'

Rough hands grabbed her face, pinching her cheeks tight. A foetid breath of air washed over her and she retched as the scent filled her nostrils. Heat spread across her face as the slap rocked her head. The leather strap around her forehead caught and she jerked still.

'Open your eyes!' The voice roared directly above her and she couldn't help but follow the command. She winced as she found herself looking into her own face as a rounded mirror was wheeled into place beside her, its oval casing hovering a few feet above her. She gasped when she saw the swelling of her left eye and the blood that still ran from the split lower lip.

A shadow moved beside her, and she could hear the metal squeal of rusty wheels as a tall tray was manoeuvred into place. It was the kind of tool tray that belonged in a garage, except instead of wrenches and spanners, she could see wicked-looking knives with curved blades and jagged teeth. A set of pliers, the grips dark with old blood, lay beside a compact saw.

'Oh, Jesus,' she said, when the realisation of where she was and what was about to happen sank in. 'Jesus fucking Christ, no.'

She started to thrash on the table, urgent need overwhelming conscious thought. She heaved against her bonds, pushed them as far forward as she could.

Another form appeared to her side and a small hand pressed against her shoulder. She couldn't make out a face but she could hear a voice; soft and cowed, it trembled as the person spoke.

'Lie back,' it said.

'Grab her shoulders,' the older voice ordered.

A gloved hand reached to the tray and took up a thin scalpel. The tip had been broken off at some point leaving a craggy disjointed edge. It caught the light from the mirror overhead, the sparkle reflecting in her fear-filled eyes.

Another gloved hand came down and pushed her skirt up, exposing her legs.

'Nice,' the voice whispered. 'Very nice.' She could hear the pleasure in his words. Even worse, she could feel his excitement as he pressed his groin against her trapped arm.

Two more hands came from overhead and pushed her shoulders down, holding her tight. She tried to look at this new person but all she could see was a silhouetted shape against the darkness.

'It's better if you don't struggle too much.'

'You don't have to do this,' she said, knowing it was useless but trying anyway.

'Yes I do,' he said, pressing the blade against the exposed skin at the top of her thigh.

When the blade bit into her flesh, she cried out in pain.

When he started to cut, she screamed.

SIX DAYS EARLIER

CHAPTER ONE

SUNDAY, 18TH

'It'll be fun.'

That's what Steve had said, and in the warm embrace of the pub, the idea certainly held its charm. Steal a car. One of the Paki ones down by the cricket field.

'Teach 'em a lesson. Show 'em who's boss,' he said, grinning like a loon.

Steve had said a lot of things over the course of the six hours they'd been drinking, a lot of it aimed at the Muslims who lived in the area. Harsh things, nasty things that left a cold feeling in Luke's stomach and an ever-growing sense of dread. Something was coming, that was certain. They'd all heard the rumours; they'd all dropped a few of their own. The Muslims were taking over. Their shops were sprouting everywhere, filled with a thousand variations of rice and hundreds more of curry powders and exotic spices. They stank of it, a sweet tang that reminded Luke of cold sweat. It made him sick. Made a lot of his friends sick. Friends like Steve, who was still going on about stealing a car.

Luke took a long pull of his pint and let Steve waffle on.

'They always park on the kerb just opposite the cricket

ground. Looks like a fucking Paki convention with their beaded seats. Stinks like one too. I say we nick one, take it for a spin then torch it.'

He didn't keep his voice down. Everyone in the pub felt the same way Steve did, Luke thought as he caught the eye of another drinker. The man turned away, eyes moving back to the young blonde with the big tits beside him. Yes, the Pakis were everywhere, infesting the streets with their weird ways and even weirder food. And when they talked, fucking hell it was like listening to someone having a fucking stroke.

The parents of the white kids were not having it. Talk was they were pulling their kids from the schools until something was done about it. Action, not just talk.

Well, Steve wasn't just talk, was he? Steve got shit done.

It had been Steve who had introduced Luke to the local chapter of the British National Party and then to their pub here on the outskirts of Savile Town. It was nothing but a short walk to the cricket ground. And it wasn't as though he was suggesting throwing a few bricks through windows or, worse, something lit. A car didn't count. A car was just a thing. Replaceable. What wasn't replaceable was their white heritage. Their white power. It was being siphoned away, they said at their weekly meetings. Time to do something about it. Take their power back. He'd heard rumours about the strong possibility of someone planning such a thing. Luke didn't like the Pakis or the Asians or the Muslims, but he didn't think he wanted to see anyone hurt. All they had to do was go somewhere else and there wouldn't be any trouble. Go back to where they came from. Fuck, if he had the chance of moving to warmer climates he'd fucking jump at it. So what if the women had to cover their faces? Some of the birds round here could do with covering up their mugs.

Instead, he was stuck here, working the rail track four nights a week for little more than pocket money while these bastards got all the handouts and were treated like fucking royalty.

Well fuck that!

'Fuck that,' he said, slamming his empty glass onto the table. A dozen other empties rocked like glass trees in a strong wind.

'Let's fucking do it!'

The car was right where Steve said it would be. While he and Luke watched either side of the road, Kevin got to work. It was just after ten at night and the road was quiet. The houses close to the cricket ground were dark; only one had a light on in the upper floor and there was no way they could be seen, tucked away behind a row of trees. In thirty seconds, he had the door open. In a minute he had the engine running.

'Hop in, gents,' he called out.

Steve got in the front seat, ripping out the beads and throwing them to the ground before sitting down. Kevin did the same. Luke got in the back.

'Jesus, it fucking stinks!' Steve cranked down a window as the car began to move. Gunning the engine, Kevin pulled on the handbrake and spun the car around, dead centre of the road. Smoke blew out from the rear tyres and there was a loud squeal as the rubber bit into the road, seeking traction in the cold silence of the night.

Thirty seconds later they were off, speeding down Savile Road back towards Dewsbury town centre, all three of them whooping with delight.

The car roared across the bridge spanning the river Calder, its dark surface reflecting the waxing gibbous moon. The sky was darkening, the stars trying their best to peek out from behind heavy clouds that drifted to their own tune. Reaching the end of Savile Road, Kevin made a hard right up Railway Street and then another onto Wakefield Road.

'Where we going?' Luke called out from the back seat, his voice raised above the roaring wind coming through the open window.

'We get to the Mad Mile, we can get onto the M1,' Steve said from the passenger seat. Kevin grunted a reply, his concentration switching between the road and the bright red warning light that was starting to flash intermittently on the dashboard. He wasn't a hundred percent sure what it meant, but judging how the car was starting to growl, he was pretty sure the engine was over-heating. Something had also begun to vibrate in the left wheel, a gentle wobble that he had to correct by oversteering to the right. It felt like the damn thing was coming loose, but that was impossible.

'I'm not sure we can make it to the motorway,' he said through gritted teeth. They were on Wakefield Road, heading through Earlsheaton so fast everything was becoming a streaky blur. The stone-faced houses that lined either side of the road were stained orange in the recently fired-up streetlights. A few people walked on the pavement, presumably heading back from the local pub. Steve was sure he saw one of them carrying a pool cue. He wore short sleeves; the night air still held a trace of the day's heat, though the tattoos that ran down the length of his bare arms suggested he didn't feel the cold.

The car lurched violently to the left, the front passenger wheel barking up the kerb to briefly run along the pavement. Kevin managed to yank the steering wheel in time to avoid hitting a streetlamp. Everyone bounced as the wheel bit into the road once more.

'Jesus, man! Who the fuck's driving... Stevie-fucking-Wonder?'

'Shut the fuck up,' Kevin bit back, just as the steering wheel ripped itself from his hands. The vibration became an earthquake beneath his fingers.

'What the fuck?' he said as the car jostled to the left once more, the rear underside striking the road at sixty-eight miles an hour. They had just made the turn around the roundabout and were dashing under the overpass and onto the dual carriageway that led to the M1 when sparks illuminated the inside of the car, throwing the occupants into momentary shades of red and gold.

They all bounced as the left rear dipped suddenly and the car was filled with the shriek of tearing metal.

As the front half of the stolen car spun to the right, crashing into the barrier that separated the two carriageways, the rear end tore away, catapulted further down the road by inertia and momentum. In the back seat, Luke screamed as blood gushed from the stump of his ruined left leg. It had been caught under Kevin's seat, his foot jammed when the car ripped in two. As the shattered edge of the car bit into the road, it sent more sparks exploding in a cascade of orange and yellow fire. The ruptured fuel line ignited with a sound like a dragon clearing its throat.

The fire rushed into the metal box, engulfing Luke, whose screams quickly died as the flames rushed down his throat. The back half of the car careened into the grassy bank of the carriageway, its steep incline trapping the wreckage. The dry grass quickly caught fire and burned brightly.

The front of the car was a crushed metal box, lodged tight within the central barrier. The metal railing had done its job; the ruined half of the car had stuck fast and not gone careening over onto the other lanes. Inside, the engine block had been forced through the dashboard, shattering the legs of both men and trapping them as glass and metal continued to rain down around them.

Oil and petrol bled out onto the road, and for those shocked first moments, the only sound that could be heard was the writhing growl of the engine and the screams of the two men trapped in the burning car.

CHAPTER
TWO

Bill Manby lay back in the bath, his eyes closed, and let the warm suds soak his body. It had been some time since he had last enjoyed the long caress of a bath with a cold beer and a good book, and he was making sure to enjoy every minute of it.

And it wasn't just the bath that he had been enjoying on this, his first long weekend in as far as he could remember. It had started on Friday with a day out to Haworth with his wife, Marie, where they explored the Bronte museum, something she had been wanting to do for years. Somehow, he had never had the time; something always came up, but this time nothing had got in the way, and his wife had shown her appreciation when they got back. Most of Saturday had been spent in the bedroom as well, the recent arguments and disagreements all forgotten, apparently. He had made them lunch and an afternoon snack, which they ate in bed before going out to the pub for drinks later in the evening. And today...

Manby let the memories of today wash over him as the water lapped across his chest. The hot tap rumbled as water poured into the bath; 'topping it off' was what he called it. He gave the tap a nudge with his toe, turning it off just as the door to the bathroom opened.

He turned and watched as Marie, still wearing her black slip and nothing else, came in carrying a bottle of beer. 'Thought you might need another one,' she said, bending down to place it on the ledge beside him. He stared down her top, taking in the sight of her naked body with a sigh of pleasure. He raised a hand and cupped her behind, fingers trailing over her skin.

'Like what you see?' she said, her voice thick. Manby was just about to answer when the sharp trill of the phone came from downstairs. Their eyes locked. A phone call just before eleven at night could mean only one thing.

Marie stood up; lips pursed into a thin line. The flush of her face had nothing to do with the rising passion from moments ago, but everything to do with the seemingly never-ending burden of being a policeman's wife.

Manby cursed silently. He had nearly made it through the entire weekend. Not once had he thought about the Shop; no one had called him under penalty of being given traffic duty for the next three months. For the first time in as long as he could remember, they had enjoyed each other's company with a lazy attitude. No rushed dinners; no snatched kisses on the way out. No sleeping on the sofa for fear of waking Marie after coming in past midnight stinking of cigarettes and office sweat.

He reached out for her, but Marie stopped his apology with a kiss.

'You get dry,' she said as she stood back. She took down a fresh towel from the linen cupboard and held it out for him as he rose from the bath. Her eyes gave a wicked dip down his body and he could feel himself blush like a teenager. 'I'll answer it.'

She left the bathroom, leaving Bill Manby wondering, not for the first time in their thirty-year marriage, what he had done right to land a good one like Marie.

By the time he came downstairs, Marie's flushed face had gone pale. One arm was wrapped across her stomach, lifting her slip to expose the luscious top of her thigh, but all thoughts of sex disappeared when he saw her face.

'Who is it, love?' he asked. His heart stopped. 'Is it Susan?'

Their daughter was nearing thirty, but she would always be that little kid who cried when the purple fairies blew off the tree in the back garden. Marie shook her head but didn't answer. Just held out the phone to him.

'I'll go get your suit out of the wardrobe.'

He took the phone from her and watched as she went back upstairs without another word.

'Bill Manby...' he said into the phone.

He listened as the person on the other end spoke. The call lasted three intense minutes, during which Manby's gut twisted tighter and tighter. He made some notes on the notepad beside the phone, scratching details down as the caller spoke to him, along with a rough plan of what he needed to do.

By the time the call had finished, he'd circled two words and underlined them several times.

Get Louise!

After hanging up, Manby went straight back upstairs. While he had been listening, his heart growing colder with each word spoken, Marie had slipped past him back to the bedroom, where she had laid his suit out. When he strode inside, she was just picking a tie from the rack that hung inside the wardrobe door.

'I'm thinking the blue,' she said, starting to pull it down.

Manby began to pull his shirt on.

'Best go for the black,' he said with a sigh.

Marie paused and turned to look at her husband. His jaw clenched and he could feel the erratic beat of his pulse in his neck. This wasn't a good sign. His blood pressure was already higher than it should be (their athletic adventures of the weekend had certainly stretched him to the limit of his exertions, fun though it was), and his work certainly didn't help. No wonder she looked so worried, he thought.

'How bad?'

His answer was a sad smile that told Marie everything.

Manby smoothed down his trousers, brushing a couple of stray hairs from the knees. Another sign that, perhaps, he was coming to the end of his own journey with the force. Perhaps Harolds had done the right thing by getting out early. Dunford, the detective Louise had replaced, seemed to be doing all right after leaving. Nights at the Tapps, drinking and playing dominoes, Sunday afternoons at the cricket. No murderers, thieves or rapists to deal with; just pints, dots and wickets. Not a bad life if he could get it.

He looked over at Marie, who was brushing down his jacket, and smiled. He already had it.

'Are you going to call Louise?' she asked. He could see his own pain and fear reflected in his wife's eyes.

'No,' Manby said as he took the jacket from his wife and pulled it on. He shook his shoulders until it fit then reached out to hold Marie's shoulders as he placed a soft kiss on her forehead.

'Bad news has to be done face to face.'

CHAPTER
THREE

Louise Miller stretched, letting a small sigh escape her lips as Karla continued to caress the back of her neck with her thumbs. It had started out as a well-earned massage, their long afternoon run together going a lot further than the planned three miles. That had been Karla's fault, a well-intentioned distraction from the sting of being passed over for promotion once again. With Sergeant Harolds retiring just as the new year began, Louise had hoped, had petitioned for the position, and from the enthusiastic comments from the DI as well as some of her colleagues, she had thought the job was hers.

The last person she expected to lose the promotion to had been Tom Bailey. *Tom-fucking-Bailey!* Louise let out a huff of annoyance as her frustration came back in a rush. He was two years younger than her and had been on the force for a year less than her. There was only one reason he'd been given the job over her, and everyone knew it.

'Are you thinking about Tom Bailey again?' Karla said, her voice muffled into the crook of Louise's neck. 'Your neck feels like a rock all of a sudden.' Her breath was warm and the way she was pressing her thumbs into the muscles along Louise's shoulders was extremely diverting. 'You need to let it go.'

'I have. I just get frustrated every now and then. It's not fair.'

Karla pressed herself against Louise, her arm snaking between them so she could hold her tighter. 'Mmm... 'course it's not fair, and it's okay for you to feel like that. Just like it's okay for you to feel this...'

Karla's hand made a gentle motion that made Louise moan softly. 'Now *that's* not fair,' she said, but she was smiling when she did so.

Louise rolled over so she was staring into the hazel eyes of her lover. No, that was too clinical a word for what the two had become over the last couple of years. Yes, at first that was what it had been all about: two professional women taking pleasure in each other, but now it was more, so much more than that. Gone was the awkwardness of the new, the fumbled words and stumbled touches replaced with the comfortably familiar. Shared looks and stolen glances; shy smiles and gentle caresses, the secret language of their love.

Karla reached up to brush a fleck of hair from Louise's face.

'Did you really expect them to give you the position?'

Before answering Louise pushed herself up so that she was resting against the headboard of the bed, her back protected from its metal frame by several layers of cushions and pillows that Karla had insisted on buying. Louise was of a more functional frame of mind when it came to bed linen: white sheets, white pillowcases. Sometimes black, blue at a push. There were certainly no pinks or fluffy lace, and in no way was there to be any silk like she'd seen when she'd visited her colleague Elizabeth Hines' home. That had been an eye opener for sure; she'd known her young friend was a lot more open and free-spirited when it came to her personal relationships, and that was matched by her choice of decoration. Hines' bedroom was an example of hedonistic excess – she'd even had a mirror over her bed!

Karla laid her head in Louise's lap, allowing her to stroke Karla's hair as she talked through her frustration.

'For a short time, yes… I did think I'd get it. After everything that had happened in the last couple of years, all the hours I've put in, the Jacobs case, the awful murder of James Willikar, not to mention all the domestic assault jobs I've been on. It was me who organised the stakeout of the working men's club down Chickenley when no one else, not even the sainted Tom-fucking-Bailey, gave it another look. How many of them would have got away with it if I hadn't?'

By *them* Louise meant the organised gang of house breakers that had been operating in and around Ossett and Dewsbury for the better part of a year. Almost three thousand pounds' worth of stolen property had been recovered along with a couple of firearms, a small quantity of drugs and nearly six thousand in cash. All out of the back of the Working Men's Club. And it had been Louise who had broken the case.

'And it wasn't Bill, it wasn't the new guy and it certainly wasn't Tom-fucking-Bailey who sorted it, was it?'

She looked down into Karla's eyes. The smile she gave back told Louise that Karla knew she was venting again and also knew better than to say anything when Louise was in this mood. The fire of her frustration was diminished by that smile, but didn't entirely go out.

'I still can't believe Bill did that,' Louise continued. 'He'd led me to believe it was going to be my promotion for the taking. "A just reward for all you've done," he'd said.' She was running her hand through Karla's hair, not realising that each successive stroke was harsher than the last until she was nearly yanking Karla's head back with every stroke.

'You know it wasn't Bill,' Karla said, gently removing Louise's hand. 'That sounds like it has Freeman all over it.'

Louise knew she was probably right. Chief Superintendent Freeman. In charge of their new unit, or at least the one who had the last say about how the Prospect Road CID unit operated. Manby had a lot of input on how the unit ran; he had managed to get Peter Danes promoted to run the Scene of Crime team, going so far as to install a fully working lab on the top floor to better handle the forensic side of cases, and to keep everything in-house as much as possible. Freeman had balked at the cost initially, but Manby had worn him down. Unfortunately, he hadn't been able to do the same when it came to the decision of who should be the next Sergeant.

Louise was about to get into it again when, thankfully, there was a knock at the door downstairs that made them both sit up.

'That'll be the takeaway. I'll get it,' Karla said, getting out of bed. As she pulled on her dressing gown, she turned back. 'Do you mind if I say something?'

Louise shrugged.

'It was a shitty thing Bill did, getting your hopes up like that—'

'A very shitty thing,' Louise interrupted.

Karla continued.

'—a very shitty thing, but who's going to be the one to pick up all the pieces when, not if, when Mr Bailey makes a pig's ear of things? It's going to be you. You know it. Bill knows it, and I think Tom-fucking-Bailey knows it too. It'll only be a matter of time before you get the slot. There's only so many times someone can fuck up and get away with it.'

It was true. Bailey had already made several errors in tactical choices regarding surveillance and had messed up the entire file on the Kilson case, which had meant a delay at court, something that should never happen if they wanted a positive prosecution. Each time it had been Louise who had sorted it out; adding two more teams to the surveillance of the flats on Church Court, where a suspected mugger lived, and it had been Louise who had stayed up all night re-ordering the Kilson paperwork.

Another knock sounded from downstairs, harder and more urgent, and Karla moved over to the bedroom window.

She pulled the curtain back, looked down, and let out a laugh.

'It's Bill,' she said to a puzzled Louise.

· · ·

Bill Manby was crouched down giving Tom a welcomed back scratch when Louise opened the door to him. As soon as the light spilled out, Tom forgot about the back scratches and darted inside, shooting past Louise to run up the steep stone steps into the flat proper. His claws could be heard on the wooden floor as he skittered straight to the kitchen for something to eat.

'Evening, Bill,' Louise said, pulling her gown tighter around her. She wished she'd taken a few extra minutes to put a jacket on, but he had knocked more repeatedly, instantly putting her on edge.

His face was taut. His jaw set hard.

'It's Beth. There's been an incident,' he began.

'It's that bloody Joe again, isn't it?' she said as she stomped up the stairs. Manby answered with a nod as he followed, closing the door behind him first. As they reached the top, Karla came out of the bedroom. She had thrown some clothes on and was pulling her boots on when Manby reached the landing.

'Hi, Bill,' she said.

'Ms Hayes,' he replied with a tip of his head. 'Good to see you again.'

Karla was a psychologist working out of an office at Dewsbury Memorial Hospital, and had helped on a few cases for the Prospect Road CID team. That was how she had met Louise, and slowly they were beginning to let those closest to them know about their relationship. Bill had been the first to suspect, but he had taken the position that it was none of his business who Louise saw, and as long as it didn't affect their working relationship, because Karla was an outside hire, they could do whatever they wanted in their own time.

And besides, he liked Karla. Thought she was good for Louise. She reminded him of Susan.

'It's Beth,' Louise said in answer to Karla's questioning gaze. Louise slipped past Karla and into the bedroom. Manby stood in the corridor as Louise started to get dressed.

'They were having an argument in the Carps,' he said, 'and it got out of hand. She's at Dewsbury Memorial.'

'Is she all right?'

'Cuts and scrapes,' he said. 'Which is a lot less than what that prick is going to get if I lay my hands on him.'

'It always gets out of hand with Joe,' Louise shouted from the bedroom. 'Karla, where did you put my top?'

'It's where it's supposed to be... hung up,' Karla replied. 'I swear this place would be littered with clothes everywhere if I didn't put them away. It's like living with an unruly teenager,' she laughed.

'So, you two are living together now?' Bill asked with a smile, eyebrows raised. Louise stuck her head out.

'No, we are not living together, no matter what she says. Or him.'

Tom had wandered from the kitchen, belly now full and on the lookout for affection. He was currently rubbing up against Karla's shin and purring like a diesel engine. Karla bent down and ruffled him behind his ears. 'Out of the two of you, I thought this little guy would be the one putting up the obstacles.'

'Can we talk about this later?' Louise said as she opened the door. She was wearing blue trousers and a white shirt. A matching jacket was slung over one arm. 'This shit with Joe; how bad is it?'

'A few cuts and scrapes,' he repeated. 'They're a passionate couple, that's for sure.'

'That's one way to put it. I can drive you to the hospital,' Karla said.

'Wait a minute,' Manby said, raising his hands. 'Beth isn't the only problem we have right now. Not that she's a problem,' he added, seeing the look that crossed Louise's face. 'There's also been a car crash on the Mad Mile. At least two dead. Fire and Ambulance are there now, but I need you to come with me, Louise. To the scene of the crash.'

'No way. No fucking way, Bill. I need to be with Beth. She's my partner, my friend, and she needs me.'

'I need your help at the scene. Karla can go to the hospital. Would that be all right with you?' he asked, turning to Karla, who nodded in response.

'Of course.' She looked at Louise, who looked ready for a fight. She took her hands and caught her eyes with her own. 'Bill's right... this time,' she added, giving him a stern look. They all knew what she meant, but now wasn't the time for that particular conversation. 'I'll go to the hospital and stay with her. I can let you know as soon as I have any news, and if you haven't heard from me, then just come as soon as you can.'

'Just call the Sergeant and he can pass on any messages,' Bill said.

Karla raised her eyebrows and pushed her top lip out with her tongue. 'That would be...'

Bill shook his head but was smiling.

'Yes, yes. Tom-fucking-Bailey. I know. I know.' He turned back to Louise, and she was pleased to see that his cheeks had coloured with embarrassment. 'Why do you think I need you at the scene?'

CHAPTER
FOUR

The scene of the crash was awash with the strobing shadows of blue and red emergency vehicle lights. Two fire engines stood to one side, a firehose snaking from one, continuing to douse the wreckage to make sure the fire wouldn't flare back up. Large overhead lights were being set up, and one flared into life, adding the surreal appearance of day to the scene.

Manby parked his car just outside the cordon and gave a wave to the officer stationed to make sure bystanders didn't get too close to what was now considered a crime scene. Louise followed him, and as they drew closer, she could see the twisted metal of the two halves of the car, now black husks, the paint having been stripped away under the intense heat, except for a couple of patches where the heat hadn't reached.

Shattered glass lay all around, catching the lights from the emergency vehicles and throwing kaleidoscopic patterns across the spilled oil. Three firefighters stood around them damping down, while another was jabbing at the wreckage, prying away sections so they could be more easily reached by the water spray. The Senior Fire Officer waved at Manby and pointed to the tape then raised five fingers. *Wait there – five minutes*. Manby waved back then turned to Louise.

'Beth's a tough one, you know. From what she said, she's just got a few cuts from where she fell. It's nothing serious.'

'*She* called you? Not the hospital? Not Joe?' Louise said. A hole opened somewhere in the centre of her chest and she felt herself slipping towards it. 'Why didn't she phone me?'

'Oh, I don't know,' Manby began, his gaze momentarily averted as a loud hiss of steam captured his attention. 'Perhaps because she knew how you'd react.' He saw the expression on her face and paused.

'I can see you're worried; hell, I am too, but Beth is a tough one, she takes no shit, especially from some of the bigger lads—'

'Usually at the Carps at throwing out time,' Louise said.

Bill continued, '—but what happens behind closed doors is a world away from how people react in the workplace. Karla will look after her. I think out of all of us, she's best equipped to handle her, don't you think?'

Before she could answer, Peter Danes came to stand between the two and gave them both a nod in greeting.

'She's a tough one, our Beth. Be up and running in no time. A few scratches and a fucked-up nose won't keep her down, so don't be worrying about her, okay?'

His cavalier attitude instantly ignited Louise's anger.

'Don't tell me what to do! She's my friend. I'd have thought you, of all people, would be a bit more concerned about her.'

Unknown to everyone at the station but Louise, Hines and Danes had indulged in a brief affair, one that had led to a pregnancy scare, which, luckily for them both, had put a halt to any further get-togethers. Louise bit at her inside lip, angry at herself for nearly letting it slip. Danes was a married man, and there was no way Manby would tolerate such behaviour in his Shop. Not with the eyes of the Chief Superintendent on their rapidly growing CID squad.

Before Manby could pick up on what she'd said, Louise turned her attention to the crash site.

'Do we know what happened?' she asked.

Danes gave a cough, happy to be changing the subject.

'An eyewitness, who nearly got clipped by the Ford Escort, says it came tearing up from Dewsbury and tried to skip through the traffic lights just as they were changing. When they got to the dual carriageway here, it looks like the stolen car ripped in two and got flipped.'

She was looking right at the mess of metal, the hiss as it cooled under the misted jet of water from the fire engine sounding like an angry snake. Only now was she starting to make out the different shapes of the car. The front half of the Ford Escort was lodged tight between the railings that divided the carriageway.

Her voice dropped to an awed whisper.

'Casualties?'

Danes shook his head and pointed to where a white sheet covered the unmistakable shape of a body. A dark stain covered most of it.

'Not much left for an ID by any relatives; we'll have to use dental records for the good they'll do. I won't be eating burgers any time soon, I'll tell you that.'

The heavy stench of burned flesh stung their nostrils, making them grimace every few seconds. She knew Danes' ill attempt at humour was an unconscious reaction to the carnage. All of them had it, a way to keep the horrors they were exposed to each and every day away from their core. For some, like Danes, it was an attitude they wore like a second skin that could be shed when they were away from the darkness and death. For others, like Louise, it was the work that protected them; they threw themselves so far into it, they became almost numb to the twisted knowledge they accumulated.

Compartmentalising was what Karla said it was called, the way Louise could switch from the evil of her day to the joys of their time together. Sometimes it bled through, one to the other, just like it had done after the Holland case, and then only last year with the suicide-turned-murder of James Willikar. The tragedy of that case continued to affect Louise; the anguished howls of Mr Willikar when he learned of the death of his son still haunted her, riding along on the edge of the wind, or hiding in the rising cry of a boiling kettle. Cold chills and shakes accompanied those brief moments when she was transported back to that time and place, but she was getting better at recognising the signs, thanks to talking with Karla.

Danes adjusted the hood of his forensic suit and continued.

'No skid marks to suggest they were going too fast, but something strange on the road back here. Come take a look.'

Water for the fire and foam to cover the spilled oil and petrol had mixed to create a sticky stream they had to step over. Louise hesitated, conscious of the fact that the oversized wellies she had been forced to wear to protect the scene would make this even more treacherous. The plastic covering she'd slipped over them to protect the scene would make this even more treacherous. There hadn't been time to find her usual work shoes; they were somewhere lost within the mess that was her walk-in wardrobe, hidden under the clutter of washing that had piled up over the last few days. For Tom, it was a wonderful landscape to sleep in, all warm and soft. For Louise, it was a nightmarish chore she had to get on top of. Karla had already mentioned the mess several times, the second and subsequent times not so subtly.

The Senior Fire Officer waved them through. The rest of the fire fighters were starting to pack away their equipment and reload the appliance. One of them switched off their strobing lights and Louise's growing migraine silently thanked him.

'There are marks where the front tyres suddenly twisted, first to the right, then to the left.'

Manby looked at the marks on the road.

'Perhaps they were going around someone?'

Danes shook his head.

'No reports of any other cars on this stretch of the Mad Mile. There were no witnesses to the actual crash, other than the one surviving passenger. We'll get a better picture of what happened when we speak to him, but that won't be for a while, if at all.'

'How badly was he hurt?' Louise asked.

Danes scratched at the back of his hood.

'Lost a leg and a lot of blood. It was a real bloodbath when I got here. Like I said... vegan from now on. Shame Beth's not here; she knows her cars and could probably tell us straight away what caused the crash. As it is we'll do a thorough examination back at the garage. Probably tomorrow, Tuesday at a push,' he added directly to Manby.

Mention of Hines made Louise conscious of how much time she was spending here instead of going to see her friend. Karla would be there by now; she should be there too.

Louise stepped closer, leaning in as close as she dared to the wreckage. That foul stench of cooked meat rose from the metal, and, beneath the mask she was wearing, her face crinkled in disgust. It was the chemical mix of burning flesh, fats, metal and fabric, a pungent perfume that coated her throat and nose.

'What am I not seeing?' she asked.

Danes pointed to the edge of the metal.

'I'm not sure. It's a pretty clean cut, almost perfect,' he said softly, as though he was speaking to himself as he ran his finger just above the line of the metal. 'And here... and here... those bumps are from welds. You can see where the metal is different here.' The section he was pointing at had a long weld mark running down its edge, its black mark standing out for a second against the bright silver of the two joins.

Danes seemed to drift away as he examined the burnt remains of the car, occasionally throwing glances back to the marks on the road and the pattern of the wreckage. He was prevented from looking further by the approach of the Station Officer, the yellow of his helmet streaked with dirt.

'Need you all to move back,' he said. 'We're going to get the separate pieces harnessed up for the tow trucks.'

He pointed back beyond the cordon. A couple of trucks sat

side by side, just behind the tape that had been strung across the carriageway, their orange lights adding to the multi-coloured kaleidoscope of the other emergency vehicles.

Manby nodded and began ushering everyone back towards the embankment. As she walked beside him, Louise stripped off her gloves. If they were going to start vehicle recovery then perhaps she could get to the hospital. A thought struck her as she pushed the gloves into one of her forensic suit pockets.

'Do we know who they are yet?' she asked.

Danes shook his head.

'That's going to be your job,' he said, 'but I can tell you it wasn't their car. If you look, there's what appear to be Pakistani adornments and a picture of a Pakistani family. Too badly burned to make out anyone though.'

'They were Pakistanis?'

Danes shook his head. 'The two dead on scene appeared to be white from what I could see. The surviving passenger was definitely white. He got taken to Dewsbury Memorial Hospital.'

Every fibre of her being was screaming to head there now, to be at Hines' side. Beyond her aunt and uncle, Louise didn't have many friends; other than Beth and Karla, she couldn't name anyone else she would walk through fire for. Maybe Manby, at a push.

It was Manby who spoke next, removing his mask and brushing his hand across his stubbled face. Louise could almost see new worry-lines carving themselves into his skin.

'With all the tension in Dewsbury right now, a group of white men stealing an Asian-owned car is not going to help matters. We need to get this sorted out and fast.'

Over the course of the last week, six more parents – white parents – had voiced their 'concern' over the level of education their children were getting surrounded by Pakistani kids in their schools. It had already led to violent arguments at the school gates at two of the Junior and Infants schools in Savile Town. The Chief Superintendent had wanted all forces in the area, including the CID team of Prospect Road, Ossett, to be ready and aware of any associated crimes that resulted from the racial tensions. Anything that looked even remotely like it was going to break out into a brushfire of unrest needed to be quashed quickly.

And it looked like that included this stolen car. This *Pakistani*-owned car; that's all people would hear. Didn't matter that the ones who stole the car and caused the crash, and therefore the resulting deaths were white. That part would no doubt get overlooked.

Pushing down her frustration, Louise turned back to Manby.

'Okay, so we have a stolen car and what looks to be a really shitty confluence of circumstances. What's the plan?'

Before he could answer there was the sound of tearing metal and the wreckage gave a lurch. The two tow-trucks had manoeuvred into position either side of one of the mangled sections of car and were now pulling it onto the back of the flatbed. One of the mechanics, a man dressed all in denim with a high visibility vest around his waist, stood between the two, giving instructions.

'Left, Dave. Left… careful. Bit more…'

Metal squealed as one half of the vehicle caught on the dividing barrier, the twisted metal refusing to let go.

'Give it some welly, Dave!' the man shouted.

In response, the engine of the closest tow-truck growled deeper and smoke began to spiral from the rear wheel as the driver rolled through the gears. It moved a fraction then stopped, the scream of tortured metal rising to join the howl of the engine.

'Cut it down, Dave!' The man started to yell another command, but in the next instant his voice was drowned out as the tow-truck shot forward, and if the driver hadn't slammed on his brakes, the truck would have slammed through the guardrail and up onto the embankment where Louise and the other members of Prospect Road CID stood waiting.

The blackened husk of the car was dragged from the railing onto the carriageway, where it landed with a heavy crash and slid across the road. As it slid to a halt, a blackened shape fell from the wrecked car to land on the shattered asphalt.

'Holy shit!'

Danes was already running down to the misshapen object, Manby and Louise close behind.

'Stand away from it,' he called to the mechanic who was walking over. 'This is still a crime scene.' The man raised his hand and moved, instead, towards the tow-truck. The driver leaned out of the window, the cigarette in his mouth spilling smoke up into the air.

'What the fuck was that?' he asked.

The other man shook his head and reached up for a cigarette, which the driver passed down. Lighting it he blew out a cloud of smoke and leaned against the door of the truck.

'Just another Paki fucking up our night. Fuckers don't know how to speak English, so how the fuck are they supposed to know how to drive a car?' He broke out in gibberish speak, which had the driver laughing so hard he let out what was presumably a beer-fuelled fart. That had the mechanic doubled up and coughing around his cigarette.

Louise stilled her mind and came up behind Danes, who knelt beside the object. Leaning over his shoulder, she couldn't help letting out a gasp of shock and disbelief at what she was looking at.

'Is that a foot?'

CHAPTER
FIVE

Bilal and Raja Wadee hurried alongside the cricket ground in Savile Town, ready to make the long trip to Hull where they worked as cargo loaders at the dockyard.

Raja sighed; they had a long shift ahead of them, nearly fifteen hours loading and unloading crates and cargo from the ships that came into the docks, most of which was then sent on transports to London. It was hard work, but honest and well paying. Much better than standing behind a counter in one of their parents' stores, being verbally abused each and every day.

'I parked it right here,' Bilal said. He walked a few steps ahead of his brother, eyes anxiously darting between the rows of cars that were parked on the roadside. 'You saw me park it. You were here when I parked it,' he continued, his head bobbing up and down as he checked each car as well as looking into the dark void of the cricket ground, 'and I know I parked it here. Right here.'

He stopped at a gap between two other cars. A gap big enough for another car to have been parked there. Small drops of oil had stained the road and Bilal pointed excitedly at them.

'See... same oil leak. Same two spots, same shape as my car. It was here.'

Raja bent to look, while at the same time giving his brother a sideways glance of disbelief.

'If anyone was going to have their car stolen, it was you. Always with you there is something going on, some drama. There is no car here and no way for us to get to work. Mum and Dad will have all the joy in reminding us it was our choice not to work the shop. I'm going home.'

He started back along the road, but the firm grip of his younger brother's hand on his arm brought him up.

'It was here, I tell you,' Bilal said. 'Someone must have seen it.' He pointed across the street to the Walton Arms pub. A single lamp burned in the window. The curtains were drawn behind it. Music and laughter could be heard coming from inside.

'That is not a good idea,' Raja said as Bilal headed across the road. 'They will not help us. They will not care.'

'They are our neighbours,' Bilal called back.

'Not by choice,' his brother replied, but he followed anyway.

The pub was filled with the sweet fog of cigarette and cigar smoke. It was nearly an hour past closing time, and the taps were still flowing as the seven regulars sat around, drinking and talking. Tables had been pulled together and a pile of crisps dumped in the centre. The bags had been opened, the contents scattered.

The owner of the pub was a large man with a cask of a beer belly and a part-shaved head, the thin stubble barely hiding the faded tattoo of a swastika. Another one adorned his neck, and across the knuckles of both hands were two words: GOOD on the right; NIGHT on the left.

'We all good?' he said, his voice thick and guttural.

Tommy Everad had run the Walton Arms pub for six years and the local chapter of the British National Party for seven. Grunts and nods came from the others around the table. Tommy leaned back in his chair and called to the girl behind the bar.

'We're done, Kelly. You can get off now.'

'She can get off on me any time of the day,' one of the men said.

Everyone laughed. He was in his fifties; Kelly said she was nineteen but her sixteenth birthday wouldn't be for another two months. If Tommy knew, he didn't care.

Kelly came from behind the bar, pulling her coat on.

'Fridge is all stocked up, Mr Everad,' she said, 'and the till balances.'

'Damn fucking right it balances,' he said, turning from the shocked girl to his friends. 'That last bastard was a real thief. Fucking nigger thought he'd try and skim my till? Gave that fucking bastard a good night.' He waved his hands in front so everyone could see the tattoos on his knuckles. 'Last time I'll give one of their kind a chance at a white man's job.'

'Too right, Tommy,' someone said. A chorus of approvals sang back.

Kelly blushed but didn't say anything. She knew the lad Tommy was talking about, had gone out on a couple of dates with him, but since he was beaten unconscious by Tommy Everad and a couple of his friends she hadn't seen him. He hadn't taken the money either; she knew that, having seen one of Tommy's friends lift the two twenties when his back had been turned. He had caught her staring, and when she'd gone to the loo, he'd snuck in behind her and pushed her up against the wall. A boozy warning to keep her mouth shut while one hand rummaged beneath her skirt. When his thick fingers began to push inside her knickers, she'd squeezed her eyes closed.

'Trust your own, is what I say,' Tommy continued. 'Knew you'd do right, love. Get yourself home and I'll see you next Friday night. Before I forget, here's your pay.' Tommy took a roll of banknotes from his pocket and peeled off a couple of tens. He held it out and she took it from him, hoping he hadn't seen her flinch when his fingers touched hers.

'Thanks, Mr Everad. I'll see you next week.'

'Ben... go lock the door after her, will you?'

A young man dressed in denim jacket and jeans stood and walked behind Kelly as she hurried to the door. Tommy gave a look at her backside, the skirt swinging side to side and riding up a little as she walked. He mimed grabbing it and everyone laughed again.

A moment later she was out of the door. Ben watched her walk down the street, passing two men heading back towards the pub. The closer one was waving his arms and pointing back in the direction from which they came.

'Shut the fucking door, lad. It's colder than my wife's cunt in here.'

Ben laughed. 'Maybe I should go warm it up for you, Eddie,' he said as he shut the door. The latches dropped into place with a metallic double-clack.

'Saves me having to do it,' the man called Eddie said. He turned to Tommy. 'So, we got a plan yet?'

Tommy sat at what could be classed the head of the table, a pint glass almost lost within the meat of his fist. He took a long swallow, let out a roar of a belch and slammed the glass down, shaking the table.

'We?' he growled. 'What's with this "we" shit? You think you've got the brains to be thinking for the rest of us, do you, Eddie?'

Eddie paled. 'Didn't mean anything by it. Was just wondering, like. The lad's looking forward to it nearly as much as me, so it'd be good to have some'at to tell him.'

'You a fucking pig?' Tommy leaned forward; his eyes locked onto Eddie.

The man next to Tommy was Donald Sheen, a thickset ex-miner who now drove buses between Leeds and Dewsbury. His eyes were glazed, the lids drooping. He gave Tommy a shunt with his elbow.

'Smells like one.'

'Shut the fuck up, Donny,' Eddie said, getting to his feet.

Now it was Donald who got to his feet. The red glaze of beer was replaced with the burning fire of anger.

'If you want a fucking fight then I'd be happy to fucking oblige.'

Eddie was about to reply when there was a double rap on the door.

Everyone fell silent.

'Who the fuck is that?' Tommy said. 'Ben... Go see who it is and tell them to fuck off.'

With a resigned smile – there was always trouble between Eddie and Donald at every single meeting – Ben went to the door and looked out of the window beside it. He turned back to everyone gathered in the room. Each one was a fully paid member of the Savile Town Loyalist Committee chapter of the British National Party, which made their new visitors particularly unwelcome guests.

'It's only a pair of fucking Pakis,' he said.

Tommy's smile was as cold as his eyes.

'Let them in.'

'This isn't a good idea,' Raja said again as the metallic clicks of locks being pulled aside echoed in the small doorway. If his brother heard, Bilal gave no sign.

Light from inside the pub spilled out as the door was cracked open. A man with dirty blond hair, and dressed head to foot in light denim, peered out.

'What do you want?' he said.

From behind him came a couple of beer belches that made Raja wince.

'So sorry for intruding,' Raja said, giving a slight bow of his head that made his brother cringe with shame. 'We were wondering if anyone had seen a Ford Escort parked just over the road and by the cricket ground earlier.'

Bilal hated the way his brother sounded. Apologising for

wanting to speak to someone was not how it was supposed to be. They had every right to talk to them, to ask them questions; they were just as much a part of this community as anyone else. More so probably; the Wadees ran a string of shops in the Dewsbury area as well as Ossett, and while not the sort of work the two brothers enjoyed, both preferring the manual labour of dock-working, food, drink and papers were sold to the families who lived close by and had been for many years now.

'Come, Raja,' he began, giving his brother's arm a gentle pull as he started to move away from the pub door. 'We have disturbed them, and they don't know anything about your stolen car.'

'Did he say we stole their car?' someone said from inside the pub.

Raja knew instinctively he had made a mistake in coming here, but it was too late.

The man at the door reached out, grabbed Raja by his shoulders and pulled him inside, twisting to the side so he could push the startled man into the centre of the room.

'Raja!'

Bilal turned to run, but before he could do so he felt himself grabbed from behind.

'Let me go!' he shouted as he was dragged back towards the pub. A shadow fell over him as a large figure moved out of the pub to help grab him.

'Shut the fuck up, Paki.'

He felt the cold trickle of spit land on his face a moment before the punch came. It connected with his jaw, snapping his head back and to the left. Stars danced across his vision and then he was aware that he was being lifted up. A moment later the loud bang of the door shutting was followed once more by the metallic click of locks and chain.

They had indeed made a mistake in coming here.

Another punch, this time to the back of his head, rocked him forward and he fell to the floor.

He landed beside his brother, who was now curled up, his arms protecting his head against the flurry of kicks coming from the group of men standing around. He heard the dull thuds of their kicks as they landed and the heavy groan of his brother.

'Please…' Bilal said, but before he could continue to beg for them to stop, a heavy metal-shod boot caught him on the cheek, and everything went black.

CHAPTER SIX

He followed as the two Pakistani men were dragged outside the pub, their cries for help muffled by hands around their mouths. The beating they'd already sustained was nothing compared to what was to come. He felt a tingle of excitement run through him.

The slam of the pub door behind him was like a gunshot in the silence of the night, echoing off the large industrial bins and stacks of empty bottles waiting for pickup. The rear of the pub was filled with rubbish, dirt and dead cigarettes, but no one could see the small group of men lost in the overhanging shadow of the building.

He watched for a few minutes as the beating continued, each member of the group getting a few licks in before the next one dived in. When it came to his turn, he gave a chuckle and shook his head.

'I ain't touching their kind with my skin,' he said. 'Dirty Paki; who knows where they've been?'

Laughter now echoed around him and he smiled. He wasn't dumb, not like the other members of the group. He might share their hatred, but that was where the similarities ended. They were dumb, stupid animals acting on instinct. Not with cold logic. They were punching the Pakis with bare fists. Fists that left marks, split skin and shared blood. All signs the pigs would be looking for when the men went crying to them. And they would.

Not one of the group had the stones to do what was needed. There was only one way to end a threat and that was to cleanse it totally from existence. He was more than happy to do that, but it had to be done right. Not this way. Not so... sloppily. They had no idea what they were doing, just playing at being big tough guys. How difficult was it to knock a few brownies around? Anyone could do that, as they had proven. But what he did was so much more subtle. So much more... refined. They would get caught, easily. Quickly. Especially if they let these two brownies go. Which they would.

He wouldn't.

He had ways to make them disappear. People would come looking, of course. That was natural. Inevitable. But the way he did it... much harder to find. And chances were, they wouldn't even realise they were missing to begin with.

But there was no way he was getting caught up in this, and that was why he was leaving.

'Got to head off anyway. Lad's on his own.'

Against a chorus of calls that challenged his heritage, his mother's choice of father and his sexuality, he slipped down the closed alley beside the pub. As he walked away he could hear the beating resume. The heavy thud of boots striking the two bodies on the ground filled his blood with an energy he was only too well aware of.

'Work to be done,' he whispered.

Coming to the end of the alley, he paused. There would be repercussions from what was happening behind him in the dirty alley of the pub, repercussions he didn't want to be involved in. There would be further ones from the plans they had been talking about. Plans for next Saturday. Those he wasn't so sure about.

Another groan came from behind. He had to make sure he wasn't seen and so he waited.

When nothing happened, he stepped out from the dark alley, brushing away a damp leaf that had attached itself to his shoulder, and onto the pavement of Savile Road.

There was no one else around, at least no one he could see, and even if he was being observed, what would they actually see? A figure stumbling from the alley of the pub; what was so wrong with that? Someone needed a piss, and the thick bushes provided a perfect place to do so. Nothing weird about that; how many hundreds if not thousands of times had that happened over the years?

No, if anyone saw him, they'd dismiss him as just another punter needing a slash after a Sunday session. And if they did think he was a bit suss... Well, by the time they'd found a copper to speak to, he'd be long gone. He'd learned that one the hard way, years ago, way back when he started exploring his new hobby. Mistakes of the past never to be repeated.

And with his new protégé, there was so much more to learn, more secrets to be revealed. New skills to learn. He was good; the boy would be better.

The sound of a scream was cut off sharply behind him. He paused as a light came on in a house nearby and he slipped into the shadow of one of the trees that lined the road. A dark anger rose inside him. Stupid! They were so stupid!

He cursed and stomped and hit at the air as the rage threatened to take him. It clawed its way up his throat, burning his insides with its fire. The urge to vomit was nearly overwhelming, and it took all his effort to stop himself from splattering his rage all over the pavement.

His mind reeled and a dizzying wave rocked him. He reached out and used the small wall of the cricket ground to steady himself, both physically and mentally. The cold touch of the stone, chilled by the falling night air, punched through his hot rage. He dragged his hand along its rough ridges, savouring the rasp as his skin was pulled taut, the flesh tearing in small places.

He'd done everything to make sure nothing ever led back to him, and here they were, those stupid, ignorant fucks, stomping on a couple of insignificant Pakis. Six months, the longest he'd ever been allowed to play, and these idiots... this should have been fucking fool proof, and yet here he was, the fucking fool!

Pain exploded in his head as he punched the trunk of the nearby tree, his arm and fist slipping through the bars of the metal cage that ringed the trunk in a green circle. His teeth bit down on his lower lip and he tasted blood. The copper tang brought a smile to his bloodied lip.

It had cleared his mind, the pain. It always did, whether inflicted on himself or another.

He knew what he had to do.

A quick look up and down the street told him what he already knew; he was alone. Good.

Pulling his collar up against the cold of the night, he started walking towards Dewsbury town centre and a taxi home. To him.

And her.

CHAPTER
SEVEN

Louise looked out of the window at the passing scenery as Danes drove to Dewsbury Memorial Hospital. They sat in silence, both lost within their own thoughts. It was past midnight. They were both tired, the stress of the incident compounded by the knowledge that their friend was also in hospital, put there at the hands of someone she trusted. A growing anger burned in both of them.

It was Danes who broke the silence, slamming his hand on the steering wheel so hard and so suddenly it made Louise jump in the seat beside him.

'What the fuck was she thinking?' he said, slapping the steering wheel again. 'As soon as he raised his hands once, she should have called it over. Right there and then.'

'It's not always easy to do the right thing,' Louise said, surprised at the crashing wave of anger that rolled off Danes, 'especially when there's love involved.'

He was married; what had happened between Hines and him had been a one-night mistake, one that could have ended both their careers and his marriage if she had become pregnant. Her boyfriend, Joe, hadn't known what had happened either. As far as Louise knew, Hines had never told him about the suspected pregnancy. Perhaps he had found out... Was this what had caused whatever happened tonight?

It had been tough on her, she was young with a promising career ahead of her, Hines had been asked to join the detective branch after the Holland case and she had certainly proved herself over the last couple of years.

Louise had seen it happen before. That had been back in Manchester – Debbie Hayward, another rookie officer who had fallen for one of the training officers. They hadn't been careful; they had been seen. The rumours spread through the station like wildfire, burning everyone it touched. Nearly burning Louise as well, as she did her best to look out for Debbie. For her friend.

It had all ended horribly, tragically, that night in Manchester. In the Crescents.

In Hulme.

'Louise?'

She turned to see Danes staring at her.

'What?'

'You didn't hear a word I said, did you?'

'It probably wasn't important,' she replied, trying to inject a little humour into the darkness of their night. 'And keep your eyes on the road. Last thing we need to happen is to be in an accident of our own. Manby would be really pissed off then.'

Danes laughed, and a moment later, Louise joined him.

It felt good.

After another moment, Danes cleared his throat.

'So, I guess you know about me and Hines.'

Louise looked at him.

'Is that a question? Doesn't matter. Yes, I know and I don't care. It's over, right? One and done.' He didn't say anything, keeping his eyes on the road. 'Right?'

The car turned onto Halifax Road, and a few moments later they were parked in the hospital car park. A former workhouse from the eighteen hundreds, Dewsbury Memorial looked imposing, with its tall stone walls and crenellations giving it the appearance of a castle rather than a modern hospital.

'You find out about our suspect,' Louise said, climbing out of the car. 'I'm going to see Beth.'

Danes shrugged and locked the car door.

At this time of night, the only way into the hospital was through the Accident and Emergency department. There were two columns of seats in front of the reception area; three rows of plastic chairs sat empty on the left, while the right had about a dozen people scattered amongst them. Talk was a hushed cloud of whispers and low arguments, fuelled for the most part by cold caffeine and hot tempers. A young mother cradled a child in one arm, the other held at an awkward angle at her side, an obvious break. A man muttered angrily at her, his words not carrying to Louise, who stared at him with professional interest.

She couldn't switch it off; the way she saw through the masks and the lies, the false fronts and the tears. Her aunt would see a young family, all tired, all cranky at having to visit the hospital after a careless accident. Clothes pulled on in the late hours of the night without any thought of appearance; hair unkempt and uncombed; the baby brought along because there was no one to babysit while they waited to be seen. What Louise saw was worse, much worse, the result of multiple past experiences. What she saw lurked beneath the surface in plain sight: the pale, haunted skin that suggested drug use, the faded bruises on the neck, cheek and exposed skin of the mother's arm when she moved to keep the baby still. The greasy, nicotine-stained fingers, the eyes red with tears. Panicked looks when the baby started to make a noise, first to the man and then to the receptionist behind the glass. *Has she seen? Did she hear?*

Does she know?

Louise saw the pain and the fear and worse: felt them both a hundredfold, knowing there was nothing she could do.

She saw the two drunks sleeping it off on the back row; the homeless man pretending he had hurt his leg so he didn't have to feel the wooden bench beneath his back for one night. She saw the couple arguing over how long they were waiting while his hand bled onto the floor in small drops, the skin puckered around the nail that had been driven into his finger, the result of a late night, drunken attempt at a home improvement. A woman wearing a colourful Pakistani dress sobbed into a handkerchief, her face covered by the shawl wrapped around her head. She sat alone, isolated from the others by an invisible barrier. Distance had been given, unconsciously or not. Louise sadly suspected it was the latter.

Louise Miller saw it all. All the darkness, both in and out.

'Can I help you?'

The receptionist gave a tired smile. Monday morning. The tired start to another week. Louise smiled back.

'My name is Detective Constable Louise Miller. I believe Elizabeth Hines was brought here earlier?'

'The domestic?' Louise nodded.

The receptionist looked at her paperwork, flipping back a page. Contrary to the calm of the reception area, it appeared it had been a busy night after all. 'Yes. Came in shortly after eleven and taken straight through for treatment.'

'How bad was it?' Louise asked, dreading the answer.

So far no one had actually said to her what Hines' injuries were, or how badly she had been hurt. All through the journey from Ossett to Dewsbury, Louise had been steeling herself for the worst. No matter what the doctors said, no matter what Beth's injuries would turn out to be, Louise vowed she would help her recover, whatever it took. However long it took, Hines wouldn't be alone.

'I'm afraid I can't say,' the receptionist replied with an apologetic shrug, 'but I can say she has been given a bed for the night in the general ward, so it can't be life threatening.'

'She's fine,' a voice said from behind her.

Louise turned to see Hines' on-again off-again boyfriend Joe as he came out of the main hospital. He had a few cuts to his forehead and one hand was bandaged. Blood spotted his collar. A moment later the doors opened again to reveal Karla Hayes. Her eyes were hard, her jaw set.

'Is he still here? He tried to get in her room.'

'What the fuck are you doing Joe?' Louise said. 'I heard—'

Joe's face turned into a snarl of annoyance.

'Doesn't matter what you heard. Doesn't matter what happened either; I was still concerned, why wouldn't I want to see her?'

Karla came to stand beside Louise. The two exchanged a private glance, Louise's eyes sparkling at the look mirrored back.

'Just go,' Karla said to Joe. 'There's no way you're getting to see her tonight. If again.'

Louise turned to glower at Joe.

'I should arrest you right now, but I'm pretty sure Beth wouldn't want me to. What the fuck she ever saw in you, I'll never know.'

She knew she was being spiteful, but she couldn't help herself. It wasn't as if Hines was totally innocent in all this drama, but she was her friend. Joe was just a bartender.

'Don't be stupid,' Joe said, his voice rising enough that the people still waiting in the cheap seats looked over. 'And I don't take relationship advice from queers. Yes, I know about you two,' he continued with a wicked sneer. 'Beth told me all about you. You want to know what I think?'

Joe's face swiftly changed into a pained look of surprise as Peter Danes grabbed him by the scruff of his neck and physically walked him out of the building, the bartender's feet barely touching the floor, scuffing the polished linoleum as Danes dragged him along. The doors hissed open and the cold morning air blew in briefly as Danes pushed Joe out.

. . .

As soon as he was free from Danes' grip, Joe whirled round. He took a step forward. Danes took two.

'Think carefully, twinkle-toes,' Danes said.

'Fuck you!'

Danes shook his head.

'Don't think so. Not my type.'

'I know you,' Joe said. Tears were streaming down the young man's face. 'You're the married guy she was fucking. Yeah, I know of you. Question is, does your wife know of you like I do? What do you think she'd do if I told her?'

'Like I give a fuck,' Danes said.

He turned away and walked back inside the building, leaving a confused Joe standing outside in the cold. Alone.

'Well, that was certainly interesting,' Louise said to Karla as Danes walked up. 'Old meets new.'

'There's nothing going on between us,' Danes said. 'It was a one-time mistake.'

'Nearly a costly one,' Karla said. Danes' eyes flashed.

'What does that mean?'

'Let's all leave it alone,' Louise said. 'We're here for Beth, right? How is she?'

'Banged up but okay,' Karla replied. 'Apparently they got into a fight that became a shoving match, and Elizabeth ended up falling through one of the glass tables in the Carps. Oh, don't worry, she got a few good licks in herself,' she added, seeing the concern spring to the lips of both Louise and Danes. 'Broke a pool cue over his arm, she did. That Sergeant of yours was here, but he's done nothing except take a statement from Joe. Didn't even speak to Elizabeth. Seemed he was more interested in the person from the car crash than one of his own officers.'

'Seriously? I knew he was a waste of space, but this is beyond a joke. Where is he?' Danes said.

Before Karla could say anything else, the doors slid open and a man barrelled out, nearly knocking into Danes.

'Careful,' Danes said. The man didn't seem to hear him and, from the seating area, a woman's voice called out. It held a lyrical tone yet was clearly edged with worry.

'Danesh!'

Louise looked up. She knew that name. She recognised that voice.

The Pakistani woman in the colourful dress stumbled from the seating area and fell into the man's arms, sobbing. He held her and patted her back, his cheek pressed to the top of her head.

'They are all right,' he said. 'Hurt, but all right.'

'Mr and Mrs Wadee?'

The two parents turned to Louise. Both were crying. Mr Wadee – Danesh – wiped at his tears with the sleeve of his suit.

'I am sorry, but we are… Ms Miller. Is that you?'

Louise put her hand on his shoulder.

'What happened? Are you all right?'

Mr Wadee nodded. Mrs Wadee kept her face pressed to his chest, her own body rocking with tears.

'We are fine, yes. Thank you. But it is our sons; Bilal and Raja. They have been attacked. They have been hurt.'

Danes stalked down the corridor, his feet stamping hard, the echo of his steps like gunshots. He turned a corner and found Detective Sergeant Tom Bailey standing in the corridor, hands shoved firmly into his coat pockets as he talked with a white-jacketed doctor. The conversation seemed heated; Bailey's cheeks were red and the doctor was clearly impatient with the Police Sergeant.

'For the last time, there is nothing my patient can tell you tonight. He is in too much pain and has been sedated. We only just got his foot from the crash scene. He will be asleep for the next few hours. Lunchtime tomorrow will be the earliest I can let you speak with him, if at all, as he'll be going into surgery as soon as he is capable.'

'Now listen here, you fucking—'

Bailey stopped himself, clamping his mouth down so tight, Danes could hear the man's teeth clash together. Danes watched as Bailey took in a long deep breath, trying to control himself.

'Ay up,' Danes said, pulling the attention to himself. He gave Bailey a clap on the shoulder then turned to the doctor.

'Hi. Peter Danes. I lead the Scene of Crime team that's handling the vehicle collision in Ossett. I understand you've been looking after one of those involved?'

The doctor visibly relaxed.

'Yes. As I was saying to your colleague, the gentleman has suffered severe injuries, including burns across eighty percent of his body and, as a result, is unconscious. The medication given to handle the pain he is in means it is very unlikely he will be in a position to talk anytime soon. If at all.'

'Thank you,' Danes said. 'As soon as he is awake, though, we would like to talk with him. With your permission of course, Doctor…?'

'Kavel. Sanjay Kavel.'

Danes smiled and shook the man's hand.

'Thank you, Doctor Kavel. I'm just going to have a chat with my Sergeant if you don't mind, and then I'd like to see any of his personal items.'

'Of course. I'll have one of my staff take you to them.'

'Thank you again,' Danes smiled.

Doctor Kavel gave a cold stare at Bailey before moving away down the corridor. Danes watched him for a moment and then rounded on Bailey.

'What the fuck is your problem?'

'What do you fucking think? We've got two dead and the bastard that knows what happened is lying in a bed all nice and comfy. That sanctimonious arsehole is stopping the investigation of an offence. I'm not having it.' He stared at the retreating form of the doctor, who pushed through a door and disappeared. 'Fucking Paki!'

Danes was startled by the man's reaction. Startled but not surprised. There were those on the force, some he called friends, who held deep prejudices, a them and us mentality that Danes had never understood. While they never came out and voiced their racism as Bailey had done, he knew by their tone or choice of words how they really felt about members of the Muslim community. It was a shock to him; the colour of a person's skin had never been a factor in how he treated them. What mattered was their actions, their words. He took everyone at face value; if you acted like a prick, it didn't matter if your skin was white, brown, black, yellow or unicorn pink. You were a prick. It was simpler to think in those terms, Danes had decided years ago, than tarnish everyone with the same racial brush. If he did that, then there'd be no one left. He knew a lot of pricks, and while they were a rainbow of skin colours, most of them were white.

Just like the one standing in front of him right now.

'What's happening at the crash site?' Bailey asked, tearing Danes away from his thoughts.

If you were a proper Sergeant, you'd fucking know. It really should have been Miller.

'The car's being recovered and taken to the garage for inspection. But we've also got the situation with Beth. Let's try and find some coffee and you can get me caught up with what Joe said.'

Karla got them all tea from a vending machine while Louise sat with the Wadees and listened, as Danesh recounted the story of what had happened to his sons as best he could. They had been found in Savile Road in Savile Town by a passing taxi. Luckily for them, the driver had stopped and, seeing their beaten faces, radioed the taxi base, who in turn called the police. They were brought to the hospital and their parents informed.

'Bilal has a broken jaw and Raja is lucky not to be blind in his left eye,' Danesh said.

He stopped and took a deep drink of the weak tea. Vanita Wadee kept her hands in her lap; Karla held them, hoping that the distraught mother would be able to take a little solace from the gesture.

'What were they doing in Savile Town?' Louise asked.

Danesh gave a smile only a frustrated father could give.

'They have a flat of their own over one of our other shops. They didn't want to continue in the family business and so chose manual work at Hull docks. Better pay, worse hours, but they are, as they say, "out from under us". Such is their choice.'

Louise could vaguely remember Raja and Bilal from a couple of visits to the shop below her flat. The Wadees were her landlords as well as the owners of the local newsagents and grocery shop. She had been surprised to see the young men wearing jeans and t-shirts, not the usual dress of Pakistanis. If there had been any tension between parents and siblings, Louise had never seen it. Such is their choice, their father had said.

Not all lifestyle choices were as readily accepted. Louise knew this first-hand; coming out to her aunt and uncle, her adoptive parents following the death of her own when she was a child, had been one of the hardest things she had ever done. It had taken some time for Aunt Fiona to come round; Uncle Bernard had accepted her news immediately with a hug. This had been just before she left for Manchester and the police training course; by the time she returned to Ossett her aunt had accepted that her adoptive daughter was gay. That didn't stop her from trying to set her up with several single men though. Thankfully now she was with Karla, that had stopped. In fact, they seemed to love Karla almost as much as her.

'They were beaten looking for their car.'

'Why would they do that?' Karla asked. 'I mean... why would someone attack them?'

'It's Savile Town,' Louise said, as if that answered everything.

When she saw her partner's perplexed look, she continued. 'It's been going on for some time now. Some parents got it into their heads that their children weren't being given the same kind of education, same level of education, as children in other schools in other areas of Dewsbury.'

'I don't get it.' Karla looked at Louise then at the Wadees. 'Why would it be any different?'

It was Danesh who answered. 'The parents complaining are white,' he said.

Louise sighed. 'Sadly, that's true. They say that their children aren't being taught white values.'

Karla shook her head. 'I mean, just what are white values anyway?'

'Christian beliefs, not Muslim, is my guess. But what does religion have to do with learning your ABCs and 123s?'

'Nothing at all, and if any of those complaining have ever set foot in a church in their life, I'll drink all the tea in that vending machine.'

That had the desired effect Karla had been aiming for. The tension broke and everyone laughed. Everyone except Vanita, who simply smiled through her tears.

'Are the police looking into it?' Louise asked.

Danesh told them what the police had said: without witnesses there wasn't a lot they could do. Officers had been sent to the pub where the siblings had said they were attacked, but no one was there.

'Do you want me to do anything?' She could talk to Manby in the morning, perhaps speak to the desk Sergeant at Dewsbury station. Do a follow up with the taxi driver who had found them.

Danesh Wadee smiled, but his words chilled her soul.

'Nothing will change.'

CHAPTER
EIGHT

MONDAY, 19TH

The school run was in full flow. A steady chain of parents and children streamed along the pavement, an ever-changing kaleidoscope of people of all ages, sexes and race. Some went willingly, others complained with every step. Encouragement was given through slapped legs and yanked arms. The cries of the wounded mixed with the joyous shouts of those excited to see their friends once again. Parents shouted tired greetings across the road as they passed each other. Some joined together into groups, the weekend gossip passed back and forth between the parents in loud voices that drowned out the shouts of the children.

Savile Road gave way to South Street, and Freddie Bowler laughed as he threw the bright red koosh ball to his best friend, Imran Alvi, who caught it one handed. No parents walked the two friends to school; Freddie's mum lived on her own, his dad long gone before he was even born, and she was getting ready for work, while Imran's worked in the corner shop a few streets away.

'Pass it back,' Freddie called.

'Mine now!' Imran shouted back as he took off down the street. Freddie laughed and chased after him. They ran down South Street and turned on to Warren Street, where the Savile Town Junior and Infant school was.

Imran paused, giving Freddie enough time to catch up to him. He reached around his friend and grabbed the koosh ball from unresisting fingers.

'Nice try, Immie,' Freddie said, giving his friend a playful punch to the shoulder. 'Go on, run on and I'll throw it to you.'

Imran didn't move. There was a big crowd outside the gates to the school and it scared him. He could hear them shouting, chanting almost. It reminded him of the packed football crowds he saw on television, and it filled him with the same fear.

'What's up, Immie?'

Freddie stood beside him, staring at him as though he didn't understand why his friend had stopped playing their game. Only then did he see the fear in Imran's eyes. Only then did he hear the crowd's words.

'Pakis out! Pakis out!'

Imran turned to Freddie.

'I don't like this,' he said.

'They don't mean you,' Freddie replied, not believing his own words.

Two women, mothers dressed in the same colourful dresses Immie's own mother wore, clutched their children closer to their bodies as they walked between two lines of angry looking parents. Why they were shouting at them, Freddie didn't know, but he recognised some of the words being yelled; his father had said the same kind of things when he got back from the pub, fuelled by John Smith's and gin.

Neither of the children saw who threw the bottle but they heard it smash against the brick wall of the school, quickly followed by the scream of one of the mothers. Milk spattered the wall, and where the broken bottle landed a white pool began to form. Glass covered the pavement and Freddie was shocked to see that one of the women was bleeding.

'Come on, Immie,' he said, taking his friend's arm. 'We can sneak past.'

Imran tore his arm away, yanking the coat from between his friend's fingers so fast that it left a smooth burn on Freddie's fingertips.

'Watch it!' Freddie cried. 'That hurt!'

'I'm not going in,' Imran replied.

He was already backing away even as the chants began to get louder and more repetitive.

'Pakis out! Pakis out! White schools for white kids!'

When a loud voice called out for the Pakis to all fuck off home, Imran turned and ran.

CHAPTER
NINE

Elizabeth Hines was about to pull on her shoes when Karla Hayes appeared in the corridor outside the ward. Every part of her body hurt, and each movement seemed to find yet another aching joint, pulled muscle or twisted tendon that sent a sharp pain along every nerve. The sudden memory of being thrown through the glass table knocked every other thought out of her mind and she rocked back on the bed, just as Karla came to stand beside her. The image of Joe standing over her, his face twisted in anger, filled her mind and she shivered.

'Did you sleep well?' Karla asked, coming to sit beside her on the bed.

Hines swallowed and nodded but stayed silent. She didn't trust her voice not to break and tears to come pouring once again. She had cried quietly to herself in the middle of the night, her legs tucked up into her chest despite the pain, her face pressed into her pillow so she didn't wake the woman in the bed opposite. She had held the secret of what had happened between her and Danes for so long, hoping that Joe wouldn't find out. His anger was always like a spit of oil in the pan, flaring only when something triggered it, something trivial like a dirty plate being left on the sink, or the way she answered him.

'Do you need any help with these?' Karla asked, holding up her shoes.

Hines smiled, and lifted one foot, then the other, allowing Karla to slip the shoes on.

'All sorted,' Karla said, getting back to her feet. 'You got everything together?'

Hines looked at the bed and the small table beside it just to make sure. Other than the near-dead flowers Joe had brought in last night, leaving them with a nurse who didn't know better, there was nothing left that belonged to her. She knew just how lucky she had been; it could have been so much worse.

'Where's Joe?' she asked.

Karla had expected this. It was a natural reaction, a morbid itch that the brain had to scratch following such a traumatic event. Grief took on many different forms, and in her capacity as a psychologist she had seen if not all of them, then most.

'He's being dealt with,' she replied, remembering how Danes had bodily thrown him from the hospital, but Hines didn't need to know that. The camaraderie between those who worked in dangerous roles like the police, fire brigade or military was a fascinating subject to study but also a paradoxical puzzle, both totally understandable and yet inaccessible to those on the outside.

'I should speak to him.'

Karla shook her head.

'Probably best to leave it for now. Come on, we need to get you home and back into bed.'

'I need to go to work,' Hines replied. As she spoke, her words sped up as her train of thought ran away from her, fuelled no doubt by the stress and anxiety of what had happened. 'I've so much to do,' she continued. 'The report on what happened, for a start. Manby's a stickler for procedure, and getting a witness statement as soon as possible is always high-up on his shit-list.'

'Bill can wait, and besides, he told me to take you straight home,' Karla replied after listening to Hines' argument. 'They've got their hands full with the crash and the two dead bodies without having to be worrying about you at the same time.'

Louise had told her all about the grisly accident when they'd got home in the early hours of the morning. Karla had been mesmerised as she listened to Louise's description of the burnt car and the foot of the survivor that had dropped from it. It all added to the bizarre mystery of what had happened that night.

'Say that again?' Hines said. 'What car crash?'

Louise sat at her desk, her hands clasped around her mug, taking comfort from the warmth of the coffee. It was just after nine in the morning; Karla should have picked up Beth by now and be on the way to the younger detective's home where she was under strict instructions to lie up and fully recover. A night's stay in hospital was enough to get over the immediate effects of the attack, but she would need time for her body to fully heal. Louise knew only too well how long that could take; she still had scars from the crash that had taken her parents' lives when she was only a child. One ran up her back and across her shoulder blades where glass and hot metal had cut into her. Only Karla had ever seen her scars, all of them. She smiled, remembering the soft touch of Karla's fingers running up her spine and the feel of her lips taking away a little of their sting away with each gentle kiss.

'Penny for them,' a gruff voice called out.

Louise looked up from her coffee to see Detective Inspector Bill Manby standing in the open doorway to his office. Like her he was still wearing the same clothes as last night. *Or was it this morning?* her tired mind asked.

He leaned against the doorframe as he pulled a packet of cigarettes from his jacket pocket. He fumbled one free, lit it and put pack and lighter back, all in one single motion. He took in a deep pull, held it, then let the smoke out slowly. Louise watched, mesmerised, as the cloud spread out then rose slowly to the ceiling.

'I thought Marie wanted you to give up?' Louise asked as she came over, cup of coffee in hand, to stand beside Manby. His eyes were tired shells, his skin pale and drawn, his lips a thin line that clamped tightly around the tube of the cigarette. He looked as though he had aged ten years overnight.

Louise suspected that if she dared look in a mirror, what stared back at her would be just as bad.

The road was still closed, which meant traffic diversions being set up. The 'Mad Mile' of the A638 dual carriageway fed the M1 from Ossett and Dewsbury. With links to Leeds and the north, and London and the south, it was an artery that couldn't afford to be blocked for long. Hundreds of haulage trucks used the route every day; there was no way it could be allowed to back traffic up in the surrounding streets that led into Ossett itself.

And that all meant headaches for Manby as he negotiated with the different divisions. Add to that the calls from Chief Superintendent Freeman at the West Yorkshire Police Headquarters in Wakefield, with demands for constant updates, and it was no wonder Manby looked ghastly.

'One won't kill me,' Manby replied. 'Want one?'

She smiled and shook her head. Louise had over a hundred packs of Regal Blues stored away in her cubby hole wardrobe at home, packs she had bought over the years in memory of her dad, who had smoked religiously. Every now and then she would light one and leave it burning in an ashtray on the windowsill. When she did that, her dad was back in the room, his presence as thin and wispy as the smoke, but there nonetheless. She always enjoyed the memories that the smell brought back, however brief they were.

'I'll stick with this,' she replied, holding up her coffee mug. The drink was cold and bitter, and if she was being honest, she would much prefer to be downing a cold pint of Carling rather than the stale brown slop that passed itself off as Prospect Road coffee. Manby headed back into his office, indicating that Louise should follow him.

'Any word back from the hospital yet?'

'Nothing yet,' she replied, 'and the doctor says he doesn't hold out much hope for him. Too badly burned. They're not even going to try and reattach the foot.'

Manby grimaced. 'Has anyone been able to identify him yet?' There hadn't been a wallet or any other form of identification on him when his clothes were removed at the hospital.

'Not yet, and even if there had been, chances are anything would have been burnt beyond recognition, anyway. A little good news; we've got names on the two who died on scene.'

Manby sat at his desk, stubbed out the corpse of one cigarette and lit another as Louise continued.

'Steve Smith and Kevin Roberts. Both lived in Ossett. Officers are at their home addresses right now and we should have more information later this morning.'

'Good stuff. And the car?'

Louise took a seat. 'The DVLC should get back to me around eleven this morning. I'll look at the report and take it from there.'

Manby smiled.

'Another case of hurry up and wait, then?'

'Isn't it always?' she said. There was only so much they could do in any given case before they had to wait and let the process play out. 'In the meantime, I'm going to check up on what happened to the Wadees. I know the family and I just want to make sure everything that should be done is being done.'

'Good idea,' Manby said. He sat back in his chair and let out a long sigh. 'Not exactly the end to my break I was planning on.'

'Did Marie blow her top?'

It was no secret that the DI and his wife had been having problems, and getting dragged in from his first proper break in months must have been a real kick in the teeth.

'She was surprisingly okay with it,' he said with a smile, 'but I doubt she'll let me off the hook as easily next time. And speaking of hooks; when are you going to take yours out of Bailey? If you should be mad at anyone it's me.'

'Do you really want to talk about this now?' Louise said. She could feel the flush of anger already rising to her cheeks, the wound of being passed over for promotion to Sergeant still raw.

'Do you really want to talk to your DI like that?' he replied, his own anger poking through his words. 'I had to make a decision, and on paper Tom Bailey was the better candidate. That doesn't mean you need to take every opportunity to drag him down, and especially not in front of other officers.'

'Because he's a man,' Louise said. 'That's the only reason why he got the job. He was the better candidate? I have a better clearance record; I've not been dragged before a disciplinary hearing and I know how to co-ordinate a crime scene. Bailey barely knows what day of the week it is. Instead of being on scene at the crash last night and co-ordinating the start of the investigation, he was at the hospital with an unconscious suspect, something any uniform could have done.'

'He was also at the hospital checking up on Beth at my request, or had you forgotten?'

His words were a cold, harsh slap that she knew he instantly regretted. His expression softened.

'I can remember being passed over for promotion several times myself, but I'm sure it's harder for you. I get it. I do, but being passed over this time is not your shame; it's mine. Maybe I could have fought harder for you, but it wouldn't have changed anything. Minds had been made up long before I got involved. It'll happen, I'm sure of it. Just not yet.'

'Fine,' Louise said, her voice dropping its edge.

She knew he meant what he said. She also knew he was probably as gutted as her that she hadn't got the job. More, knowing him. He always fought their corner, both hers and Hines'.

'Fine,' she repeated. 'So, while he's at the hospital, who's running the show back here? The car, the crash and now the Wadees. That's a lot to be left hanging in the air, don't you think? And I've not even included what we should be doing for Beth.'

Manby's smile didn't fill her with the confidence she'd wanted. In fact, it unnerved her even more.

'Well, that's yours. You wanted to show what you can do as a Sergeant; here's your chance.'

Louise was shocked.

'You want me to be acting Sergeant while Bailey sits in a hospital? All the work and none of the recognition?'

'If you fuck up you'll certainly be recognised,' Manby said with a wink.

Louise said nothing. The look on his face told Louise he knew he had totally missed the mark with his attempt at a joke.

'What I mean is, this is a chance to show the Chief Superintendent just what you can do when called on. Instead of moaning about it and being all Missy Pessimistic—'

'Missy Pessimistic?'

'Instead of being that… be Polly Positive.'

'Are you drunk?' she asked, but she couldn't help the laugh that crept into her voice.

'Grab the opportunity by the balls… and squeeze. Show them why they should have picked you instead of Tom-fucking-Bailey. Take advantage of the situation…'

'Without looking like I'm taking advantage,' Louise finished. 'Got you.'

Manby stubbed out his cigarette just as his phone began to ring. 'Well… go get on it.' He lifted the phone, greeting the caller with his usual gruff response.

Louise rose from her chair and left his office, silently closing the door behind her.

CHAPTER
TEN

Louise was just making another brew when Hines walked up behind her. The kettle was beginning its shrill whistle and she was lost in her thoughts about how best to organise the workload now that she was in charge of the investigations when she felt a tap on her shoulder.

She turned to find Hines grinning at her.

'What the hell are you doing here?' Louise asked, before throwing her arms around her friend and pulling her into a giant hug. She hurriedly let go when she felt Hines tense up and heard her sharp intake of breath. Louise stepped back and regarded her friend with concern. 'Karla should have taken you home and you should be resting up.'

Hines shrugged her coat off, hanging it over the back of her chair. 'I told her to bring me here. I can't be sat at home twiddling my feet when there's work to be done, and besides, you need me. With me gone out of the office that would leave you free to take down Bailey without anyone stopping you.'

'About that,' Louise began, pointing to the chair for Hines to sit in. She grabbed another cup from the side. 'There's been a little change. Fancy a cuppa?'

• • •

They were both sitting at their desks, a stack of folders between them, their mugs of tea now accompanied with a pair of biscuits pilfered from the absent Sergeant's desk. Hines lifted hers, took a sip and grimaced. 'I swear your tea making skills are getting as bad as mine,' she said. Louise answered with a shrug as she took a bite of biscuit.

'You know, they always taste better when you're not the one to buy them,' she said. Crumbs fell from the side of her mouth and she brushed them away. 'He might be a prick but he does buy the best biscuits.'

She looked over to Bailey's desk: it was pristine. No stacks of folders, no scattered pieces of paper with hastily written phone messages on them. No tea-stained mugs with old tea going mouldy through neglect; his Leeds United mug was as clean as the day it was kilned. *I suppose it's hard to get untidy if you're never at your desk*, Louise thought.

She looked at her own desk and winced.

Three towers of folders balanced precariously next to each other, creating a small wall between her and Hines' desks. A four-tiered paper tray overflowed on every level, a mix of official forms, procedural guidelines and one or two glossy magazines that her aunt kept palming off on her when she visited. Plucked from the almost encyclopaedic Sunday papers her uncle got each week, the pages were packed with the sorts of shenanigans only those with celebrity status could get up to.

And get away with.

If a member of the public, rather than a musician in a popular band, was found driving with three times the legal limit of alcohol in their blood, and a prostitute lying across their lap, they would, at the very least, spend time in the local cells instead of getting their pictures in every glossy mag in the land and, presumably, shifting a few thousand more copies of their really bad pop song. Then there were the articles about who was dating, who was marrying and who was divorcing; for some it seemed they were in a revolving door of relationships, depending on how much their star had dimmed in the public consciousness.

And yet Louise still read them, finding a little self-indulgent distraction in the glamour of celebrity madness from the selfless drudgery of police work. After a day dealing with the drug dealer who happily pushed his trade on those already down on their luck; the street-walker who offered her body each night so she could feed her baby; or the family man who now broke into homes and stole jewellery after his job was stripped from him as crudely as he had once stripped the coal from the land; after dealing with such sorrow, anger, and in several cases, death, reading about the extremely privileged lifestyles of the rich and famous was the very least she could do to keep her sanity. Reading might be pushing it, she thought, as she looked for a particular form amongst the stacked papers. The articles were little more than puff pieces used to fill the spaces between the sparkly pictures.

'What are you looking for?' Hines said.

She reached forward to stop a stack of papers sliding out of the tray as Louise pulled a sheet with a fast sweep. Her face turned cold when she saw what Louise had pulled out.

'No,' she said, in tone that suggested she was trying to end the conversation. Louise's expression didn't change. 'No,' Hines said again, but her voice broke a little. 'I'm not... I'm not doing it.'

'This isn't a request, Elizabeth,' Louise said.

Hines' head shot up at the use of her first name in such a way. Louise tried a different tactic.

'What did you think was going to happen? You were in a fight. A fight! There are witnesses, people who care about you whether you like it or not. People who saw what happened and have come forward and made their own reports. The police were called to the Carps. You were taken to hospital in an ambulance. If you think this is just going to go away, that this time is just going to be like all the others, then you're wrong. Just plain wrong. Even worse, you're naïve.'

She put the form on the table and pushed it towards Hines. For a moment the younger officer just looked at it, her chest rising and falling rapidly. Each breath was followed by a sharp wince as the wounds she had suffered last night bit once more.

'No one's talking about pressing charges, though they should. No, wait,' Louise said, seeing that Hines was about to protest.

Her raised hand cut Hines off, and so did her raised voice. An officer standing at the door that led to the upstairs lab turned to look. Louise ignored him but still lowered her voice.

'You don't want to hear it but you were assaulted last night. Assaulted by someone who is supposed to care for you. To love you. You were thrown into a glass fucking table, or had you forgotten that? You spent a night in hospital. You should be fucking livid about what happened and demanding that arsehole gets brought in and thrown in a cell, and let me tell you this: it took everything to stop Danes from doing just that. If not worse. Joe's lucky all he got was thrown out of the hospital last night and not given a right fucking kicking. I'd have joined in and stomped on him once or twice myself given the chance.'

'You were at the hospital last night?'

'Of course we were. We had to deal with the car crash first, but as soon as we got the preliminary investigation out the way, we came straight over. By the time we got there, though, it was late and you were asleep.'

'I vaguely remember seeing Karla and, I think, Joe, but it was all a bit groggy. You were there?'

Tears had started to run down Hines' cheeks. Louise didn't say anything, just reached across the table between the gap in the pile of files, and placed her hand over her friend's trembling fingers. She gripped twice with an encouraging smile.

'What happened, love?'

Hines took her hand away, moving it to her mug of tea, which she raised to her lips. It was hot and loaded with sugar. She stared across its brown surface with red rimmed eyes. When she began to speak, her voice fell to such a hush that Louise had to lean forward in order to hear her.

'He wasn't always like this,' she began, her words a perfect mirror for the dozens of similar victims of domestic abuse that the pair had spoken to over the last few years.

This was how every such interview began, with the victim trying to justify why they were now sitting with blackened eyes, bruised ribs and bleeding lips. It was their fault; they shouldn't have burned the dinner, shouldn't have said no to sex, shouldn't have talked back. He worked all day; he'd had one too many, that was all. He'd pushed too hard, not meant to hit her with his fist. It was her fault; she'd pushed him, threatened him, threatened the kids. Threatened divorce. Not his fault. My fault. Blame me. Everyone always does.

But Elizabeth Hines wasn't like the women Louise had spoken to before, at least not in that regard. Where she differed was the rod of steel that ran through her very core, the strength of self she could rely on. For the vast majority of victims, the women had once had the same strength but it was lost, trodden down so deep within their soul that for some, it was never found. But not Elizabeth Hines.

'He wasn't like this until I told him about Peter. About the possibility I was pregnant. Then he changed. Just like that. In a way it was my fault... I cheated. Not Joe. But that doesn't excuse how he acted. That doesn't give him permission to lay hands on me, and that was the one and only time he ever did. I think he scared himself more than me; I certainly don't fear him. How could I... I've seen his dick, and let me tell you—'

'Please don't,' Louise said.

'—it's nothing worth talking about.' She waggled her little finger in the air, making them both laugh.

Hines winced, clutching at her side.

'Fuck, that hurts. We'd both been drinking. He said something. I said something back. Then I pushed him and he pushed me and I fell into the table. I'm not making excuses for him, but it was my fault as much as his. I've already told them I'll pay for the damage.'

'Yes, I've got that from the witnesses. You were more bothered about the mess than the cuts you'd taken. Apologising all the time you were waiting for the ambulance to turn up.'

Hines put her head in her hands.

'Oh, God. There's no way I can go back to the Carps now. How fucking embarrassing is that?'

'You can go back any time. Joe not so much.'

The owners had already told Louise that Joe was probably going to be fired. The word *probably* troubled her. Dominic was a fair man, but he also had a business to run, and no matter what she thought of the man, Joe was a good worker. She'd already decided to wait until she'd got Hines' statement before telling her about Joe's likely sacking – there was a good chance she'd clam up if she knew.

'So that was it? Those other times...?'

'It was just arguments. Loud ones, to be sure, but nothing like this. I promise,' she added, seeing Louise's questioning look. 'I promise.'

Louise took a cap off a pen and handed it over.

'Fine. Now write all that down and we'll call it quits.'

With a sigh, Hines took the pen and began to write. Louise smiled and wandered over to Tom Bailey's desk again to see what other treats she could find.

It had taken nearly half an hour for Hines to write down everything that had happened. Twice she had to scrap the paper, but Louise was pleased to see she took up another form straight away and continued on until she was happy with the two sheets of her statement. By the time she was finished it seemed as though a weight had been lifted from her shoulders; her face had lost some of the stone-like countenance that had

worried Louise into thinking she was goir
the papers and walk out. It wouldn't l
had given up on something imp
mattered.

Louise had spent the time Hines was w.
initial notes from the crash scene, gathering the p.
and studying the measurements and statements from u.
witnesses whose houses overlooked the dual carriageway on
Gawthorpe Lane, so that when it came to deliver the morning
briefing she had everything she needed. A surge of excitement
shot through her at the big opportunity she was being given by
the DI, but it was short lived as she realised once again that it
was probably being done to placate her over the fiasco that had
been the Sergeant's promotion. Why had she even considered the
possibility that it would go to her? Even Karla had warned her
not to get her hopes up too much, but she had, thinking that all
the hard work and long hours she had put in actually meant
something.

'Fancy another?' Hines said, pulling Louise out of her
thoughts.

The twin sheets of the statement were now in Louise's in-tray
and Hines was reaching for her mug.

'I'm fine,' Louise said. 'All filled out?'

Hines scowled and sat back down.

'As much as I can remember. I'm not pushing for charges
against Joe. I want that known and I put it in the statement.'

'I wouldn't have expected anything less, but we have it on
record now, and that's a big first step.'

'It's the only step. I'm not—'

Louise held her hands out, tapping the air to try and still the
panic that was rising in Hines' voice.

'I know. I know. Sorry Beth… I'm not trying to push you here,
but, look. I care about you, you know that, right? A lot of people
care about you.'

The crumbling tremble of Hines' lower lip told Louise all she

to know. Now was not the time to push. Now was the
ɔ heal.

And with that statement all done and finished with, we have
ɔmething to fall back on. Just in case.'

'The only thing I'm falling back on is my bed tonight. So...
this crash on the Mad Mile. Care to fill me in on it, Acting-
Sergeant Louise-not-Tom-fucking-Bailey Miller?'

Louise looked around, worried someone had overheard
Hines' remark. Luckily, everyone was busy getting their own
paperwork and heading into the large office used for the
morning briefing session, so no one had heard. She turned back
to find Hines sniggering softly into her mug.

'Not funny,' Louise said, but she couldn't help a smile playing
around her lips.

There were a dozen uniformed officers in the briefing room along
with Peter Danes. Detective Inspector Bill Manby sat at the back
and talked softly to a smartly dressed officer who Louise had
only met once before. Chief Superintendent Freeman was a stern
looking man, his chin pointed under the neatly trimmed beard.
Every line of his uniform was crisp and looked sharp enough to
cut; the buttons of his jacket shone like polished gemstones, and
his tie was just this side of perfect. His hat sat on his lap.

Hines saw Louise looking and turned in her seat.

'Why's the Chief Super here?' she asked. Louise didn't
answer. A hot ball of nervous energy started to boil in her stomach. Was he here to check on her? Had Manby said something to
him, or had Bailey? No. It couldn't have been Bailey. He was at
the hospital still waiting for the survivor of the crash to wake up.
Wasn't he? Or had he heard that Manby was letting her take the
lead and had called his friend, the Chief Superintendent?

'Whenever you're ready, Miller,' Manby called out.

Was that a smile on his face?

Louise gathered her notes, cleared her throat and strode to the front of the gathering. For the next ten minutes she went through everything they knew so far, what had led up to the crash, the fatalities on-site and the nature of the one survivor.

'And the car?' Manby asked.

'We have a potential lead that links with the assault in Savile Town. We should have confirmation from the DVLC shortly. Both sections of the car have been recovered and taken to the garage. Forensic and engineering examinations are currently taking place and we should have an update...'

Louise turned to Danes, sitting in the front row. He turned so he could answer his DI directly.

'Sometime this afternoon. If you come along around one?' Louise nodded as he continued. 'Due to the damage the vehicle suffered it has been proving difficult to get the usual markings that would tell us where the car came from, but I'm confident we'll have it confirmed by the DVLC. As to why it came apart like it did. I've a few ideas but need to have more before I can say anything with any certainty.'

'Any more about the survivor?'

'Still working on that, sir,' Louise replied. She tried to ignore the slight shake of the Chief Superintendent's head. 'Sergeant Bailey is at the hospital, and as soon as he has anything pertinent to add to the investigation I am sure he will.'

Manby hid his smile behind a cough.

'I have every confidence in Sergeant Bailey,' the Chief Superintendent said, half to Manby, half to the rest of the room.

'That makes one then,' Hines whispered just loud enough for those nearby to hear.

A ripple of laughter sounded, cut short by a pointed cough from their DI.

'And the two Wadees,' Manby said before the Chief Superintendent could jump in. 'What's their story?'

Louise briefly checked her notes.

'It was really just chance that we came across them at the hospital, though they had reported the attack on their sons already. Both men were in Savile Town, their car was apparently stolen and they went to a pub to ask about it, where they were attacked. We are operating under the belief that the car that crashed was their stolen car.'

'Allegedly attacked,' Chief Superintendent Freeman said.

He rose to his feet in a smooth motion and strode to the front of the room.

'From what I understand we don't have any witnesses to this alleged attack, do we? Or the theft of the car? Nor do we have any evidence to suggest any other assailants; is that correct?'

Louise felt another ripple through her body, but this time it was a mixture of anger and resentment rather than excitement.

'We have their statement, sir,' she replied as calmly as she could. 'We also have their injuries. They were definitely attacked; there's no allegedly about it.'

'Brothers fight,' he said, not letting go. 'Have you considered that this was nothing more than a family argument?'

'A family argument between brothers that have no history of such behaviour? An argument that nearly left one brother blind in one eye? I highly doubt it.'

Louise turned from the Chief Superintendent to look at Manby with disbelief. He patted the air before him, a *slow down* gesture that only infuriated Louise even more.

'What is this?'

The Chief Superintendent sat on the edge of the table and looked out over the gathered officers.

'It is no secret that the relations between the Muslim and Christian communities in Dewsbury and Ossett have deteriorated in recent weeks. Reports of protests outside schools, parents taking their children out of class and, well, let's call them squabbles with some of the youths in the area... all of that has led to rising tensions. The last thing we want is for this to blow up out of all proportion and get out of control, especially following the horrendous events in Liverpool only a couple of months ago. We must ensure we tread very carefully.'

'The Wadees have put in a formal complaint, and Dewsbury Police will be looking into every aspect of this,' Louise said. 'Being sensitive to the issues for *all* involved.'

The Chief Superintendent shook his head.

'No. I've already spoken with Detective Inspector Manby on this issue and we are in agreement that you and WDC Hines will take charge of the investigation as you have a current relationship with the Wadees. Isn't that correct?'

'Well, yes, but…'

The Chief Superintendent rose from the desk.

'Excellent. All settled then. With any luck this will all blow over in the next week or so. Just a bit of pressure building like it always does in mixed communities such as ours. Sign of the times and all that. Good to see you all. Keep up the good work, everyone. Manby, I believe you promised a full breakfast over at Jenny's.'

He was already out of the door and heading through the office, adjusting his hat as he walked. Manby stood and let out the breath he had been holding.

'Well, that could have been worse,' he said. 'Just go take a full and proper statement from the Wadees, see what there is and tell them you'll look into it. If there's more to what they say I'm sure you'll pick up on it, and you can say to the Chief Superintendent that you did all you could. Everyone wins.'

'I don't think the Wadees would agree with you on that,' Louise said. 'This is why people don't trust us. It's more about the politics than it is the actual crime.'

Manby let out a sigh just as his name was called again by the Chief Superintendent.

'Just for once, do what I ask. Please.' With that said, and without waiting for an answer, Manby left the briefing room to join his boss. Louise stared daggers into his back as Hines came to stand beside her.

'Think of it this way,' she said as Louise began to gather her belongings. 'You won't have far to go after speaking with them.'

'Fancy a drink at mine after?' Louise offered. 'Maybe a bite to eat as well?'

'Good idea,' Hines replied as a uniformed officer came over. 'Hey, Philip. What's up?'

'You've a visitor,' he said, pointing through the room to where a man stood.

The man's jacket was torn in three places, the hood pulled up over his head. He held a dirty white carrier bag in one hand, while in the other a cigarette smouldered. When he saw Louise and Hines, he waved.

'Great,' Hines said with no enthusiasm. 'Scruffy Pete.'

CHAPTER
ELEVEN

Pete Williams clutched his hands around the mug of tea, apparently oblivious to the heat of the recently brewed cuppa. He drew it close, his arms pressed tight against his chest as he held his face over the steam rising from the mug. Known as Scruffy Pete throughout the pubs and betting shops of Ossett, Wakefield and Horbury, he was also a frequent visitor to the various police stations as a keen dispenser of information, as well as an occasional reluctant guest. His usual run-ins with the law were the result of too much booze and too little self-control, his hands dipping into the pockets of those who stood at the bar with him. It was never anything serious with Pete, a frustrating fact that made dealing with him problematic. Scruffy Pete had the ear of the local criminal underworld; the nefarious whisperings of drug dealers, car clockers and other associated thugs somehow found their way to him and then, in exchange for money or looking the other way when he was caught lifting someone's wallet, he was off back to the local nick.

Since moving back to Ossett, Louise had somehow become his favoured contact, probably due to the fact that she always made sure he had warm food inside him whenever they met, but today, Pete wasn't here to give information. He was here to get it.

Since his sister had gone missing six months ago, Pete had made weekly visits to the Prospect Road police station to find out if there had been any developments. Helen, a known local prostitute who worked in and around Ossett, Wakefield and Leeds, had disappeared shortly before Christmas last year, and despite their best efforts, there had been no sign of the young woman.

Best efforts? If putting her picture up on the bulletin notice board at the entrance to all police stations in the West Yorkshire area was best efforts, then yes, that's what they'd done, Louise thought as she watched Pete take a tentative sip of his tea. His face contorted into a grimace – Pete, who had been known to drink a cup of piss on a dare for a five-note – but he drank it down nevertheless.

'How have you been?' Hines asked.

'Okay,' he said.

He put down the mug and reached for the Texan bar Hines had given him, and began to unwrap it, his dirty fingers struggling to gain purchase on the thin paper. There was a slight slur to his speech as though his tongue was too big for his mouth, and when he looked at her, Louise could see that his eyes were unfocused. They were red rimmed as well, as though he had been crying for a long time. She knew different; the smell of stale beer clung to him in the same way her Lou-Lou perfume clung to her. Its scent gave her a headache, but she wore it because it had been a gift from Karla at Christmas. Pete's scent, on the other hand...

'When was the last time you had a bath?' she asked.

Pete didn't look up, just continued to struggle with the chocolate bar as he stared into the murky depths of his tea. Louise looked over at Hines, who shrugged her shoulders – *I don't know.*

When he didn't move, Louise gently touched his hand. He jumped, throwing the bar to the floor and knocking the table with his leg. Tea sloshed all over his hands. If he felt the scald, he didn't show it.

'I'll get that,' Hines said, reaching for the Texan bar under the table.

She put it down next to Pete and began to mop up the spill with tissues from a box on Louise's desk.

'Can't be having tea soaking into the paperwork,' she laughed.

'It's been six months,' Pete said. His voice was that of a child's, small and lost against the vastness of his worry. 'Six months and no one has seen or heard anything from her.' He raised his head, his eyes seeking Louise's. 'Have you found out anything? Do you know where she is or where she went?'

Hines finished mopping up and bunched the tissue into a ball. With a deft flip of the wrist, she launched it through the air and directly into the waste paper bin next to Manby's office door. Pete didn't even look.

'We've not heard a thing, Pete. Sorry,' Louise said.

'Where is she?'

His voice broke and he began to sob, his shoulders shaking. Bits of dirt and dust that had gathered on his coat fell off as he shuddered under the weight of his grief. It was apparent he hadn't been taking care of himself, more so than usual. Louise knew that most times he would cadge a bed from one of his drinking buddies after a day's session, or stumble back to the small house he shared with his sister on the Broadowler estate. But, since her disappearance, everything seemed to have fallen apart even further for the man. He barely ate, rarely washed and, judging by the thick bush of scrappy beard that clung to his face, never shaved.

'I don't know what to tell you,' Louise said, moving her chair a little closer so she could rest a hand on his shoulder. 'You obviously know your sister better than anyone, better than me and Beth, that's for sure, but in our experience, when someone with a history like Helen's goes missing, it's because they chose to disappear.'

'She wouldn't just leave me,' he said.

Louise's heart broke. It always did when she listened to the family members who were left behind, their desperate need to find answers blinding them to what everyone else saw as clearly obvious.

'I'm sure she didn't want to hurt you,' Hines said, taking over from Louise. 'I know how close the two of you were.'

'Are!' Pete shouted. 'We are close. She isn't gone! She isn't... She can't be.'

His shoulders sagged and he crumpled in on himself, head bowed as though in prayer. Louise knew that it was unlikely that he had ever seen the inside of a church, and if so it had probably been to filch the collection plate. For a few minutes neither Louise nor Hines said anything, letting the man regain his composure in his own time.

The low murmur of the room filled the silence as other officers went about their tasks. Some threw looks as dirty as Pete's jacket in their direction. Not everyone felt the same about the man; some saw him as a criminal nuisance, one that should have been locked up long ago. Others figured he was adept at hitting those officers up who were considered a light touch, the WDCs being the most obvious targets. Either way, no one other than Louise and Hines showed any concern over the man's missing sister; she was just another prostitute who had moved on. Leeds or even London; both were serviced by the nearby M1 motorway and Louise had no doubt that Helen could be very convincing if she needed a lift, especially with Clays, the late-night haulier that ran out of Ossett.

Perhaps she could ask around, see if any of the drivers had picked up a hitchhiker back in December? Off the record, of course. She wouldn't want to get them in trouble with their employer, who would, no doubt, frown on such things. She didn't want to get them in trouble with their wives, either.

She was about to say as much to Pete when the phone on her desk rang, its three-tone warble indicating an external call. She silently asked Hines if she would be okay looking after Pete and, after getting a reassuring nod, picked up the phone.

'Miller.'

The voice on the other end of the line was a high-pitched nasal tone that set her teeth on edge.

'DC Miller, it is Edward Hollings calling. PC Hollings. I have been stationed with Detective Sergeant Bailey at Dewsbury Memorial Hospital.'

'I know who you are, Ed. What can I do for you?'

'DS Bailey asked me to give you a call with an update. The poor fellow who was brought in last night just passed away. DS Bailey thought you should know.'

Shit. That was not what they wanted. With all three of the men in the car now dead, it would be a lot harder to find out exactly what happened.

Across the desk Hines had an arm about Pete's shoulders as he continued to sob quietly into his folded arms. With his head down Louise could see his crown; his hair was thinning at the top and there was what appeared to be a deep cut running from the crest of his head down the back. The sort of wound one got when struck by something hard. It had scarred badly when it healed. How old it was she couldn't tell. Louise gave a quick nod to catch Hines' attention, then indicated that she should have a look.

'Did he say anything?' Louise asked into the phone.

'He just asked me to call and let you know the man had died,' Hollings replied. Louise sighed.

'No... not Bailey. The man. Did he say anything before he died?'

'I don't think so. You'd have to speak with the Sergeant. Or the doctor. He should be back in a moment.'

'Where is he?'

There was a long pause on the other end of the phone, long enough that Louise could make out the sounds of the hospital in the background. Hushed voices spoke and the swish of cubicle curtains filled her ear as she waited for a reply. When it came, it wasn't what she had expected.

'I don't know.'

'What do you mean? Where's DS Bailey?'

She could hear the nerves in the Police Constable's voice.

'He was here a few minutes ago, and then he spoke with the mother of the deceased, and they left the hospital together.'

That was new.

'The mother turned up? Do we have a name?'

PC Hollings perked up.

'Oh yes, we have a name and an address. Luke Ellis. Lives—'

'On Broadowler estate,' Louise interrupted. She looked at Pete, a plan beginning to form in her mind. 'Thanks, Hollings. Best get yourself back to the station. I'll have a car come pick you up.'

Without waiting for a reply, Louise hung up the phone. After giving an officer instructions to go and collect PC Hollings from the hospital, she turned to Hines and Pete. He had sat up and was wiping at his eyes, Hines passing him several tissues in a constant stream.

'Come on, Pete,' she said, standing up. 'Let's give you a lift home and maybe take a look at her room again.'

A smile lit his face. 'Really?'

Louise nodded, worried at the sense of false hope she was giving the man. 'Grab your stuff.'

It wouldn't hurt to take another look, and after they'd done that, they could make a visit to the Ellis residence and see what Tom-fucking-Bailey was up to.

CHAPTER
TWELVE

He waited until the boy had gone to school before pulling the clothes from the washing machine.

Breakfast had been toast and tea, hastily put together at the last minute as they had both slept late. His fault; he had got in somewhere around four in the morning and fallen instantly into a deep and dreamless sleep, exhausted by the previous evening's events. It was the washing machine hitting the final spin cycle that woke him, its loud thumps as the machine rattled against the fixtures either side echoing throughout the house. After realising the time, he had bellowed for the boy to get up and, after throwing on fresh clothes, gone downstairs to prepare breakfast.

He threw a five-pound note to his son and ushered him out of the kitchen door, ignoring the boy's protests. The lad was keen to learn, that was certain, but he needed time to think. Needed time to plan what to do next.

Last night, before the pub, before he had gone to see her, he had known what he was doing. It was the same thing he had done for nearly ten years. Always the same. Always the same schedule. Nothing got in the way. Not his fear, nor his doubts. Certainly not his wife, though she had suspected towards the end. Nothing had got in the way until last night, and he had acted rashly because of it.

Because of them.

Those idiots in the pub, with their prejudices and their hate. He knew what he was, knew what he was capable of, what he'd done. But them... *children. Overgrown children with a child's thoughts. A child's reactions. Spoilt brats that demand and cry when they don't get their own way.* That's all it was about, the blacks and the browns. The yellows and those diluted by multi-racial couplings. He didn't care about any of that. Didn't care about the colour of the skin.

Because inside, beneath the skin, everyone looks the same.

But they had gathered together, a schoolyard gang of bullies who drank and told tall tales to big themselves up in the awed sights of those that shared their hate. *BNP... British National Party?* he thought, dragging the clothes he had been wearing last night from the washing machine, draping them over the clothes horse in front of the fire. *More like Bullies 'N' Pricks.*

He laughed at his own joke and then checked each item as he draped it over a metal arm of the clothes horse, making sure all the stains had come out. A vision of her face danced before his eyes and her soft moans and weak whimpers echoed in his mind as he bent and lit the fire. Its *whoomph!* as it roared to life and the sudden blast of heat that washed over his face startled him and he fell back, knocking the clothes horse and sending it crashing to the living room floor.

'Damn and fuck!' he cried out, the red rage instantly falling over him once more. In anger and frustration, he lashed out with his foot, kicking at the small table that stood beside his chair. It crashed to the ground, throwing the photo frame that stood on it onto the tiled raised surface around the fire. Glass shattered and the frame broke, the picture slipping out.

He reached for it, ignoring the cuts to his fingers as he pushed through the glass. Picking it up, the image of his wife and the boy shortly after his birth blew the red mist aside as it always did. Seeing the boy, new to the world, still to be new to his world, filled him with hope. Hope for the future. Hope for his future.

The phone rang, bringing him out of his thoughts. Checking to make sure the clothes weren't too close to the fire, he went into the hallway and answered the phone.

'Yes?' He listened for a moment then, shifting the phone from one ear to the other, reached for his jacket hanging on the coat hook beside the phone. 'I know… sorry. Had a rough night with the lad. He was sick so we're running a bit behind. I'll be in shortly… No. Don't worry, I'll work through lunch. See you in twenty minutes.'

He hung up.

'Prick.'

All further thought about what to do with her would have to wait till later. Probably until after the boy got home from school. Maybe they could figure it out.

Together.

CHAPTER
THIRTEEN

Broadowler estate had spread like a bruise across the backside of Ossett, the original pre-fabricated houses of the mining community changing over the years into a sprawling council estate of brick and dirt, expanding from twenty homes into nearly three hundred over the course of a decade. Once the choice of home for the working miner, Broadowler had now become synonymous with crime, a place to dump the unfortunate and the unworthy. Quite how that was decided, which camp you fell into and by whom the decisions were made, was still unclear. All that Louise knew as she looked out of the car window at the unkempt gardens filled with strewn rubbish and discarded toys, and the smashed and boarded windows on every other house, was that if you lived in Broadowler, either you had given up, or been given up on.

Probably both.

Hines was driving; Scruffy Pete sat in the back, finally gnawing on the Texan bar. He growled lightly as he chewed through the thick chocolate and caramel, worrying it like a dog with a bone until the bar broke. His lips smacked loudly as he chewed, the sound rippling down Louise's spine like ice water.

She turned her attention back to the houses as they passed by. Curtains were drawn across most of the downstairs windows, and a few of the bedrooms as well. Privacy was a currency greater than money down here, in the twisting maze of Broadowler. It could be bought. It could be sold. What went on behind the stained lace or the Union Jack or Leeds United flags, with the rips in the cotton and the blood, was no one's business but your own. If you heard shouts or screams, you turned the television up. If you had a knock on the door, you turned it up louder.

And if the police came down the street, just like Louise and Hines were doing right now, you pulled the curtains across even tighter and also flicked on the radio.

'I'm down there on the left,' Pete said, around a mouthful of chocolate.

'I know where you live, Pete,' Hines said. 'I've had to bring you back several times, or had you forgotten?'

'Just there,' he said, ignoring her. 'Next to that van. Number Twenty-One. That's us.'

That's us.

A cold shiver ran through Louise. He was still clinging to the hope that his sister was going to be coming back, that she was all right and nothing bad had happened to her. She supposed that could still be possible. Like she'd said, sometimes people just want to get away for a bit, and if anyone had good cause to get away for a bit it would be Helen Williams.

Hines pulled the car over and parked just behind the white van Pete had pointed out. Its back windows, one in either door, were painted over with black paint. Some enterprising soul with a sick sense of humour had scrawled CLEAN ME: I LOOK LIKE A PAKI into the dust that covered the vehicle's side door. Pulling her seatbelt off, Hines reached into her pocket and took out her notebook. She began writing down the licence plate.

'Just in case,' she said, seeing the look Louise gave her.

They all got out of the car and headed into the overgrown

garden of 21, Davison Drive. A rusty slide lay on its side, weeds overgrowing what had once been yellow plastic. If there had been a pathway leading to the house, it too was lost beneath tangles of weeds that stretched either side and threatened to trip those unwary or foolish enough not to take care as they approached the house.

The metal bin beside the front door was covered in stains both the police detectives did their best to ignore. The furrowed lid clung on to the crest of the mountain of rubbish crammed inside, one handle missing, the other lying forgotten beside the bin.

Forgotten, Louise thought. *Like the rest of Broadowler.*

Pete didn't bother looking for a key; he simply pushed open the door and stepped inside, disappearing into the darkness as the two detectives hesitated on the doorstep. They could hear him banging around inside, as he made his way into the living room, calling out for Helen as he did so.

'After you,' Louise said, holding the door open.

It felt sticky to the touch. From somewhere inside the house came a startled cry followed by the sound of breaking glass.

Hines moved forward, Louise right behind her.

Stale air filled their nostrils as they entered the living room. The curtains were pulled across, throwing everything into a murky haze, broken only by a thin stream of light that struggled to find the floor under the discarded newspapers, food packaging and empty cans of Special Brew and dandelion and burdock pop.

Pete stood in the doorway that led into the kitchen. The smashing glass they had heard was a pint glass he had knocked from the small side-table that now lay on its side. He clutched his knee and moaned.

'Jesus, that fucking smarts,' he said through gritted teeth.

He hopped on one leg, clutching the wounded knee with his hands.

'Maybe if you opened the curtains, you'd be able to see where you're going,' Hines said.

She made a move to do just that. Pete stood up, the pain in his knee forgotten.

'Don't do that,' he said. 'I don't like the light. It's too bright.'

Hines let the curtain drop, thankful to not feel its grimy slime on her skin any longer. She wiped her hand on her trousers.

'Maybe you could see to clean up a little as well. Jesus, Pete... this place is a mess. No wonder Helen decided to get away for a bit.'

'I prefer it like this,' he said. 'The dark, I mean. The rest...'

His voice trailed away. His shoulders sagged and his head drooped.

'Tell you what,' Louise said, hoping to stop Pete from dissolving into a sad mess, 'how about Hines gives you a hand getting this place ship-shape while I take a look in Helen's bedroom? What do you say, Pete? You don't want her coming home to an untidy house, do you?'

At the mention of his sister coming home, his head lifted and there was a soft sparkle in his eyes. 'She's coming back?' he asked.

'I honestly don't know, Pete. Maybe. Maybe not. I don't know, but if she did and she saw...'

Louise swept her arm around. Pete nodded enthusiastically, already reaching for a stack of newspapers that were leaning against the tatty sofa.

'She would not be happy,' he said, grabbing the papers up. 'Not happy at all.'

'Good. That's settled then.' She turned now to Hines, who stared at her with daggers in her eyes. 'It won't take long.'

Hines surveyed the wreckage of the room.

'You're kidding, right?'

'I meant looking in Helen's room. I doubt there's anything there that will tell us where she went.'

'Then why are we here?' Hines asked.

Louise looked back to Pete, who was now gathering up the scattered cans from around the room. He had a smile on his face and was humming a tune.

'That's why,' she replied.

CHAPTER
FOURTEEN

Helen Williams' bedroom was in stark contrast to the dark, smelly rubbish tip that was the rest of the house. As she'd climbed the stairs to the first floor, her shoes occasionally sticking to the carpet as though she was walking in some underground grunge-bar as opposed to a Wakefield City council house, Louise had seen the torn wallpaper with old stains across it; the rickety banister with notches scraped out of the wood, and the chipped window that shone dirty light through its shattered pane. This room looked nothing like that. Other than the layer of dust that came with six months of vacancy, there were no strips of wallpaper hanging from the walls, no broken windows and no rubbish scattered across the floor. Love filled this room, touched every surface. A pleasant scent still lingered on the air; Lulu perfume, a reminder that Helen Williams was her own woman and not defined by what she did. Her room was testament to that.

Louise looked around and saw nothing of the streetwalker. Saw nothing of the dark acts Helen was forced to perform, had performed too many times. Too many nights walking the streets, stalking the streets, looking for her next mark. Her next hand-job for a tenner. She had known the woman for two years, talked to her on a regular weekly basis, usually in the Carps on a Sunday night between belting out songs at karaoke with Hines – Hines loved the karaoke; she'd also loved Joe for a time and look at how that had turned out.

The sudden thought of her best friend and work colleague being at the hands of that man-child sent a surge of anger through Louise. Her cheeks flushed and her fists involuntarily clenched tight at the very thought of him laying hands on her...

Louise took in several long breaths, her eyes closed, a technique Karla had shown her that was supposed to help with sudden bursts of anger. While it helped, pounding Joe's face would help more. She smiled and continued looking round the bedroom.

The chats with Helen had been quick ones by necessity, snatched conversations over a pint, over the pool table or, more usually than not, over the foul stink of a porcelain well, its stained sides testament to the lack of hygiene in the cramped confine of the ladies', the dull thump of muted music a backdrop to their meetings. It was there that Helen had told Louise about the rise of violence against the girls she worked alongside. Whether on the streets of Wakefield, Leeds or even Dewsbury when she didn't have enough ready cash to get into the major cities nearby, more and more of the girls were being attacked by the men they were servicing. Sometimes it was a slap and nothing more, a little extra spice for the man that helped him maintain or even get an erection. But there were times, Helen had said, when the slap became a punch, sometimes to the gut, sometimes to the head. And then there were those who grabbed the throat and squeezed with both hands, only letting go when their own release had been achieved.

'Are you done?'

Louise turned to see Hines standing in the doorway. She was munching on a biscuit with one hand. In the other she held a battered-looking diary.

'There's nothing I can see here that's out of the ordinary,' Louise said, turning her back on the room.

'This whole room is out of the ordinary when compared with what's downstairs. I don't know how she managed to stomach it, living with Pete in this mess. I've pulled the curtains back and cracked open windows in the front room and kitchen to try get some air in.' Hines grimaced. 'It stinks of old socks and cigarettes. Christ, but it's a mess,' she said, taking another bite of biscuit.

Louise noted the crumbs falling to the carpet. The clean, crisp carpet. If Hines noticed that she was as guilty now of adding mess to the house as Pete, she didn't say.

'Even Danes and his SOC team would struggle with this, and they dealt with the aftermath of the Franks Abattoir incident down the bottom of Healey Road.'

'I can hear you, you know.' Pete's voice lifted from the stairs where he was loitering, waiting for the two detectives to come back down. Louise grinned; the Scene of Crime clean up team were four hardy individuals whose task it was to make presentable what was now coated in the detritus of violent acts. The blood, the shit and the piss; all the offal of men's depravity to each other was to be cleaned away so that the stains of death and fear were gone. Or at least invisible to the untrained naked eye of the survivors, those left behind to deal with the sorrow and pain of what had befallen their lives. Louise knew only too well that the horror was never truly gone; pushed aside perhaps. Pushed down and ignored, definitely, but the marks were still there if you looked, and knew what you were looking for.

Karla knew. Karla had looked past Louise's own outward cleansing and hadn't turned away when she discovered the stains of her past that Louise tried so very hard to scrub away.

'I found this,' Hines said, breaking into Louise's thoughts, 'but it makes no sense,' she continued, holding the diary out to Louise. 'It's gibberish. All weird names and numbers.'

Before Louise could say anything else, raised voices from outside caught their attention. Angry voices. Violent voices.

'Erm, ladies...' Pete said from the landing, his voice wavering. 'I think you should see this.' He had come up the stairs while they were talking and was now standing beside Hines, a worried expression on his face. 'I don't know what's going on, but it doesn't look good.'

He pointed to the window, just as another voice gave a pained yelp. Louise rushed over and pulled the pink curtain aside. For a moment she just stared, and then she sucked in a startled breath.

'What is it?' Hines asked, now standing beside her friend. She tried to look past Louise and down into the street below, but she couldn't get the angle. 'What's going on?'

'It sounds like an argument is just about to turn violent,' Louise said. 'Come on.'

'They're fucking crazy,' Pete said, stepping to one side as the two detectives emerged from the bedroom doorway.

'Who is it?' Hines asked as they rushed downstairs.

For a moment Louise didn't answer, but when she did the exasperation in her voice was unmistakable.

'It's Tom-fucking-Bailey!'

CHAPTER
FIFTEEN

'Sergeant!'

Louise shouted as she ran out of the Williams' house, Hines close behind her. In the street right outside, Detective Sergeant Tom Bailey stood face to face with a large-set man, their noses nearly touching. Both had red faces; Bailey's was from anger, the other man's from a powerful slap that had left red marks across the cheek and brow. It must have been from Bailey, Louise thought, noting the way her Sergeant was shaking his hand, doing his best to let the sting fade away in his mind if not in reality.

'What's going on, Sergeant?' Hines called from behind Louise.

'I got this handled,' he replied without turning. 'Nothing to worry your pretty heads over. This is between me and Gerry. Isn't that right, you pikey prick?'

'What you say now?' Gerry replied. 'What you fucking say?'

'Guess my little tickle knocked your hearing out, you old pikey fuck. Now, are you going to tell me what your Luke was doing in a stolen car or do I have to drag your fat arse down the nick for a quiet chat in your good ear? While it can still hear,' he added with a lopsided grin.

'Wait… this is Mr Ellis?' Louise said.

Shock wouldn't let her mind comprehend what she was seeing. Surely she was wrong; Bailey couldn't be picking a fight with the father of the deceased, could he?

'Are you insane?' Hines apparently had the same thought she did and wasn't afraid to voice it.

'Soon as he came in, he started throwing accusations around just a half second before he started throwing his fists,' Gerry Ellis said. His words were directed to Louise and Hines, but his eyes never left the Sergeant. 'We're grieving, me and the wife. She were the one who went to the hospital and saw him. I was at work.'

'If you call bending your arm in the pub, work,' Bailey spat. 'And you ain't answered my question, pikey.'

'See?' Gerry said. 'See what he's like? Racist. Racist that is.'

Bailey's laugh sent a chill that grabbed each nerve down Louise's back and twisted them.

'You ain't black, you dumb pikey. You're as white as I am, so I ain't being racist. Fucking retard,' he added for good measure, setting Gerry off once again.

The man swung a fist, which Bailey easily dodged, ducking low and to the right then throwing a fast punch to the man's generous gut, knocking the wind from him and sending him reeling back several steps to clatter into the Sergeant's police car. The wing mirror bent under the sudden weight then snapped off, bouncing off Gerry's head as he slumped to the ground.

'You broke my fucking car!' Bailey shouted. He towered over the man, fists clenched as he continued to shout down into the man's upturned face. 'You fucking pikey fuck. Like father like fucking son. And you fucking wonder why he's now cold on a slab. Just take a fucking look in the mirror.'

'Sergeant Bailey! That's enough!'

Louise grabbed Bailey by his shoulder and pulled him upright. Without turning he threw her hand off him with a powerful shrug of his shoulder.

'Get the fuck off me.' His voice was a gravelled growl, low and cold and full of threat.

'I come round here to let them know about their Luke, and out of nowhere this pile of useless shit comes barrelling into me.'

'You were touching my wife!' Gerry shouted. 'My son's hours dead and you're in my kitchen pawing at my wife!'

'I was fucking consoling her,' Bailey said, finally turning round. His face glowed with smug satisfaction and contempt. He gave Louise a once over, his eyes trawling over every inch of her, lingering on her chest before travelling down her body. The corner of his lip curled when he reached her hips. 'Women like a bit of consoling now and then. Ain't that right?'

'You're bang out of order, Bailey.' Louise said.

'Out of order? He's out of his mind. What were you thinking, Bailey?'

Hines said. She brushed past him to reach down to Gerry and help the man to his feet. They both moved to the small wall that lined the Ellis garden where Gerry sat, as Bailey retrieved the smashed pieces of the wing mirror.

'That's *Sergeant* Bailey to you. To you both. You'd be best remembering that.'

He started round the car, opened the driver's door and threw the broken mirror onto the passenger seat. The engine rumbled to life, a slow throaty cough that ended with a blast of black smoke from the exhaust. Two loud bangs like gunshots echoed round the estate. Leaning over the passenger seat, Bailey wound the window down and called out, 'I'll be getting this fixed and sending you the bill. Pikey.'

Before Gerry could respond the car moved away, a couple more exhaust shots sounding its departure.

'I'm so sorry,' Louise said once the car had moved round the corner, vanishing from sight, if not hearing. 'I honestly have no words.'

'He's a bastard and a prick,' Gerry said.

'You'll get no arguments from us,' Hines said, drawing a brief smile from Gerry. 'Want to tell us what it was really about?'

'No,' he said.

CHAPTER
SIXTEEN

The stench was overpowering, an almost physical presence that threatened harm if too much was inhaled. She took in small breaths as fast as she could through her mouth so that she didn't have to smell the blood and the shit that stained the air, but even then she could taste it on her tongue as it coated her flesh on the way into her lungs. What was worse was the burning shame that it was her blood, her shit, that she could smell and taste.

For six months – *is that how long it has been? It feels like a lifetime* – she had endured the taunts, and the touches, the looks and the sounds, kept in this cold warehouse. The chain on her ankle was colder, the metal as tainted with rust as the air was with her decay. Whenever she moved it didn't so much rattle as groan, the sound her only companion when they weren't with her. The weight of it she had become accustomed to. At first it was an anchor to her, a device that kept her as trapped here as her brother had kept her trapped in Ossett.

Pete.

What would he be thinking now, six months with her gone? Had he even noticed or did he just think she had skipped town once more, lost in Leeds with their junkie acquaintances? Had she used her mouth and her body to gain a ride to one of the cities she was always talking about? London; Manchester; Liverpool. Edinburgh was always a special time on those rare occasions they had gone, but the history and the buildings and the people had caught her attention, filling her head with a million what ifs: if she could just get a foothold on life, a single, simple, thing that a billion people took for granted every single day, if she could do that, just do that one simple thing, she could get away. Start again. Start fresh.

And she had been so close. So close. They both had. She had been putting money aside for them both, keeping it secret so that Pete couldn't piss it up a wall, or turn it into another drug fuelled haze of conspiracy thoughts and paranoia.

But she was the one on the chain, right? Not him. She was the one used every other day. Used by them both. Her flesh was red where they pawed at her. Squeezed. Pinched and pulled. Bit even. They used her in ways even she hadn't considered, in ways her johns hadn't tried; and at least they had paid. These two freaks, the old one and the young. The boy who had clocked her in the other warehouse, the one next to the church, had been wary at first despite his initial enthusiasm. His reluctance had angered the older one, the father, obviously. He had had to be shown what to do and he had followed instructions *very* well. The faded marks had been replaced with bright new ones every couple of days, the hot pulse of them adding to the fire of hate that sustained her. Kept her going.

Kept her alive.

She drew on it every day, feeding off its strength. Whenever she started to feel numb, she recalled the latest degrading session, looked at the fresh marks on her body. Her arm was a fishing-net of scars where he had practised with the knife. Most weren't deep. A couple were. They had bled for days. They had thrown sanitary pads to her, taped them to her wounds, ripping them away when they started to turn brown.

All she had to do was think of that and her hate was back, feeding her. Fuelling her. Keeping her alive.

She took in another breath, this one long and deep and through her nose. She gagged as her stomach heaved and threatened to throw up the slop they had left for her to eat. It looked like dog food but tasted like chilli-con carne, despite it being cold. Not the boil in the bag kind she cooked for her brother on a Saturday night when they couldn't afford a take-away; this was from a can. It had more taste even though it looked like shit. Whatever it was, it had kept her alive, that along with the bucket of water she was to drink from. The older one came in the morning to top it up; the young one – *Ian? I think his name is Ian* – came in later in the day. Probably around four. Afternoon. After school, she suspected.

Helen Williams pulled on the chain again, her dirty fingers trembling as they closed around the metal link. Every day she did this at least ten times, pulling as hard as she could, pulling until her head hurt and her eyes hurt, and the pressure in her lower body built until she nearly soiled herself.

Once or twice she had, crying afterwards as she felt its warmth on her thighs and buttocks. She had cleaned herself using her drinking water, squatting over the bucket and splashing the cold water onto herself, rubbing away the mess while she cried hot tears of shame.

And still she tried. Every day she tried, never giving up. Never giving in. Thoughts of escape didn't cloud her mind though; she knew she wasn't leaving this place alive. They had told her that already. She didn't think too much about her brother either, because she knew she would never see him again. To do so would only raise false hope, and she had none. But what she did have, what kept her trying the chain each day, pulling hard against its iron grip, was that roaring hate in her heart. Hate towards the two men who kept her here, used her here.

Would kill her here.

Her hate gave her a little more strength to do what she needed to do.

Gritting her teeth and ignoring the pushing pain behind her eyes, Helen pulled on the chain with all her strength of will. The growl of frustration rose from her chest, thickening in her throat, pushing out the vile taste of decay that languished there like a dead thought until it became a scream of anguish. The sound echoed around the empty warehouse, bouncing from the bare brick wall to come back to her, taunting her. Mocking her.

In anger she threw the chain to the ground, and that was when she heard it.

The laughter.

It mixed with her own cries until that was all she could hear.

He stepped forward, appearing as if from the very shadows themselves. He held a twisted grin on his face and a wicked knife in his hand.

Helen dropped the chain. It clattered to the stone floor of the warehouse, landing with a heavy thud.

'I'm sorry,' she said. All thought of hateful vengeance had left her in a warm rush, running down her leg to pool beneath her bare feet. Ignoring the heat of her own fear, Helen knelt, raising her head. 'I'll do whatever you want.'

'I know.'

As Harry Peterson walked towards her, Helen never took her eyes from the knife.

CHAPTER
SEVENTEEN

Hines visibly tensed as the pair headed once again inside Dewsbury Memorial Hospital. Louise saw it; the momentary hesitation at the door, the clenching of Hines' fists mirroring the staccato twitch of her jaw. The bruise on her cheek was starting to colour now, but, to Hines' credit, she hadn't tried to hide it beneath makeup. Instead, she seemed to wear it like a badge of honour, and yet she paused, her eyes darting left to right before settling ahead.

'You okay?' Louise said.

She lightly touched Hines' arm, noticing the violent flinch that vanished in an instant as Hines stared straight ahead. The doors opened, pushed wide by a porter as he wheeled an elderly gentleman out of the building and into the warm sun.

'Morning, ladies,' the man said from his seat. A blanket covered his legs and he clutched the patterned top with arthritic fingers.

'Morning, William?' the porter said. 'It's gone three.'

'Don't be ridiculous,' William said, giving the porter's hand a soft slap. 'It's Thursday.'

Louise smiled at the man as he was wheeled away, grumbling that he'd be late for work if the porter didn't get a move on.

If Hines had noticed this, she didn't give any indication. When Louise turned back to her, she saw her young friend licking at her lower lip, catching it between her teeth and chewing nervously.

'It's all right if you want to stay here,' Louise said, pointing at the seats in front of the reception desk. 'I can speak to the Wadees on my own.'

'I'm fine,' Hines snapped back, then added a little more softly, 'Sorry. I didn't mean... It's just that...'

'It's all right,' Louise said again. 'You want to sit for a minute?'

Hines shook her head.

'No; it's getting on.' She gave her shoulders a shrug as though throwing off the invisible shackles of last night's experience. 'I'm not letting that prick stay any longer in my head than necessary. I've been mulling over what to do all day and that's it. I'm done. I'm out. He can become a distant memory like the others.'

'The others? How many have there been?' Louise asked with a smile. It was no secret that Hines enjoyed male company, and why shouldn't she? She was young, beautiful, intelligent and always up for a good time. Some took that to mean she was easy, a bed-hopping nympho who couldn't keep her legs together. She'd heard the whispered rumours round the Shop, the tall tales and short sightedness of their colleagues. Their male colleagues, that was. They were the ones laughing about her, calling her out on behaviour that if any man was seen to do would be praised, worshipped even. Their few female colleagues understood for the most part; there were one or two who laughed along with the men, trying to fit in by going along with the jokes and the looks, the name calling and slut shaming. That had been different today though, when they heard what had happened. What Joe had done. Then things had changed. Attitudes had shifted slightly as one of their own had been attacked. One of their own had been hurt.

And that didn't happen. Ever.

'It doesn't matter,' Louise continued, seeing the mock annoyance on Hines' face. 'I was joking. Are you still coming to mine tonight? I'm cooking, and I know Karla's looking forward to seeing you.'

'So she can analyse me? Check up on the poor little punched girl.'

'No, it's not like that at all. I thought it would be nice for you to have some company instead of being alone in your house. It's up to you though. No pressure at all. You like lasagne, right?'

Now it was Hines' turn to laugh.

'No pressure. Right.'

The Wadees were all together in the ward. Bilal and Raja were in beds, side by side. Both men were covered in bruises; Bilal's face was swollen where the broken jaw had been reset, while half of Raja's face was swathed in bandages, a protective cover over his left eye. Vanita Wadee sat between the two beds, her hands holding one each of her sons', while Danesh leaned against the windowsill, arms folded across his chest.

When he saw Louise and Hines walking towards them, he pushed off the windowsill and raised his hand in greeting.

'Ms Miller, it is so good to see you again, but I am shocked as to why you are here.'

'Hi, Mr Wadee,' Louise said. 'We wanted to come and see how everyone was and perhaps speak with your sons directly about what happened to them. If they are feeling well enough,' she added, seeing the worried look on Vanita's face.

Hines was in the process of pulling up a chair when Danesh spoke again. The man's voice was strained and thick with emotion.

'But I thought there was nothing that could be done. That is what the police we spoke to last night said.'

'That was Dewsbury police,' Hines said. She squirmed as she struggled to find a comfortable position in the hard plastic chair.

Louise chose to stay standing.

'We work a little differently,' she said, 'and besides, how could I not at least listen to what happened and see if there's anything I can do to help?'

'We,' Hines said, sitting forward in the chair and fixing Louise with her eyes. 'See if there's anything *we* can do to help.

Louise smiled and nodded to her colleague and friend. Hines smiled back.

Bilal sat up in the bed, and gestured to his mother to hand him the pad of paper and pen that lay on the small table beside him. Rather than do as he asked, she instead took his hands in hers.

'No, Bilal. Your handwriting is worse than your father's. These ladies have important things to be doing and can't be wasting their time trying to figure out your words. Let your brother talk.'

Bilal turned, a wince of pain at the movement quickly becoming a grimace.

'It's okay,' Louise said, seeing the man's growing distress. 'Let your brother talk, and if there's anything you want to add, write it down and we'll take it with us. We're not going to be rushing through this, I promise you.'

He nodded and winced again when he tried a smile. Louise turned to Raja. His face was swollen and puffy, and when he talked there was a tremor to his voice, a quavering of suppressed emotion as he held back the anger and the tears while he told the two police officers what had happened to them last night.

'We went to go to work as normal, but our car... It had been stolen.'

As he talked Louise listened intently, taking in the words but also the way he told his story. The way his hands clenched into fists when he talked about being punched repeatedly; the way he kept his gaze locked on a spot on the bed sheet, his feet beneath its crumpled surface constantly shifting and moving, twitching in time with his staccato speech.

'I kept my head covered as best I could but they pulled me up. Forced me to stand while they continued to hit me. I couldn't see Bilal, there was too much blood in my eyes and it had started to swell already, but I could hear him.' Raja turned to his brother. 'I could hear you, but I couldn't help you. I tried, Bilal. I tried so hard but I couldn't break free.'

Tears were flowing now as the two brothers reached across to grasp the other's hand. Vanita cried into her hands.

Danesh turned his back to his family and stared silently out of the window onto the cold, faded outline of Dewsbury.

'And what time was this?' Hines asked, handing a mug of tea to Raja.

Following his initial statement, which she had written down studiously, Hines had gone to find the ward matron to get everyone a cuppa. It hadn't taken long before a nurse came in with mugs for everyone and a plate of biscuits that Louise had already swiped from. It was nearing four o'clock and her stomach was rumbling loudly, as they had skipped grabbing a proper lunch so they could crack on with talking with the Wadees. Karla would be mad when she found out; it had become quite an area of contention lately, Louise's eating habits. The skipped meals, the high sugar sweets and crisps Louise found herself snacking on, were taking their toll on her health. Her hair was becoming clammy, her skin spot ridden; her morning routine, once a thing set in stone, was now nothing more than a rushed cup of coffee, a quick bite of toast and time enough to feed Tom before she was out the door and on her way to the Shop. Her daily morning run had become a fortnightly event, if it happened at all. Karla had offered to join her in an attempt to encourage Louise to take better care of herself, but it still rarely happened, and now they were arguing about what she was, or rather wasn't, eating. Yet no matter how many times she tried to explain to Karla the nature of the job and the way it would constantly get in the way of a good, healthy meal, she could never make her understand.

'You have to have priorities,' Karla had said.

'And those priorities are the people I'm trying to help,' Louise had replied. 'Surely you understand that?'

Louise bit into another biscuit, listening to Raja's reply as she put her lover's advice out of her mind. Now was not the time to dwell. Now was the time to help.

'The pub was shut,' he said, 'though there were six or seven men inside drinking.'

Hines looked at Louise, who was wiping crumbs from her blouse. 'An illegal lock-in?'

'Sounds like it,' Louise replied. 'What was the name of the pub again?'

'The Walton Arms,' Raja replied.

'Opposite the cricket ground, if I remember correctly,' Louise said.

Both Raja and Bilal nodded, though the latter did so carefully. For the next few minutes, the brothers relayed as much information as they could remember about the men who attacked them, prompted by Louise when their recall dried up.

Finally, she closed her notepad.

'Okay, well our next step is to go pay a visit to the Walton Arms and have a chat. The description you've given of the men involved is a big help.'

'Shouldn't be too difficult to spot a large man with GOOD NIGHT tattooed on his hands. Find him, we find the others.'

'And then what?' Vanita's face was a mask of parental worry. Not just parental, Louise noted. There was a stark fear in the woman's eyes and in the way she clutched at her shawl, worrying at the golden tassels as a child would worry at their blanket. 'What happens when you find these men who did this? You arrest them and we then have to face the backlash from their friends. This is not good for us. This is not good for my sons.'

'What would you have them do then?' Raja asked from his

bed. 'Ignore what happened to us? Forget it like you do all the other times they attack us?'

'This has happened before?' Hines asked.

'Only with words,' Danesh answered.

Till now he had been silent while Louise and Hines asked their questions.

'Not just words,' Vanita said. 'We have had bricks thrown through the window at many of our shops. And then there's the car.'

'Yes,' Louise said. 'Your car.'

'The reason we went to the pub in the first place,' said Raja. 'Our car was stolen and we were looking for it and thought they might know something or had seen or heard something. How stupid we were to think so.'

Louise pulled her notebook out again, flipping to a new page.

'What make and model was the car, and do you remember the registration plate?'

Raja told her.

Hines and Louise shared a look.

'We know where that car is.'

Peter Danes, head of the Scene of Crime team, was dressed in a white forensic suit, complete with gloves on his hands and plastic booties covering his shoes. There were streaks of oil staining the otherwise pristine sheen of his suit, and strands of hair poked out from the sides of the hood he had half-pulled over his head.

'Afternoon all,' he said, the excitement clear in his voice as Louise and Hines escorted the Wadees into the police garage.

The Wadees stood nervously in the entranceway until Danes noticed them and beckoned them all over to the long workbench against the far wall. There, a SOC technician offered them a seat each, wiping away some of the dust that had gathered.

'This better be worth it,' Bailey said.

He stood to the side, his hands jammed in the pockets of his coat, and glared at the officer.

'Oh, it's worth it,' Danes said. 'Afternoon, Beth. It's good to see you, but shouldn't you be taking some time? You know, rest up. Take it easy for a bit.'

Louise looked at Hines and was surprised to see tears in her eyes. It took a second too long for her to answer, but when she did, Louise could hear the choked emotion in her voice, despite what she was saying.

'I'm fine, thank you very much. Can we just stop with the Hines pity party? Thanks.'

Danes' face coloured. The history between them was now exactly just that, but he obviously still cared about her.

After getting her statement, Louise had deliberately chosen not to bring up the events of last night. That wasn't quite accurate; Karla had told her not to press the issue, to let Hines talk about what had happened in her own time. She needed time to process it herself, and to be pressured by others, even those closest to her and who cared about her, would do more harm. It would be frustrating, Karla had continued, talking over Louise's heated objections, but it would be for the best, and Hines' welfare was all that mattered, not Louise's need to fix the situation, or Danes' sense of jealous protection.

He had the good sense to let the matter drop.

'And these I presume are the Wadees. Hello; we briefly met last night, but you obviously had pressing matters on your mind. I hope your sons are doing well?'

'They are healing, thank you,' Danesh replied.

Beside him, Bailey gave a grunt but added no further words of support. Louise walked over to him.

'What the hell was that with Mr Ellis?' she said, doing her best to keep her voice low enough that they wouldn't be overheard.

'None of your business, Miller. We have a history, Ellis and me. Don't fret over it.'

'That was more than a spat. It was extremely unprofessional and I can't think of a reason not to tell Manby about it.'

'Get you into his good graces, eh? And what does he get into?'

She was about to answer him when a voice sounded.

'Sorry I'm late.'

DI Manby hurried inside to stand beside Louise. He nodded a greeting to Bailey, catching the man's eye, then turned to the Wadees, his hand reaching for Danesh's own.

'Very good to see you both. Thank you for coming. Your boys are in the best possible hands, and it will be a great help to have you here.'

The two men shook hands.

'I thank you for asking us here, but I don't know what we can do to help. I don't really know what we are doing here; Ms Miller chose not to elaborate.'

'Ms Miller... oh, you mean Detective Constable Miller.'

'I am sorry. Of course, Detective Constable Miller.'

Louise smiled. 'That's perfectly all right, Mr Wadee.'

Hines gave a laugh.

'Yeah, it's not the worst thing she's been called. Do you remember that homeless crack-job down Earlsheaton last week-end? The one who pulled his dick out and told you to blow—'

'Beth!'

Everyone was staring at her.

'Never mind.'

Danes cleared his throat, bringing everyone's attention back to him.

'Now that we're all here, I can let you know what I've found.'

'Can we hurry this along?' Bailey said. 'I've a meeting. Maybe an inside line to what the Ellis lad was up to,' he added, throwing Louise a pointed gaze. Manby's quizzical gaze fell on him. Danes continued without missing a beat.

'I've been able to go over the cars that were involved in the fatal accident last night,' he said, addressing Bailey directly.

Louise noted this but said nothing. She knew there was no love lost between the Sergeant and Danes; he had been as shocked as everyone else when Bailey got the promotion.

'It was a very interesting examination, which yielded some quite extraordinary results.'

'It was a car crash,' Bailey said. 'What the hell is extraordinary about a car crash? Okay, a few fatalities, but that's what happens when a car smashes into the central divider at eighty. I'm only surprised they weren't turned into a large smear of jam.' A soft gasp came from Vanita. 'Sorry,' he added.

'He said he inspected the *cars*,' Louise said. 'Plural.'

'But there was only one car involved, I thought? That one,' Hines said, pointing behind Danes at the two halves of the car.

Both were on mechanical lifts, raised a couple of feet off the ground so that technicians could get in, around and under the vehicle to carry out their inspections. At this moment, only two technicians remained; one was lying on her back beneath the front section of the ruined car, waving a bright lamp slowly back and forth along a section of piping. The other technician, the one who had offered the Wadees a chair, stood nearby, writing down the measurements and comments the other called out.

'And there's the rub,' Danes said. He was almost rubbing his hands together with glee. 'That's not one car. There are two.'

'What the fuck are you talking about?' Bailey said. 'Only one car was brought here. That one.'

'But that's the thing. Yes, in practice it is one car. A Ford Escort. Registration A39 JJU.'

'That is our car!' Danesh said, stepping forward. 'At least I think so. It is hard to tell for sure as it is badly burned, but it looks like the car my sons were looking for last night before they were assaulted.'

'Allegedly assaulted,' Bailey said.

'How can you say this?' Danesh said, turning to Bailey, his voice tinged with anger. 'How can he say this, Ms Miller? You saw them. You saw their wounds, heard their story.'

'Fairy story, if you ask me,' Bailey said, not as quietly as he thought.

'Stow it, Bailey,' Manby said. 'Mr and Mrs Wadee... We say allegedly not because we don't believe your sons, but because it is police procedure to approach all crimes from a neutral standpoint. It is in everyone's best interests to do so, but I can assure you, we treat all allegations seriously and will investigate to the best of our abilities. I am sure WDCs Miller and Hines also assured you of that themselves.'

Manby gestured to the twin halves of the burnt-out husks of the car.

'Danes... if you would.'

'Of course. You said this was your car, and in a sense it was.'

'I know it was,' Danesh said. 'I bought it myself.'

'And we'll get to that in a moment, if you don't mind,' Danes said.

Danesh gave a nod and sat back down. Vanita gave his arm a squeeze but said nothing, her eyes on Danes.

'This isn't one car; it's two. I put a call in with the DVLC this morning, but here's the thing. It doesn't exist. At least not A39 JJU; that registration number actually belonged to a Saab that was destroyed in 1984 over in Bradford. That's strange in and of itself, but what's even stranger is the fact that this car is actually made up of two different cars: a front half from one vehicle, and a back half from a completely separate car, both welded together to make a brand-new vehicle. This vehicle.'

'You're talking about a cut and shut?' Louise said.

Danes grinned.

'Exactly!'

'A what?'

Louise turned to Hines.

'A cut and shut. Some back-street garages charge a small fortune to get your car to pass its MOT by splicing a half of another car to the original. Cheaper apparently than just fixing the problem. It was a huge issue down in Manchester. In fact, there was a gang using it as a way of making some extra money.'

'But how do you know this is two halves of different cars?' Bailey asked. 'Certainly looks like one car to me... despite being in two black pieces.'

Danes looked questioningly from Louise to Bailey and back again.

'Do you know nothing about cars and car crime? There are two different VINs, meaning two separate cars.'

Louise saw the confused look of the Wadees.

'Vehicle Identification Number,' she explained. 'It's like the fingerprint of a vehicle. It tells us where and when it was made, by who and which plant. No two vehicles have the same VIN.' A thought struck. 'Two VINs? I thought there was one, just on the inside of the bonnet.'

Danes was shaking his head.

'No. There are a couple of places the manufacturers put them, and some of them have multiple locations on one car. In this instance, we had two on the front half – the bonnet and under the footwell on the driver's side – and the rear half had a VIN in the wheel cavity of the offside tyre. Both identify their respective cars as being built in the UK, but the year code identifies the front half being built in 1974 and the rear in 1982. According to the DVLC, both cars were reported stolen, the front half from Leeds, the rear from Coventry.'

'So how the hell did they end up here?'

Louise turned to the Wadees.

'Where did you buy the car from, Mr Wadee?' she asked

'It was a second-hand car. A cheap run-around for my boys. I had no idea.'

'Of course you didn't, but if you can remember where you bought it and when, it would be a great help.'

Danesh didn't even have to think.

'We bought it from Sanderson's, here in Ossett,' he said. 'It was a good price. Very fair, I thought. I have the paperwork back at our shop.'

'Sanderson's?' Danes said. 'Everything seems to be coming back to Sanderson's.'

'What?' Bailey shook his head. 'So what? We get our cars from Sanderson's. They do our MOTs. Vehicle recovery. Doesn't mean they knew it was a dodgy car. He said it was second hand; that's what they do, init?'

The distaste was not hidden in Hines' voice.

'The Ellis boy worked at Sanderson's, and I wouldn't be surprised to find the others did too. Wasn't it the Sandersons who came out to tow the wreckage away?'

The same thought seemed to strike both Wadees as they voiced the same question.

'Did this have anything to do with the attack on our boys?'

'It's certainly something we need to look into,' Louise said.

Bailey threw his hands in the air and pushed himself off the table. He started stalking towards the garage entrance, the light outside having fallen as they'd talked.

'This is fucking ridiculous,' he said. 'Bill… are you listening to this? What the hell is this? One has nothing to do with the other, and if we're not careful, we're going to be wasting a lot of time chasing up a simple punch-up gone a little too far, as well as these poor lads who went for a joyride and paid the ultimate price. Fucking tragic, if you ask me. You waste your time with this shit if you want. I've wasted enough as it is. I'm going t'pub.'

He stormed past Louise, who managed to move aside in time to just get a hard nudge to her shoulder instead of being knocked aside by his stride. She turned to Manby, who waved away her unvoiced complaint.

'I'll speak to him tomorrow. No point now when he's in one of his moods.'

'Are you kidding?'

Manby's face grew dark.

'Now is not the time. Are we done here?'

Danes was already taking his protective suit off.

'That's about as much as I can do today.'

'Then we'll all call it a day.'

Manby again shook Danesh's hand and gave Vanita a wide smile. 'I'd like to thank you both for coming along. You've given us some good information we can follow up on in both cases. Thank you.'

'Are you okay for getting home?' Danes asked.

'Is that it?' Danesh asked. He seemed a little unsure what to do next.

'That's it for now. Like DI Manby said, your help has given us plenty to be working with now. Let us get on with it, and you get on with looking after your boys.'

Danesh helped his wife from her stool. He brushed at a speck of dirt that had darkened the colourful thread, rubbing his fingers together to dislodge it from his skin. 'And the car?' he said. 'What happens with the car?'

'That's a total write-off,' Danes said as he folded the forensic suit and placed it on the desk. 'Best thing is to get in touch with your insurance company and start looking for another car. Here, I'll walk you out.'

'We shall see you later, Ms Miller?' Vanita asked. 'We can cook extra if you like.'

'Thanks, Mrs Wadee, but Hines and I are going to go to the pub after work.'

Hines looked surprised.

'We are? Not the Carps, though. You know… because of…'

'Not the Carps. The Walton Arms.'

CHAPTER
EIGHTEEN

Detective Sergeant Tom Bailey had lied.

It wasn't something new to him, lying. He wore its seductive sheen like a second skin, slipping into it whenever it suited the situation, which for Bailey was nearly every day. It was how he had managed to keep his job to date, changing the facts to fit his narrative. A little embellishment here, a lot of bull there. He was clever though, kept it straight and believable until he could look a person in the eye and tell them the sky was the sea without blinking.

He had lied, telling them he was off to the pub, because he didn't want them to know where he was really going. Who he was really going to talk to. Questions would be asked, though he knew in his arrogance that he could twist a tale they would believe. And it wouldn't be difficult to do that, knowing the person he was coming to see.

Bailey parked his car and switched off the engine, listening to the pops and the whistles as it cooled down. It wasn't supposed to do that. They'd said they'd fixed it. They'd charged him a small fortune, even with the copper's discount, and he'd paid it. They'd said it would work now. They'd said a lot of things.

But so had he.

He'd said how he could shut them down. Close down their income stream with a single word in the Chief Superintendent's ear. That got their attention. That brought *him* to their attention. He wanted in, wanted part of it. All of it.

And he got it. Got his own little slice of the pie. Became part of their group, their gang. Their group.

A tap on his window. Thick meaty fingers with NIGHT tattooed across the knuckles.

Bailey smiled and opened the door.

CHAPTER
NINETEEN

For half-past five on a Monday evening, the Walton Arms was surprisingly full. Surprising, at least, to Louise and Hines as they pushed the doors open and were met with the raucous sounds of working men letting the stress of the day bleed away into their pint mugs. Smoke filled the air and Louise could detect a hint of something a little more exotic in its thick scent. She cast a quick look at Hines, whose stony gaze betrayed nothing, but the quick, almost imperceptible nod reassured her that Hines was good to go.

Loud voices, some raised in anger, others in jest, clashed together to make a single wave of noise, but as they headed towards the bar, Louise and Hines could snatch brief words and phrases from the melange.

'…is no way I'm going to let my kid…'

'…better a British bloke took the job than just another darkie…'

'…you down for it?'

'…at the tits on that! Nice arse too, I'd get deep in there.'

That last came from a tall man in jeans and a black shirt who leaned against the bar, his eyes roaming all over the two women. He lingered on Hines, slowly looking her up and down as he licked at his lip. The smug, lopsided grin he threw her way was filled with blatant lust and she shuddered as he adjusted his crotch with his free hand. Another man held a near-empty pint, which he drained then slapped down on the bar right in front of Hines.

'I'm getting another. What do you want?' he asked her, turning so that his body almost pressed against her arm. Hines moved away slightly; her eyes kept directly forward.

Louise ran her eyes over the bar. The usual array of bar cloths were staged at various points; their design was of the Union Flag with BNP in the centre. A stack of flyers was placed beside each. Next to Louise was a large jar filled with coins and a few pound notes. The scrawled label sellotaped to the front read FOR THOSE SOULS KILLED BY THE STATE APRIL 15. Opening her purse, Louise dropped in a five-pound note.

The barman gave her a nod of thanks as he finished pulling a pint. He placed it on the bar in front of the lecherous man.

'Owt else?'

'What you having, love?' the man said to Hines, trying again. 'My treat for such a lovely lady.'

Louise stiffened and she was about to step around Hines when the younger officer turned with a smile. 'I'll take a gin and tonic and my friend will have a lager top.'

He leaned out to give Louise a look over. She could feel his eyes lecherously crawling over her body. When they finally met her eyes, she held them in her gaze, her face flat and still.

'She seems a bit quiet. What's your name, love?' He signalled the barman to get their drinks as he moved to stand between the two women. At first there was not enough space, and he tried to edge his way between them, but neither moved. Finally, he gave up and simply stood before them, his smug smile flipping between the two. He took a long pull on his pint and wiped foam from his lips with the back of his sleeve.

'Didn't think I'd be getting this lucky this early,' he said. 'And on a work night.'

'And what do you do?' Hines said. Her voice had dropped a few octaves and almost purred. The effect on the man was instantaneous and, Louise thought, really rather troubling. Was this how Hines usually acted with men, slipping into the sultry vixen role? If so, no wonder Joe had got jealous.

'Anything with a pulse,' the bartender laughed.

'Fuck you, Bert,' the man said, but he was laughing as well.

'Three twenty-five, Nick.'

Only now did the man, Nick, turn away from Hines. 'Fuck off three twenty-five,' he said. 'No way that comes to over three quid.'

'It's three twenty-five I tell you,' Bert replied. 'Now cough up, you cheap bastard.'

Louise and Hines took their drinks and slipped away, unnoticed by Nick, who was now demanding to see Bert's price list.

'What a dick,' Louise said as they made their way deeper into the pub.

All the tables had at least one person sitting at them, but she was certain she had spotted an empty booth just beside the toilets. Not ideal, but it would allow them to view the entire pub, from the front door to where they were sitting with little trouble.

Hines sat. Louise brushed at the fake leather seating, sweeping aside some ash from the previous owner's cigarette. Dead tabs were stuck in the ashtray and a few were scattered across the table. Three empty pint glasses had also been abandoned, as had the crumpled remains of some prawn cocktail crisps.

'Jesus. Who the hell eats prawn cocktail?' Hines said as she lifted the packet and deposited it on the table next to them. 'Salt and vinegar or beef for me.'

'Dry roasted peanuts are my favourite,' Louise said, giving her glass a swirl. She looked over Hines' shoulder, back to the bar. 'Your friend is still arguing with the bartender. I don't think he's realised we're not there yet.'

'He will,' Hines said after taking a drink. 'He'll be over here soon enough. Quicker he is, the quicker we can get out. I don't like this place. Did you see the BNP flag behind the bar?'

'Yes. And the poster advertising for new members,' Louise replied.

'No wonder the Wadees got the shit kicked out of them if they came in here. What were they thinking?' Hines mused.

'They weren't. They were looking for their car. Despite everything all around them, they didn't take into account the sort of people who come in here. It's not how decent people think, which says a lot about us, doesn't it?'

'Well, maybe if they had,' Hines said, ignoring the self-jibe and staring into her glass, 'they wouldn't be lying up in hospital. Choices have consequences, even if you can't see them at the time. Every choice. Even the ones you think are good at the time but turn out to be—'

'Arseholes like Joe?' Louise said. She reached over the table to place her hand over Hines'. She could feel her hand tremble, and when she looked up, there were tears filling her friend's eyes. Louise's heart broke in two. 'You want to talk now?'

Before Hines could reply an arm came down between them, in the hand a half-finished pint of Guinness that sloshed black liquid and white foam onto the scratched wood.

'Thought you could get a cheeky free drink, eh?' Nick said, looking around them for an empty chair. He grabbed one and dragged it over, throwing a leg across the seat so he sat with the back of the chair facing the table. 'No mind... I like a lass with spirit. So, what say we down these then head off for a spot in town?'

'How about fuck off,' Hines said.

'What she said,' Louise said. 'Thanks for the drinks but you're really not our type. He's not, is he?'

Hines let out a laugh that caught the attention of those sitting nearby.

'Him... Are you kidding? Look at him. Slick hair, an over-starched shirt. And that smell…' She leaned forward and took in a deep breath. 'What the fuck is that?'

Nick bristled, his cheeks turning red. He could see people staring.

'It's expensive cologne,' he said. 'You'd have to do a dozen back-alley hand-jobs to afford this.'

Hines laughed again.

'Oh, mate, they saw you coming. You got it off Dewsbury market, didn't you? It's a cheap knock off. Probably toilet water mixed with deodorant. They get picked up every other week. Actually, now I think about it, you're the one that sells that shit, aren't you?' She looked back to Louise, who was really enjoying this exchange. 'I thought I recognised this idiot. He runs that knock-off stall on the market.'

'And how the fuck would you know that, you cheap tart?'

'I'm definitely not cheap,' Hines said as she pulled out her warrant card and waved it under his nose. 'Because I'm one of the coppers that pulled you, dickhead.'

Nick turned bright red and looked at Louise. She was holding her own warrant card in front of him, a smile on her face.

'Probably best you do one, Nick, was it? I think I heard the barman call you that, and in about twenty seconds, my colleague here will be remembering everything from your last encounter together, and chances are you'll be coming with us after all, but not the way you'd like, I'd expect. A night in the cell sound good to you, Nickie-boy?'

He couldn't move fast enough. His chair clattered against the table, his drink forgotten. People nearby laughed as he made his way to the door, where he stopped and turned round.

'Fuck you both,' he called back just before slipping out the door.

'Well, that wasn't very polite,' Louise said.

'Positively disgraceful,' Hines said, just before they both burst out laughing.

CHAPTER
TWENTY

They stayed for another thirty minutes, Hines buying the next round. Despite getting close to opening up earlier, Hines didn't take the opportunity to talk, but Louise could understand why. In here, everyone listened to everyone else, conversations were not private, and since they had shown their warrant cards the noise level had dropped and the tense atmosphere had risen. The looks thrown their way were hidden glances, the antagonism in each snatched glimpse getting more and more apparent.

Across the room someone grunted like a pig.

Hines finished her drink.

'Time to go.'

Louise nodded and stood.

'Anyone else smell pork?'

Laughter ran round the room, following them as the two police officers walked out. Louise let out the breath she had been holding.

'Perhaps not the best thing to have done,' she said as they walked towards the car.

They had parked right outside, a fact she was very glad of, as a number of blokes were watching them from the doorway of the pub.

Hines nodded as they got inside.

'Definitely not a place to bring your aunt and uncle. Seems to be nice enough for the BNP though.'

The car started and they set off. The road was relatively quiet and they made good time as they headed back to Ossett.

'Our friend Nick had a tattoo; did you see it?'

'Two daggers crossed over a shield, yes.'

'Same as on the flag behind the bar.'

'And the flyers at the end of the bar as well.'

Louise reached into her purse and pulled out a crumpled piece of paper. As Hines drove, she uncurled the paper, doing her best to flatten it out on her knees. The twin dagger logo stretched across the top of the flyer; beneath it in large red letters:

INTO THE BATTLE
Saturday 24th June, 2pm
DEWSBURY TOWN HALL
FIGHT FOR WHITE

'Fight for white?' Louise repeated after reading it aloud. 'Jesus.'

'Not exactly subtle, are they? Can they do that?'

'Stage a protest... Unfortunately, yes. The language skirts the border of good taste, but I don't think it breaks any laws. Manby will know. I'll show him it tomorrow. See what he says.'

The car came up to the top of Earlsheaton, where she paused at the roundabout. Only a few hours earlier the road had been closed off as clean-up crews finished making sure there was no damage to the central barriers or footbridge following the accident. It was clear, and a few cars and trucks continued to turn down the Mad Mile, the rush hour now over. Hines indicated and went round the roundabout, moving to the top of Dewsbury Road, where she again turned right onto Kingsway.

'So, did you decide?' Louise asked. 'Fancy a curry with me and Karla?'

Hines laughed.

'I don't think so. Early night for me for a change,' she said with a shrug. 'After spending an hour in that pub, a good long soak in the bath is what I need.'

'You sure? There's going to be plenty. I'm cooking so that means a takeaway, and like I said, Karla will be pleased to see you.'

'She'll be pleased to grill me, you mean,' Hines laughed. 'I know you've been pestering all day but I'm good. Thanks.' She dropped a hand onto Louise's arm and gave it a squeeze. 'For everything.'

Louise was about to say something when the car came to a stop.

'Here's you,' Hines said. She left the engine running, but reached across Louise and opened the door. 'Looks like your man is waiting for you.'

'My... oh.'

Sitting outside the door that led to Louise's flat was her cat. Tom glared and let out a yowl that was all urgency and admonishment at the same time.

'I guess I left him out all day. That's me in trouble.'

'Just give him some curry and you'll be fine,' Hines said. 'Pick you up in the morning?'

Louise grabbed her bag.

'Make it eight. We'll head over to Wakefield and have a chat with Mr McKensie. Shouldn't be too hard to set up a meeting. It's not like he has a full scorecard, is it?'

Hines laughed. It was good to hear. Better to see.

'See what he knows about Helen Williams? Do you think he had anything to do with her disappearance?'

'I doubt it, but at least we can then tell Pete we tried.'

Louise got out and closed the door. She waved at Hines, who nodded back once before driving away. Louise watched until the car was out of sight and then turned round to Tom.

Before she could say anything, the door to her flat opened, and Karla stood in the doorway, a bowl of cat food in one hand, a glass of wine in the other.

'Who wants what?' she said, grinning.

Tom yowled once more and slunk inside.

The food was warm, spicy and filling, and after the third helping Louise fell back on the sofa, her hands clutching her belly.

'I'm stuffed,' she said. 'That was gorgeous.'

Karla began reaching for the plates.

'I wish I could take credit for it, but Mrs Wadee came round shortly after I got here, laden with bowls. All I did was reheat it.'

'That was from Mrs Wadee? I thought you'd ordered in. I know I was going to.'

Karla laughed. 'Apparently she was very thankful to you for listening to her sons and looking into what happened to them.'

Her voice drifted back from the kitchen and Louise smiled as she heard the clank of the pots in the sink and the quiet curse as Karla struggled with the hot tap. It kept sticking; Danesh Wadee had said several times that he would come and fix it, but so far he never had, and what with all that had happened, she doubted it would be any time soon.

'Well, unfortunately I don't have much more than what they could tell us,' Louise called out. She took a sip of wine and settled further back into the sofa, her legs tucking beneath her. Fleetwood Mac played on the stereo, and the room flickered with the soft glow from the lamp mixed with the dozen or so candles that Karla had lit, placing them carefully on the mantelpiece as well as the windowsill of two of the three windows that looked out onto the road below. She ran a hand through her hair, fingers working at the knots that had built up through the day. Hines' idea of a bath sounded good and she wondered if she had time to fit one in. She was exhausted; the day's events, plus the stress from last night, had left her feeling tense as the anxiety began to slowly bleed from her. The food had helped, the wine certainly, but she could feel the headache starting to grow behind her eyes.

'You want me to run you a bath?' Karla asked, coming back into the room.

'How do you do that?' Louise asked as Karla slid onto the sofa beside her. 'Always say the right thing at the right time.'

It was Karla's turn to smile now, but instead of answering she snuggled against Louise, laying her head against her shoulder, legs tucked to the side. Tom came and sat on the sofa arm, and for the next few minutes no one said or did anything; they just sat there together, the three of them full of food and content.

'How was Beth today?' Karla finally asked.

'I'm surprised she came in at all,' Louise said. 'I for sure wouldn't have done it if my partner had attacked me like that. I'd have died of sheer bloody embarrassment for a start.'

'Did she have any problems today? Any over-reactions, outbursts, that kind of thing?'

Louise shifted and Karla sat up, allowing Louise to move on the sofa so her back was against the arm. She gave Karla a stern look but didn't say anything.

'What... I'm concerned, is all,' Karla said when it was apparent Louise wasn't going to say anything. 'I thought you would be too.'

'If you want to know how Beth is, I suggest you speak to her. Here,' Louise said, reaching back behind her to the telephone on the side table, 'let me call her and you can ask her for yourself.'

'There's no need to be like that. I'm just concerned.'

'You said that already. I'm not going to talk about her behind her back. She's my friend.'

'I wouldn't want you to.'

'Good.'

Karla sat back. 'Good.'

For a few moments silence settled between them. Tom

jumped down from the sofa and wandered out of the room, his claws skittering on the wooden floor of the hallway as he made his way back to the kitchen.

Finally, Louise put her glass down and turned to Karla.

'You said something about a bath?'

Karla smiled, a wicked glint in her eyes.

'How about a shower instead?'

CHAPTER
TWENTY-ONE

The person who stared back from the vanity mirror wasn't one she recognised. The features were the same; the slightly crooked nose that turned to the left, the hazel eyes, the cheeks with the freckles that always seemed to bloom brightest when she was either embarrassed or angry. The hair that framed rather than hid. All those parts that people always commented on, all those were the same, but the person who wore them had changed.

She pressed against the bruise that ran down the right side of her face, an indrawn breath anticipating the sting of pain as she probed with careful fingers. In her years on the force, Elizabeth Hines had been hit and punched so many times it was now just a normal facet of her working life. As natural as filling in endless forms of paperwork, but with the added adrenaline rush that always left her feeling energised, and looking for a way to keep the feeling alive. To celebrate being alive.

For a time, that had been Joe. Being with Joe, feeling him, touching him. Tasting him. They lived their lives together, fast and furious sessions that left them both sated and spent. Exhausted and exhilarated. And yet, still surprisingly hollow, all at the same time. Empty. She knew she could reach out for him and he would be there. A phone call away. No hesitation. No thought.

No thought.

She touched the side of her face again. That was how she had ended up like this. By not thinking. With this dark reminder of how out of control things could get if she wasn't careful. Hines pressed against the bruise, feeling the warm spread of pain flow across her cheek, up to her eye and behind, where it quickly sharpened into an intense flash of white and then disappeared, leaving her feeling more embarrassed than hurt.

Everyone knew. Everyone had seen what had happened, if not the incident, then at least the fall-out. Her friends in the Carps, those few who shared drinks and stories, time and company each week; they had seen. They had helped, or tried, not understanding what they were seeing, only knowing that things had once again jumped out of the normal argument that had become a staple between the two, and into something more sinister. Violent words had become violent acts, and Hines winced, not at the pain of landed punches but at the memory of what had led them both to such drastic action.

But those were fair-weather friends. Friends in name only; she only ever saw them when she went to the pub. And she only went there because that was where Joe was. She didn't care about them. Not really. Not at all, if she was going to be truly honest with herself.

'That would be a first,' she said aloud, startling herself in the cold quiet of her house. The only one she did care about was Louise. Seeing her own pain reflected in her friend's eyes just added to the embarrassment she felt. The others, Karla, Manby, even Danes; those she could handle. Each one had already taken time to speak with her, to check she was all right, to offer help, offer advice. Out of the three Karla was best placed to help, but Hines wasn't ready yet to take that step. She knew it was one she had to take, but not yet. She tried to tell herself it had only happened yesterday, but that wasn't true, was it?

This had been going on for some time. Subtle at first, the digs and the jabs, the barbed thorny words that stung almost as much as the countless tears she cried silently in bed, or when she had a snatched moment of solitude at work.

What had happened in the pub had been inevitable, a natural conclusion to an unnatural situation. And now here she was alone in the dark.

Joe wasn't here. No one was here. Just her.

'Just me.' She smiled at herself in the mirror, and was pleased to see herself smile back.

The toaster popped and she took both slices and slathered them with butter before dropping them onto the stack that was now cooling. One slice in her mouth, she grabbed the mug of tea with one hand, the other holding the tower of toast, and went into the living room where she flopped onto the sofa. Feet up on the low coffee table, she searched amidst the discarded clothes and fresh laundry that were now mixed together until she found the book she had been reading for the last three weeks. Given to her by Louise, she had got scared and put it aside until she felt ready to continue.

The book was under an old t-shirt, one of Joe's, which she threw across the room into the wastepaper basket by the door. Removing the playing card she had been using as a book-mark, she settled back, took another bite of toast and began to read.

Half an hour later she had just got to the part where Ben Mears visited the shop run by the vampire's thrall when there was a knock at the door. A quick glance at her watch caused her to scowl. Nine-thirty. After the day she'd had, and with an early start in the morning, she knew she should be in bed already, but Louise had been right; the book was addictive, if she could just get past the scary parts.

Which is almost all the book, apparently, she thought, going to the front door. The outline of the person outside was one she instantly recognised. Anger rushed through her, along with a small jolt of... what? Excitement? Fear?

Lust?

'What do you want, Joe?' she called out.

'Open the door, Beth.'

For a moment she did nothing, simply stood there in the hallway, her hand on the door and a whirling maelstrom of indecision crashing around in her mind. She knew she should turn out the light, walk back to the sofa and finish the chapter she was reading, and then go to bed. Ignore him. Forget him. Forget he ever existed.

'I came to apologise. To talk,' he said.

She knew this was a lie; he had never apologised before. Why should he start now, and she said so.

'I was wrong. Way out of order. Come on, love. Let me in. I'm freezing my bollocks off out here.'

He knocked again, louder this time. Harder. Four harsh raps on the door, so hard the glass rattled in its frame.

'Stop that,' Hines said, unlocking the door. 'You're going to wake the neighbours.'

She flung the door open wide and grabbed Joe by the shoulder. He was wearing his trademark denim jacket and a smile that went right to the heart of the problem.

'Stop being so smug,' she said, closing the door behind him.

Joe stood in the hallway, breathing hard. She took in the scent that hung in the air between them, a heady mix of his cologne, alcohol and sweat. He had obviously run here; his hair was slicked back against his forehead and several strands curled around his ears. Hines wanted to reach out to tuck them back, but she stopped herself.

Only just.

'Say what you want to say, and then I think you should leave,' she said.

He stepped closer.

'I'm sorry,' he said. 'I was an idiot.'

He stepped even closer.

Hines, head down, whispered, 'Yes you were.'

Another step. He reached out to brush his fingers against her hair. She flinched, an involuntary twitch of her shoulder.

'You hurt me.'

His hand retreated. He stepped back. His head dropped.

'I'm sorry,' he said and started to cry.

Hines looked up. Watched as he buried his face in his hands. Shoulders shaking, hair falling around his face, Joe let out soul wrenching sobs, the words he now spoke lost within their wet depths.

'I didn't mean it. I never wanted to hurt you. How could I... I love you...'

She stepped closer.

'...but I did. I lashed out like a kid angry at having his toys taken away. And I hurt you.' He looked up, and the anguish in his face, the pain in his voice broke Hines' heart all over again. 'How can you ever forgive me?'

And her arms were around him, holding him tight, his face buried into her chest, her fingers brushing his hair as she whispered soft reassurances that she would never leave him, that she loved him. His arms gathered around her, pulling her even tighter. She could feel his hot tears against her skin; his breath, that wondrous, glorious mix of cigarettes and Polo mints that was oh, so Joe, filled her nostrils, and then his lips were on hers and he was kissing her and she was kissing him back and his hands were on her, touching her, sending waves of pleasure through her even while her mind screamed at her *don'tdothis-don'tdothis-don'tdothis* and then she was against the wall and her shirt was pulled up and his lips were on her and there was fire all around them as passion, and lust, and anger all rolled into one sweet sensation and the world fell away as easily as their clothes.

. . .

They had made it as far as the sofa in the living room, crashing together amongst the discarded clothes, rolling together as good sex overrode good judgement. And it had been good, Hines thought, stretching out, enjoying the feeling of their sweaty skin pressing against each other in the hot heat of the room.

The air stank of sex and cigarettes; Joe had lit another, using her mug of cold tea as an ashtray. His back was to her, partially covered by the blanket Hines had snatched from behind the sofa to keep them warm. Neither had wanted to move upstairs to the bedroom, to pause their passion long enough to climb stairs. Now they languished on the sofa in the comfortable embrace of each other.

'I could kill for a cuppa,' Joe said, reaching down to tap more ash into the mug.

'You know where the kitchen is,' Hines said from behind him. Her voice was thick with sleep, as a happy and content fog began to settle over her. She didn't know what time it was; it couldn't be much later, it had been fast. Furious and passionate, yes, but still quick. But that was all right because everything else was all right now, wasn't it? They were together.

She stretched her arm out, hooking it around Joe. In response he moved away from her, swinging his legs out so he could sit up. Her arm fell down into the warm spot he had been lying in.

'Come back here,' she said sluggishly, reaching for him once more.

Joe pushed her hand away, immediately grabbing his clothes up.

'I throw you a fuck, the last thing you could do is make me a damn cup of tea.'

It was like she had been slapped again. Cold realisation sloshed over her like a crushing wave, punching through whatever veil of hope she had foolishly draped over her eyes.

'What?' she stammered. Sitting up, she clutched the blanket to her, feeling its warmth bleed away as fast as her heart was beating. 'What's wrong?'

Joe pulled his jeans on and stood. Angrily he snatched at his t-shirt and began yanking it down over his head.

'This. This was wrong. This was a mistake.' He turned and looked down on her.

'You're a mistake.'

It was like being punched all over again and Hines fell back against the sofa as though she had been struck by his fists instead of his cruel words.

But then the anger ignited within her once more. She could feel it rise up, throwing aside her fears and her doubts.

'You fucking prick!' she shouted, struggling to her knees. 'I'm the one who threw you a charity fuck. One last ride before I ditch you like the bad habit you are. Get the fuck out of my house!'

His head whipped side to side as he looked round the room.

'Where did I put my fucking shoes?'

'Those dirty rags are in the hallway. With your jacket.'

She held the blanket tight around her body, very conscious of the fact she was naked underneath. She could still feel him inside her, feel the power of their lovemaking, and yet here they were arguing once again.

But this time felt different. This time felt like the end.

'You're a fucking joke!'

Before she knew it, Joe had spun round, his hand around her throat, the other grabbing the back of her head, tugging her hair so that her head tilted back at an almost impossible angle. She could feel her neck begin to spasm as muscles contracted and twisted under his grip.

'What did you fucking say?'

His voice was a raspy growl, and as he spoke flecks of spittle landed on her face. His fingers at her throat tightened and she suddenly had trouble breathing.

'I... I...'

'*What did you fucking say?*' He was almost screaming in her face now, his body pressed against hers as he towered over her, their noses touching.

She pushed against him; her hands flat on his chest. It wasn't working; she couldn't get leverage.

And now he had two hands at her neck. Somewhere a bell was ringing – *is it my phone?* – and the lights were starting to dim. At first the television disappeared, then the bookcase. On her right the door to the hallway began to fade, and then it too was gone. All she could see was the horrid face of Joe staring down at her, his lips pulled back to reveal teeth biting into his tongue. Blood trickled down his chin and began to spatter onto her face.

He looks like a vampire right out of that book, she thought. An overwhelming urge to pee gripped her and another, more wicked, thought flashed across her mind: *I'm going to piss on the sofa*.

And then the pressure was gone and the room swam back into existence as Joe fell away from her.

'You fucking bitch. Look what you made me do!'

Hines was gasping for breath, clutching at her throat where his fingers had pressed tight. Her mind rocked and rolled, swayed and swam as she stood up. The room tilted and for a second she thought she was going to end up on the floor, but everything steadied, long enough for her to grab the mug of tea that now held ash. Summoning every last ounce of strength she had, Hines threw the mug at Joe.

He never saw it coming. He stood slightly bent at the waist, hands on his thighs as he caught his breath. He looked up just as the mug, its contents trailing behind it like a clumpy cloud of ash and tea, connected with his temple. With a startled grunt he fell back, blood flowing from a deep cut. He staggered back two steps, tripped on the rug and fell to the floor.

Hines quickly stood over him in an intense rage, throwing punches and kicks as hard as she could.

'Get the fuck out!' she screamed with each kick. 'Get the fuck out! Get the fuck out!'

'Jesus… Fuck off!'

He tried to block her attacks with his arms, covering his head as best he could. Blood flashed across the wall as he dashed for the door, staining the books on her shelf as he passed.

In the hallway he grabbed up his shoes and was reaching for his jacket, slung over the banister when Hines stormed out of the room.

'Out!' she screamed again.

As she passed the bookcase she grabbed up a large book, another Stephen King doorstopper of a novel, and with a single swing, she flung it at Joe.

This time he was ready and dodged, but not before striking his toe on the bottom of the door as he pulled it open.

'You crazy fucking bitch!' he yelled, stumbling out onto the porch. He made a couple of steps before tripping and falling over. His startled cry of pain made Hines laugh.

'Hope you broke your fucking neck,' she cried out. 'Stay the fuck away from me!'

She slammed the door shut and so never heard his colourful reply.

Her back to the door, Hines slid down until she was sitting, legs tucked up so that she rested her chin on her knees. Arms tight around her, she hugged herself, breathing hard.

Why had she thought anything would be different? But it had been, hadn't it? Not him. Not Joe. He was the same. He would always be the same. Pleasant to the eye but a monster inside, and that monster would always be there, always ready to come out with a harsh word, and then with harsher actions. That was a dark truth, *his* dark truth, hidden within his very soul. He would always be the same.

But she wouldn't be.

She didn't have to take that any more.

She didn't deserve to be treated like that.

No one did. And not this time. This time she had fought back almost immediately, not giving him a moment's victory. He'd thought she'd submit again. He'd thought he'd won. But not this time.

And never again.

She stayed like that, arms around her body, her victory hug tight and comforting, until the cold chill of night began to nibble at her skin.

Slowly, wincing with the movement, she got to her feet. With deliberate and careful steps, she climbed the stairs to the bathroom.

'Never again,' she said and smiled at the power of those two words.

CHAPTER
TWENTY-TWO

'Never again.'

He checked his watch. It was just after two in the morning and his body ached. The places that hurt the most were his wrists, the right one more than the left. He could feel the hot throb of his pulse just below the surface, see the skin twitch with each angry beat. The heat ran up his arm to his shoulder where it flared, a white supernova of pain. If he was worried, he gave no indication; his eyes were locked on her.

Like a discarded doll, she lay still and unmoving on the table before him. Her hair, once shiny and smooth, now spread out around her head in dirty, greasy strands that were twisted together like old tree roots. His eyes travelled her body, captive on the table, bound at the wrists and ankles with metal chains, the links old and rusted.

Her clothes had long since disappeared, cut away from her body with scissors as rusty as the chains. They lay discarded on the floor, sodden by rainwater that had fallen into the abandoned building, dripping down with a sound that echoed throughout, like the moan of lost memories.

He smiled as they washed over him. Oh, the things he had done. The sounds he had elicited from her lingered, warming him deep inside. The scent of her filled his nostrils and he inhaled deeply, leaning in so that he could take as much of her in as possible.

One last time.

Face mere inches from hers, he sighed as his senses flooded with the very essence of the woman. She was still there, barely. Her perfume had long since faded but there were moments it slid in, drifting across like an ocean breeze.

He smiled again.

All her bravado, all her fight was now gone. Cut from her in small slivers, each slice removing another layer of her resistance. She had been strong at first, barely moving when he slid the blade across her skin, opening her flesh to reveal the wonders within. It was only when the boy had come to stand beside him, to stare into her very being as he worked that she had become frantic. Desperation overriding sense.

But he had anticipated that. Done what was needed, and now she lay unmoving. Untalking. Silent. Obedient.

He smiled again. 'Not long now,' he said. His hand reached out to caress her one last time. It drifted down her body, savouring the feel of flesh and dirt and blood under his fingertips. He closed his eyes as they dipped inside her one last time, his movements drawing a pained moan from her, and a soft sigh from him. Memories of taking her in all the ways he could possibly imagine rushed through him; watching as the boy took his turn and feeling so proud, so very proud.

'Not long now,' he said again.

CHAPTER
TWENTY-THREE

TUESDAY, 20TH

The interview room at Wakefield Prison was in stark contrast to the remainder of the building. For a start the walls had been painted a bright, warm red, not the cold white of untreated brick that were the cells. The table filled the centre of the room, and around it had been placed four wooden chairs that made Louise think of being back in school. Minimal practicality was the order of business here, not comfort. It was a functional room, one to be used and abused, as the saying went.

They had been sitting here for fifteen minutes, having been led here by an officer who gave neither name nor interest. There had been no offer of a hot drink and it didn't look like one was coming any time soon.

The same could be said for their visitor.

'How long are they going to be?' Hines asked.

It was the first thing she'd said all morning since picking Louise up. As soon as she'd got in the car, Louise had seen the bruises on her neck, as well as the redness in her eyes. Not a hangover, and she was sure Hines hadn't been crying hard enough to cause such a reaction, so that, along with the bruises, left only one thing, and she had said as much. Surprisingly, rather than the heated explosion Louise had expected, Hines had simply concentrated on driving, almost destroying the gear box as she wrenched through each one. The engine had growled angrily, echoing off the buildings either side of the road as they made their way through Horbury, and still Hines had said nothing.

She turned to find Louise staring at her.

'What? Oh, just let it go.'

'I can't,' Louise said, 'and you shouldn't want me to. In fact, you should be screaming the house down until we drag that arsehole into the Shop, perhaps bouncing him off a wall or three along the way. Look what he did to you...'

She reached out but Hines flinched back before she could touch her neck.

'You can't argue away those marks. I can see the damn outline of his fingers, and that's not from some kinky sex game gone awry either, before you say anything. That's assault, pure and simple. What the hell were you thinking, seeing him again after what he did on Sunday?'

'It's complicated,' Hines began.

Louise could feel the anger flare in her chest, its copper tang bitter in her mouth.

'It's not complicated. Not in the slightest. In fact, it's so fucking easy even you should understand it. He hits you; you have to dump his arse, preferably after giving it a kick or two. Or are you really that stupid?'

Hines' cheeks had gone bright red and her fingers had tightened into fists on the table. For a moment Louise thought she was going to lash out, to strike at her, and, honestly, if she had it would be a step forward. Better than just accepting the bad situation she was in.

But instead of striking out, Hines took in a long deep breath, held it until Louise thought she was going to start turning blue, and then let it out very, very slowly. Her eyes rose and locked on to Louise's, holding her in place until Louise realised that now she was the one holding her breath.

The pause before the storm. Louise braced herself.

'You're right.'

The breath Louise had been holding exploded out in a single rushed cloud that left her feeling slightly light-headed.

'What? I'm right? You're agreeing with me, no argument? Who are you and what have you done with the real Elizabeth Hines?'

'You know you're not really funny, don't you?' Hines said, but she was smiling as she did so. 'Look, I get it. I really do. And last night was the last time. I promise. He's not going to be coming around any time soon, anyway. Not after getting hit by a mug and then *It*. Surprised it wasn't a murder, to be honest,' she added, laughing.

Louise was not impressed.

'You can't go hitting people with Stephen King novels. You might damage the book. And using your mug of tea… That's pretty cruel. Did you make him drink it?'

Both were now laughing, the turbulent tension between them calm waters once more. When she had finally gathered herself, Hines sat back, visibly more relaxed than she had been just a few moments earlier. The colour had returned to her skin, and despite the bruising at her neck, Louise thought the younger officer looked a lot healthier and more relaxed than she had seen her in months.

'Why are we here?' Hines asked again. 'It's been six months since the Willikar case and McKensie only just got sentenced. I'm guessing we're the last people he wants to be seeing right now, don't you think?'

'Don't you think it a bit strange that Helen disappeared at the exact same time that McKensie was killing the Willikar boy, and all because he had seen him with her?'

'You think he killed her as well?'

'That's what we're here to find out,' Louise said, just as the door to the room swung open.

Daniel McKensie was marched inside, flanked by two stony-faced guards. He was dressed in a light blue shirt with matching trousers that had been torn at the knee and down one leg. His shirt had what looked like dried blood on it, and his left cheek was a swollen disaster. Without a word he was driven to the chair on the other side of the table, the meaty paws of the guard nearly swallowing McKensie's entire shoulder as he pushed him into it. Still saying nothing, the two guards left the room. The door swung shut behind them, and there was the distinctively loud *click* as the door was locked.

'Cosy,' Hines said. 'What happened to you?'

'Funny, I was going to ask you the same thing.' He waved a nicotine-stained finger at the bruise on her neck. 'Get a bit rough, did he?'

Ignoring his remark, Hines turned to Louise.

'D wing, isn't it? We know a few people on D Wing. Owe us a few favours, I expect. I wonder if they make house visits?' As she said this last she turned slowly to stare at McKensie. He visibly paled.

'No need to be like that. I can be friendly.'

Still ignoring him, Hines started as though she was getting ready to leave. Her chair screeched back across the floor and she began pulling on her overcoat.

'Guess he doesn't want a little extra help in here keeping some of the other animals off his back. They don't like those who mess with kids; not the done thing, is it? Well, if he doesn't want us to get them to leave their hands off in return for a pleasant chat, then that's his doing. I'll get the car ready.'

McKensie jumped to his feet as Louise nodded over to Hines and slid her own chair back.

'No, wait!' he said, hands raised. 'Wait! I'll talk with you. What do you want to talk about?'

Hines paused at the door.

'Helen Williams.'

McKensie looked from one officer to the other. He shook his head.

'Who?'

Louise pulled her chair back in. Hines turned round and grabbed the back of her chair.

'Seriously? You don't remember?' When he simply stared back at her, mouth limp, eyes flared, Hines sighed and sat back down. 'Helen Williams. The woman you went to the warehouse with just before you saw James Willikar. You remember him, I guess?'

Now it was McKensie's turn to sigh. It was a long drawn-out breath, almost a death rattle of regret.

'It was never supposed to happen,' he said after a long pause.

'What was... killing James Willikar or killing Helen Williams?'

'Wait; I might have killed the boy—'

'Might have?'

'—but I never killed the whore. Is that what you think? That I killed her?' His voice dropped and he leaned forward. 'Is she really dead?'

Louise didn't answer. Instead, she flipped a few pages in her notebook. Read a few lines, flipped another couple of pages then looked up.

'What did you do with her?'

'Nothing. She blew me, we got spooked by those damn kids—'

'One of whom you killed,' Hines jumped in. McKensie kept his eyes on Louise.

'—and I ran. Last I saw her, she was talking with the tall kid.'

The tall kid. The one with the buzz-cut.

The one with the creepy smile.

A cold weight settled in Louise's chest. McKensie sat back in his chair and shrugged but Louise gave him no further thought. One thing, one name, filled her mind.

'Peterson.'

In the car, Louise sat silently as Hines drove back to Ossett. The day had changed; the clouds that had started so white and fluffy were now dark and angry. The sky had flipped from blue to grey, as though the colour had been leached away until all that remained was an afterimage of the day.

Peterson.

Again, that name had come up during the course of an investigation.

A shiver ran down her spine and she shook it away as best as she could, but the thought still remained: *Peterson.* She closed her eyes and instantly she could see the boy, see the smile that filled his face but never reached his eyes. He stood dressed as he was the last time she had seen him, dressed in choral attire at the midnight mass. He was at the front of the throng, and when he passed by...

That smile.

That smile that knew things.

'Why did Manby say not to look into the Peterson kid?' Louise suddenly asked.

Hines shrugged.

'No idea. If I remember right, something about a lack of evidence. Nothing that tied him to the place. No evidence he was anywhere near either the warehouse or the churchyard. Just another weird and troubled kid.'

'I guess you're right. Do you think we should talk with him anyway, or am I just wasting our time?'

As much as it hurt to admit, perhaps there was nothing to Helen's disappearance. She was a drug addict and a prostitute. It happened all the time. Walking the streets, injecting or snorting or drinking what she earned from renting out her body to name-less strangers every night, eventually the terrible reality would all come crashing down, pushing her to do even more dangerous acts just to survive. And so what if she had done one, then got a coach or a train so that she could run from her situation here? Who could blame her? And here Louise was, wasting her time and raising the hopes of Helen's brother, who was just as guilty for putting his sister into that position.

You can't save them all, Manby had said, after introducing her to the Williams siblings, *but you can help them along the way and get something useful in return.*

But Louise wanted to save Helen from herself. Just like she did Hines.

'Damn it!'

Rain had begun to fall and the windscreen wipers were strug-gling to keep up with the downpour. The blades swept across the glass, but when they came back they screeched like the wail of a dozen angry foxes. A clump of dirt was smeared across in a dirty rainbow's arc, making it even harder to see out.

Slowing the car, Hines leaned forward and wiped her hand across the window.

'You know the dirt's on the outside, right?' Louise said, laughing.

'Ha-ha, funny bugger. The garage said they'd fixed this but it's even worse.'

As if in answer, the blades gave another groan, shuddered a couple of times and then stopped working altogether.

'Sanderson's?' Hines nodded.

Louise might talk with Manby, suggest another chat with the Peterson kid, but she doubted anything would come of that. Sanderson's, however…

'Seems now's a good time to get them looked at, don't you think?' Louise said with a sly grin.

Maybe there was nothing they could do for Helen Williams,

but there was something they could do for the other cases they were officially working on.

'What about Bailey?' Hines asked.

Louise settled back in her seat as Hines threw the car into a new gear.

What indeed?

CHAPTER
TWENTY-FOUR

Detective Inspector Bill Manby sat in his office and silently wished for the day to officially come to a finish. He looked over at the clock and saw he was a good six hours from clocking off time, but on the other hand, he was just thirty minutes from slipping out and grabbing an early lunch. Yes, if he could just make it through a couple more reports he could reward himself with a few quick ones in the Carps.

He reached for the cigarette that had been leaning limply in the ashtray. The stack of paperwork had been taunting him since yesterday. Two days into the week, the tower of case reports, interview transcripts and requisition requests was already taller than his chipped mug. Some of it was holdover from last week – the muggings on Church Street Park and The Green; two car thefts, one in Ossett centre, one in Gawthorpe, and the five-way punch-up that took place Saturday night in the Horse and Jockey – added to the multiple calls that had come in directly, the usual small-town complaints and grievances. While their task was to handle the growing threat of serious crime in the area, they still had the daily grind to deal with. The traffic violations, the neighbour disputes, the husband too quick with his fists and the wife too fast with the household chequebook.

Tapping ash into the glass tray his wife had bought him at the bring and buy down at the cricket field a few Sundays ago, Manby despaired at the never-ending stream of chaos that was modern day policing. Alongside all the usual, he also had to manage his team, the dynamics a constant rolling wave that repeatedly crashed against itself. He drew in the final dregs of the cigarette, savouring the taste one last time. Marie had made it clear she didn't want him smoking any more. Very clear. Her words still stung in his head, almost as much as the slap on his hand where she'd swatted away a tab when he unconsciously tried to light up after his breakfast that morning. He rubbed at the back of his hand, smiling around the cigarette as he took in the last of its offerings.

He was grinding it into the wasteland of ash in the tray when the door opened. Chief Superintendent Freeman strode in, hat under his arm and a stern expression on his face.

'Morning, David,' Manby said, rising from his chair and extending his hand. 'I didn't know you were coming along today. Have I forgotten another meeting?'

Freeman smiled and placed his hat on the desk.

'No meeting. Not officially, anyway. Far as that lot out there knows, this is just a surprise spot inspection.' He pulled a chair out and sat. 'We've got some things to discuss.'

'Sounds serious. Cuppa?' The Chief Superintendent nodded and continued to pick at a loose thread on his jacket. Manby walked to the office door, opened it and called out for two mugs of tea. The girl wasn't at her desk but he was sure someone would answer the call, especially if they knew what was best.

He turned back. 'Won't be long.'

'Close the door then and let's talk.'

Feeling like something bad was about to be dropped on him from a great height, Manby did just that.

. . .

When the knock at the door signalled that the mugs of tea had arrived, Manby was shaking with rage. He called out and waited as the officer who had been unlucky enough to be given the job of delivering the tea to the bosses strode in and placed the mugs on the table.

'No biscuits, treacle?' the Chief Superintendent said, tipping the officer a wink.

Startled, the young woman threw Manby a *what-do-I-do?* look, but all she got back was the reddened glare of her DI.

As soon as the door shut behind the retreating police officer, Manby let out the breath he had been holding in a long exhale.

'And you're absolutely sure about this?' he finally said.

'The operation has been going on for seven weeks now. The intelligence is considered credible, the details of which pose a very real threat.'

'Multiple verifications?'

The question was a stupid one and Manby regretted asking it almost as soon as the words had left his mouth. Of course it was verified, cross checked against multiple sources and deemed credible. The Chief Superintendent wouldn't travel from Wakefield HQ, break operational procedure and fill him in if he wasn't absolutely convinced he needed to know.

'I can't fucking believe it,' Manby said. He needed a cigarette but he'd just smoked the last one. 'We'd heard about the kids being taken out of the schools over in Dewsbury, but here in Ossett as well now?'

'Five this morning. We had a call from our inside man, who said a small protest had been planned for outside South and North Ossett schools. We sent a couple of men but they said nothing major happened. A few names were thrown about, and a couple of kids got into a scrap. We actually got more calls from concerned parents wanting to know what the police would do to stop them doing this again.'

Manby was still trying to get his head around what he'd been told.

'The British National Party protesting outside schools.'

'Well, people who hold a similar world view. There's not been any official word from the party.'

'What about what your inside man had to say?'

The Chief Superintendent blew on his mug of tea before taking a sip. His face crumpled and he put it back down on the desk.

'Needs more sugar and about another five minutes of stewing. Our bloke has been inside for about five months. At first it was a fishing exercise; we'd heard rumours but nothing concrete, so we put someone in. It was a few weeks before they trusted him enough to bring him below the surface.'

'Sanderson's garage. A fucking nest of racists. We work with them. Your Ruth is married to Sanderson.'

'My sister always was good at making bad choices.'

'How did we not see this? We've been using them for years. You got us the contract in the first place.'

'Don't remind me. I was just as shocked as you, more in fact. Doesn't look good when the Chief Superintendent's own sister is married to the man whose garage workers are members of a deeply racist political party. Casts a bit of a shadow and gets a lot of people asking a lot of very uncomfortable questions.'

'I can imagine,' Manby said.

'Needless to say, now we know they're planning a protest in Dewsbury centre this Saturday, we can look at closing them down.'

He passed a small folder over, which Manby took and opened immediately.

'I can't believe they were able to get the legal go-ahead to hold this rally,' he said, his eyes roaming down the official paperwork. 'Who the fuck would think this was a good idea?'

'Good idea or not, it's all legal and above board. They're allowed to hold up to 500 people for a two-hour gathering in Dewsbury marketplace on Saturday 24th June. This calls for additional policing to be arranged, and we'll need some help from you and your team as well.'

'Of course. Whatever you need.'

'Put a plan together, and Thursday we'll brief the team fully. Till then, keep this between us.'

'Do you think this has anything to do with the Wadee brothers?'

The thought had jumped into his head almost as soon as the Chief Superintendent had started speaking. Too many coincidences, too many linked variables. The stolen car had belonged to the Wadees, who had been beaten up looking for it, probably by a bunch of BNP racists. The idiots who had stolen the car from Savile Town worked at Sanderson's garage, the place that had sold the car. And then there was the car itself, a cut and shut piece of shit that had finally fallen apart with tragic consequences.

And the owner of the garage was married to the sister of the Chief Superintendent.

This couldn't get messier if he tried.

Yes, it can.

'That's for you to figure out,' the Chief Superintendent said, rising from his seat. He gathered his hat and put it on, wiping the brim with his hand. 'I'm still in overall command, but I want you and your team to be taking the lead on this so there's no chance of anyone questioning the legitimacy of any arrests. This is a fucked-up situation, Bill. You can see that, right? You can see the position I've been put into?'

Manby could not only see it, he wondered how the Chief Superintendent *hadn't* seen this coming. CS Freeman gave a smile, didn't wait for an answer and departed, leaving Manby in his office with his conflicted thoughts.

There had always been rumours about Colin Sanderson. About his links with extreme-right gangs. There had even been rumours that not all the business carried out on the premises was legit, but being linked with Chief Superintendent Freeman meant that cheeks were turned and eyes looked the other way on more than one occasion. And now it looked like it was all coming back to bite the Chief Superintendent in the arse in a big way.

Jesus, but if there was ever a time he needed a cigarette it was now. Instead, he'd settle for a pint and a pie.

CHAPTER
TWENTY-FIVE

The Carpenters Arms was always popular at lunchtime. Along with the stacked rolls that came from Jenny's Café over the other side of the marketplace, an assortment of hot pies, served with mushy peas, buttered bread and a pint, was available for the lunchtime crowd. Today was no exception, and the pub was busy. It was so busy that Dominic, the pub's owner, was serving tables with hot food.

Manby had a table always reserved for him and he was surprised to find that this was already occupied by an old couple.

'Sorry, Bill,' Dominic said, as he walked past him, carrying a stack of dirty dishes back to the kitchen. 'We're pushed for space today.'

'And staff by the looks of things,' Manby said.

Behind the bar, a young girl was taking down a customer's food order, scrawling it onto a scrap of paper. As he watched, she scratched what she had written out, and started again. Beside him, Dominic gave a sigh and rebalanced the plates in his hand.

'We had to put one of the cleaning staff behind the bar.'

'Joe still here?'

'Out back. Delivery just arrived.' Dominic's face darkened.

'Don't start, Bill. I don't like what happened any more than you, but I need him right now. We had words, and it seems like he had another round with his lassie and came off worse this time.'

A cold anger settled on Manby. He had promised Hines he wouldn't get involved. With Susan now living away, Hines had become a surrogate daughter. Oh, he never admitted to such, but if he was honest with himself, he knew that was how he regarded the young woman. The thought of that arrogant young prick laying hands on her... He tried to shake the thought away but couldn't.

He stood at the bar and waited to be served. The sound of the kegs being rolled from the truck and down into the cellar filled his head. He could see Joe in his mind, all arrogance and flair, a substantive arsehole lacking any substance at all. No character of good intent. Manby smiled when the young girl asked what he'd like and he placed his order. What he needed to do was forget about Joe; if Hines wanted to do anything, she would, and if and when she did, he would be there to help her. He just needed to let things take their course. Even Marie had commented that Manby was blind where Elizabeth Hines was concerned. He treated all of those under his command like family, always willing to listen, always ready to help with work or personal problems alike. But Hines, who reminded him so much of Susan, was like the second daughter they had never been blessed with.

Some could have forgiven Marie for being jealous, of thinking that Manby was crossing a line with his young, female, officer. Working close together on cases, late most nights, even a few overnight stakeouts... the rumours were always there, just lurking behind the covered smirks and smiles. The boss and the bimbo, they would whisper. He knew it. Marie knew it, but she also knew the truth of it.

But she was right; where Hines was concerned he was more than a little invested; the protective father she didn't have.

His pint delivered, Manby was waiting for his food, standing at the far side of the bar nearest the game room, when Joe came in, red faced and sweating.

'Pull us a pint of Johns, Carrie,' he said, wiping at the back of his neck. 'Pulling those monsters in has got me all hot and bothered.'

A couple of men, friends of Joe's no doubt, cackled and gave him a nudge. They all looked at the young girl behind the bar.

'Bet she could give you a rub down, all right.'

'What I wouldn't give…'

Laughs all round.

Manby stared into his drink. *Breathe in… breathe out…*

'What about that lass of yours?' one of them was saying. 'You still banging her?'

'Or she's banging you by the look of it. What happened there?'

Manby looked up just in time to see Joe pull back from the man's hand, which was stretched out to touch at his temple. He swiped at the hand and gave the man a push to the shoulder.

'Fuck off, soft lad,' he said, laughing. 'Like she could do anything. Got this after I'd done her good.'

White heat began to flood along Manby's nerves. His hand tightened around his glass. The liquid, brown and still, was a deep chasm into which he tried to focus all of his growing anger. *Don't listen*, he told himself.

Don't.

'Threw my last one into her last night. So, feel free to give her a go,' Joe was saying. 'She likes it rough so don't hold back, big guy.'

'Don't you know it,' the man was saying, and then Manby was beside them both and his hands were around their necks.

'Oi, what the fuck you doing?'

'Hey! Fucking nonce, what is this?'

Manby said nothing. He dug his thumbs into the soft area of flesh where neck meets shoulder and pressed. Hard.

Their yells of pain became stammered protests as Manby, his hands still clutching their necks, marched them through the side door, past the toilets and out the back into the car park. The delivery truck that had just dropped off the beer had already left, leaving behind a large puddle of oil on the ground.

Manby threw the men forward with a single jerk. They staggered and turned round, faces flush with anger.

'What the fuck do you think you're doing?'

'Who the fuck do you think you are?'

Manby raised a hand and pointed right at Joe.

'You.'

For a moment, Joe was puzzled. He looked from his equally baffled friend to the small group of people who had gathered by the door to watch, and then back to Manby.

'What are you playing at? You can't do that. I'll have you done. You're a fucking copper and—'

'Shut the fuck up.' Joe shut up.

Manby's words were as cold as stone. His eyes never left Joe's. Didn't blink once. He didn't say anything else. One minute Joe was standing, glaring silently at Manby, the next he was lying on the floor, his upper lip smeared across his cheek, his nose crooked and spilling blood, his eyes closed. Two fast punches that Joe didn't see coming, until it was too late.

Manby turned to Joe's friend, who raised his hands and backed off several steps.

'I don't want any trouble,' he said, stammering so hard it sounded like he was standing in the Arctic Circle rather than the damp, oil strewn car park of the Carpenters Arms.

'Then leave. Right now. And forget whatever was said about Ms Hines. I hear you went anywhere near her; I hear you even so much as picked up the phone and tried calling her, I will come and find you and you'll join your mate here.'

'Hey… I don't know what the problem is between you two, but I don't want anything to do with it. Hines is off-limits. Got it.'

'Good. Now fuck off.'

'But my pint—'

The look Manby gave the man cut off any desire to finish drinking right here and right now. Without another word he walked away, jamming his hands in his pockets. A moment later, he was jogging and then he was gone. The spectacle over, the small crowd moved back inside the pub.

Manby knelt down beside Joe.

'Let's you and me have a little chat,' he said, lifting the groaning man by the scruff of his shirt.

When Manby came back into the pub, his pie was waiting at the far end of the bar, along with a full pint and a whisky shot. He was wiping his hands on a paper towel from the toilets, its pulpy brown texture quickly becoming little more than mush.

Dominic broke away from serving at the bar to hand Manby a beer towel.

'This'll be better. You feel better?'

'A little.' He swallowed the whisky in one, savouring the bloom of heat in his throat and chest. 'More now. Thanks.'

'Dare I ask where Joe is? He's supposed to be manning the bar.'

Manby took a bite of pie, chewed and swallowed.

'He's been taken over to the station. Won't be back. In fact, it's probably a good idea to start looking for a new bartender. I think Joe will be moving on after a bit of self-reflection in the cells.'

'Self-reflection? Is that what we're calling it now? Not that I'm saying he didn't deserve it; he's always been trouble, that one, but trouble with a good-looking face.'

'The worst kind,' Manby said.

'Had to talk to him more than once about hitting on the girls when he's supposed to be working. Had heard the rumours about what he sometimes did with them, but I thought it was talk. What happened Sunday was an eye-opener all right. If I could have fired him there and then I would have. But you know how it is. I thought he was all talk.'

'It wasn't talk.'

Dominic poured Manby another shot of whisky, and one for himself. He raised the glass.

'Fuck that arsehole, then,' he said and drained his drink.

CHAPTER
TWENTY-SIX

Sanderson's Garage was located on the wide corner that curved from Ventnor Way onto The Green in Ossett, right next to Dearden Street. It had operated in the area for many years, a successful enterprise to which almost everyone who owned a vehicle brought their respective cars, vans and bikes for their annual checks, MOTs and general repair work. It had garnered a reputation for fast, reliable work, work that didn't always come cheap, but it did come guaranteed to be complete. If they said it was fixed, it was fixed. If they said it needed work and the cost would be this, then you knew exactly where you stood. Nothing hidden. Nothing slapped on at the last minute to bump the price up.

That was the reason given, along with the excellent work, when they landed the contract with the new police unit based out of Prospect Road. With few cars and a limited budget, and needing the work to be done locally rather than wasting time or money transferring to the dedicated internal police garage over in Wakefield, several businesses were approached in and around Ossett, but only Sanderson's met all the criteria. The Chief Superintendent himself oversaw the search, and when he signed off on

Sanderson's he made it very clear that there was no one better suited to the job.

'Is it true that Sanderson is married to the Chief Superintendent's sister?' Louise asked as they waited at the traffic lights on Prospect Road.

Their car gave another low grumble, a warning sign that it would soon be needing its own tune up. Hines balanced the biting point as she stared at the lights, willing them to change to green. It didn't do to keep the engine idling this way; the car didn't as much need a tune up as a complete overhaul.

'Married for three years and still going strong, from what I hear,' Hines replied. 'They had that rough patch last year, but it all seemed to work out.'

That *rough patch*, Louise recalled, had led to the Chief Superintendent being extremely prickly for a few weeks, hanging around the station and lurking over everyone's shoulders, making things very uncomfortable for days on end. Finally, the pair had sorted things out and the Chief Superintendent had gone back to his office in Wakefield HQ. Hines turned quickly to Louise, a grin on her face.

'But from what I hear, Ruth Sanderson still likes to hang out with the mechanics every Saturday night, while hubby is out on a call, if you catch my drift.'

Louise smiled. Whenever there was gossip, there would be Hines, lapping it up.

'In fact,' Hines continued, 'I heard that Ruth gets a gold star service herself. You know, spark plugs lubed up, oil changed, tyres rotated.'

'I get it,' Louise said with a laugh. 'Lights changed.'

The car rolled forward and turned left.

The rain hadn't yet reached Ossett, choosing instead to linger over Horbury, but the sky was slowly turning darker by the minute. As the car pulled to a stop, and they got out, they were surprised to see Sergeant Bailey's car parked outside the garages. They were even more surprised to see the animated conversation Bailey was having with a young mechanic. They were standing close to one another, close enough in fact that to anyone who didn't know better, it could appear that they were having an intimate conversation instead of an argument. The young mechanic, his jeans and jacket stained with engine oil and grease, gestured wildly, his arms raised and spread either side of the Sergeant. It looked like he was getting ready to deliver a double handed karate chop, and the thought made Louise speed up, no matter her personal thoughts of the man

'What's this all about?' Hines said, matching Louise's pace.

'No idea, but it doesn't look good,' Louise replied, her eyes locked on both men. 'Does he have to argue with everyone? First the Ellises—'

'And we still need to find out what that was all about,' Hines said.

'—and then earlier with the doctor in the hospital,' Louise continued.

As they got closer, Bailey turned and saw them approach. He leaned in closer to the young man, one hand on his shoulder. All appearance of an attack had been dropped by the mechanic, who simply stood and listened to whatever the Police Sergeant was saying. Louise could hear the low murmur of voices, the thick tang of Bailey's Yorkshire accent rising with the occasional word.

'…careful…'

'…not the best…'

'…seven-thirty. You better…'

'Do you think it's all getting to him?' Louise asked Hines in a low whisper. 'The pressure, I mean. The job isn't suited to everyone, and people react to the change in circumstances in ways totally out of character.'

Hines grinned and gave her friend a playful nudge.

'Has Karla been giving you more psychology lessons in between snogging sessions?'

'During, actually,' Louise said with a laugh.

The argument between the two men seemed to be over now,

the young mechanic wandering away towards the nearest of the buildings. Bailey turned towards them and stood, fists clenched at his sides as they came up to him.

'Thing with Bailey is,' Hines continued, 'and you have to take this into account… he's always been a dickhead.'

'What do you two want?' Bailey said.

'I rest my case,' Hines said. Louise laughed while their Detective Sergeant stared at them. 'Hello again, Sergeant. Everything all right?'

'Everything's fine. I asked why you two are here.'

'Car's playing up again, Sergeant,' Hines said before Louise could cut in. 'Scrapers are doing fuck all and the engine keeps skipping.'

'That's you not knowing how to drive it right,' he said, moving back towards his own car. 'Best thing to do, get someone else to drive.'

'Who was that?' Louise asked, pointing to the young man who was now disappearing inside the garage.

'No-one. Just someone who should know better,' was the gruff reply.

Before Louise could ask anything else, Bailey started the engine. Unlike their own police vehicle, this one roared into life like an angry puma.

'Wait. Where are you going?' Hines called out.

If he heard her, Bailey gave no reply as he put the car in gear and drove off, not even looking at the two women as he drove past.

'What a dickhead,' Hines said.

'No argument there. Did you recognise the man he was talking to?' Hines shook her head. Louise sighed with a shake of her own. 'You really should pay more attention. In the Walton Arms. He was there, standing at the far end of the bar. You did see him, because for ten minutes you couldn't take your eyes off him. Same shirt, but he was wearing a denim jacket and black jeans—'

'With the Black Sabbath patch on his arse pocket,' Hines said. 'Now I remember.'

It was Louise's turn to smile.

'Of course you'd remember that. What do you think?'

'Definitely worth having a chat. You know… police work and all that.'

Louise stared at Hines, who smiled back as though butter wouldn't melt in her mouth.

'Unbelievable,' Louise said.

She knew it was all front, Hines' way of coping, but still…

'Don't you know it.'

The groan of the metal door was lost beneath the pitched battle that was taking place across the garage length. On one side a mechanic was cutting through the rusted frame of a car, raised off the ground on a hydraulic lift. Sparks flew around the man as he cut, their short lives flashing bright as they bounced off his un-masked head. If he noticed them showering around his unprotected head he gave no indication, just kept his face tilted down as he pressed the saw through the frame.

The other side of the garage screamed with the sound of an engine in distress. It revved like a wounded animal, throaty one second then a lofty cry that rose painfully before crashing into silence once again. It echoed around the garage then began all over again.

Hines was saying something, but Louise couldn't make it out over the din.

'What?' she shouted, cupping her mouth in hopes it would allow Hines to hear her. Or at least read her lips better. Instead, Hines shook her head and pointed.

Between the two clashing tasks, the dissected frame and the screaming engine, the young man they had followed inside was sitting on the edge of a cluttered desk, talking to a man in a repurposed car seat. With his back to them, neither Hines nor

Louise could make out who the man was, but it appeared he was in charge. *Sanderson himself.*

With a nod, Louise started across the garage floor, Hines a step behind her.

The man in the denim jacket looked up. He leaned forward, tapped the seated man on his shoulder and pointed to their approach. Slowly the chair turned.

The man grinned. His face was large, round and reddened by what Louise could only suspect was a good dose of alcohol. Whisky, probably. There was a scent of it lying just beneath the oil, petrol and cigarette fog that hung in the air, coating everything. She knew she'd need a good long bath at the end of the day. The thought was particularly warming.

At a single wave of his arm, the cacophony of industry within the garage suddenly ceased. The soft *spackle-hiss* of cooling equipment drifted in the air, but all other noise had stopped.

'And what can I do for you lovely ladies?' the man said. 'Oh, I know you. You're the skirts from the cop shop.' He turned his face to the young man sitting on the desk. 'These two lovely creatures are detectives from Prospect Road. Our very own cop duo: Perky and Snatch.'

'That right, Mr Sanderson?' the man asked. He turned to look at Hines and Louise. 'I've seen you before.'

'And we've seen you,' Louise said, doing her best to ignore Sanderson's remark. 'At the Walton Arms over in Savile Town.'

The man jumped off the desk. 'That was earlier. Are you following me? What's this about?'

Colin Sanderson reached out to pat at the man's stomach in a gesture that Louise found strangely disturbing. 'Hold fire, Ben. No need to get worked up now, is there?'

Ben was having none of it. 'I don't like being followed, and I certainly don't like being followed by coppers. Even if they are a nice bit of gash.'

'Ben...' Sanderson warned.

'That's all right, Mr Sanderson,' said Louise. 'We're used to it.'

'I'm sure you are. As you can see, we are very busy right now. If this is about the car we picked up for your lot the other day, then that's all been taken care of. Dropped it off sharpish like was asked. Even told your Sergeant about it earlier.'

'We saw him just as we arrived,' Louise said, 'but we're not here about the car accident just yet.'

'Just yet?'

'I'm sure DS Bailey mentioned the fact that several of your workers were involved in the incident, or hadn't you noticed that they didn't turn up for work?'

Sanderson plucked a pack of cigarettes from the desk, pulled one out, lit it and slowly exhaled smoke into the air.

'We get a lot of turnover here,' he said. 'A few lads do a couple of shifts and realise it's not for them. Means nothing.' He handed the pack to Ben, who did the same.

Louise and Hines stood and watched, waiting for Sanderson to continue. A cold prickling began at the back of Louise's neck, running down her spine. She was suddenly very aware how exposed she and Hines were; there were six large men in the garage, and none of them appreciated the detectives' presence. Slowly Louise shifted her handbag on her shoulder, dropping her right hand inside. Her fingers closed around the short shaft of the billy baton, and she took a small modicum of comfort from its feel.

In response, Hines moved slightly, instinctively putting a little distance between her and Louise, so that if needed, there would be room to move. One hand in her pocket, Louise knew that Hines had hold of her own truncheon.

'So why are you here?' Sanderson asked again, cutting into her thoughts.

'We're investigating a serious assault that took place in the late hours of Sunday.'

'At the Walton Arms,' Hines said, staring directly at the man known only as Ben. 'Do you know anything about it?'

'People fight all the time,' Ben said. 'Especially drunk people. What of it?'

'The victims of the crime suffered very serious injuries, and it was their car that your colleagues had stolen. A car that, strangely enough, had been bought from this very garage, but that's something our Sergeant is handling. We're only interested in anyone who may, or may not, have been witness to the assault. You go to the Walton Arms, don't you?'

'You know I do.'

'And your last name would be?'

Ben stood stock straight, hands at his side clenching into fists.

'None of your fucking business.'

He stared right at Hines. She held his stare.

'Well, that's not very friendly, is it, Ben?' she replied. 'You might as well tell us your surname now, here, where we're all still being friendly, or we're just going to have to insist you come with us for a more intimate chat down at the station.'

'You want to get intimate, buy me a pint, then blow me. Slag.'

Louise stepped forward. 'That's it. You're coming with us, Ben.'

She pulled the baton from her handbag, reached out and took his arm with her left hand. He gave it a yank, pulling her forward and off balance just enough so that he could try and slap the truncheon from her grasp.

Louise gasped but held on to her truncheon. Using the momentum of his swing, she raised her arm and brought the baton down on his shoulder.

Ben cried out in pain and fell back, right into the waiting grasp of Hines, who had moved round the still-seated form of Colin Sanderson to get behind him. She threw her arms around Ben's chest and grasped him, her own baton held across his neck.

'Don't fucking struggle,' she said, leaning in so her lips were right to his ear. 'Slag.' To emphasise her point she squeezed just enough to make his eyes bulge. She then relaxed her grip a little so that he could breathe.

'Didn't need to be this way, idiot. Arms behind your back,' Hines continued. She was breathing hard, the adrenaline making her cheeks burn as she got her handcuffs out.

Louise turned to the other mechanics, who had started forward.

'Don't even think about doing anything stupid,' she said.

'Do as she says,' Sanderson said, rising from the chair. 'Can I apologise for my colleague's behaviour? Perhaps you and I can come to some sort of arrangement, what with us working closely with your Chief Superintendent and all?'

Hines finished cuffing Ben then, one hand on his shoulder, started shoving him towards the exit.

'We don't work like that,' Louise said. 'Didn't need to be like this, Mr Sanderson. What with car thieves, serious assault and now attacking a police officer in the course of their investigations, it seems you need to get your house in order, don't you think?'

'We'll get Mr Tallingate to sort this out, Ben,' Sanderson said.

'No problem, Mr Sanderson,' he replied.

Hines gave him another push forward.

'Shut up,' she said. 'See you all later, gentlemen.'

Sanderson glared at Louise.

'Anything else?'

'As a matter of fact there is,' she said with a smile. 'Our car's having a couple of problems. Do you think someone could take a look?'

CHAPTER
TWENTY-SEVEN

The journey from Sanderson's garage to the Prospect Road police station only took five minutes but to Louise it felt like hours. Sitting at the pelican crossing opposite the Town Hall, waiting for Myrtle Watts to dawdle across, Louise couldn't help but let out a *tut* of frustrated displeasure.

'What?' Hines said.

'Why did you come this way? You should have just gone down the Green then left onto Prospect Road.'

'This way is easier.'

'How?'

'It just is.'

Louise wasn't buying.

'How? How is it easier?'

Throwing a quick glance at their charge in the back seat, Hines leaned closer, hoping he wouldn't hear.

'I don't have to cross over the road,' she whispered.

Ahead of the car, Myrtle had finally reached the other side. She gave a wave as Hines started the car rolling forward. Louise waved back.

'What do you mean... Are you serious?'

'I don't like crossing traffic,' Hines said, ignoring the snort of laughter from behind. 'Easier to go this way, then I can just turn in without having to wait for traffic to clear.'

'Fucking women drivers...'

Hines slammed down on the brakes, and in the back, Ben, who had chosen not to wear a seatbelt, was thrown forward so hard that his head hit the back of Hines' seat. He cried out in pain then slumped back.

'Ow, you fucking bitch. That fucking hurt.'

'I think it was meant to,' Louise said with a smile.

After booking Ben in at the main desk and leaving him briefly in the care of PC Martins, who would take him through to Interview Room 3, Louise and Hines got down to work in what was affectionately known as the pen. This was where the detectives worked. Each had been given their own desk, complete with access to the Police National Computer. Notes were typed up, copied into the computer and filed away. It was a long, laborious process, and if there was any way to speed it up, any shorthand cuts that could be made without drawing too much attention from the higher-ups, then they would be happily employed. For Louise, the only shortcut was making sure her own notes were as thorough and detailed as possible. Copying them from her pocketbook onto the system didn't take as long, she found, if she had already done most of the work.

Hines, on the other hand, was struggling.

'Is that an e or an a?' she asked, holding her pocketbook out for Louise to squint at.

'A w,' Louise said, handing the pocketbook back.

Hines peered at it, turned the book round a few times then looked up. 'That makes more sense,' she said, then continued to tap away at her keyboard. Louise stood.

'You nearly finished?'

'I will have by the time you make a cuppa. Two sugars, if you don't mind.'

In the small kitchen area on the other side of the pen, Louise filled the kettle and switched it on. She spooned coffee into her Star Wars mug – it bore a photo print of the crew in the Millennium Falcon cockpit on one side, Princess Leia aiming her blaster on the other. It was a gift from Karla, found waiting for her on her pillow when she came home from work. She had entered the flat to the sounds of the Star Wars theme playing, Tom asleep at the top of the steep flight of stairs that led from the ground floor to her flat. Louise had squealed, actually squealed, when she saw what was waiting for her, and she now refused to drink out of anything else at work. Into a cracked mug she dropped a tea bag, poured in water and idly stirred it while looking out across the pen.

The few officers in the room kept throwing shadowed glances towards Hines. Head down, fingers angrily stabbing at the keyboard, she didn't notice. But Louise did.

'Hey, Martins,' she said, walking over to the officer who had deposited Ben into the interview room. 'What's with everyone?'

He was ripping open a pack of chocolate digestives when Louise came over and he offered her one.

'You weren't here when it happened,' he said, his voice as low as he could make it. 'She doesn't know.'

He turned and looked over at Hines. 'DI Manby said not to tell her.'

'Tell her what?' Louise's voice had grown icy and loud enough for Hines to hear.

'What's going on?' Hines called, getting up and heading over.

'That's what I'm trying to find out.'

'Hey, those going spare?' Hines asked, pointing at the biscuits. Without waiting for an answer, she scooped them up and dropped a couple into her mouth. 'What's going on, and why can't you look at me without blushing?' she asked, biscuit crumbs spilling from the corner of her mouth.

Martins, one of the new intake of recruits that had recently joined the expanding team, looked like a startled deer, caught in the open with nowhere to hide. 'I... you see... I...'

'Oh, for God's sake,' Louise said, turning to Hines. 'Manby's in one of his moods, and it seems it's something to do with you.'

'With me? What the hell did I do?'

'More likely, what haven't you done? Did you put in the claim form for your replacement skirt? What about the report on the Earlsheaton burglary from last week?'

'You were there when I handed it in.' Hines took another biscuit from the pack and nibbled on it, her nose scrunched tight as she considered what she could possibly have done to upset her boss. Louise smiled at her puzzled expression, thinking how cute she looked. How could Joe possibly...

'It's Joe, isn't it?'

Hines stood stock still, a panicked expression on her face.

'What about Joe? Martins?'

If the young officer had looked spooked before, he looked positively terrified now. Hines' tone left no room for manoeuvre. He raised his hands and surrendered to the inevitable. 'Look, you didn't hear it from me, but there was a little incident between your Joe and Manby at lunchtime.'

'One... he's not *my* Joe, and two... what do you mean, a little incident? Where are they?'

'Downstairs in the cells. Manby had him brought in and took him straight down there. The doctor's with them now.'

Hines threw the biscuit she had been about to eat onto the table.

'The fucking what now?'

There were ten identical cells in the basement of Prospect Road police station, five on either side of the single corridor. At the head of the corridor, just beyond the door that led to the stairs back up, was a small desk and single chair. A lamp sat on the desk and a bored looking police officer was flicking through today's *Sun* newspaper when Hines burst through the door. She grabbed the clipboard and quickly scrolled her eyes down the list of names. It didn't take long to find the name she was looking for; only three of the cells were currently being used.

Her footsteps echoed off the walls, the clack of her heels shotgun loud as she paced towards cell number seven, the only one with its door open. Louise quickly followed, throwing the confused officer an apologetic look.

'Don't be doing anything stupid,' Louise said to Hines' back.

'I don't need anyone fighting my battles for me,' was the angry reply, her voice ringing hollow, 'and I certainly don't need my boss sticking his nose into my business.'

Manby stepped out of the cell into the corridor.

'And I don't need one of my detectives caught up in a case of domestic violence. It's not good for you and it's not good for the station. We're all still under the spotlight, or have you forgotten?'

Hines stood in front of Manby, breathing hard. Louise came up beside her. Placed a calming hand on her friend's arm.

Manby turned from the fury on Hines' face to the soft, enquiring expression on Louise's. She wanted to know almost as much as her friend about what was going on, but she also wanted to make sure no one said or did anything to jeopardise either friendship or job. It was obvious Hines had been going through some tough things lately; the last thing she needed to do was make it worse by saying something that caused her to lose her job.

Manby seemed to reach the same conclusion, because he let out a big sigh. 'I suppose my little speech applies just as much to me as anyone else,' he said. 'Maybe more.' He stared at Hines with hard, grey eyes, squinting in the harsh bright light of the corridor as he looked over her. Instinctively her hand rose to the fresh marks at her neck. 'I figured,' he said. 'I don't feel as bad now.'

He nodded towards the open door of the cell. Hines went past him and inside.

'What did you do?' Louise said. She couldn't keep the slight note of amusement from her voice. Manby picked up on it and smiled.

'Not as much as I'd have liked,' was his reply.

CHAPTER
TWENTY-EIGHT

Joe sat on the edge of the cot, his head tilted back as the doctor examined his nose. Bloody tissues were scattered on the mattress and a few littered the stone floor. He moaned as the doctor pressed against the side of his nose, hands clutching the mattress with each sharp wave of pain.

'Relax, Mr Everad,' the doctor said, taking a step back. 'It doesn't look like anything is broken. You just have a tendency to bleed like a stuck pig.'

'He does,' Hines said from just inside the doorway. She leaned against the doorframe and watched as the doctor finished his examination. 'Remember when you cut your hand taking the glass from the pot washer at work? It broke apart in your hand and you sliced your palm open. Didn't stop for hours.'

'But I still finished my shift,' Joe said, his voice thick and nasal. 'Ow... fuck's sake, that hurt! Are you done?'

The doctor's reply was accompanied by an exasperated sigh.

'Best thing you can do is keep a cold compress on it to stop the swelling.'

'I should do him,' Joe said, wiping at his nose with another bloody tissue. 'Rat his arse out to his boss. He can't do this, you know. He's a copper. He can't just go beating people up for no reason.'

Hines moved aside to let the doctor leave. She thanked him with a smile and a quick touch of his arm. Joe saw.

'What was that?'

Hines laughed. Not *with* him, not with some joke or funny statement he had made, but for the first time that she could recall, she laughed *at* him. All the concern she had felt had evaporated as quickly as ice in water. And Joe knew.

'Are you sleeping with him as well? Were you fucking that old dick as well? What the fuck is it with you and old men?'

'You really are an idiot,' she said. 'To think I was actually worried about you when I heard you were here. Well, that lasted for a second. Right until you opened your mouth.'

She turned to leave, but Joe reached out and grasped her arm. Instinctively Hines grabbed his wrist, twisted twice and pushed him away.

Rubbing his arm, Joe glared at her.

'I'm going to make your life a fucking misery.'

'That's the worst marriage proposal ever,' Hines said, then walked out of the cell, leaving Joe alone.

Louise watched as Hines crossed back to where she was standing with Manby, finishing a brief about the day so far. She had tried to find out what had happened, but gave up after Manby refused to answer. *Fair enough*, she thought. *If he wants to keep it to himself, that's fine.*

Looking at the red bruise on his knuckles, she could guess anyway.

'All done?' Louise asked.

She was happy to see a smile on Hines' face. They had heard Joe cry out in pain and Louise would have rushed in, if not for the gruff 'Wait!' and Manby's hand softly touching her arm.

In answer, Hines came right up to Manby and threw her arms

around him in a giant hug. Her face came up to the top of his chest and he briefly rested his chin on the top of her head.

'Thank you,' she whispered.

For a moment, Manby said nothing. Louise could see the emotion in his eyes, knowing that he thought of Hines as another daughter, his own away in Leeds. Louise knew he missed her terribly.

Gently he moved back, holding Hines out at arm's length.

'Okay. Enough of that,' he said. 'We've enough going on round here without this soap opera bullshit distracting everyone. I take it there won't be any more... incidents, shall we call them?'

'We're done. One hundred and ten percent,' Hines said, nodding.

'You want to file official charges?' Manby asked as the three started back to the stairs.

Hines shook her head.

'It's done. It's over. He knows if he tries anything then he's not going to get dragged in as much as kicked in. But can I ask a favour?'

Manby stopped, holding the door back upstairs open.

'Go on.'

'How about next time, you let me sort it out?'

'Because my way, the lad had a chance of surviving,' he said with a laugh. 'I'll let him stew down there for a few more hours then let him go with a stern word. I don't think there'll be any further noise from him. Now don't you two have someone to interview?'

As the three made their way up the stairs, Louise tapped Hines on the shoulder.

'You know, you can't actually have more than a hundred percent. Someone very arrogantly told me that once.'

'Fuck off,' Hines laughed.

CHAPTER
TWENTY-NINE

Armed with coffee for their prisoner and mugs of tea for themselves – Louise was getting used to Hines' way of making it – the two detectives entered the interview room. Ben sat at the table, arms folded across his chest, eyes closed, head down. He wasn't snoring but he was breathing deeply. Slow, deep breaths in; long expulsions as though he was doing his best to control himself. His jacket was draped over the back of the chair, his pockets having been gone through by the officer who had checked him in.

He hadn't asked for a solicitor. He hadn't asked for a drink; in fact, according to the police officer who had sat outside the room waiting for the detectives to arrive, he hadn't spoken a word since being brought in.

And even now, as Hines put the coffee in front of him, he still didn't speak. He did, however, open his eyes and look up.

'Sorry you've been sat here all on your Jack-Jones for a bit,' Louise said, pulling a chair out and sitting down opposite. 'Just had a few other things to attend to. You know how it is.'

His answer was to slowly drag the coffee cup closer. He took a breath of it and winced.

'Be glad it's not one of Hines' teas,' Louise said.

He moved his eyes to the tea and looked up. 'A brew's a brew.'

'Fair enough,' she said and passed the mug over. 'It's your funeral.'

'I am sat right here, you know,' Hines said. 'Last time I'm making you a brew.'

'Can I have that in writing?'

'It's not bad,' Ben said, lowering the mug. 'Although I prefer less sugar.'

'It speaks,' Louise said. 'It speaks crazy talk if it thinks that that tea tastes good, but at least it's a start. I don't suppose we can get your full name now, can we?'

Ben took another drink of tea as he considered her request. Louise had seen this countless times, but never under such circumstances. Normally those who refused to talk, to even give their names, had already been linked to some crime or other, or at least to someone associated with a crime. Not with Ben; all they had was a tenuous link from Sanderson's garage to the pub where the Wadee brothers had been attacked – the Walton Arms. He didn't match any description the two brothers had been able to provide, not that they had been given a lot to go on: white, young and angry. After visiting the pub, that accounted for 99% of the clientele.

'Lewis,' Ben said. 'My last name is Lewis.'

'Well, that's certainly a start, Mr Lewis. Thank you.'

Ben smiled. 'Well, how could I refuse after you so politely invited me?' His hand went to his neck, and his fingers rubbed gently. 'You've certainly got a way with words,' he said with a wry smile at Hines. 'And I see you've had your own conversation lately.'

Her hand went to her own throat involuntarily. Louise wasn't having any of it.

'Cut that out, Mr Lewis,' she said, 'and tell us about what happened at the pub late Sunday night.'

'Which pub?'

'Stop being a daft sod. You know the one. The Walton Arms.'

'The one in Savile Town, or the one over Batley way?'

A flicker of uncertainty washed over Louise and she could feel Hines physically tense beside her. Of course they meant the Savile Town pub; that's where the Wadee brothers went and were attacked. Their car was stolen from that area, and that was where they had seen Ben Lewis, sitting as comfy as you please.

But she hadn't known there was another pub with the same name, and not all that far away. Could the boys have got the location wrong? It was highly unlikely; why would they lie about it, and what could they possibly gain by doing so? More questions to be answered, even when they weren't legitimate lines of enquiry. The Wadees were the wronged party here, not this slimy joker sitting in front of them, smirking around his tea.

He liked Hines' tea... of course he was a wrong 'un.

'Cut the shit out,' Hines said. 'You know damn well we mean the Saville Town pub. The place where there was an attack on two young men in the early hours of Sunday morning.'

'You mean Sunday night, don't you? At least get it right if you're going to accuse me of attacking someone.'

'We never accused you of anything, Mr Lewis. We just want to find out what you know. I take it you're a regular there?'

'What makes you say that?'

Hines leaned back in her chair, drawing Ben's attention to her. His eyes roved across her body and she played into his scrutiny, arching her back slightly so that her chest pushed forward. It was a dumb tactic, but it seemed to work. Especially on ones like Ben Lewis, apparently. His face had reddened and he shifted in his seat, trying to find a more comfortable position. Hines smiled.

'Oh, come on now, Ben,' she said, drawing his name out. 'A young lad like you. Fit looking. Got a good job with money to burn. Seemed like you were comfy on that stool at the end of the bar. Like you belonged there. You certainly didn't seem out of place there. Like you fitted in.'

'It's a good pub,' Ben said. 'Trouble only finds you if you're looking for it.'

'And trouble found the two men who came looking for their car, right? Is that what happened?'

'Like you said, I belonged there. Those two Pakis didn't. You were there. You know what sort of place it is.'

Hines sat forward. 'And what place is that, Mr Lewis?'

He grinned. 'The sort of place that Pakis shouldn't go. Bad enough they're over-running the schools, stinking our kids out with their spicy foods and their rags for clothes. It's not right. Gibbering away like fucking monkeys in their made-up language. They know we don't understand them; fuck knows what they're saying about us. And then they try coming to our pub? No. Fuck that. We draw a line with that.'

As he spoke his face reddened further, this time not with lechery but barely contained fury. Louise watched as he leaned forward, arms on the table, fists clenched, jaw twitching.

'I don't give a fuck what they said. They shouldn't have been there, and whatever the fuck happened to them was well deserved. Fucking Pakis; what did they think, coming into our pub?' he added with a sneer.

'And that would be a BNP pub, right?' Louise asked.

Ben snapped his head up. 'What of it? The British National Party is a legitimate voice of reason, one that stands up and speaks out against the rising black and brown wall that threatens to crush the true and legitimate white voice in this country.'

'Wow,' Hines said. 'That's almost word perfect from the recruiting literature.' She pulled the flyer she had picked up at the pub from her bag and slapped it down on the table between them. 'Is that what this protest is all about? Did they see this shit when they came in? Did they say something you didn't like? Is that why you and your lot beat them within an inch of their life?'

His grin never left his face. If anything, it got more intense. He picked up the flyer.

'Should be a fun day,' he said. He dropped it back down. 'You should come. Speak out with your white brothers and sisters. Or are you in their pocket as well? Are you one of those bitches that likes to ride a black pole? Make some bounty babies?'

'You're an angry man, Mr Lewis. I'm starting to understand why you'd do what you did.'

'I never said I did anything, or that anyone did anything to them. Though I could understand if they did; Pakis always have that condescending arrogance about them, so that would need putting in its place real damn quick. We have to protect ourselves. Do what's white.'

Ignoring his infuriating smirk, Louise was shocked by his language. Shocked, but not surprised. Angry, but not surprised.

'Did you think that one up yourself? It's not as clever as you think, and neither are you.' She got to her feet and indicated to Hines to do the same.

'We never said the men who were attacked were Pakistanis.'

Ben's face fell.

Louise grabbed the flyer and the two detectives left the room.

'There's nothing to hold him on.'

Manby was reaching for his overcoat, the day almost at an end. He had nearly managed to escape when Louise and Hines had collared him and asked that they be allowed to hold their prisoner overnight. Listening to Louise, he could see that whatever the man had said, it had got to her. Riled her up to the point where she could very easily keep him locked up and the key conveniently misplaced, perhaps forever.

'He's a racist arsehole,' Hines said.

Manby shrugged his coat on.

'That may be the case, but if we were to lock up all the racists just because they're racist, then we'd be out of cells in seconds. A few of the newer officers around here would be in there as well,' he added, with a sad note of reality in his words.

Louise wasn't giving up, but Manby cut her off. 'Let him go.

The Wadees description doesn't match him. He hasn't said anything that really incriminates him, and besides,' he added, throwing a nod into the pen, 'his solicitor has arrived.'

Louise looked over to see a tall, expensive suit wearing a thin-framed man. Hair greased back; spectacles balanced precariously on the sharp bridge of his nose, which he dabbed gently with a bright white handkerchief.

'Do you really want to get into it with him now, or would you rather get home to Karla at a decent hour for a change?' Manby said, drawing her attention back to him.

Louise sighed. 'And what do I say to the Wadees?'

Manby picked up his briefcase. 'Tell them the truth. We're looking into it.'

Without another word, he left the two detectives standing in his office, nodding a greeting as he walked past the solicitor and doing his best to ignore the frustrated anger that he was feeling. Every instinct was telling him that this Ben Lewis was balls deep in the events of Sunday, and that, with a little more time, they could get it from him. But he had to follow the rules, to play the game and do it the right way.

And besides, Marie was waiting at home with a shepherd's pie for tea, and for once he wasn't going to be late.

CHAPTER
THIRTY

As soon as those two had walked into the pub he'd known it was time to finish this and move on. The boy wouldn't be happy. It had been his gift to give, his time to shine, and shine he had. Glowed like a new born sun with each new visit.

But over the years, through his varied experiences, he had learned the need to recognise the signs. To adapt. To change when necessary. To ditch the old and move on to the new.

It was time to ditch this last one. He smiled at what he had in mind, a twisted plan that would throw confusion and fear into the path of those who sought him.

And that was the part of the whole thing that excited him the most, and it would excite the boy just as much in time. He knew that almost as well as he knew what needed to be done.

This would be different though. It was too easy, the rush of the kill not as strong as it had been at the start, those years ago. The first one he would always remember, and he wanted the same for the boy. He wanted the same thrill to course through his boy's veins for years to come, and so this would be different. A test for sure, not just for him but for those who would no doubt be tasked with its investigation.

Night had fallen, so it was easy to make his way back to the warehouse undiscovered. He had expected a stronger police presence after the events earlier in the week; the stupid beating of those Pakis had drawn the attention he had feared, but other than the two detectives in the pub earlier today, the same two who had gone to his place of work, there had been nothing said. Nothing done. One of those involved had been spoken to, apparently, taken in and questioned, but he was out and crowing in the Arms as proud as could be. For them, nothing had changed.

The talk on the street whispered about the protest at the weekend. A perfect hunting ground. He would take the boy and they would hunt the next one together. Father and son on the prowl. His heart surged at the thought, and as he lifted the long knife he felt that familiar stirring. Excited, his breathing increased as blood rushed to all the right places.

On the table she lay bound, gagged and totally naked. He ran his hand across her one last time. She didn't move at all. Not even when he pressed his lips to hers, savouring the taste one last time.

Not even when he pressed the tip of the knife against her navel.

When he pushed the blade into her weak and fragile body, she moaned softly.

When he began to draw the blade back and forth, cutting her flesh, she screamed into his mouth...

CHAPTER
THIRTY-ONE

WEDNESDAY, 21ST

The cool, crisp air bit into Gerald Dillinger's face as, beneath his feet; the wet dew of morning grass slushed with each step. The path along the bank of the River Calder stretched away to Dewsbury and beyond, a journey he had taken with his dog Freddie several times, but today Gerald wasn't appreciating it. The air was cold, there was a little rain hidden in it, and his head was pounding from too many pints at the Tapps at the top of Healey Road.

Just thinking about his long walk back up the hill filled him with dread. *Why didn't I bring the car?* he asked himself for the fifth time, bending down to pluck the sodden tennis ball from the grass. Freddie danced around his legs, his eager face staring up at him. With a deft flick of his wrist, Gerald threw the ball a little further down the path.

'Just one more time, lad,' Gerald called after the retreating shape of his dog. He checked his watch; eight-thirty. He had a meeting at eleven with the accounting department and then lunch with his wife, so if he was going to have time for a bath he'd have to set off back now.

'Come on, Freddie,' he shouted down the empty path. 'Time to be going!'

He waited a moment or two, and when there was no movement, he called again.

'Freddie! Come on! We have to get going…'

A rustle in the long grass ahead, and the dog leapt out onto the path. Gerald smiled.

'Good boy,' he said, unfurling the leash he'd kept bunched up in his hands while the dog chased the battered old tennis ball. 'Come here and we'll make a start back. No, wait… Come here!'

Gerald's heart fell as the dog bounded off the path once more. With a sigh, he jogged forward, calling the dog's name until he stood right where he had last seen Freddie. The grass here was tall, nearly to his shoulder, and quite thick. The close proximity to the river meant that the ground was more marshy than firm, and he could feel his feet beginning to sink into its embrace.

'Freddie, for the love of God, come on!'

Gerald pushed his hands into the thick tall grass and parted the stalks like Moses parting the Yam Suph. He could see the dark shape of his dog, front paws forward, head hunkered down, hindquarters raised as it worried at something on the ground. A low buzzing noise filled Gerald's ears and straight away his skin began to itch.

'Whatever that is, drop it right now, Freddie,' Gerald said. He stepped forward carefully, shoes squelching in the mud and threatening to be sucked off his feet. Eventually he got to his dog and patted its rump, trying to get its attention. 'Freddie… Freddie, drop that. Drop…'

His voice fell away.

Gerald grabbed the dog around its middle and pulled it back, eliciting a whine of protest that mixed with Gerald's own fearful cry.

In the kodak-snap of an image that had burned itself on Gerald's mind, he had recognised the soft curves of a woman's legs lying in the grass. What he didn't see was her torso, because that was missing above the ragged cut of her waist.

Unable to help himself, Gerald bent over and threw up this morning's tea onto his muddy shoes, as Freddie licked his own bloodied muzzle.

CHAPTER
THIRTY-TWO

By eleven o'clock, the area immediately surrounding the grisly find had been sealed off by police tape. The pathway was closed to the public; the only people standing around were the members of the SOC team, led by Peter Danes. He was bundled up in a forensic suit, his imposing height making him easy to spot when Louise and Hines arrived.

They had parked their car at the bottom of Healey Road amidst the jumble of other emergency service vehicles. There was the Scene of Crime van, which housed all the equipment and transported the four-man team to each crime scene, alongside two ambulances, three police cars and Manby's own car. It had taken a minute or two to find somewhere to park, but eventually Hines was satisfied. This part of Ossett was an industrial land-scape of old mills and warehouses, along with one of the oldest pubs in the area. Boon's End was a hundred yards down the street, away from the bustle of activity that led to the canal pathway where the body had been discovered, and there was a small space just in front where Hines could squeeze the car in.

A huddle of people stood outside the pub, most with a drink in hand as they watched the bustle of police activity. Louise recognised one of the women sitting at a wooden table, a fag in one hand, a pint of ale in the other. She gave a nod of recognition, which was returned with a wave of the near empty glass.

'You not working today, Linda?' Louise called out.

'Early shift today,' Linda replied. She sucked in smoke and blew it out of the side of her mouth almost instantaneously. 'What's going on down there?' she called out.

'I'm going to find out,' Louise shouted back. 'You have any idea?'

'I heard it was a dead girl. It's always a dead girl, int-it? When's it going to be a lad that gets their throat slit or guts punched out? Don't seem right it's always the girls that are getting slain, does it?'

'She's got a point,' Hines whispered.

'I could think of one or two of the male persuasion that could do with being taken down a peg or two, permanent like,' Linda continued. 'Starting with my Larry.'

That got a loud chorus of laughter from those gathered nearby, along with a few hearty backslaps. 'Oi... watch me pint,' she shouted out. 'You want one, lass?'

Louise waved her off. 'Maybe later. Work and all that.' She pointed down towards the river.

'Aye,' Linda said, getting to her feet. 'You take care, and give your Fiona my best, will you?'

They continued down and round the corner towards where the riverbank began. They passed under a stone bridge that connected two warehouse yards together and then found the pathway that eventually made its way alongside the Calder. An officer stood at the entrance to the pathway and took their details, handing them plastic booties to slip over their shoes.

'I hate these things,' Hines said, struggling to pull the frail plastic over her left foot. 'Even with small heels like these, they never stay on.'

'That's why I wear pumps,' Louise said. 'There's Danes...'

'He doesn't look happy.'

'When does he ever look happy?'

As he came closer, Louise could see that something was decidedly wrong with the head of the Scene of Crime team. Normally he would hurry over to brief them on the scene before they visited it, eager to dispense what he'd learned so far. Since taking over the team, their procedures and practices had become second to none, with many of the region's new recruits now coming to Danes for training. It was just another example of how far their experimental police unit had come in such a short space of time.

But there was no spring to Danes' step this time; no mugging for an audience. In fact, Louise noted, he looked pretty sick. Like he'd had too many whiskies and not enough sleep. As he drew closer, both detectives were shocked by how pale he looked.

'Jesus, Danes. Are you all right?'

As well as the sickly pallor, Louise noted the short, shallow breaths he was taking, an exercise she recognised only too well as one done to maintain composure. An anti-anxiety exercise. He didn't reply immediately, and Hines took the time to finish fiddling with the plastic on her shoes.

'You're not going to need those,' he said finally. His voice was as sickly as his skin, a watery quality to it that filled Louise with worry. As he reached up to pull his hood back, his hands trembled, adding yet another layer of concern. 'We've processed the scene, photographed and videoed from every possible angle, and collected any foreign items from the immediate area for examination. Officers are doing a perimeter search up to and including this pathway down to the riverside and we've put in requests for any closed-circuit security cameras from some of the warehouses in case they were able to capture the vehicle that was used to transport the... the remains,' he finished after a short pause.

'The remains? We really need to see,' Hines said, moving around Danes and heading to the area where three suited SOCOs stood. They weren't doing anything more than talking to each other, another strange factor that had Louise's nerves on edge.

'Don't say I didn't warn you,' he called after her. 'A statement has been taken from the man who found her, but he was in such a state of shock he's had to be taken to the hospital himself. His wife came to collect their dog just a few minutes ago, but you'll be able to get his statement from the boss.'

'What has Manby to say about this?' Louise asked, staying next to Danes.

She watched as Hines greeted the SOC officers, their warding gestures doing little to deter the detective from moving past them to look beyond the tape.

'Doesn't matter. This was my call. No need for the police surgeon to visit. She's definitely dead, and not by long.'

'So, a she. Any ID?'

Danes shook his head. 'No clothes, no shoes. No purse, nothing.'

'Description?' She had her notebook out ready for the routine of height, hair, eyes, complexion, identifying marks, state of the body; all the details she would need to begin her investigation. She was certain Manby would want her to get right on it, and there was no sign of Bailey anyway, so she might as well get started.

Danes was now as white as the suit he wore.

'Red nail polish. Long legs. Skin dirty. That's all I have right now.'

'Oh, come on, Peter. No need to be territorial about it.'

'I'm not,' he said, 'but that's seriously all I have.'

'Don't be an arse about this.'

He sighed and slumped against the nearest car.

'I'm not being an arse. That's all I have. The legs to the lower waist just below the belly button. That's all there is.'

It was at this moment that Louise turned, just in time to see Hines double over and vomit into the tall grass beside the riverbank.

· · ·

She had to see. Despite the warning from both Danes and now Hines, Louise had to see for herself.

Carefully she moved through the tall grass and dipped just enough so she could pass beneath the police tape, helpfully raised by Grace Fellows, one of the Scene of Crime officers tasked with waiting for the van that would transport the remains to the police mortuary in Dewsbury.

Louise nodded her thanks but Fellows had already turned away, leaving her alone. She inched forward towards the small tent that had been erected over the body. Was it a body, could you really call it that when all there was were legs?

In her career Louise had seen some pretty bad things, scenes of blood and violence that everyday folk couldn't even begin to imagine. She had lost count of the number of bodies she had been witness to, the deaths all violent and brutal. Most had been fast as well, but there were ones that had been dragged out, their torturous cuts and beatings carried out over days, weeks, and in one particularly nasty case that had gained above-the-fold head-lines in all the newspapers for the fifteen weeks of investigations, months. *The Dockside Slasher.* That's what they had called him, that nasty perverted sicko who had stalked women as they walked alongside the docks of Manchester back in eighty-four, slashed their throats from behind and dragged their bodies into the dark shadows of the docks where he carried out what he called experiments.

'When you need to puke, do it over there.'

Louise turned to see Hines standing on the other side of the tape. She couldn't help but feel a sense of pride at seeing her colleague, now looking as pale and shocked as the more experienced and senior detective, right back in the thick of it. No hesi-tation. No second-guessing; there was a job to be done and she was the one to do it. Or at least be part of the team that worked the case.

Louise nodded and moved closer.

The sound of flies was amplified by the confined fabric of

the small tent. It echoed within, filling Louise's mind with the crawling sensation of bugs and insects on her flesh. The fabric of her own protective boilersuit crackled loudly around her head and already she was beginning to feel claustrophobic. Her head was becoming hot, and her hair, which she wore tied in a ponytail, was scratching at the back of her neck, adding to the unnerving feeling that was slowly gripping her. Despite earlier dismissing the need to wear protection over their shoes, when Louise insisted she take a look for herself, Danes had similarly insisted on her suiting up correctly.

'This is a bad one,' he had said, handing over one of the white suits. 'No way I am letting anyone mess up on this.'

His pallor, coupled with the oddly out of character no-bull-shit tone, told Louise everything.

And here it was.

At first her mind didn't register exactly what she was looking at, protecting her at least for a few seconds before the awful realisation sank in. She had seen this dozens of times before, her mind was saying. Just another woman lying in the grass. Another victim. Another death. Probably sexual in causation as the body was naked; she could see her genitals, see the small patch of hair, and just above, the faded mark of a tattoo. Red, yellow and blue in a pastel colour, splotches either side of a green oval. Wings. They were wings. The wings of a…

Oh, no.

A terrible void suddenly appeared in her chest, swallowing her revulsion enough that she was able to kneel down beside the remains. She kept her eyes trained on the feet, ignoring the jagged cut of the waist and the disturbing thought that the tall grass beyond should be crushed down where her head and body lay, instead of standing undisturbed.

Photos had been taken, but the body…

I have to call it the body. Doing that means it's nothing different from what I've seen before. Doing that keeps me from thinking about what has happened to this woman. Doing that keeps me from going insane.

...hadn't been moved, as far as she was aware. The grass around didn't look disturbed. She couldn't blame Danes and his team; she didn't want to touch this either. She didn't want to be anywhere near this right now, but she had a job to do.

Reaching out, she looked up to see Fellows watching her.

'Have you still got the camera?' Louise asked. The officer raised it. 'Good. Can you take pictures as I move the right foot?'

Fellows stepped back under the tape and stood over Louise.

Keeping her eyes trained on the foot, Louise carefully lifted it. The *snap-snap-snap* of the camera sounded behind her, Fellows firing off shots, burning film. Danes wouldn't mind, although Manby might get testy about wasting resources, but Louise already knew that everything would be thrown at this. She also knew that, later today, she would be giving someone the worst news possible; a loved one had been taken from them. A loved one had been murdered.

She turned the ankle and saw the heart tattoo, and that faint shine of hope that this woman would be found alive became a dark, deep pit of disappointment.

'Over here!'

Louise rose, turning her attention to the sudden bustle of activity further down the pathway. The call had come from another of the Scene of Crime officers working beyond the tape. Tasked by Danes to scour the immediate area for any signs of who had deposited the horrific find, the search area had slowly expanded further and further out. Now, 500 metres down the canal pathway, several white-suited forensic technicians waved people over. One was already taking pictures by the time Louise got to them. Danes was already there too, directing the photos.

'And another there...' He pointed to where the grass had been flattened under the weight of three black bags; two small, one large. 'Make sure you get the position of the stalks, and that depression. Could be a footprint. Have Mark try a cast.'

The SOCO nodded and set about their task.

'What is it?' Louise asked.

'I'm guessing the other half,' Danes replied. 'Jesus, this is sick.'

'And those two?' She pointed to the smaller bags. Danes took a deep breath.

'Let's find out.'

After making sure they had been properly recorded on camera, Danes pulled at the first of the bags. Louise saw that it had been tied in a single knot. She also noted that the ground beneath it was damp. The buzzing of flies grew louder as he cut through the bag with a knife, just below the knot. To one side, the *click-click-click* of the camera continued, a forensic officer making sure everything was captured on film in real time. Louise crouched next to him, the two sharing a look before he pulled the neck of the bag open.

'Oh, Jesus fucking Christ…'

The stench that clawed its way out of the bag was an almost physical being. It punched through the nostrils and forced its way down the throat, finding its way to the stomach where it began to roll and churn. Mesmerised, Louise forced herself to keep her eyes on the contents as her mind struggled to make sense of what she was seeing. Finally, she gave up. Fortunately, or rather unfortunately, depending on your point of view, Danes knew exactly what they were looking at.

'Stomach,' he said, the single word forced from between clenched lips. He waved a gloved hand in the air, and signalled with three fingers followed by a closed fist pulled down. When Louise continued to stare at him, he gave a shrug. 'We need a number three container. One of the bigger ones,' he explained. 'Sometimes we can't always talk directly so I came up with a shorthand.'

Louise couldn't help but smile, despite the horrific surroundings.

'Nerd,' she said. 'What about the other one?'

The other one turned out to be the kidneys. A full and proper examination would confirm whether the two grisly finds were directly connected. The third, and largest, of the bags had been opened by another SOC officer by the time Danes and Louise made it to them, the black plastic carefully cut away and peeled back to reveal the body inside.

Like the bag found earlier, it too contained half a body, this time the upper torso.

'Looks like we have a matching pair,' Danes said, standing to one side as photos were taken.

'No, we don't,' Louise said, her voice shaking as she stared into faded open eyes that saw nothing. 'The legs belong to Helen Williams. That,' she said, pointing at the torso, 'isn't her.'

Danes let out a soft whistle. 'Jesus. What the fuck is going on?'

'I don't know,' Louise replied. 'But I intend to find out.'

They found Scruffy Pete sitting on one of the large planters in Ossett marketplace, chewing on a fish butty and reading the day's sporting pages. Beside him was a large plastic bag, the sides bulging enough so that Louise knew what was inside. The clink of bottles confirmed it; a liquid lunch. Probably tea and tomorrow's breakfast too, by the sound of it. Immediately her mind returned to the black bags she'd seen earlier, her stomach doing a quick flip.

He looked up as Louise and Hines approached, a big beaming smile on his face. A chunk of fish fell from the corner of his mouth, bounced off his shirt and landed on the bench beside him. As he tried to grab it up, a bird swooped in and snatched it, taking flight before he could bat it away.

'Always the birds trying to eat my lunch,' he said. 'I sometimes feed them...' His voice fell away when he saw the dour expression on their faces. His eyes dropped back to the scraps of fish butty that lay nestled within yesterday's news like an afterthought.

'Pete...'

He gave a cough and looked up.

Louise's heart broke as she saw the tears rise there, saw his lip tremble and his hands begin to shake. This wasn't from the beer or the drugs, not this time.

'I sometimes feed them,' he began again, "cos who else will if I don't? Helen said that about me, she did. "Who's going to look after you if I don't?" she said.' His voice had taken on that watery element now, breaking in waves as he fought back the tears that Louise knew would surely come.

It just needed to be said. Just needed to be confirmed.

'Always looking out for me was our Helen. And she'll be back. She knows I can't keep on top of things without her help. She'll be back.'

Louise sat next to him. Hines crouched before him and placed a hand on his knee.

'I'm so sorry,' she said.

Pete ignored her and turned to Louise instead.

'You could be wrong.'

'We're not.'

'But you could be. Right? You could be wrong. You lot have been wrong before, you can be wrong now.'

'The butterfly tattoo on her groin. Her ankle tattoo. The heart with your initials...'

Pete's hand fell on Hines', the nicotine-stained fingers gripping tight, crushing her hand within his. She winced but didn't pull her hand away. Louise put an arm about his shoulders and softly pulled him towards her. At first he resisted, but coaxed by her soft whispers he gave in, slowly drawing her into a hug.

Hines rose and stood silently before them as Pete pushed his head into Louise's shoulder and wept.

CHAPTER
THIRTY-THREE

Louise was glad the day was over. She had had bad days before, days when all hope and joy in life had been swallowed by terrible events and sights, but none compared to seeing the complete devastation in Scruffy Pete's eyes. As the knowledge that his sister, missing now for six months, was in fact dead became a terrible reality, the grief overwhelmed him and they had had to call the doctor to help bring a modicum of calm to the distraught man. They had tried showing him a picture of the other woman, but he either hadn't recognised her, or was too distraught with grief to remember her. Either way, they had been forced to abandon any further questioning.

With a friend tracked down and promising to watch over Pete, Louise and Hines had left, and returned to the station. After a few hours of paperwork, and with neither of them able to concentrate, Louise had suggested a drink. That was three hours ago, and as the day turned to night, their faces were bathed in the soft orange glow of lamps in the window of the Tapps pub. Outside rain fell, creating chaotic patterns on the glass that reminded Louise of the tears falling down Pete's face.

Since arriving and sitting with their drinks, neither had said much. Occasionally they would both look up at each other and offer a wan smile, but finding words was difficult as the stress of the day began to bleed away. Images kept flicking through Louise's mind, swift blasts of colour that mixed and wrapped with each other, creating a dark kaleidoscope of horror and pain.

The red toenails, the strokes of the brush clear to see, blended into the red of Pete's eyes, worn out from crying...

The jagged edge of flesh where Helen's upper body should have been, warped into the scrap of fish flesh discarded by Pete and quickly snatched away by a waiting bird...

Legs and no body...

Tears and no hope...

And then there was the other woman. Body and no legs...

Two halves of women. No whole.

A cold shudder ran through Louise's entire body. Hines saw it, tried to smile and gave up.

'Look who I found lurking outside.'

Both women turned to see Karla. She held three glasses by their stems in one hand, while the other clutched the neck of a bottle of wine. Behind her was Manby, shaking out his coat. Depositing it on the coat stand by the door, he came and stood by their table as Karla took her seat. She kissed Louise on the cheek and got a smile in return.

'Tough day,' Manby said.

Karla was pouring the wine and she held the bottle out to Manby. 'Are you joining us?'

'Let me grab a glass, and another bottle or two. That's not going to last us.'

Louise watched as he walked back to the bar and waited to be served. She gave a small laugh. 'You know it's bad when he's on the wine,' she said. 'Thanks for this, love.'

'Thank your boss. He called me to let me know what had happened.'

'Did he tell you everything?' Hines asked. She continued to stare into her wine glass, giving the liquid a soft swirl.

'He told me enough. Not the details, just the substance.'

'Bad enough, we know,' Manby said from behind them. He carried a tray on which were two bottles of wine, a glass and a whisky. He set them all down on the table and pulled up a chair. 'No need to give everyone nightmares.'

'Too late for that,' Hines said.

Manby let out a puff of a laugh. He took the whisky and drained it before pouring more wine for everyone, including himself. He lifted his glass and gestured for everyone else to do the same.

'To absent friends,' he said, offering the same toast Louise's uncle always gave.

It made her smile, despite the terrible circumstances. Everyone drank. Everyone sat silently. Manby reached to the windowsill behind Louise and pulled a box of dominoes from a stack of boxed games. He deposited the dominoes onto the table and started turning them all over, shuffling them together.

Louise watched. The clink of the pieces as they clashed together was somehow soothing. She leaned into Karla, taking comfort from her warmth.

'I'm glad you came,' she said.

Karla kissed the top of her head.

With a smile, Louise sat back up and reached for the wine. There was still so much to do. What happened to Helen Williams, and the other as yet unidentified woman, was not an accident. There was a sick individual out there, someone who had taken Helen, kept her for months and did... that. They would hunt this person down; they would find them and lock them away. Louise swore that to herself, swore that to Pete and most importantly, swore that silently to Helen.

For a moment it all felt too much, too big for her to deal with. Death she could deal with, normal death though, not this. Whatever this was.

As if sensing this, Karla reached down and took her hand.

She gave it a soft squeeze, her thumb idly rubbing Louise's skin.

Louise looked into Karla's eyes and everything felt a little better.

Manby stopped shuffling the pieces.

'Fancy a game?'

'Why not?'

CHAPTER
THIRTY-FOUR

THURSDAY, 22ND

Louise's head hurt. The wine finished, whisky had taken its place as tales of the Williams siblings were passed about, the various war stories a heady mix of humour and pathos. By the time she had left with Karla, staggering up the hill towards the flat, her mouth was numb with Highland Park scotch. They had collapsed into the flat, clutching each other as they made their way up the steep, stone steps, the decorative red strip of carpet that ran down the centre of the stairs a recent addition.

Tom, Louise's cat, lifted his head to watch the women bounce down the small hallway and stumble into the bedroom. With a yawn, he resettled and went back to sleep.

That had been last night, and now Louise sat at the counter in the kitchen, nursing a cup of coffee and a gutful of regrets. Karla, on the other hand, was exceedingly chipper, singing to herself as she prepared toast and jam, much to Louise's annoyance.

'Can you please dial it down a notch?' she said. Her voice was raspy and her throat felt like Tom's scratching post. She took a sip of coffee, hoping it would alleviate some of the discomfort. It didn't.

'I have no sympathy for you,' Karla said. She brought the plate of toast over and sat beside Louise. 'You should eat something.'

Lips clamped tight, Louise shook her head. Karla scowled.

'How are you supposed to concentrate today if you've got a hangover?'

'I don't need a telling off. I need a new head.'

Smiling, Karla ran her finger down Louise's cheek.

'Looks fine to me.' She glanced at the clock on the wall above, let out a sigh and got up, taking her cup and plate to the sink. 'I have to get going. Will you be all right getting to the station?'

Louise turned on the stool to face her.

'I'm fine. I'm hungover, not dead. See you tonight?'

Karla leaned in for a kiss.

'I was thinking we could go to the pictures in Wakefield. The new *Hellraiser* came out last week.'

Louise made a face.

'Ugh. After the week I've had so far, the last thing I want to see is more blood and gore. When's the new *Indiana Jones* film?'

'Next week. Wait... What's on in Dewsbury?' Karla started rifling through the stack of papers Louise kept piled up on the edge of the breakfast counter. She found the *Ossett Observer* and leafed through until she found what she was looking for. 'There's a science fiction one out tomorrow if we wait. *They Live*. By the same director who did your favourite, *The Thing*.'

Louise sat straighter.

'Ooh. John Carpenter. I do like his films. How about we go tomorrow instead?

'I was hoping to go out tonight, but okay.'

'Tonight, we'll go to the Lotus in Wakefield. I'm pretty sure by then I'll be hungry, and what's better than a Chinese on a Thursday?'

She wasn't as sure as she sounded about this. Already, unbidden images of the black bags and their contents were flashing through her mind.

'Even better, let's order in and have an early night?'

'Deal.'

Karla stole another kiss and all but flounced out of the kitchen. Louise shook her head with a smile, regretting the movement immediately.

Way too early to be that chipper.

After finishing her coffee, Louise had a shower, got dressed and headed to the door. Tom sat at the top of the stairs, washing his paw. He looked up as she approached and craned his neck so that Louise could scratch him.

'See you later, big guy,' she said, scratching him behind his ear. 'There's water in your bowl and biscuits beside it. Try not to eat them in one go this time.'

The day was warming up, and so she kept her jacket tucked over her arm as she walked along the Green and up into town. The rumble of traffic around her was like the drone of bees lingering just on the edge of hearing. The air was filled with the acrid stench of exhaust smoke mixed with the light scent of flowers from the gardens that she passed by. She missed the garden of her aunt's home, where growing up she would run around the lawn or up into the rosebed at the back. Her uncle kept a compost heap fed by the food scraps from their meals and discarded lawn cuttings, and in her child's mind this was a magical mountain, protected by a dour dwarf who would send her on adventurous quests. After moving in, some of those magical moments were lost.

She smiled at the memory, promising herself she would go visit her aunt and uncle and their magical garden later next week.

After a ten-minute walk, Louise was in the station, waiting as the kettle boiled. More coffee was needed to quell the pounding in her head. *There is not enough coffee in the western hemisphere to calm this troubled beast*, she thought. She added the water, stirred and poured milk.

'Any water left?'

Hines walked in and Louise was dismayed to see that last night's alcohol party appeared to have had no effect on the woman. First Karla and now Hines... What was it with these two? Her skin glowed, her hair shone. There was a spring to her step that Louise hadn't seen for some time.

'How do you do it?' Louise asked, automatically dropping a tea bag into a fresh mug.

'The wonders of youth,' Hines laughed.

'Piss off. You're only a couple of years younger than me. Wonders of youth, my arse.' Her voice trailed away as she looked around the pen. 'Is Manby in yet?'

While Louise had drunk quite a bit last night, and was suffering for it now, Manby had drunk even more. It was no secret he had been close to the Williams siblings, Helen especially. He had taken her under his wing, done his best to help her where he could with money, food and clothing. He had even let them both sleep in his and Marie's spare bedroom just before they got their first house. Manby had helped with that as well, putting down the deposit and covering the first month's rent. Her death had hit him hard; not finding all of her only added to his distress, and his solution had been to drink even more.

'He's in the briefing room upstairs with the others.'

'The others? What others?'

Hines blew on her tea.

'It's a right gathering up there. Chief Superintendent Freeman, Danes, Manby. A few others. Here early too. I was in just after nine—'

'What?' Louise was shocked.

Hines ignored her.

'—and there were already about eight or nine of them up

there. From what I gather, some of them are part of a special task force from Dewsbury.'

As she spoke, another group of police officers, a couple carrying cables and one an overhead projector, made their way across the room and through the door that led upstairs. Louise and Hines watched them go.

'Let's go,' Louise said, a note of anger barely contained.

As Louise came into the room, she noticed that DI Manby and Chief Superintendent Freeman sat at the head of a rough square of tables. In the centre was another, smaller table on which the overhead projector was being set up. The white wall behind the senior officers was being used as a screen, despite the large dark crack that ran down and right through the image being set up. Until only last week, this room had been a storage closet, and not all the renovations had been completed. Prospect Road was still very much a work in progress, even three years after its inception. Louise recognised the Walton Arms just before the projector was switched off.

Most of the chairs were now occupied, but they were able to find two seats together right at the back. A moment later, Manby got to his feet and walked over to the flip chart. 'Okay, everyone. Quiet down and we can get started. Is everyone here?'

A hush fell over the room as Manby flipped the top sheet over.

OPERATION LIGHTNING STRIKE was written in big black letters.

'What's this?' Hines whispered.

Louise shrugged.

'You've all heard the rumblings over the last few weeks,' Manby began, 'and we've seen an increase in conflicts between the white and Muslim communities. A lot of this has been in and around the Dewsbury area, and while the force there has been dealing with each situation, the fact that it has escalated to the point where parents are pulling their children from schools amidst intimidating protests means we have to take stronger action. This Operation Lightning Strike is one line we're taking.'

'Sounds like a Chuck Norris film,' someone said.

Laughter ran round the room.

'However it sounds,' Manby said, regaining the room's attention, 'this has been running now for six months. I'll hand it over to Chief Superintendent Freeman, who will continue the brief.'

'Six months?' Hines whispered again. 'Did you know anything about this?'

'News to me,' Louise replied.

'A few years ago, we identified several groups affiliated with the British National Party in and around the Ossett, Dewsbury and Wakefield areas,' Freeman began. 'Wakefield have experience with this, having dealt with the Wilkins gang back in early eighty-two, and their dedicated unit naturally handled any upswing in racial crime there. Our focus, or rather your focus, as a relatively new unit, whose catchment area now includes Dewsbury, is the group that operates out of the Walton Arms pub in Savile Town. This area has seen a huge rise in confrontation between the two communities, resulting in the alleged assault on two young men in the early hours of Sunday morning.'

Louise and Hines shared a look. Louise raised a hand and Freeman nodded at her.

'That connects with the stolen car from the area and the RTA that ended with the death of three individuals,' Louise said. 'And from our initial investigations to this point, it appears that certain people from the Walton Arms and Sanderson's garage are very tightly connected.'

Freeman nodded as she finished.

'And that leads me to the next stage of Operation Lightning Strike. The group has organised a protest to be held this Saturday in Dewsbury town centre. They have applied through the correct channels and it has been approved. While we may not agree with their rhetoric, they have the legal and legitimate right to protest, and as long as it remains lawful, we will do our jobs and protect those rights, as we would for anyone.'

A rumble of voices ran through the room. Louise wasn't sure how many were in favour and how many were against this event. She knew some of her fellow officers shared the same views as the BNP, to a lesser or greater extent. She had seen the differences in the way they treated white and Muslim victims of crime. The former were treated with sympathy, empathy and in a timely fashion. The latter were lucky if the report was ever filed. Too many times she had seen the officers in the pen laughing about 'just another nagging Paki.' It stung to see such behaviour, and while she knew it was a minority amongst her fellow officers who behaved in such a way, like their sexist and misogynistic behaviours, it still lingered. It hurt to see the noble calling of a police officer tarnished in that fashion.

'We have had an undercover officer inserted into the BNP group for the last five months. I'll hand it over to him, and he can brief us all on the situation as it stands.'

From the back of the room, a young man dressed in a denim jacket and jeans strode to the front of the gathered police officers. As he passed by, Hines saw the Black Sabbath patch on his jeans and let out a gasp.

She nudged Louise in the ribs.

'It's that jumped-up prick from the other day.'

'It's actually Sergeant Benjamin Harris,' he said with a smile. 'Special Operations out of Wakefield.'

'Harris? Not Lewis? I knew he was fucking lying to us,' Hines said. 'How's your neck?'

Ben gave it a rub.

'Sore, but no need to apologise. You didn't know.'

'Did you hear me apologise? I don't fucking think so.'

Laughter broke out again and it took Manby a second or two to get everyone back under control.

'Sergeant Harris has been undercover now for some time,

garnering information about the Everad clan of the BNP. The recent events have complicated matters in one aspect—'

'—and made several other areas a lot clearer,' Harris added.

He took a seat on the edge of the table and flipped the chart to its next blank page.

'We knew about Everad... That's Tommy Everad, who owns, albeit in name only, and runs the Walton Arms in Savile Town. Head of the local chapter of the BNP, Tommy is known to have his fingers in a lot of dodgy pies, along with his legitimate pub business. I went in looking for bar work, and slowly worked my way into the group. Meetings were held in the pub, and it was Tommy who made the arrangements for the protest on Saturday.'

Louise looked at Hines. Mention of the Everads had chilled her; she could see the tension in Hines' face. She could also see the questions exploding in her friend's mind: *Does all this have anything to do with Joe? Does Joe express BNP tendencies?*

Freeman jumped in.

'He came to me with all the paperwork and we walked round Dewsbury town centre looking for the best place to hold their rally. We came to an agreement that it would be held in front of the post office, opposite the Town Hall on Wakefield Old Road.'

'Right in the centre? Are you sure that's wise?'

Louise turned to the speaker. A man dressed in a Metallica t-shirt, with short hair and silver earrings, was shaking his head. 'There's too many routes of egress from that position,' he was saying.

A couple of his colleagues beside him were nodding in agreement.

'The permit is for up to and including five hundred people. They're not expecting much more than that, and so this seemed the most agreeable position for all concerned. The mobile command unit can be parked on the side street next to the Town Hall. We're going to have cordoned off the far end of the marketplace with tape… Can you put up the overhead of the centre, Jim?'

A moment later the bright light of the projector flickered on, to be quickly replaced by a grainy overhead photograph of the marketplace.

Freeman continued, 'Here, here and… there, those three places as well. Cordon tape will be secured at these points, and a strong line of officers at each one will make sure no one sneaks through. The only entrance and exit to the rally will be here at Foundry Street, with officers checking people in and out.'

'That's going to piss off a lot of the shops,' someone else said.

Louise couldn't make out who it was, but they were right. Judging by the positioning of the cordons, all the shops in the centre, about two dozen including the Black Bull pub.

Harris jumped off the table and came and stood in front of the map.

'It's only for an hour or so,' he said, 'and we've already spoken to most and they're happy with it. Well, maybe happy isn't quite the right word, but they'll put up with it just to get it over and done with.'

Louise sat forward.

'I take it we'll have uniformed officers on the inside of the cordon, patrolling?'

Harris nodded. 'As well as plain clothes and undercovers.'

'And in case everything goes to shit, we'll have crowd control officers in full response gear in vans at several spots. Here, here and here. We're ready for anything,' Freeman said proudly.

Louise wasn't so sure about that.

'What has the community response been to this rally? There's a definite connection now to the Wadee assault… Can you offer any more information in regard to that?'

The questions came from Hines, who hadn't taken her eyes off Harris all the time they'd been talking, Louise noted. The man had got under her skin at their last meeting – and she'd nearly split his – and to find out he was one of them… Very surreal. The questions were good ones, too. Just because this rally was loom-ing, and all the complications that came with correct policing of such an event, that didn't mean that everything else they were dealing with should be cast aside. The assault on the Wadee brothers was obviously directly tied now to the Walton Arms, and by association, the BNP group. If anyone had some inside information, then that would be Harris.

'And what about the cut and shut?' Louise added. 'We have the stolen car, the deaths of the car thieves, the apparent cut and shut operation operating out of Sanderson's garage, and now we have someone who is directly connected to all of that. You. Sergeant Benjamin Harris. So, what gives?'

She couldn't help it. Louise could feel the anger building as she was speaking and she knew it wouldn't help. They were supposed to work together, but it seemed she had been left out of a lot of things recently, and she couldn't help but think it was because she was a woman. They both were, she added realising that Hines was as just as big a part of this now as she was. They were partners now, not just work colleagues. Their three years together was testament to their partnership. When Louise had been passed over for the Sergeant's position, there had been one consolation. It meant she could continue to work with Hines without the issue of rank getting between them.

'All good points,' Harris said. 'The pair of you. Good work, by the way.'

Patronising prick, Louise thought.

'We haven't done much more than find the obvious links between the three cases. Wadee assault, Wadee stolen car and subsequent car crash. We also have the murder of Helen Williams, and a second woman, now. Do you think those are connected in any way?'

'I don't see how. They might be a lot of things…'

'Racists, Twockers, cutters…'

Harris ignored her. '…but murderers they certainly aren't. How about we talk more about this after this brief?'

Manby cleared his throat and stood.

'Well, getting back to the rally, you'll all be required to report at 5a.m. Saturday morning.' A chorus of groans filled the room. Manby ignored them. 'There's going to be a duty sheet up in the pen that will have your assignments for the day. I'll have that posted later today, so make sure you check it and know what you're doing and what to bring. There's an info sheet here on the desk with a couple of faces we're looking for, and Harris is going to hold one more briefing just before we set out. Any other questions?'

There were none and the room began to empty.

Hines and Louise got out of their chairs and went straight over to Harris. Without waiting for everyone to get out, Hines rounded on the undercover officer.

'What about in the garage the other day? What do you call that?'

'Intimidation. Nothing more. Like what they did with the Wadees.'

'Then you do know who did it,' Louise said.

'I do, but it wasn't me, for a start.'

'But you did nothing to stop it.'

Harris shrugged.

'What could I do without breaking my cover? Shit happens.'

'Shit happens? … These two were clocked within an inch of their lives. Bilal is lucky to be able to speak and Raja to be able to see out of his eye. It was those goons in the garage, wasn't it? I remember one of them having bruises on their knuckles. Fresh ones. Pretty stupid to go beating up a couple of strangers, especially ones that had their car nicked from right outside the pub. And stupid to have nicked it in the first place. Seems like this BNP gang is full of real geniuses. I bet the boss wasn't happy.' She took a deep breath. 'Everad, right?'

'You've pretty much nailed it spot on,' Harris said. 'Except Everad was one of the ones that did the kicking. When he found out about the car being nicked he went livid. Probably would have done the three lads in if they hadn't been killed. From what I've seen, he has a way of getting rid of people who antagonise him. Several close associates who angered him haven't been seen since. New suppliers now.'

'It doesn't surprise me,' Hines said. 'The Everads always think and talk with their fists first.'

'You know them?' Harris asked.

'She dated Joe Everad,' Louise said, finally able to jump into the conversation.

Harris'eyebrows rose.

'Really? The son? I wouldn't have thought he'd be your type.'

'Oh, she has lots of types,' Louise said, drawing an angry glare from Hines, 'but what we don't have is a reason not to go and arrest Everad and his crew for the assault on the Wadees.'

Harris said nothing. He sat on the table, his hands resting on his knees. He looked lost in thought, as though weighing up the best option to take. Finally, he settled back, his hands coming together on the top of his head as he let out a long sigh.

'Just take a moment to look at this big picture. We have Everad – runs the Walton pub, runs the BNP group. Members of the group nick a car, crash it and die. Sad, yes. Regrettable, yes, because that's three fewer inroads into what's really happening here.'

'And what is that?' Louise asked.

She was getting irritated again. Even worse, she was getting hungry. The hangover had finally gone, and the caffeine had worn off, leaving nothing but a hungry hole in her stomach. The last thing she needed to be doing now was playing puzzle games.

Harris checked his watch.

'It's lunch. Fancy a pint and a pie?'

CHAPTER
THIRTY-FIVE

'How do you think Everad is able to fund the running of the pub, or the organisation of his chapter of the BNP?' Harris asked around a mouthful of steak and onion pie.

They sat in the far corner of the Carpenters, the table usually reserved for DI Manby. He was stuck back at the station in his office, talking strategies with the Chief Superintendent. Louise had seen the jealous look he had thrown them when they announced they were nipping out for an early lunch. The unlucky joys of being the boss, she supposed. Perhaps if Tom Bailey had been there he would have put a stop to their short break, but he wasn't... another mystery to add to the growing list.

'It's not from nicking cars, that's for sure,' Harris continued. 'And that's what we wanted to find out. Over the last year or so a lot of cash has been rolling into the region, financing businesses like the Walton Arms in Savile Town and the groups that meet there. It was decided to put someone in, gain their confidence and learn as much about their operations as possible. Guess who drew the short straw for that?' he grinned.

Hines was fascinated. 'How long have you been on special assignment?' she asked.

'Eight months now. Five over in Bradford and Batley, and then the last three back here.' Hines watched as he took another bite. Her own food was sitting on her plate going cold. Louise, on the other hand, was still starving.

'Are you not finishing that?' she asked.

Hines shook her head, so Louise pulled the plate before her, sliding it on top of her own empty one. She reached past Hines to grab the salt and vinegar and lashed both liberally over the chips and pie.

'Can you pass the Daddies sauce as well?' she asked. 'Can't believe you're not eating. This is gorgeous.'

'I remembered that Joe probably got them,' Hines replied. 'I don't want anything of his in my mouth again.' She paused, grinned and gave Louise a playful punch to the arm. 'You know what I mean.'

'So, you two were close, I take it?' Harris asked.

'Well, if she was—'

'We had an on again, off again sort of thing going.'

Louise was shocked at the casual description of their tumultuous relationship.

'The man was a prick and a bully. He put you in the hospital just a couple of nights ago, or had you forgotten?'

Hines rounded on Louise.

'That's none of anyone else's business,' she hissed. 'Don't be so dramatic. Put me in the hospital, indeed. You make it sound like I was at death's door.'

'He assaulted you in public and you got smashed into a glass table.'

Hines wasn't backing down. Harris took a drink and watched the argument play out before him. 'We fought. I fell. The hospital was Dominic's idea, more to cover himself and the pub than to make sure I was all right, I think.'

'It's obvious you can take care of yourself,' Harris jumped in. 'My neck is still sore. You're pretty good at handling yourself.'

Hines smiled. 'Thank you,' she said.

Louise shook her head and turned to Harris, her angry stare causing him to flinch back. 'For a woman, is that what you're saying? Pretty good at handling yourself for a woman?'

'Well... yes,' Harris said. 'Look, it's just a fact. She's small both in terms of size and strength when compared to me. I'm a good eight to ten inches taller. I have more muscle mass, but she was able to handle the situation the other day. She used her training well, and controlled me to the point where I was easy to subdue and arrest. Your average woman wouldn't be able to do that.'

'Your average woman?' Louise waved away his objection before he could voice it. 'Oh, you'd be surprised what we can do when the situation warrants it,' she continued hotly. She was still fucking sick and tired of this masculine bullshit. Because she had tits she couldn't fight?

'I meant it as a compliment,' he continued. 'I'm sorry if it pissed you off. Perhaps I could have phrased it better?'

'Are you asking me or telling me that?'

Harris laughed, raising his hands. 'Truce... truce.'

'Are these all finished with?'

Standing by their table was Dominic, the owner of the Carpenters pub. His face was red and sweaty, his apron stained with food. Louise quickly dropped the last forkful of chips and pastry into her mouth as the landlord reached down to scoop up all the plates.

'It's good to see a lass with an appetite,' Dominic said. 'Hungry today, lass?'

'Absolutely starving,' Louise replied.

'And how are you feeling?' Dominic said, turning to Hines. 'Still coming to karaoke Sunday, I hope?'

'Karaoke? You sing as well?' Harris asked. Hines visibly blushed.

'She's one of the best, and no one's going to hold what happened last week against you. He's gone, by the way.'

'I know,' Hines replied. 'And yes; I'll be in on Sunday. Thanks.'

'No problem,' Dominic said as he carried the plates away.

Harris checked his watch.

'I think we should be getting back, but before we do I want to run something by you. It's obvious you can handle things, and you've a good eye for details. I'd like to have a quieter chat about Joe; see if there's anything he might have slipped out about his dad, if that's okay with you?' Hines nodded. 'Also, how about you join me in the crowd on Saturday?'

'That's a terrible idea,' Louise said. Hines threw a withering stare at her as the three rose from the table. 'Think about it. Those men who saw you choke out Ben at the garage are members of the BNP group as well. Right?' she added, turning back to Harris. His response was a simple nod of the head. Louise continued, 'They've seen you. They know you are a police officer.'

'I can dye my hair,' Hines said carefully. Louise could see she was getting mad at her obstacles, but she could also see that Hines was starting to question herself. 'But they'll still recognise me, won't they, and then they'll put two and two together and...'

'...and work out I'm a copper as well.' Harris opened the door and waited as Louise and Hines stepped past. 'Let's think about this...'

Outside the sun was shining. A few benches had people gathered around them, but Louise noted there was no sign of Scruffy Pete. Thursdays were his betting days; his giro would be in and he'd normally be out spending. Not today, though. Today he would be lucky to get out of bed, she was sure of it. The curtains would be drawn against the day; despair and sorrow had collapsed on him like a demolished building, crushing him beneath its weight and trapping him with only his dark thoughts as company. Louise made a mental note to go to check on him later.

Hines and Harris were walking side by side, Hines listening

intently as Harris continued to outline his plan. His crazy plan, Louise thought. Pure madness. Another thought struck; was she really upset about Hines being put in another dangerous situation, or was she a little bit jealous that Harris hadn't suggested she be the one to accompany him? Being passed over for promotion, even to a knuckle-dragger like Bailey, was one thing; to be as easily dismissed in favour of her friend and colleague was something Louise didn't want to face.

Karla would laugh when she told her, and of course she would confess her insecurities, probably over another glass of wine.

Suddenly the pair stopped and turned to each other.

'That's so fucking obvious,' Harris said.

They high-fived each other and turned to Louise. Hines' entire face was grinning. Louise groaned. This usually meant trouble was brewing.

'What?'

'We have the answer to what to do with the guys from the garage. Go ahead… It was your idea; you tell her.'

Hines grinned even wider. She told Louise what their plan was, and as she did so, Louise's smile slowly grew until it matched theirs.

They were right.

It was obvious, plain and simple.

'Let's do it!'

There were three cars in the garage but only one was being worked on when the police van rolled up outside and six officers dived out. Sanderson's Garage was quiet on a Thursday afternoon, save for the metallic clatter as a tool was dropped to the stone floor.

'Stand fast!' With shouts of warning, the police officers charged inside, truncheons drawn. 'No one move! I said don't move!'

Three of the mechanics obeyed. The fourth, the one who had dropped the wrench, scooted off to the side, disappearing through a doorway marked OFFICE. Louise walked in and watched as the mechanics were all cuffed and then brought to stand before her.

'Keith Wallis; Eric Merchant and George Kent. You are under arrest for the assault of Bilal and Raja Wadee on Sunday evening...'

'Jog on, Charlie,' one of the men said. The other two laughed as their rights were read out. None of the men seemed bothered. Not the first time they'd worn silver bracelets, that was for sure.

Louise's eyes scanned around the garage, immediately captivated by the car that was being worked on when they had arrived. Another Ford Escort, its rear wheels were off and what looked like the exhaust system lay on a dust sheet nearby. More noticeable were the two licence plates partially hidden by the same dust sheet, the corner hastily thrown over in an effort to conceal.

She was just reaching down to lift it when a spanner bounced off the table in front of her. It spun through the air and hit the rear of the car with enough force to dent the metal.

'What the fuck is this?'

Standing in the doorway of the office, face as red as the last time they had been here, was Colin Sanderson. He glared at Louise, and she knew immediately that, this time, the angry redness of his face was down to her presence rather than booze. 'This is fucking bordering on harassment, you know,' he said, idly fingering another tool he held in his hands. 'And what did you do with my lad from before?'

'Mr Lewis? You'll have to speak to your solicitor about that. Soon as he turned up we had to let him go.'

Sanderson was already picking up the phone.

'Too fucking right I'll be talking to him,' he said as he started to dial.

Louise walked over and put her left thumb down on the

plunger, cutting the call off. With her right hand she took the receiver from Sanderson.

'You can call him from Prospect Road,' Louise said. 'You're coming with us, too.'

'This is a fucking outrage, you bit... AAHH!'

His words died off as Louise twisted the man's arm up his back with one hand, the other grabbing his shoulder. A moment later he was being marched quickly towards the waiting maw of the police van.

As they neared, Louise propelled Sanderson towards the waiting clutch of a PC, who caught him and shoved him unceremoniously into the back of the van. Sanderson's protests were silenced behind the slamming metal cough of the door.

Listening to the muted cries of outrage coming from the van, Louise hoped Hines and their new colleague were having an equal amount of success.

CHAPTER
THIRTY-SIX

The second part of the plan involved the Wadees directly. While Louise went to Sanderson's garage to arrest the men Harris had pointed out as being directly involved in the assault, Hines took a car and drove to the Wadees' shop on the Green. After a brief explanation, and many reassurances, the entire Wadee family were being transported to the station in two cars.

They arrived just as Louise was dodging the spanner thrown by Sanderson and were taken into one of the interview rooms, where Manby and Harris were waiting. As soon as Bilal saw Harris, he grew angry and started towards him, fists clenched.

'Wait, wait,' Manby said, putting himself between the two. 'He's a copper.'

'He was there that night,' Bilal spat. 'He was there when we were attacked.'

'What is this?' Vanita said.

Danesh stood in the doorway, visibly shaken.

'Mr and Mrs Wadee,' Harris said, stepping forward. 'My name is Benjamin Harris. I am an undercover police officer with a special division tasked to infiltrate hate groups like the one your sons regrettably encountered last week.'

'You were there,' Bilal said again. 'And did nothing.'

Harris' head dipped and for a moment he said nothing. When he raised his face, Hines noted that shame filled his face, but in his eyes burned a determination that she found compelling.

'It is hard to explain, I understand that, but I hope you will allow me to try. Please, can you sit? All of you. I will have drinks brought if you wish. Tea... coffee?'

Bilal stepped forward and Harris tensed, ready to accept any blow the man would throw. Instead, and surprising everyone in the room, including Bilal himself apparently, what was offered was a handshake. Harris took his hand and they shook.

'I will listen to what you have to say, and if you could get a can of Coke, I would be most appreciative.'

His smile was wide and honest. Harris smiled back.

'No problem.'

With drinks brought, Harris spent fifteen minutes in the interview room alone talking with the Wadees. As they talked Louise arrived with the men they'd arrested, and she was just beginning to fill out the required paperwork when Hines joined her at their desk in the pen.

'How did it go?' she asked, dropping into her chair. Louise gave a non-committal grunt and continued wrestling with the paperwork. 'Ben's talking to the Wadees.'

'That's good. How do you spell causal?'

'What's the context?'

Louise sat back and began to read from her report. 'From the intelligence provided by Sergeant Harris, we know that Mr Sanderson employed Messrs Wallis, Merchant and Kent, along with the victims of Sunday's car crash. We also know that Messrs Wallis, Merchant and Kent attacked Bilal and Raja Wadee, so we conclude by causal reasoning that Mr Sanderson sanctioned both the stealing of the Wadees' car and their subsequent assault.' She looked up. 'What do you think?'

Hines shrugged. 'Not sure about the use of the world by

implication, and that's a pretty flimsy foundation for an arrest, don't you think?'

'This was your idea, you and your new best friend.'

Hines laughed.

'The idea was to arrest the three who did the actual assault, not Sanderson.'

'Yes, well... he's a prick and deserved it. He threw a fucking spanner at me.'

'You probably deserved that,' Hines laughed. 'I've wanted to throw a thing or two at you in the past. Add that about the spanner into the report though.'

Louise shrugged but started to type.

'Only in the past? So, what's next?'

'Ben will do the line-up with the brothers, and once the men have been identified they will be arrested, formally charged and put in the system. Sanderson will be trying to get their solicitor involved but the victim identification will mean no bail. They'll be off the streets and away from the rally, leaving it open for me to get in the thick of it.'

Louise finished her report and saved it to disk.

'Are you sure you want to do this?' she asked. 'You have nothing to prove, you know. What happened with you and Joe...'

'Has nothing to do with this. Jesus Christ, Louise. Why does everything have to be about me and Joe?'

'What happened is important. You see that, right? You understand that?'

'What I understand is that everyone treats me like a porcelain doll, scared that I'll break.'

It's not your body we're worried will break, but your spirit, Louise thought. Biting back a reply that would only pour more fuel onto the fire of their argument, she instead decided to change tactics.

'Okay. Fair enough,' she said. 'You know what you're doing. Just promise me that if things start to feel too much, you'll talk to me.' She put her hand on the table, halfway across the desk.

Hines looked at it for a moment then reached out, taking Louise's in her own, their fingers intertwining.

'Of course,' she said, 'and don't think I don't hear what you're saying. What you're *really* saying. I do. I really do.'

Her voice choked. Louise squeezed her hand. Hines squeezed back then let go.

'Right. What's next?

CHAPTER
THIRTY-SEVEN

DI Manby had read hundreds of case reports. Seen thousands of crime scene photos. The images of devastation and loss, of pain and sorrow, were forever marked in his mind, grisly mementos of misery inflicted on others.

The smashed-up living room, trinkets scattered, glass shattered... The bruised faces, the broken limbs... The faces of the dead, their sightless eyes staring accusingly back from their celluloid hell, daring him to avenge them.

Too many of these photos, too many of these memories.

And now he was looking at more pictures that would return unbidden to his dreams, twisting them into nightmares that he endured as part of his job. This was something they never taught you when you joined the force; they never told you what would be asked of you, what would be drawn from you. The sacrifices you were made to make, along with your family and loved ones. Too many times he had woken in the dead of night, a scream twisting behind his lips, or a cold sheen of sweat coating his goose-pimpled flesh, soaking through the sheets that would need changing once again. His wife, Marie, had accepted this hidden cost to their marriage with grace and love, doing what was needed to be done with no complaint, taking her husband into her arms to hold him against the unseen threats until he fell back asleep.

The blank face of a woman now stared up at him from the photo in his hand. He was only too well aware of the way the sheet that covered her chest fell away to settle flat on the mortuary table where her legs should be. His stomach rolled and another wave of dizziness washed over him. This just didn't happen. This was beyond anything he had ever dealt with, the evil of the act beyond comprehension.

Putting the photo down, he lifted the post mortem report.

The report made for grim reading. His eyes traversed down the page, taking in the details. Taking in the horror. Two bags had been found with her. Stomach in one; kidneys and liver in the other. Black bags, the sort he used to take the rubbish out, to drop in the bin ready for Tuesday pickup. Like the scraps of food brushed from his plate, she had been discarded.

His eyes wandered back to the photo of the legs. Helen Williams' legs. An enlarged photo of the heart tattoo on her ankle. Why do… that? Why cut them in half like that? For what possible reason? Easier to move, perhaps? Less weight?

'Jesus Christ…'

His hand fell to the drawer beside him. The glass neck of the bottle tinkled against the white porcelain of his cup as he poured the amber liquid, his hand shaking. It took two attempts to screw the cap back on. The last time he had opened the bottle had been for Bailey's promotion to Sergeant, a decision he was already regretting. Louise had told him what Bailey had done at the Ellis house, the language he had used. He had known Tom Bailey for seven years, and he'd always suspected he had strong views about foreigners. Thinking back over the man's career, he now saw the pattern; the arrests that needed medical attention, the complaints that fell on deaf ears. He saw it now for what it was and again regretted the decision he had been forced to make.

And now this. Two women; one known, the other still a mystery. Both victims of the same evil.

A knock at the door brought him from the dark path of his thoughts. Glancing up, he saw DC Miller and waved her in.

Louise entered, closing the door behind her. She took the seat opposite and reached for a mug.

'A little early for that, isn't it?' She held her mug out. Manby glanced into the pen beyond, making sure no one was watching, and poured.

'Not for this,' he replied with a nod towards the stack of folders on his desk. 'Take a read and tell me what you think.'

For the next five minutes, they sat in silence, Louise reading through the reports, Manby turning over the details in his mind.

When she had finished, Louise took her mug, drained it and held it out for a refill. Manby obliged, topping his own up for good measure. This time he didn't check the pen. 'Well?'

'Putting aside the obvious horror of it all, the basics: two dead women, two different halves of their bodies found at the same dumping site. One very recent kill – that would be Helen – the other... well, evidence and an initial examination suggests killed within the last year and the body stored in some way. Probably a freezer, Danes says, but he'll need that clarified by the pathologist. It's good enough for me, though.'

'So, missing for a year,' Manby said, 'at the least.'

'And that indicates that she was probably another prostitute or drug user. Low priority.' Manby bristled at that but Louise wasn't having it. 'Oh, come on, Bill. Even with your association with Helen, her case wasn't treated as a top priority. Just another runaway street tart, or she'd gone off with her dealer. Never mind her brother's worry. Never mind that she was getting her shit back together. Just another statistic.'

'Helen Williams was never just a statistic,' he said.

'To you, deep down, maybe not,' Louise conceded, 'but as far as the system was concerned, yes she was. You might not like to hear that truth, but truth is what it is. You can't change it to better suit your outlook on things. Truth hurts and truth also heals, and you have to take both as they come.'

She pulled four folders from the stack and spread them out on the desk.

'I've checked. Four women who have gone missing over the last ten years, two of them in the last five. No updates, no follow ups after the initial investigation. And that includes Helen Williams. Now we have the remains of two women. I'm guessing that the torso is one of the other missing women, not a fifth. That links them together, or at least initially points me in that direction.'

'But why cut them in half? Why dump two halves together?'

'I think we should let Karla take a look at this. Perhaps she can put together a profile for us.'

Louise sat back with the forensic report on the torso and sipped at the whisky as she read. A dozen stab wounds, most centred around the breasts. Only a couple were deep cuts. She looked at a photo of one such cut. Clean. Neat. Penetrated at least four centimetres between the third and fourth ribs into the superior lobe of the lung. She looked at another photo, a similar wound, but this one was ragged. The rib had taken the blade.

A thought began to form.

'Pass me the report on Helen.'

Manby fumbled for it, found it and slid it across the table. Louise started reading, her eyes flipping between two photos.

'I think he's practising,' she said, and then proceeded to describe the differences between the wounds. 'Here, on Helen's thigh. This cut... It's almost like it has been carved like an after-disco kebab.'

Manby paled but said nothing.

'But this one here. See how different it is. Smooth, like a chef's carvery.'

'Can you please stop with the food references? I'll never eat anything again at this rate. So... he's learning?'

'Practising his craft,' Louise said.

The thought chilled her.

'But again, why cut them in half?'

'Again, Karla may be better suited to answer this, or at least hypothesise on it, but think about it. If he leaves one victim, that's one line of enquiry for us to pursue. That's tough as it is, we both know that. Finding all the people to talk to, the friends, the relatives. Work colleagues. And then following up on everything they tell us. Now factor in another victim; that's the workload doubled, and we're already being stretched pretty thin right now.'

'Do you think he knows that?'

'I have no idea,' Louise said, 'but if I was going to try and draw the investigation away, I would aim to throw as much chaff in the way as possible.'

'Chaff?' Manby asked. 'They're not chaff. They're people. People with families who care about them. People who love them. They're not chaff.'

He looked at his empty mug, looked at the whisky bottle and thought better of it. Making sure the cap was screwed tight, he dropped it back into his drawer, shutting it away.

'They are all of those things, but to us, they're a lot of work. Two victims and all the work that entails. The horrific nature of the bodies. Bags with innards in, and the close relationship of one of the victims with the Detective Inspector who runs the investigation. That's a lot of shit to wade through already. Add on top of that the assault, the upcoming protest and the car crash, all active investigations…'

Manby suddenly sat up. Louise could see that the same terrible thought had taken hold.

'The car. A cut and shut. The two victims.'

Louise nodded, her blood cold. 'One top. One bottom. The human equivalent.'

A deep silence fell between them as each contemplated what had just been said.

Finally, Manby spoke.

'Jesus… Does that mean they work at Sanderson's as well? Just what the fuck did we get into here?'

Louise had had another thought. One perhaps even more troubling.

'The wounds. I said that they appeared as though he was practising. What if...' She took a breath and ploughed on, determined to say the unpleasant thought as fast as possible. 'What if he wasn't practising. What if he was training someone?'

CHAPTER
THIRTY-EIGHT

'She was mine!'

Ian Neal Peterson screamed into the cold, dark cavern of the warehouse, his voice echoing around the building like thunder. It rattled off the prefabricated metal that had been secured over the windows, their surface dusty and covered in cobwebs.

Harry Peterson stood silent amidst the tumult of his son's fury, watching as the boy picked up another wrench and threw it against the wall. It hit, gouging a track in the brickwork to clatter to the stone ground, its own echo adding to that of his son's voice, which still lingered. He had known there would be a reaction, had even hoped for one; that way he would know he was doing the right thing, but this? This was beyond anything he had ever hoped for. Ever dreamed.

For so long it had just been him and his passions. Those dark desires he had been forced to hide from those closest to him. Lies compounded lies, his true nature buried beneath a false skin that he found so much more disgusting than anything he had been compelled to do.

And it was a strong compulsion, a driving need to sate his thirst. The cries of exquisite torment; the look of anguished terror in eyes that couldn't comprehend what was happening, who chose to disbelieve even when the very truth was laid before them in bloodied strips.

How many years had he travelled this path alone, hiding his actions, planning his needs in the shadows of his marriage? And then they were blessed with his son's arrival. Not conventional by any means, but welcomed nonetheless. Straight away he knew they were kindred spirits; he could sense it in the boy's demeanour. The way he cried when he was hungry; the way he manipulated his mother with sounds and looks. And he took to it so well, so easily, when the time came. Watching at first, taking direction occasionally.

And then his first tentative steps, taken on his own initiative.

Oh, what a proud father he had been. What a proud father he was.

Even now. Standing amidst the storm of his son's petulant rage.

'She was mine and you took her from me,' he cried, throwing another spanner. This one hit the trolley workbench with enough force that it rolled a couple of feet.

'She had to go,' Harry said. 'It was her time.'

'But I hadn't finished. You told me that last time. I hadn't finished.'

Harry smiled.

The slap came out of nowhere. He hadn't thought about it, hadn't expected to do it; it just happened. The sound of his palm striking his son's cheek was an explosive retort, harsh and sudden, over as soon as it had begun. There was no echo, no reverberation, just a split second of noise and the startled look in his son's eyes.

He watched as they filled with tears, but he made no sound. Made no outward sign at all. It was as though he was carved from the same prefabricated metal that coated the walls of the warehouse in which they stood, able to be moulded and shaped by strong actions and divine purpose.

'It is done,' he said. Ian nodded, silent. 'We will find another,' Harry added.

For a long moment, Ian said nothing. His lower lip trembled as he fought back tears. Harry could not have been prouder. Then, almost a child's whisper: 'You promise?'

Harry smiled.

CHAPTER
THIRTY-NINE

Once again, Louise found herself surrounded by shadows as she stood in the front room of Pete Williams' home.

Gone was all hope from the man she knew as Scruffy Pete. He sat slumped in the chair, his legs hanging over the arms, his head reclined against the tatty backrest. His face was drawn and pale, the bags beneath his eyes betraying his body's desire for sleep, and his mind's determination to refuse. The redness Louise saw could just as easily have been from the drugs he had obviously consumed; scattered around the room were the tools of the heroin user, the air heavy with its stench.

One arm dangled down the side of the chair, the other lay across his lap, fingers barely clutching the can of Tennent's. His eyes were closed. A thin trickle of liquid seeped from his mouth; Louise wasn't sure if it was sleep drool or unswallowed lager.

'Pete,' she said, as gently as she could.

He hadn't acknowledged her, not when she had knocked loudly on the door and windows, and not when she had made entry, banging the door open with a well-placed kick. The frame had splintered, but an hour or so's work and it would be good as new again.

But not Pete. It would take more to fix him. As she watched, he moaned something unintelligible, his body tilting to the left. The can also tilted and liquid spilled out, soaking into his trousers.

A lot more.

Brushing her skirt free of grey hairs from a cat she had never seen, and the sticky wrapper of an old, forgotten sweet, Louise went and crouched beside Pete.

She reached out, her hand carefully taking the can from him.

'Pete.'

His answer was a low moan, deep and guttural. Louise suspected he was annoyed at her interruption, frustrated from whatever foggy, drug-induced mindscape he currently occupied, wandering free from the hurt and the pain of losing his sister. The mix of alcohol and heroin was a tightrope across an abyss of oblivion that he walked with reckless contempt. A single misstep and he would plunge into its dark embrace, never to wake.

Putting the can down, she moved her fingers to his neck, checking for the twitching beat of his pulse. It was there. Barely, but it was there. His skin was clammy, and when she examined them, his eyes were pinpricks.

Stepping back, she looked around the room. She couldn't see a phone anywhere.

Without another thought, Louise went back outside to the car. She opened the back door and ran back to the house. Pete needed hospital treatment; she didn't know if it was a true overdose or just a really bad hangover, but she couldn't take that chance. With no phone in the house, there was only one course of action she could take.

She was surprised by how light he was, but then realised that most of his meals came in liquid form. As carefully as she could manage, Louise carried/half dragged Pete to her car.

Within the hour, Pete was admitted to Dewsbury Memorial, where he was given fluids and treatment for heroin overdose, and his system flushed of any remaining alcohol as best they could by making him throw up all the shit he had taken the night before. When his clothes were stripped from him, the doctors and nurses were horrified by his near skeletal state.

'That explains how you could carry him,' the doctor said over his clipboard. 'Weight is at least three stones under what is normally expected of a man of his size. Extremely dehydrated and malnourished. Obvious marks of a heroin user...' His voice trailed away.

'So, he's going to be okay?' Louise asked.

She had sat in the waiting room for two hours, working her way through the only magazine available while waiting to hear of his condition. If anyone asked, she could talk about holiday excursions to Llandudno in great detail, thanks to this brochure. A vague memory of a holiday chalet near the beach drifted across her mind but then disappeared.

'If by okay you mean he won't die today, then yes. He's okay. You are the one who drove him here?' Louise nodded. 'That was a risky action to take, but one that undoubtedly saved his life. You are also the one who dealt with the Wadee brothers and the car accident Sunday night, am I correct? I am Doctor Kavel. Sanjay Kavel. I treated the man they brought in. The man who sadly passed away.'

Louise confirmed she was aware of both incidents.

'We've just made an arrest in regards to the Wadee assault.'

'That is good to hear,' Kavel replied. 'Though somewhat surprising.'

Louise frowned.

'Surprising? How so?'

Kavel indicated for Louise to sit once more. She did so, moving the magazines so that he could sit beside her. He smoothed the creases from his white coat and ran the seam of his trousers between two fingers, bringing it to a sharp point once more.

'I too was once attacked. Less than a month ago. Very similar circumstances. I went to the wrong place, had the wrong skin colour. The wrong language. When I realised, I tried to leave but they wouldn't let me. They attacked me, at first with words, calling me a stinking Paki.' Louise flinched.

Kavel saw and carried on. 'They called me curry-breath while they hit and punched me,' he said.

'This is terrible. And you reported it?'

Kavel's laugh was devoid of any humour. Louise sadly recognised it; had heard it too many times. Had even laughed it herself on many occasions when she had been the one not listened to. The one not heard. The one not seen.

'Of course I reported it. I then followed up a day, a week, a month later, and every time I got the same answer. Not a priority. Will be looked into, but not a priority.'

Louise flinched inside. She had said those same words herself. Too many times, perhaps. Said not to comfort or reassure the victim, but to silence her own conscience. There was a growing number of crimes to be looked into, and only so many hours that could be devoted to each. Louise knew this as a realistic fact of the job, but still she struggled with the practicality of it all. She had to look into the faces of those she was disappointing, hurting all over again because of her apparent dismissal. A victim all over again.

Kavel waved aside her rote reply of apology.

'It is of no concern now,' he said. 'I am only glad that this instance was taken more seriously than my own. But have you not seen the growing hostility to us? Something must be done.'

'It will be, I promise you,' Louise said, and something in her words or the way she locked eyes with the doctor as she spoke made Kavel sit back.

'I believe you believe that,' he said. 'But I doubt anything will change. But it is good to see that someone is at least trying.' He stood with a smile. Mr Williams should be up to a visit now, but only for a few minutes. He has a long, arduous journey to health ahead of him and needs his rest.'

As Doctor Kavel walked away, already swamped by a group of nurses with their own requests and needs, Louise wondered how bad things could really get before there was any true change.

Pete was sitting up in bed drinking Kia-Ora through a straw when Louise walked onto the ward. For a moment she didn't recognise the man; he had been given a wash, his hair had been combed through and possibly washed as well, and his face had been shaved clean of the scraggly beard. His skin was still pale and a drip fed liquids into his body but he looked... well.

'Thank you,' he said in response to her comment. 'And not just for that. If you hadn't come when you did...' His voice trailed away. 'We used to drink these as kids.' His eyes drifted to the box of juice, but she knew he wasn't looking at it. He was looking at what it represented. At who it represented.

Looking at a box of Kia-Ora and seeing Helen, the way Louise looked at packs of Regal Blues and saw her dad.

'I'm so sorry, Pete,' Louise said, placing her hand on his arm. His eyes stayed locked on the Kia-Ora, but Louise saw the tears fill them and begin to roll down his face. She gave his arm a gentle squeeze. 'Can I ask you a few questions? About Helen and her friends?'

His answer was a silent nod.

Louise reached into her bag and pulled out four photos she had taken from the missing persons' files that still needed closing. One by one she placed them on the bed. Even through the sheets, she could feel how frail the man was; his legs were nothing but bony contours.

'These are women who have been missing for some time, and this one we found shortly after finding Helen. Do you recognise any of them? Were they friends of Helen? Did they...'

'Work together?' Pete shook his head, a slight wince at the

movement flickering in the corners of his eyes. 'I don't think so. Wait... her.'

He pointed to the picture of the woman who had been found by the canal.

'Mary King. She works Savile Town and Dewsbury. Worked,' he corrected himself. 'Down by the Walton Arms, and sometimes in the centre.'

'The Walton? Are you sure?'

Pete nodded.

'She lives in a downstairs flat a few streets away. She would go in there, and me and Helen would sometimes go along for a few.'

He struggled to sit up further, Louise helping by bunching his pillow into a fatter shape. He smiled his thanks and finished the juice before continuing.

'Not a nice pub that, the Walton,' he said. 'I didn't like going there. Rough place. Rougher people.'

'I know,' Louise said. 'What can you tell me about it, or the people there?'

For a moment Pete didn't say anything. Louise could see the indecision take hold, the fear rise in his eyes, but it was only for an instant.

'Will this help Helen?'

'I think so,' Louise said. 'And Mary.'

'It's not a good place. It attracts bad people.'

Louise smiled. 'You make it sound like the Overlook,' she said.

Pete waited for her to continue with a quizzical look.

'The haunted hotel? Stephen King?'

'I'm not a big reader, and not horror. Too much of that as it is. I just finished *The World According To Garp*. John Irving... now there's a writer.'

'John Irving? I never would have thought...'

'That someone like me would read literature? Girlie mags and fag packets is all I could manage, right?'

'I'm sorry,' Louise said. She was genuinely shocked. 'It's just that, you know, how you live. How you… look.'

Pete's smile was wistful.

'Everyone has a history, right? Anyway, the Walton. Bad people go there to do bad things. You know how there's a BNP group there, run by Joe's dad?'

'The Everads. Tommy owns the pub, but we only just recently discovered the connection to the BNP.'

'Tommy doesn't own it. Oh, he acts like he does, talks big and tough all the time. Throws his money around almost as much as his fists. Or at least the fists of those he employs as his muscle. Ask anyone and they'll say that Tommy Everad owns the pub, but he doesn't. Someone else does. I don't know who, but I've overheard them a few times talking on the phone.'

'Someone local?'

Pete shook his head.

'Didn't sound like it, but from what I gather they put the money in, bought it out from under the original owners back in seventy-nine. Did the same with a few other businesses in the area.'

'Really?'

'A couple of restaurants, some other pubs. A few others I think, I don't know.'

'Who would know?'

Someone buying up businesses from outside the area was a red flag. Could be nothing; could be something. Whatever it was, it was something to be checked out.

But not a priority.

'It doesn't matter,' Louise said before Pete could reply. 'Tell me more about the people in the Walton Arms. Anyone you think I should be looking at?'

'I've only been in a few times,' Pete said, 'and my memory's a bit shit. I'm not sure I can be of much use. Oh wait… there's a new lad. I say new, he's been there a few months now. Fairly young. Blond hair. Always wears denim. Seemed very pally with Tommy, like another bit of muscle perhaps.'

Ben Harris.

Doctor Kavel chose that moment to make a reappearance, concerned that Pete wasn't getting the required amount of rest. Louise stood, and before she knew it, had leaned down and pecked Pete on the cheek.

'Careful. That's how they all fall for me,' he said with a smile. A genuine one, Louise noted. His eyes sparkled, and this time not from tears.

'Thanks, Pete. You've been a big help, and I am so sorry about Helen. She was nice. I liked her.'

'She liked you too. And that bear of a boss. Bill has always been good to us; I don't know why.'

She gave his shoulder a squeeze.

'Because you're good people, Pete. I'll check in with you soon.'

Louise was three beds down the ward when Pete called out. She turned to see him sitting up, waving at her. Ignoring the tut of disapproval from Kavel, Louise walked back, her heels click-clacking on the floor.

'There was a bloke in the pub who was always a bit weird. Not in any blatant hands in the air way, but there was always something just off about him. He had a few dates with Mary. Helen too, but that was years ago. After his wife left him.'

'They got divorced?'

'Not sure. She left him and their kid. Went to her sister's in Scotland, he said, but everyone thinks she ran off with another bloke.'

'Could be something. Could be nothing. Can you remember his name?'

'Course I can. Peterson. Harry Peterson.'

A cold chill ran through Louise.

Peterson.

CHAPTER
FORTY

He was still angry. Angry and a little horny. She always got him worked up whenever he thought about her. And he thought about her all the time. Fought his anger and his desire, two powerful emotions she aroused in him, encouraged in him. Demanded from him.

From the very start, that first time together was a violent, passionate release. An angry fuck that had left them both sated and panting like beasts, their hearts pounding, their bodies slick with their sweat mixing together. Hot breath against hotter flesh.

He could still feel her now, feel her wrap around him, grip him. Legs and muscles squeezing him, coaxing every last drop of him. Consuming his love, drinking it all in even as he breathed in her own passion.

They claimed each other, marked each other with their love, and it had been the same ever since.

But alongside this fervent love was a raw anger, just below the surface of each of them. Past deeds, past lives. Past acts of depravity and wanton desires. The shame burned within them, drawn out by the other.

At first it had just been when they fucked, but then it bled into their daily lives. They moved in together too quickly, a three-day chaotic maelstrom that left them battered and spent, the rooms overturned. When they came, their howls were both screams of pain and release; neither could tell which.

And then he had slapped her. Just a game. Just something fun. She had laughed.

She had laughed!

So, he did it again, and she hit him back.

Just a bit of fun. Just a bit of a laugh. Slap and tickle, right?

But then the palm became a fist, flying both ways along with the taunts and the slurs, the slurred speech a nightly happenstance.

God but he loved her. Wanted her.

The shadows wrapped around him as he stood opposite her house, crouched behind the park wall and hidden from view by the thick bushes. Behind him the park was quiet. The day over, the schoolchildren who hung out after the end of day bell had all gone home, called in for tea hours ago.

This was his spot. He had sat here before, waiting. Watching for her to come home, on those days when they had thrown each other aside. Praying she was alone. Praying she hadn't replaced him yet. The copper didn't count. A mistake, she had called it. A drunken fuck that meant nothing more than a change of underwear. What if she'd moved on? Moved on to her boss. Manby. Maybe she preferred old dick now?

The only other person who had been here since was the dyke. That bitch who looked down on him. He still bristled, thinking how she had talked to him at the hospital. How they had all talked to him, like he was a piece of shit or something. He knew he'd fucked up, they both had. That was why he had been there, that was why he had gone. To say sorry. To make up for it, but they had been there. Danes, married Peter Danes who had thrown a fuck into his girlfriend, but had he said anything to anyone? No. He'd kept his mouth shut, like she'd asked.

The dyke bitch and her dyke girlfriend had laughed at him. *I bet if I threw a fuck into them they'd be laughing on the other side of their faces. Fuck the dyke right out of them!*

He could feel himself getting hard at the thought.

Headlights splashed across him and he ducked as a car turned onto Northfield Road. A police car. It stopped in front of her house and she got out. His dick became rock when he saw her, his heart thudding so loud in his chest he was sure she would hear.

Elizabeth Hines laughed as she reached back and opened the rear passenger door. A man got out, his denim back to him. He carried a Co-op bag in one hand, a small backpack slung over his shoulder. Laughing together they walked up to the house and went inside.

Joe waited another twenty minutes before moving from his place behind the wall. The police car had driven off after dropping Hines and her guest. The front room light hadn't come on, but the landing light upstairs did, shining through the front window of the guest room.

Making sure there was no one around, Joe dashed across the road and down the side of the house, avoiding the strip of loose gravel he had put down. Hines had said she wanted to start growing stuff – plants and things, he thought. He couldn't remember. He hadn't been listening, just enough to catch what she wanted him to do. Not the why. Enough to score points that would keep her happy. Keep her sweet.

That was weeks ago, and he could see she hadn't done anything with it yet. Typical of her. All grand schemes but no follow through. Just like she had been with him. Just like she had been with all the men in her life. Jumping into bed with a married man, no thought of the consequences.

Well, there were consequences, all right.

He would make sure of it.

He moved slowly down the side of the house, past the door

that led into the kitchen and to the back of the house. The gate was shut, the hedge it was set into, thick and uncut. He tried the handle; it gave and the gate swung open. Making sure no one was looking he slipped inside and shut the gate behind him, being careful not to drop the latch.

The garden was dark, illuminated by a thin strip of light that came from the living room window. The curtains had been drawn against the encroaching night, but a small triangle of space had been left between the two.

Joe crouched and squat-marched to just below the window.

Voices could be heard within. Voices and music. Queen. 'Crazy Little Thing Called Love.' One of her favourites.

He scootched closer. Lifted himself up to steal a glance inside.

There she was. Back to him. His eyes travelled to her arse, tight in the skirt she wore to work. He could feel her in his hands. Feel her spread against him. She was turning the music down.

'What are you doing in there?' she called out.

A man's voice calling back.

'Trying to find your glasses.'

'Check the sink.'

She never washed up.

'Got them!'

She turned round and Joe ducked back, hoping he had fallen into enough shadow that he wouldn't be seen. The garden was dark, no streetlamp light could find this from the road. Only the thin sliver of light from the living room spilled out. He was safe.

For now.

She was taking her shoes off. Falling onto the sofa. Laughing as a man's figure crossed the window, glasses of wine in his hands. Denim jacket. Black Sabbath patch on the cheek pocket of his jeans.

'Wine okay?' he asked.

I know that voice.

'I'd rather have something else,' Hines replied.

He shrugged the jacket off. 'Why, Detective Constable Hines, I am shocked. I don't know what to say.'

'Well, Sergeant Harris. How about you don't say anything and just fuck me?'

'Let me grab the curtains,' the man said. He turned and Joe's blood ran cold.

The blond hair. The denim. The patch.

He knew this man. More importantly, his dad knew this man. And worse, this man, this fucking rat, knew his dad. Was part of his club.

Ben Lewis was Sergeant Harris.

A fucking copper!

CHAPTER
FORTY-ONE

The Chinese meal eaten, Louise and Karla sat on the sofa bathed in the glow from the television. Channel 4's new series, *Traffik*, about the illegal drugs trade, was playing silently, their interest already lost as the length of the day took its toll on them both. It had been Louise who had wanted to watch it, and Louise who had turned the sound down, dragging herself from Karla's embrace to go to the television to do so. On her way back, she grabbed the wine bottle and topped up both their glasses.

Back in her warm embrace, Louise nestled against Karla's shoulder, sipping at her wine and enjoying the feel of Karla's fingers in her hair.

'That feels nice,' she murmured. 'You give the best head scrunchies.'

'Happy to do so, love,' Karla whispered before placing a soft kiss on Louise's head. 'Good call on the Chinese. I'm podged.'

'Me too. Where did you put the fortune cookies?'

'Me? You dished up.'

'And you said, "leave the cookies, I'll bring them when I clear up".'

Karla pointed to the plates on the floor beside them with her wine glass.

'As your honour can see, I haven't taken the plates through yet.'

Louise shifted, sitting up so that she could playfully give Karla a push.

'Hush, muskie. Get me cookies.'

Karla laughed and got up.

'Slave driver.'

'Cookie denier.'

Karla leaned down and they kissed. She bent and picked up the plates.

'What did your last slave die of?'

'Not getting me my damn fortune cookie. Now mush!'

She slapped Karla on the bottom as she headed back to the kitchen.

Louise listened as Karla's footsteps retreated down the corridor to the kitchen and then rose and walked to the window. Looking out onto the funeral parlour opposite she was reminded that, at some point over the next few days, she would be called upon to liaise with the parlour for the funeral of Helen Williams' remains, such that they were.

'Can they actually perform a ceremony for... you know, half a body?'

Louise turned to see Karla standing in the doorway. Tom brushed against her ankle, his large frame snaking between her feet, his purrs loud and throaty. Over the time they had been spending together, Tom had grown to accept scratches and fusses from Karla almost as much as he had done from Louise. She had been strangely jealous of the bond between Karla and Tom; it had been faster in coming than theirs had been, but she was pleased to see they got on.

A nice start to a family. She caught that thought and held it deep down. Soon. But not yet.

'That's a nice smile. What are you thinking about?' Karla said.

Louise shook her question away with a wave and a grasping motion.

'Never mind. Cookie,' Karla laughed, as she stepped over Tom, careful to avoid his large bushy tail, which was almost as thick as one of Karla's coat arms. 'About the body: I've never heard of someone being dismembered in such a way; not even the Ripper did that as far as we know.'

'Sadly, it happens more than you'd think, and it's only getting worse,' Louise replied. This was one of the driving factors behind the CID unit at Prospect Road, the reason she had come back from Manchester.

'I don't know how Pete is going to get through it,' Louise continued, turning back to the window. She drew the blind down just as Tom jumped up, trapping him behind the slats. He yowled for a second then settled down as she raised it just enough that he would be able to slip under.

'He'll get through it,' Karla said. 'Pete, I mean. He has no choice.'

'That's a bit harsh and cold,' Louise said, taking her seat once more.

'The reality of a situation usually is. But it is much better to face that, than bury your head into wild imaginations and fantasies. Which do you want? Red or blue?'

She held out the fortune cookies. Louise gave a soft smile.

'Everything comes down to a choice, doesn't it?'

'Sometimes. Not every time though.'

She threw the two cookies to Louise, who caught them easily. When she pulled two more from her pocket Louise let out a laugh so honest that Karla joined her. 'There's always another option if you look hard enough,' she said.

As they lay in bed, feeling the warmth of their lovemaking slowly turning into sleep, Louise asked a question that had been festering in her mind until the point came where she had to voice it before the notion drove her mad.

'The name Peterson came up again today.'

Karla's reply was muffled against Louise's neck. 'Go to sleep, love.'

'Do you remember the name? Ian Peterson. He was a patient of yours around the time of the Greene case. Suffered from sleep paralysis.'

'He didn't,' Karla murmured.

'Sorry, honey, what did you say? Do you remember him?'

Reluctantly Karla turned away from Louise and wiped at her eyes. She was exhausted and full. Sleep was battling, determined to drag her beneath its warm embrace.

'Ian Peterson. He didn't suffer from sleep paralysis.'

'But I thought he was in the same group therapy as the Greene girl.'

'He was but he had bad dreams, an offshoot of the sleep paralysis and treated very similarly. What has this to do with anything?'

'The name came up again today. Well, his dad did. Harry Peterson. What do you know about him?'

'Can we talk about this tomorrow? Go to sleep, love.'

She rolled over and was snoring a few moments later.

Louise lay in bed, staring at the ceiling and wondering where Harry Peterson fitted into all this until she fell asleep. When she started to moan, Karla rolled back and drew Louise to her until her soft cries drifted away.

Finally, they fell asleep together, watched from the window by Tom until he, too, curled back round and went to sleep.

CHAPTER
FORTY-TWO

His father slept hard. Whether it was from the stress of the last few days, or from the beer he'd consumed, it didn't matter. He slept hard. And dreamed hard dreams.

His body twitched and turned under the sheet, legs kicking out in spasmodic movements, resembling the death throes of the hanged. Their final moments were a torment of pain, desperation and fear as they clutched for one more breath. Just one more, and if they could just kick hard enough, fight hard enough, they would draw in that sweet lungful of air and fight on for a few seconds more.

That was how he looked in the bed, breathing hard and kicking his legs. Like fighting to live for one more second.

What dreams were running through his head, what torments clawed at him?

The sound he made could be mistaken for snoring, but only the calm and the at-ease snored, content with their life and their lot. They went to bed with the day's troubles put aside or, even better, dealt with and now forgotten as easily as the last rainfall. They went to bed happy and free from worry, knowing neither the cold clutches of fear nor the hot embrace of anger that clouded their nights and tainted their dreams.

That was where the sound his father made came from, the depths of his own fear. It dragged itself from his being and rolled around the room, careening off the sparse furnishings; the scratched and splintered wardrobe with its missing door; the vanity table with two of its three mirrors smashed into a spider-webbed nightmare that reflected the room in hundreds of bizarre patterns. The chair where she'd sat and combed her hair and covered the bruises and the cuts. The chest of drawers where he had found his father's diary and discovered part of his horrible truth. The same chest of drawers from where he had sneaked his mother's underwear into his own room, using it to sate his own pleasures.

His father snored again and rolled over to his side.

Ian Peterson stood beside the bed and watched, the knife in his hand reflecting the thin ray of moonlight that stole into the room through the torn curtain.

He stared down at his father and pondered what to do.

She had been stolen from him. Stolen by this man who slept and snored like a troll. She had been his gift to his father, but also a gift to himself. He had shown he could do what needed to be done, had proven himself, and he ached with hate inside that the finality had been stolen from him. The cutting blow.

He had seen his father do it several times now. The first time he had been sick and passed out, coming to with his father standing over him, tied to the table now himself.

'Cut or be cut,' his father had cried into his face, the tears of rage spilling down onto his son's upturned cheeks to mix with the boy's own.

The next time he had stared and not moved, except to help with the bags.

And she should have been his first. She should have been the one.

But this bastard that slept and snored and farted out last night's beer into the skunk of the room had stolen that from him.

What could he take instead?

Ian Peterson lifted the knife and tested the blade with his thumb, wincing ever so slightly as a red line was opened along his flesh and blood began to run.

Oh, what indeed...

CHAPTER
FORTY-THREE

It was late but the Wadees were still up.

Bilal and Raja sat on cushioned seats at the table, their parents clattering still in the kitchen.

'We should go home,' Bilal said.

He tensed when he spoke, being careful to talk only in short bursts, as his jaw was still mending. The painkillers helped; they had made sure they were not haram before accepting them, and, satisfied by Doctor Kavel's reassurance, Bilal had taken the maximum possible without being dangerous. Kavel had said many other things during their stay. Things that sounded right to ears still ringing from the blows of uneducated thugs.

'We should stay until we are well again,' his brother replied.

His face had recovered some, the swelling having subsided. He still wore the eye-patch, though, he was starting to see a little now, mainly just a coloured blur.

'Why rush things? Let us enjoy Mother's cooking.'

As if in answer something hissed and spat in the kitchen, followed by their father's triumphant cry.

'I guess he didn't burn the rice this time!' Bilal called out with a laugh. He immediately regretted it as a jolt of pain ran through his jaw and down his neck.

Hearing his father laugh back in response was worth the pain.

'Idiot,' Raja said.

'Moron,' Bilal replied.

He reached into his pocket and pulled out a sheet of paper, which he passed to his brother.

'We should go.'

Raja took the note and unfurled it. Green writing in a cursive hand. Simple. To the point.

Saturday 24th
Rally Against Cultural Extremists
2PM – Dewsbury Market Place

'For what reason should we go?' Raja said, dropping the note to the table. 'This is a bad thing to do. There will be many of them there and it will only turn violent. I do not wish to be part of that violence.'

'We are already part of it,' Bilal replied angrily. He ignored the pain flaring in his jaw. Some things were more important than pain. 'We are already in it, victims of hate.'

'And yet you wish to use your hate to fight. Bilal… brother, that is wrong. We don't win by becoming like them.'

'We are nothing like them!' Bilal shouted, slamming his fist on the table.

Raja did not flinch but his parents came running from the kitchen.

'What is all this noise?' Vanita said. 'You will disturb Ms Miller upstairs.'

Danesh, still wearing his suit jacket and trousers, stood in the doorway of the kitchen stirring a pot of beef stew. He locked eyes with his sons in turn.

'You wish to go to the rally.' It was not a question. Bilal nodded. 'And do what?'

The question was simple. The answer, far from. Bilal hesitated. It was Raja who answered for him.

'He wants to fight. He wants revenge.'

'A natural thing,' his father replied, 'but foolish and wrong.'

'They attacked us! They hurt us, nearly cost Raja his eye and me my jaw. They come into the shops and they call us names, throw their money on the floor so they don't have to touch us. They complain about our clothes, our food. Our very existence, and they hurt our children by protesting outside the schools with their banners and their vulgarities.'

'And what will this accomplish?' Danesh spoke softly to counter the heat of his son's words. Vanita went back into the kitchen to finish the late evening meal.

'It will show them that we are not afraid of them,' Bilal said. He looked over at his brother, who nodded back. 'We should not be afraid of them.'

'Then we shall go. All of us together. To show them we are not afraid.'

Bilal went to smile but thought better of it. Raja caught the gesture and laughed.

'Do not smile, brother, in case your face falls off.'

Bilal couldn't help but laugh, and when he did there was no pain.

CHAPTER
FORTY-FOUR

FRIDAY, 23RD

Louise sat at the window, a cup of tea in her hands as she stared out into the rain. It was just after five in the morning and Tom had woken her early to be let out. Wincing at the cold, she had gone downstairs, the cat thumping softly behind her. Opening the door, they were both met by a swirling gust of rain and cold wind that blew in, making Louise gasp in surprise and Tom scoot back up the stairs. So intent was she on getting back into the warmth, she didn't laugh when Tom missed the top step and thumped onto the one below. He gave a plaintive yowl, then disappeared into the bathroom where his litter tray was. If he could have slammed the door behind him, she was sure he would have done.

She had tea ready for herself, and a bowl of tuna chunks for Tom, by the time he came out. Seeing the bowl, his purrs went into overdrive, and he munched softly while she looked out into the rain-covered day and thought about the rally tomorrow. That was the pressing case now; Helen Williams and Mary King would have to wait, if only for a day.

Beside her, on the small table where she would sometimes sit and read, was her uniform. Tomorrow she would be in full parade best, complete with chequered hat and cravat, just another WPC amongst many. She had been assigned to one of the cordons, her role to check people who wanted to go inside to the rally itself.

Word had come down that a counter-protest was being organised, totally unofficial and unauthorised. Louise hoped it wasn't true, because that would immediately put another line of tension into an already taught situation. She knew why the Muslim community wanted to protest against the BNP; hell, if she could, she'd be in the rally herself. Would even carry a sign or shout through a bullhorn. Anything to get rid of such a hate-mongering group. There was no place in modern society for such a thing. *Just as there's no place for anti-feminist views*, she thought with a sad laugh.

There would be a time when this sort of thing was relegated to the distant past. She only hoped that time would be soon.

A rumble of thunder drew her attention, and she was just in time to see lightning crackle off in the distance.

'Looks like it's over Huddersfield,' Karla said from behind her. She came into the room, pulling her jacket on. Her briefcase sat by the door, being carefully investigated by Tom to see if it could be eaten in any way. He gave it another sniff then wandered down the corridor to the bedroom and a much-needed sleep.

'You're leaving early?'

'I have an early meeting at Wakefield Prison. A parole hearing and I have to give a psychological review. If it was up to me, the bastard would just be hanged and have it all over and done with. But we live in a society that believes in rehabilitation.'

'As do you. Everyone gets a second chance with you, which is lucky, otherwise we wouldn't be here right now.'

Karla smiled and picked up her briefcase. 'Meet for lunch?'

Louise shook her head.

'It's going to be a busy day. We're getting everything in place for tomorrow so I'm not sure how late I'm going to be.'

'I guess going to the pictures is out then.'

It wasn't a question, and Louise could hear the disappointment in her voice.

'I'm sorry,' she said. 'See what I mean about second chances?'

'More like third and fourth now. Give me a kiss, I need to get going.'

Louise watched her leave from the window, giving her a wave as she drove off. Her reply was a quick blast of the car horn and then she was gone.

Elizabeth Hines answered the door with a bath towel wrapped around her head and another about her body. Seeing the look of shock on her face, Louise was instantly wary.

'Morning,' she said cautiously. 'Running late, are we?'

'I'm on light duty today in preparation for tomorrow.'

'Manby signed off then on you getting a little more involved, did he? Come on, let me in. It's chill as a grave out here and the rain's on the way.'

Hines threw a quick, glance back into the house.

'Or am I intruding on something?'

'No. Of course not,' Hines said, taking a step to the side. 'Come in. Fancy a cuppa?'

'I'd kill for one.'

Hines pointed Louise to the kitchen then disappeared back upstairs. As she busied herself with the cups, Louise could hear whispered voices from the room above, followed by the heavy tread of someone on the stairs. Definitely not Hines. A small ripple of disappointment rattled its way through Louise at the thought of Hines throwing herself into another meaningless encounter so swiftly after everything that had happened with Joe.

When the door to the living room opened, she expected to be

confronted with yet another nameless alcohol-fuelled conquest. What she didn't expect to see was a half-naked Sergeant Benjamin Harris, barefoot, dressed in jeans and nothing else.

'Good morning, Detective Constable,' he said as he tousled his hair, still wet from the shower. 'Could you make me a coffee or at least leave me a little water? Thanks.'

Louise stared open mouthed as he walked across the room, taking his shirt from the back of the sofa.

'What the hell is this?' she said, all thoughts of making a brew gone. 'What are you doing here? Although that looks pretty obvious.'

'Oh, it's not like that,' Harris laughed, pulling on his shirt. 'I came round to discuss tactics for tomorrow and it got late. I just stayed over in the spare room.'

'Yeah, right.'

'Seriously. Nothing more going on here than two colleagues working together.'

Footsteps came bounding down the stairs as Hines called out, 'Where's my little love-cannon?'

She came into the living room and Louise's caustic reply died on her lips as she stared at the purple-haired woman dressed in an Iron Maiden t-shirt, long black, pleated skirt and black Doc Martens boots. Several earrings hung down; two crosses and a pentagram.

'Is that a nose ring?' Louise asked.

Hines laughed and pulled it out.

'It's a half ring. Fake, like the earrings as well. Though I do like this one,' she said, giving the pentagram a playful twist. 'What do you think?'

She stood in the centre of the room and gave a turn.

'You certainly look the part,' Louise said, her head spinning. 'What's going on?'

Harris, now fully dressed, took a seat.

'Going into the crowd tomorrow, my job is to keep an eye on three of Tommy's main thugs. They've been tasked with starting a fight at some point during the rally. They'll be taking their girl-friends along as well, and they usually get wind of when the shit's about to start. Having Beth tag along as my girlfriend, she can get the nod to us before anything happens and we can shut it all down a lot faster than waiting for it to kick off. Safer for everyone.'

'And Manby signed off on this?' This sounded a lot more dangerous than Louise had expected. Wandering through a crowd was one thing; getting up close and personal with these thugs was something altogether different, and Louise said as much.

'I'm not going to say that there isn't a risk,' Harris said as he pulled on his boots, 'but that's a part of the job, and, from what I've seen, and been at the end of, Beth can take care of herself.'

'You have no idea what Hines can or can't handle,' Louise said. 'She may talk tough but you may have noticed she can also get hurt, or did you think those bruises were from overzealous bedroom play?'

She gave him a look that suggested she knew *exactly* what they had been up to.

'Hello,' Hines said from the corner of the room. 'Do I have a say in any of this?'

'If I had my way, you wouldn't,' Louise replied. 'Do you not see how dangerous this is?'

Hines stood her ground. In the flowing skirt, t-shirt and jewellery, she certainly looked the part. She sounded the part, acted the part as well. Louise knew she was strong; she had borne witness to countless times when Hines had been confronted, both physically and mentally, and each and every time she had come through it. Not always unscathed, true, but she was stronger for each experience.

They both were.

Hines said nothing. Just stared at Louise, defying her to speak.

The whistle of the kettle broke through the tension, a half-time reprieve.

'I'll make a brew,' Hines said. 'You two sort this out. Coffee, Ben?'

'Please. White. No sugar.' He looked at Louise. 'It's the best option we have,' he said, 'and I'm going to be right there as well so it's not as though she's going to be alone.'

Louise sat. She knew he was right; they both were. That didn't mean she had to like it. She was going to be stuck on the side-lines, little more than a glorified attendant, taking names and marking people off against a checklist of known agitators.

Hines came back carrying three mugs. She passed one to Harris, the other to Louise.

'So that's all settled then,' she said. 'I'm looking forward to it, if I'm being honest. Didn't you do some undercover work back in Manchester?'

Louise nodded but didn't say anything. Her time working the Hulme estate, as a rookie police constable, both in uniform and undercover, had been a trial by fire, one she was better off leaving where it belonged: in her past. She had learned a lot, but lost even more. There were nights when she still heard the screams. When the scent of burning flesh filled her nostrils, as much a ghost of the past as the names Denise, Charlie and Becky were. She still saw their faces from time to time, hanging in front of her, fading in and out, as insubstantial as the breaking of a storm's clouds.

And what a storm it had been…

If she could help Hines avoid even a fraction of that kind of pain, she would.

'So, it sounds like everything is covered then?' Louise said instead, changing the subject.

Everyone knew what Hines was doing, and chose to accept it and move on. There was nothing to be gained in arguing.

'Did you speak with Pete?' Hines asked.

For the next ten minutes, Louise filled Hines in on what had happened with Pete Williams, finding him at home and getting him to the hospital.

'He mentioned a name, someone who goes to the Walton Arms and knew both Helen and the other victim, Mary. Peterson.'

Harris sat forward; his coffee forgotten.

'Peterson? Harry Peterson?' Louise nodded. 'He works at Sanderson's garage as a mechanic and tow truck driver. Bit of a weird guy. Apparently his wife ran off a few years ago, and if you believe the stories, he had her done in when he found her cheating on him.'

Hines now leaned forward. 'He has a son, right?'

Louise nodded. She had first been made aware of Ian Peterson during the Greene case, and then again only last year as he was caught up in the apparent suicide of his friend James Willikar.

Daniel McKensie's words came back in a ghostly whisper: *Last I saw her she was talking with the tall kid.*

The one with the buzz-cut.

CHAPTER
FORTY-FIVE

Louise left Hines with Harris as they prepared for their incursion into the BNP rally. No matter what she might think, Hines could handle herself, and it was a pretty good plan. Staying out of sight was a good idea, too, and she was glad that there was nothing going on between them; the sexual banter she had heard was them getting into character as boy and girlfriend. With everything still very complicated when it came to her relationship with Joe, the last thing Beth needed was to be dragged into another high-tension affair.

At the station she busied herself with paperwork, completing several reports she had been putting off over the past week while she looked into Helen's disappearance. Now that she had time, though, all she could think about was the constant reappearance of the Peterson name. It tickled at her the way a cough sometimes tickled the throat, a determined presence lurking at the back, in the shadows. Waiting. Waiting for the right moment to strike.

Like Peterson, perhaps?

She shook that away. Conjecture, supposition. No facts. No evidence. Just coincidence.

Just coincidence.

She didn't believe in coincidence, just like she didn't believe in God. Harry Peterson knew both Helen Williams and Mary King. The Peterson boy had been close to James Willikar and knew Joanna Greene. People close to the Petersons seemed to have an awful habit of winding up dead. Or missing. The wife had left them.

And the father worked at the Sanderson garage, the same one that the thugs who beat up the Wadees worked at.

Now was that coincidence?

Eventually all the paperwork was completed. The smashed windows of Charleston Street (the Bromsgrove kids); three charges of shoplifting and two of verbal assault. Details filled in; statements taken. Finally. The smashed windows were from five weeks ago, the oldest of the shoplifting nearly a year. Too long. Much too long, but priorities had to be made, choices taken.

Just like with Helen. Not a priority, just another missing prostitute. Their words, not hers.

But Helen knew Mary, and Mary worked Savile Town and the Walton Arms. Then there was the physical assault on the Wadee brothers and their stolen car. All of it emanating from the Walton Arms, the same pub that was homebase to the damn BNP in the region.

The Walton Arms.

Run by Tommy Everad. *Owned and paid for by whom?*

More questions than answers.

Tommy Everad. Father of Joe, who used his fists on his girlfriend in an escalating series of domestic disputes. Like son, like father? Could he be the one responsible for Helen? For Mary?

Things were starting to coalesce, to draw together, but, like trying to catch snowflakes, they were all melting through her fingers.

From upstairs came the voices of the officers gathered for the first wave of cordons that were being set up tonight in Dewsbury centre. They had been up there all the time she was working on the reports, coming down only to grab a quick bite to eat. Only now did Louise realise she had worked through lunch. Her stomach growled in response.

Looking at the clock, she saw it was just past five. Where had the day gone?

When her gaze hit the white tower of paperwork, there was her answer.

She was just tidying away the last scraps of notes and folders when Manby entered the pen. He had spent the day with Chief Superintendent Freeman, finalising all the details for tomorrow's operation, and he looked as haggard as she felt.

'Fancy a pint?' he said, reclaiming his jacket from the hook just inside his office door.

'I'm meeting Karla at the Tapps if you'd like to tag along?'

As they walked down Prospect Road to the pub, the rain from earlier in the day tried to make a comeback, spotting the pavement. The sky was already darkening with clouds overhead.

'Fingers crossed it pisses it down tomorrow and the whole damn thing gets cancelled,' Manby said, pulling his collar up against the chilly air.

'I doubt they'd cancel,' Louise replied.

She knew how stubborn these sorts of groups could be. Determined and arrogant, they would happily stand in the pouring rain and catch a cold and fever, just as long as they were able to make their stand against whatever false slight they felt had been dealt against them. This was no different to the riots that took place in Moss Side in Manchester, back in eighty-one. Right after she had joined the force and in her first months of training. Racial tensions had flared up, fuelled by mass unemployment in the area.

Louise could see the same happening here; same fire, just a

different kindle. It hadn't helped that the police in Manchester were accused of aggravating the situation by clamping down hard on the black youths, using excessive force when they were sent in to quell a gathering that was quickly getting out of hand.

'Hopefully things won't be too bad,' she mused.

'We can but hope,' Manby said, opening the door to the pub.

As usual the inside of the Tapps was warm and inviting, the fire crackling in its hearth and soft jazz playing on the speakers, at a level where conversation could still be had without having to lean in and shout directly into the listener's ear.

Karla was already at a table and she waved them over. She rose and gave Manby a kiss when he approached.

'It's so good to see you again, Bill,' she said. 'Let me get you a drink.'

'I'll get it,' Louise said. 'Same again,' she added, pointing to the near empty glass of wine.

'I got here early,' Karla explained with a smile. 'Please, Bill. Sit.'

Shrugging off his coat, Manby took a seat opposite.

'How are you doing?' he asked.

'I'm good. Better now the day is over, but, I'll be honest, I'm not looking forward to tomorrow.'

Manby nodded gravely.

'The rally. Same here. I've spent way too much time dealing with this, and the sooner this is over, the better.'

'Why on earth did they grant them a licence to hold a racist rally right in the centre of Dewsbury? It's beyond explanation.'

Louise arrived bearing drinks for all. Glasses placed, she put the tray on the next table and sat beside Karla.

'Do I get a kiss?' she asked, 'or is it just my boss that gets one?'

They kissed. Manby smiled.

'What?' Louise said, taking her glass of wine. 'Do we embarrass you?'

Manby shook his head.

'Not in the slightest, love. I think it's nice.'

'You old perv,' Karla laughed, then reached out to briefly touch his hand when she saw his cheeks reddening.

'I'm joking.'

'That wasn't what I meant, but fair play,' he said with a grin of his own. 'No, what I mean is, it's nice you can, well, you can be yourself. Be open.'

'If it's good enough for Freddie Mercury, it's good enough for us,' Karla said.

'Fuck off. Freddie Mercury isn't gay.'

Louise and Karla shared a look.

'He's the flamboyant lead singer of a band called Queen.'

'I know. I like Queen. Bohemian Rhapsody. Flash. Now that's a movie. Flash fucking Gordon. No way the man that sang that is gay. No way.'

'You know that liking music by a gay man does not make you gay, right? It doesn't work like that.'

'He's not gay,' Manby insisted. 'Anyway, we're getting off the point. I was just saying that it's good to see you not hiding.'

'This is a good place,' Karla said, indicating the pub around them. 'Good place. Good people. Not everywhere is the same. We couldn't sit like this in, say, The Horse and Jockey.'

'Jesus Christ. Fuck no. You'd get your head kicked in. Or worse. In fact, a few years ago, we had a young lad beaten half to death. Now no one said it was because he was gay, but he was and that was exactly why what happened, happened.'

'And I bet nothing got done about it, right?'

Manby shrugged.

'It was just another fight in another pub. It wasn't...'

'A priority, I know. We say that way too much,' Louise said. 'But a hate crime is a hate crime. Doesn't matter if it's to do with a person's sexuality or the colour of their skin. Hate is hate.

That's why I can't understand why we're letting this damn rally take place. All we're doing is giving them space to voice their hateful speech.'

'Which they have a legal right to do. If they follow the law, and so far, they've crossed all the 't's and dotted all the 'i's. We just hope they fuck up in some way.'

'Them fucking up means someone's getting hurt,' Louise said.

Karla put a calming hand on Louise's arm.

'Now, not necessarily. They could come out and say something that is prohibited by the law.'

'That's right, and that's what we're thinking is going to happen,' Manby said. He took a long sip of his drink and wiped foam from his moustache. 'Word is that Tommy Everad is going to speak, and there's no way that clown of a man can stop himself when he gets worked up.'

Karla nodded along.

'Yes, if he gets up and starts calling for Muslims to be attacked, or angry protests to be held outside schools or something like that, then he can be arrested. Inciting violence is still a crime, especially when done in a public forum.'

'So that's why this is going ahead?' Louise asked.

Manby shrugged.

'Yes and no. Yes in the fact that once we learned it was happening, that was the plan that was fashioned. No in the fact that palms were obviously greased here and relationships taken advantage of.'

'Sanderson.'

'Can't prove anything untoward happened, but it's a little odd how quickly it was put together, and with the authorisation given by Freeman.'

Conversation fell away, and the three sat quietly for a few moments, Louise sipping at her wine. Tommy Everad headed the BNP and wanted a rally in Dewsbury. Some of his people worked for Sanderson. Sanderson arranged for the rally to take place. Was Sanderson a member of the BNP as well? Harris was working there, so he should know. Also working there was Harry Peterson. How was he caught up in all this?

More questions to be answered.

With all these thoughts swirling around in her head, Louise took another drink and tried to figure it all out.

CHAPTER
FORTY-SIX

The Walton Arms was packed. Music played loudly and the rumble of conversation was a steady bass line beneath it. Nearly everyone in the pub was wearing a BNP patch. Some carried signs that had been scrawled onto big sheets of cardboard: PAKIS GO HOME. OUR COUNTRY. WHITE IS RIGHT. Nearly a dozen of them had been stacked on the table and more were being added to with each new arrival.

Colin Sanderson drained his pint, slammed the glass down on the table and let out a belch that ran on forever, culminating in a chorus of laughter and applause from the crowd gathered around the table. At the head, Tommy Everad laughed harder than everyone else.

'Good to see our friend Mr Tallingate was able to sort everyone out. To Mr Tallingate!'

He raised his glass, and those around him did likewise. Sanderson smiled and banged his fist on the table, his glass empty.

Out of the corner of his eye, Tommy could see his son Joe over in the corner at the far end of the bar. He was talking to the barmaid; she was laughing at something he had said. Turning, he caught his dad's eye and beckoned him over.

'Get this man a drink,' Tommy said, indicating Sanderson's empty glass. 'I'll be back in a moment.'

He walked through the pub, greeting those members he hadn't said hello to yet. They had arranged for all the members to arrive by 9p.m., when Tommy would give a quick speech about tomorrow's event and outline what was expected of everyone. Hands clapped him on the shoulder or reached out for a handshake, which he took warmly and willingly. Tommy had taken control of this chapter of the BNP and raised it from the scraps of its beginning into what was now rightly feared as one of the most influential in the area.

Hadn't it been members of his group that had brought attention to the dire need for white values to be restored in their schools, first by protesting at parents' evenings, and then by more direct action? Pulling the kids out of the schools had sent a warning to the governing boards that they couldn't be denied their white rights. That they were watering down white culture in the region by including all these third world cultures. Cultures... ha! They weren't even that. They barely had running water where they were from, no wonder they didn't want to go back. Here they stole all the jobs from the white man, sucked up all the dole when they lied about not having work and then had the audacity to drive around in cars that the true citizens of Britain should be driving. Well, they had shown them, hadn't they? They'd stolen a few back. Cut them up and sold them on.

It was a grand relationship with Sanderson, one that his son had suggested, and one that had borne such great fruit. Money, reputation, and contacts. Looking at Joe now though, he could see there was something wrong. Something was troubling him, despite the flirty stares and laughs exchanged with the barmaid, Kelly.

'What's up, lad?' Tommy said, coming to stand beside his son. 'Still smarting from the beating you got? Kelly, love. Lads at the end need a topping off.' Kelly nodded and walked off.

When Tommy had heard what had happened at the Carps,

his first impulse was to strike his son. Letting someone beat you like that, let alone an old copper, was bad for his reputation. Not Joe's; his. Couldn't be having that, so another lesson was taught. He had originally sent Joe to Ossett in the hopes he would be able to start a new chapter of the club over there in the Carps, but that had proven impossible. Dominic, who owned the place, was a staunch supporter of the Pakis and any talk that threatened that was put down quickly. Another lesson learned the hard way.

'It's Beth,' Joe said.

'There's no need for any further contact with that bitch of a copper,' Tommy said, leaning in. 'You let it get too far as it was, soft lad. In and out, that's the way it was supposed to go. Get some insight into what they were doing, and a bit of gash at the same time. Not go all love-eyed and limp dicked over her.'

'She's working with another copper.'

Tommy laughed. 'Well, that's no big fucking surprise, is it?'

'It's Ben,' Joe said, with no small amount of perverse satisfaction. 'Your little pet project.'

Tommy's laugh died instantly. He stared hard at his son as this information worked its way through his head.

'All right.'

He gestured for Kelly to come over. When she did he leaned in and spoke directly into her ear. Joe watched and said nothing. Tommy finished speaking and leaned back.

'You got that?' She nodded. 'Good girl. Come on, Joe. We're off upstairs.'

The top floor of the pub had been turned into living quarters. Five rooms: two bedrooms, a kitchen, a bathroom and the room Tommy and Joe Everad now sat in. Just big enough for a desk and three chairs, it was where Tommy did all the paperwork needed for running both a pub and a chapter of the British National Party. The chapter's flag hung on the wall, along with a Metallica poster and a collection of Page Three beauties from the

Sun. Their vacant smiles and pert breasts stared down on the two men, who sat opposite each other.

Tommy poured them both a whisky.

'Are you sure?'

'I saw them both together last night, Dad,' Joe replied.

He felt the flush of anger again at seeing them, laughing and joking. Touching each other. He knew she was a slag, putting it about as much as she did. She'd fucked that other copper, Danes, so why wouldn't she fuck the new lad on the team?

How had they not seen it?

'Are you sure he's a copper? He could have just been dicking her.'

'She called him Sergeant Harris.'

'Fucking bastard! A fucking pig in our pub. In my fucking pub, sneaking his fucking snout into my business. Club business. Fucking bastard!' Tommy said again, slamming his fists against the wall and ripping the faded three-year-old picture of Samantha Fox.

'You think they're planning something for tomorrow?' Joe asked, pouring them both another drink. His father's face was red with anger.

'Of course they're fucking doing something!'

He snatched the drink from his son and drained it, then threw the glass against the wall with a feral scream that made Joe jump. Glass fragments scattered all over the desk.

'But we're going to do something first,' he said, wiping snot from his face. 'You got a picture?'

Joe nodded. He had taken a couple of Polaroids.

A knock at the door sounded. Tommy opened the door.

'Glad you could make it. We've got a pig problem. Fancy making a few hundred quid?' The man nodded. 'Good. Joe. Give him the photos.' Joe did.

The man looked at them.

'That's Ben.'

'He's a fucking copper.'

No reaction.

'And her? I've seen her before. Not with that hair though.'

'Consider her a bonus. She's a pig as well. Find them tomorrow and get rid of them. Will that be a problem?'

Harry Peterson looked at the photo of Elizabeth Hines with her shock of purple hair and felt an excited tingle run through his body from prick to heart.

'No problem at all.'

CHAPTER
FORTY-SEVEN

SATURDAY, 24TH

The threatened rainstorm had passed, leaving the day to start cloudy but dry. Dewsbury town centre was normally busy on a Saturday afternoon, with shoppers making their way to the open market just beyond the Town Hall. Today, however, their way was hampered. Police tape and barriers had been erected along all the in-roads to the centre of town, leaving the market stalls quiet, their owners angry.

Louise stood at the far cordon, opposite the swimming baths. Four metal barriers had been placed across the road, preventing access, and tape, strung from each end barrier to a lamppost to stop pedestrians walking in. With nine other officers placed along the cordon, they had so far stopped a couple of dozen people. None had been wanting to join the rally; they all wanted to go to the market and were frustrated that they would now have to walk all the way around the back of the Town Hall to get there.

Music danced in the air, a pulsing beat that vibrated through the street. Even this distance away, Louise could hear words in the music but couldn't make them out. Part of her didn't want to; she knew they would be filled with anger and hate. She had seen the people as they made their way into the rally area, and she was stunned to see they didn't look like monsters. They didn't have horns; their feet weren't cloven hooves. They didn't breathe fire and they had the right number of arms, legs and heads.

They looked like her. Like Karla. Like Aunt Fiona and Uncle Bernard. Like DI Manby, and Danes. Like Scruffy Pete. They looked like her neighbours.

They weren't monsters. They didn't speak with forked tongues, but she still didn't understand their language, would never, *could* ever, understand them.

She looked at the line of people waiting to be let in; some carried signs, some wore the patch of the BNP. She thought of Hines, dressed in her black leather skirt and jacket. A tasty treat for the eye and the arm. Ben's latest conquest. Would it work? Would they see through the disguise? And what would this really accomplish anyway? Here she was doing line duty when Hines was in the thick of it, trying once again to prove she could hold her own.

Louise could feel the frustration growing and she threw a look back to the rally itself, hoping to get a glimpse. All she could see was a steadily growing crowd, their faces merging into one blank wall of white.

Ridiculous.

'Never ending, isn't it?' The officer to her right gave her a smile. 'Only a couple of hours to go, love, but I hope your shoes are a lot more comfortable than they look.'

Until now they had been. Now she could feel the cobbled stone of the street beneath them. Sighing, she lifted her clipboard and turned to the next person in line.

'Name?'

. . .

The stage was set. The music playing. Trestle tables had been put up in front of the small stage, by three black leather jacketed men, each bearing the crossed sword motif of the Walton Arms BNP chapter on their backs. Leaflets were arrayed across the tables, the men handing them out to all who approached. Two collection tins were chained to the tables, loosely enough for them to be held out to passers-by. They rattled heavily.

The crowd numbered over two hundred by this point, spread throughout the area provided for them, with space for more. Tommy Everad stood on the stage, waiting for his time to speak, and looked out into the crowd. He was pleased with what he saw. Some he recognised, most he didn't. Some would be ones who had tricked their way inside to try and disrupt their legal right to protest. Some would be ones who wanted to hear what they had to say.

And some were his own, scattered throughout the crowd to ensure its continuance. Just in case.

He smiled.

Just in case.

It wasn't usual for Hines to wear a leather skirt and she was regretting choosing it. Jeans would have been so much better. She carried a small backpack with her radio, truncheon and a few other items over her right shoulder, her hand jammed into the pocket of her jacket. Her other hand held Harris', their fingers interlaced as they walked through the crowd.

As well as the literature tables, the group had also set up stalls selling food and drink, and the mixed smells of hot dogs, onions and frying chips made Hines' mouth water.

'Fancy something to eat?' she asked, giving Harris' hand a squeeze. 'I'm hungry.'

'How can that be? You had a full fried breakfast this morning before we set out. And half of mine too.'

'Come on, lover boy,' she said, nuzzling into his shoulder. 'Get your lady some food.'

Harris leaned in as though to kiss her cheek.

'You're certainly playing your part,' he whispered. 'I've seen three of the ones Tommy uses to kick things off. No, don't look. They're just by the stage right now. I expect a few more are scattered in the crowd itself, but they won't have anything that shows they're part of the BNP. Those ones will be later made out to be "outsiders" trying to cause a riot.'

He finished by kissing her neck. Hines felt the shiver run through her body and hoped he hadn't noticed.

They headed towards the food stand.

'After this, we'll go to the stage where the others are. I'll leave you with the other girlfriends…'

'I'm your girlfriend, am I?' Hines teased.

Harris ignored her, but he did give her a playful nudge.

'I'll leave you with them, so you can find out if anything is going to kick off. I'll be doing the same.' He turned to the man behind the food table. 'Two dogs. One chips, please.'

'Ay up, Ben. How's things? Not a bad turn out, is it?'

'Looks good. Got you slaving away again, have they? This is Simon,' Harris said to Hines. 'Anytime we get our lot together, this bastard comes out and feeds us. Not bad grub either. How's the kids?'

The man ladled onions over the hot dogs, then without asking squirted tomato sauce over both.

'Fucking annoying as always. Wife's got them at the baths.'

'Not here with you?'

Simon leaned forward, handing the hot dogs over. Into a paper cone that would look better on Blackpool beach than a Yorkshire marketplace, he scooped chips.

'Best not to be here,' he said with a wink. 'Just in case.'

Harris took a bite of his hot dog. Sauce ran on his chin and Hines reached up and wiped it away with her finger. She put it in her mouth and sucked it clean, her eyes on Harris. When he started to cough, she let out a laugh, then took a bite of her own.

'Fiery one there, Ben,' Simon said. 'Better looking than the last one.'

Hines gave a curtsey and turned to walk away. Simon leaned in.

'Word is it'll be on fairly quick. Some Pakis are trying to do a counter-protest. Watch yourself.'

Harris reached up and shook the man's hand.

'You too, fella.'

He caught up to Hines, who was standing just by a large planter. Nothing grew inside; the soil was littered with dead fags, food wrappers and crushed beer cans.

'Seems a pleasant chap,' she said. 'Not a bad cook either.'

'The man's an arsehole. Beats his wife each week at least once, then brags about it. Rumour is his kids aren't his, but if he's at an event, good chance it will kick off, and he's all but confirmed that. Ready to go be with the others?'

Hines nodded.

'And if it looks like it's kicking off, I'll give you the warning wave.'

'Or in dire circumstances use the radio. Let's hope it doesn't come to that.'

Hines bit through her hot dog, onions dripping onto her t-shirt. She wiped them away, leaving a smear of tomato sauce across the white lettering.

'I honestly doubt they're going to do anything more than beat their chests and scream obscenities at each other. It's pretty sad, truth be told.'

'And dangerous. So, watch yourself.'

'You watch me,' Hines said, dropping the sauce-smeared napkin onto the ground. 'Who's this, lover boy?'

They were at the pamphlet desks where a thickset man in all leather stood handing out the literature. His beard was thick and bushy, his glasses mirrored. He wore a bandana around his head, tied and hanging down his back. 'You got another skirt, Lewis?' the man barked. 'Man, you must be hung like a horse.'

Hines grabbed Harris' crotch.

'You better believe it, and it's all mine now, right, baby?'

'Later, Sweetstuff,' Harris said, removing her hand and giving her a stern look. 'Hey, Dan. where's the ladies? I gotta drop this temptress off and then catch up with the boss.'

'They're over there,' the man said.

He pointed to an area just to the left of the main stage. A group of six women, all dressed in either leather or denim, stood in a small circle. Each had a drink and most were smoking. One held a sign saying WHITE POWER.

'You go to the girls,' Harris said. 'I got business to attend to.'

She reached up on her tiptoes and gave Harris a huge, wet kiss.

'Don't be too long,' she said. 'I get lonely. Catch you later, handsome,' she added, giving Dan a wink.

With that. she wandered over to the other women and got chatting with a tall blonde almost immediately.

'Where did you get that firecracker?' Dan asked. 'And does she have a sister?'

'One of a kind,' Harris laughed, giving Hines a lingering look. He turned back to Dan. 'Where's Tommy?'

'He's just about to go on. He's been asking for you. This way.'

With one last look at Hines, Harris followed the man to the back of the stage.

There she was. With the rat. Easy to spot with the purple hair, talking to that tall bitch with the long legs and blonde hair. Any other day he could have had her instead, but he'd been given a task and he was determined to carry it out.

Get rid of her. Simple enough. No questions asked. He'd done it before. Would do it again.

He just had to wait for the right moment.

Luckily for him, he was patient.

Practice makes perfect.

Keeping her within his eyeline, he moved closer.

Tommy Everad took to the stage. A microphone had been set up and it whistled with feedback when he first started talking, the crowd jeering until it settled and they could hear him speak.

He spoke with an arrogant confidence, borne of a deep, dark hate that ringed his every word.

'Friends. We have gathered here today to celebrate our white power. Thank you all for coming!'

Cheers rang out.

Louise's blood ran cold as she listened to them. No one else was being let through the outer cordon now, but she noticed that the number of people standing just beyond the barriers was growing in number.

A ripple of concern crackled on the radio from another cordon, noting a similar growth in numbers.

Behind her, Tommy continued speaking, his voice carrying cleanly.

'We have all seen it recently. The way our schools are contaminating the supreme white culture by including so many children of other races, most notably the Pakistani.'

More cheers. He let them continue for a moment before carrying on.

'But it is not only our schools under attack. Have you noticed the jobs are disappearing? First the mines, then the mills. Even the shops that once were proud to display our British heritage, even now they are being overrun. And is this right?'

A chorus of 'No!' rang out from the crowd.

'Is this right?' he yelled again, the microphone once again exploding with feedback, quickly drowned out by the crowd's heated reply.

'What is right?'

'WHITE IS RIGHT!' came the reply, fuelled by the BNP members dotted throughout.

Standing behind the stage, Harris watched as Tommy whipped the crowd into higher levels of frenzy, getting the chant going. 'WHITE IS RIGHT! WHITE IS RIGHT!'

'Getting 'em going, isn't he?' Dan said beside him.

Harris nodded. Another member from the pub had come to join them; a third stood just behind them all. Something itched at the back of Harris' mind, but before he could do anything he was struck on the side of his face by an almighty punch. His head rocked to the side and he fell into the grasping arms of Dan.

'You fucking pig!' Dan said, before slamming a headbutt into the startled officer. Black stars exploded in his vision and everything became a helter skelter of colours and sounds.

One thought ran through Harris' mind as he struggled to remain conscious.

Beth!

The women were clustered together, arms raised into the air and chanting along with the rest of the crowd. Hines stood with them, feeling the electric surge of the crowd. She had been to several concerts, and this was a similar feeling, a shared experience, a shared mindset that everyone somehow tapped into.

Banners were being waved; fists pumped into the air. From somewhere within the crowd a bottle was thrown across the dividing barrier to smash against the window of the Yorkshire Bank. Luckily the window didn't break, but the bottle shattered into a million pieces. The crowd cheered.

Bodies started to surge then, to ripple like a human wave. It started somewhere over towards the swimming baths. That was where Louise had been stationed. Panic began to rise in Hines and she looked through the crowd to the stage, hoping to catch a glimpse of Harris. All she could see was Tommy Everad on the stage, arms raised, still chanting into the microphone.

'Time to go,' one of the women said. She threw her cigarette down on the ground and stomped it beneath her high heel. Hines was about to follow when she felt a hand grip her elbow.

She turned to stare into the face of a man she faintly recognised but couldn't place.

'You've to come with me,' he said.

The other women were walking away, totally ignoring this man. His breath stank of old beer and cigarettes and something else. Something rotten.

'Ben sent me to get you.'

'Ben? Where is he? And who are you?'

The man smiled. It sent a shiver down her spine.

'I'm Harry. Come with me.'

Rushing her along, Harry Peterson began to lead Hines through the crowd.

Louise didn't know what happened.

One minute there had been a peaceful gathering; the next a full riot was taking place. Anti-rally protesters had gathered beyond each of the cordons, keeping a distance, remaining quiet until they weren't. They surged forward, over-running the barriers and the police officers.

Louise had been knocked aside, and then a placard had struck her in the face, sending her to the floor. A surge of bodies swarmed over her, knees catching her, legs battering her. She felt a foot stamp on her side and cried out in pain.

And then it was over and they were beyond her. They swarmed into the marketplace, knocking aside those who had gathered for the rally. She could hear glass break and shouts of anger and pain overtake the chanting. Fights broke out, and over the radio she could hear DI Manby scream for units to get into position.

The riot they had all feared had begun.

CHAPTER
FORTY-EIGHT

The mobile police unit had been set up down the side of the Town Hall. Inside were monitors linked to video cameras carried by officers and placed at several key locations around the rally. From here the crowd was closely watched, and officers co-ordinated. It had been a junior officer who saw the first surge by the swimming baths, but moments later, each of the seven officers manning the monitors was calling for perimeter units to converge as more people swelled past the cordons.

When the fighting broke out, DI Manby had called for specialist officers armed with shields and batons to intercede immediately and separate the two groups.

Snatching a radio, he jumped out of the mobile police unit and started running towards the back of the staging area. Screams filled the air, along with the barked commands of his officers. The thud of bodies against the riot shields made him wince; this was getting out of hand.

'All senior officers: Berlin. Repeat; Berlin!'

Berlin was the code for getting a wall of police between the two factions. It was easy to tell which ones were the BNP, the majority at least; they wore the patch on their arm or the backs of their jackets. Or they carried banners and placards that they were using to batter their opponents. The others, Manby didn't know who they were. Counter protesters, locals fed up with the violent, hate-filled rhetoric coming from these bastards.

He had sympathy for them, but not for how they had chosen to act.

He ran down the hill and into the crowd. Perhaps he could collar Everad. Get him to call out to his lot to stop.

And pigs might fly, Manby thought.

He had just reached the back of the stage when he saw Harris being jumped by three men. He saw him go down and quickly ducked under the tape and grabbed the neck of the nearest. Throwing him around he grabbed the man's jacket and pulled it up, covering his head. Two quick punches and the man went down.

'Oi, fuck-face!' Manby yelled.

The second man paused in kicking Harris on the floor and started to turn. He didn't make it. Manby smacked him with his radio. Blood and teeth flew and the man threw his hands to his face, crying out in pain. The other man ran off.

Manby knelt by Harris and gently turned him over. As he did, Harris brought his arms up, covering his face and swinging his elbows, trying to connect with his unseen assailant.

'Get off me! Fucking get off me!'

'Easy lad. Easy. It's me. It's DI Manby.'

He gripped Harris' arms, lowering them. 'Jesus, they did a number on you, didn't they?'

'Where's Beth? These fuckers knew I was a copper. Where's Beth?'

Manby's blood ran cold.

Hines had gone with Harry Peterson willingly, the mention of Harris reassuring her. As the crowd surged and descended into chaos around them, he had steered her beyond a cordon and towards a van parked on a side street. Police armed with shields and batons rushed by them, ignoring them both. One officer knocked into Hines and he stopped to apologise. Recognition flared in his eyes, but before he could say anything, another officer grabbed him and pulled him away. He looked back; she shook her head and he moved on.

Behind them she could hear the yells and sounds of fighting.

Stopping by the van, Harry brought out keys and unlocked the side door.

'We're getting out of here before the pigs crack down.'

He pulled the door open. As it swept back, she could see written in the dust CLEAN ME: I LOOK LIKE A PAKI.

Something snagged in her mind.

'Get in.'

Hines stayed where she was.

'Where's Ben?'

Harry looked around as more people ran past, getting away from the fighting.

'Where's Ben?' she said again.

'Just get in, for fuck's sake,' he said angrily. 'We're meeting everyone back at the Walton Arms.'

This was new to Hines and she took a step back.

'No one said anything about that.'

In an instant he was right in her face, his hand grasping hold of her arm with a vice-like grip.

'And no one said anything about a fucking copper trying to sneak her way in, either.'

Before she knew it, his head connected with hers. She fell back, landing on the metal floor of the van. She tried to kick out but was groggy and missed him completely. The punch to her stomach knocked the wind out of her, and as she gasped for air, she felt her legs being bundled up and shoved unceremoniously into the van.

He jumped in beside her and pulled on the door, slamming it shut and plunging the van into darkness.

Her throat burned as he closed his fists around her neck. She battered at his arms, the pressure building in her head and her eyes beginning to bulge. His gasps as they struggled sent a sickening wave of his breath across her face and she fought the urge to vomit, even as she fought for breath. Her boot heels clanged off the metal floor of the van, two harsh raps.

Then darkness claimed her and she lay still.

Harry Peterson fell back, exhausted.

For several minutes he sat still. Quiet. Catching his breath. Making sure no one came knocking on the van. Surely someone had seen it rocking as they fought? Someone must have heard?

Patience. Patience was key.

He leaned over the woman. The police woman. Young. Pretty. Her breath was slow and shallow. Still alive.

Good.

His hands wandered over her body, testing her contours, feeling her curves. She would be good. She would work.

The boy would be happy again.

Outside, the sounds of the riot continued, but no one came knocking. He slid the door aside and got out, quickly sliding it shut.

Getting into the front, he started the engine. Checking both mirrors twice, he turned the wheel and set off, his new prize unconscious in the back.

'Where is she?' Manby yelled, slamming his fist into the wall beside Tommy Everad's head.

They were in a side street just off the marketplace. A couple of officers blocked the entrance with their shields, so no one could see what was happening.

Tommy's grin was a bloodied smear, his lower lip busted by a truncheon to the face. One eye was swelling and his jacket had been torn, the BNP patch hanging by a thread.

'Mr Tallingate is going to finish you,' he said, then spat a thick glob of bloody phlegm onto the pavement. A couple of teeth lay in the mess.

'Maybe,' Manby growled, 'but not before I beat the fuck out of you. Where is she?'

'I have no idea who you're—'

The punch came out of nowhere, slamming into Tommy's gut, doubling him over. If Manby hadn't been holding him against the wall he would have fallen. Manby shoved him back, hard against the wall, hands on Tommy's shoulders, with enough force that his head cracked against the stone. Tommy yelled out in pain and Manby slapped him across the face.

'Where is she, you fucking prick? What did you do with her?'

'He's not going to say anything,' Harris said. 'I've known him long enough to know he's an arrogant fuck. He'd rather stay silent and get a kicking than talk.'

'Fine by me,' Manby said. He grabbed Tommy again and dragged him forward, one leg sticking out so the BNP leader fell over it. He hit the ground on his right shoulder then rolled onto his stomach. Instantly Manby's foot lodged itself in the crook of his neck, even as he pulled Tommy's left arm up and back.

'Talk!'

Tommy screamed as pain shot down his arm.

'*Bill!*'

The DI turned to see Louise standing in front of two police officers.

'Let me through,' she said, pushing her way past the two men. She dragged Joe with her, his face equally bruised and bleeding.

'It's all turned to shit out there. What the fuck is this?' she said.

'Beth's missing,' Harris replied.

'And this cunt knows where,' Manby added, giving the arm another twist. 'What did you do? Learn who she is and decide to send a message? Was that it, you piece of shit?'

Tommy cried out again but remained otherwise silent.

With a frustrated growl, Manby dropped the man's arm and took his foot from his neck. He instead kicked Tommy in the ribs and stepped back, breathing heavily. A moment later he turned and looked at Joe.

'What about you, soft lad? What the fuck do you know?'

CHAPTER
FORTY-NINE

Driving out of the centre of Dewsbury proved harder than Harry Peterson had originally thought. Stuck waiting for a road to clear from protesters, it was apparent that two groups of youths were now fighting in the streets, while, at the same time, police officers armed with riot gear were trying their best to get everything under control. All they were doing, though, was adding to the chaos as officers struck out with their batons indiscriminately.

The fighting had spilled out onto the side streets and roads that ran around the marketplace. A big push from the police had sent a huge portion of the crowd back along Savile Road towards Savile Town, the direction he was trying to go.

Running battles continued all around the van. Bottles, bricks and wooden slats bounced off the sides, thrown by protesters and police alike. Dewsbury had become a warzone.

A gap appeared in the road ahead, and Harry drove forward, carefully watching either side to make sure no one jumped out in front of him. The last thing he needed was to be stopped by the police and his van searched.

Seeing the usual road blocked by a large group of people and police, Harry turned right instead. There were other ways to get to the warehouse, but first he had a stop to make.

. . .

Tommy Everad had been arrested along with a dozen other members of the BNP chapter that operated out of the Walton Arms. They had been placed in several police vans, along with a few of the counter protesters. A couple of raps of a truncheon kept everyone in line as they sat waiting to be taken to the station for charging. Medical teams gave aid where needed, some with questioning looks at the wounds inflicted. No one said anything.

In the mobile police unit, Manby wiped at his face with a wet cloth. Harris and Louise stood in front of Joe, who was sitting on a chair, his hands handcuffed behind his back. His face was a worsening purple bruise. The image of Bilal and Raja Wadee flickered briefly in Louise's mind – *a little poetic justice*, she thought, then immediately regretted it. One didn't justify the other.

'If you thought you were in the shit before, Joe,' Louise began, 'then that's nothing to what's going to happen to you next. This is nine levels of seriousness above giving Hines a slap now and then. A lovers' tiff. Rough sex taken a little too far?'

Joe smirked and Louise wanted to slap it right off his face. Instead, she took a deep breath and continued.

'That sort of stuff we can understand. It happens.'

'What would a dyke like you know about it?' Joe sneered.

Harris cuffed him across the face.

'Be polite,' he said.

Joe spat blood but kept silent.

Like father, like son.

Louise grabbed a chair and sat directly in front of Joe.

'Look. I know you still have some feelings for Beth. How could you not, what… were you together two, three years?'

'Off and on,' he replied smugly. 'Felt more like a life sentence.'

'And that's what you're going to get unless you tell us where she is!' Manby shouted, throwing the cloth down onto the side.

'We know you told your dad about Ben and Beth. And that your dad then decided to do something about it. Couldn't be seen having a rat in the nest, could he? What did he do? Come on, Joe. We know you didn't order it. Just like you didn't order or take part in the Wadee assault. That's not your thing.'

Manby leaned over Joe's shoulder until his face was right by his ear.

'You're a coward. A man who hits women to keep them in line. Or at least that's what he tells himself. Tells his mates down the pub. You remember doing that, don't you? You remember telling your mates how you'd just thrown a last fuck into Beth and that they were welcome to give it a try. You remember that, don't you?'

Manby now moved so that he was standing right in front of Joe, almost straddling him.

'You remember what happened next as well, don't you?'

Joe's mouth twitched. A nerve in his neck looked to be having a fit and his eyes had filled with tears. Louise took over.

'Joe. What did your dad do? Tell us and we can help Beth and that can help you.'

For a moment it looked like the Everad stubbornness had been passed down the line, but then Joe shook his head, wincing at the pain it caused.

'There's a guy at the pub who sometimes gets rid of things for Dad.'

'Is that what he's going to do?' Louise asked. 'Get rid of Beth?'

Joe shook his head.

'He'll put a scare into her. Take her somewhere miles away, scare her and leave her. He won't hurt her, if that's what you're thinking. Dad doesn't do that. He doesn't kill people or have them killed.'

'Did he get the Wadee brothers attacked?'

Joe laughed, unable to stop himself.

'Of course he did. He's not going to have a Paki come into his pub like he owns the place. But he made sure they weren't hurt too bad. Just a message they wouldn't forget. Same thing he will have done with Beth.'

'Name!' Manby roared.

'Peterson. Harry Peterson.'

Louise looked at Manby. Her blood had gone chill.

'Peterson!'

Ian Peterson heard the van pull up outside their house and was at the door just as his dad reached it.

'I thought you were at the rally?' Ian said.

'Got given a special job, and a special prize,' Peterson said, moving past his son into the house and up towards the bathroom. 'Grab your coat. I'm having a slash and then we're off.'

'Off where?' Ian shouted up the stairs. His answer was the bathroom door slamming shut.

Twenty minutes later they were in the van and heading towards Savile Town again. Fleetwood Mac's 'Go Your Own Way' played on the radio. Ian had his window down, arm out. A cooling wind blew through the cab.

'How was it?' Ian asked again.

'The rally turned to shit. Idiots. No conviction in their beliefs, just a desire for another punch-up and a pint.'

'I don't understand then,' Ian said, turning to his dad. 'Why did you go?'

The smile Harry gave never reached his eyes.

'I wanted to watch them. All of them. Scurrying like ants, feasting on each other's hate. Bouncing off one another. Idiots,' he said again, spitting the word out. 'Idiots!'

He slammed his hand on the steering wheel. The van rocked to the side, one wheel bouncing off the kerb, threatening to send the vehicle crashing into the wall.

'They argue over race, over the colour of their skin, but that doesn't matter. *This* doesn't matter,' he said, reaching over to pinch Ian's cheeks between stained fingers. 'This doesn't matter. It never mattered. Never. Flesh is nothing but a bag, one shaped in pleasing lines, yes. Yes, I grant you that. Pleasing lines that catch a man's eye, and turn his head and stain his soul. If you're not careful, they will turn yours too. Like your mother did mine.'

They drove in silence for a minute or two. Ian stared out the window, thinking over what his father had said, trying to make sense of it all. Emotions warred within him, as they had done for years. Was he wrong, doing what he had? His urges... were they of the flesh too, or was that something else?

'True beauty lies within,' Harry continued, 'hidden beneath the flesh. Your mother's true beauty was revealed to me when she left. I found it beneath the false skin she wore. Like I showed you.'

'Like you taught me,' Ian said. 'I was so close with the last one. I had nearly uncovered her truth. Just like you showed me. I was so close!'

Harry smiled and this time his eyes sparkled.

'We have new truths to find, son.'

The van slowed as he turned onto an industrial estate.

'And we will find them. Together.'

CHAPTER
FIFTY

Within the hour, the riot in the centre of Dewsbury was brought under control. The marketplace was a ruined, chaotic mess. Shop windows had been smashed and benches overturned, and the cobbled pavement was spattered with the blood of the rioters. Amongst the litter were the fallen placards, their words of hate smudged under scuffed boot prints. The banners that had been strung along the front of the stage had been ripped down, torn and burned in several places.

Louise stared out of the window of the mobile police unit. A dozen officers in riot gear still stood in a line, their imposing look quelling any further outbreaks, while several more officers walked among the few who remained, moving them on. Questioning some. Shoving others when they talked back.

She turned to Joe, still seated. Still handcuffed.

'Where was he going to take her?' she asked.

'I don't know,' Joe replied. He was crying now, snot dripping to mix with the blood on his shirt. 'I don't know.'

'Think!' Louise shouted in his face.

Her hands itched to close around his throat, to throttle good sense into him. This was all his fault; everything came back to him. He and Hines had met at the Carpenters, got talking. Got to fucking. All but moved in together. Had she known about his dad, about his hateful beliefs? Had Joe shared them? Did he share them now?

Questions. Too many questions and no answers.

No. Only one question mattered. And Joe had the answer.

'Where would he go?'

'I don't—'

Louise waved him off. She stood and started pacing.

'It wouldn't be his house. Certainly not work. Not to the garage. Not to Sanderson's. So where?'

Manby laid a hand on her shoulder. His voice was a soft breeze. 'Louise…'

She shrugged him away.

'WHERE?'

'A warehouse! He does some work for the garage in a warehouse in Savile Town. Not far from the Walton Arms.'

The description he gave was clear enough for Harris to recognise exactly where it was.

'Isolated enough. Accessible,' Louise said, once he had identified it.

Manby was nodding.

'And the canal is close by as well. Could easily have walked along it to where Helen and Mary were found. In fact, I think there's a dirt road that runs alongside. At least for some part. He could easily have done that.'

Manby stared at Louise for a moment.

Louise had gone pale.

'If Peterson has Beth…'

Reaching into his pocket, Manby pulled out a set of keys.

'Go!' he yelled, throwing them to her. 'Take my car.' He turned to Harris. 'Go with her! Move it!'

As soon as they had gone, he snatched up a radio.

'Get me Chief Superintendent Freeman!'

. . .

They leapt from the police unit and ran to the car. Seconds later they were tearing away, the chaos of the rally-turned-riot left behind them.

'Are you going to tell me what you know about Peterson?' Harris said. He held onto the dashboard as Louise threw the car round a corner.

'A woman went missing just before Christmas last year. Helen Williams. Prostitute who worked the bars around Ossett but also in Wakefield, Dewsbury and Leeds. We found her, or her legs at least, just a few days ago.'

'What? Say that again. I knew there was a new murder enquiry, but... her legs?'

Louise nodded.

'And we found the torso of another woman. Another prostitute. Mary King. She worked—'

'The Walton Arms area. I know her. Knew of her, at least. Her torso? Fucking hell.'

'Two women, two halves. No whole. We found some internal organs in black bags nearby as well. We're still waiting to find out who they belonged to.'

'And you think Harry Peterson did this?' Ben asked. He pointed ahead. 'Take the next left. I've known him for a few months and can't say I've ever seen any behaviour that would indicate that level of depravity. I knew there was a bad background to him. I'd heard the stories. Rumours and pub gossip for the most part.'

Louise braked heavily, throwing them both forward, as an Eddie Stobart truck pulled out slowly from a junction.

'Fucking bastard!' she yelled, pressing heavily on the horn.

She swung the police car out and overtook, ignoring the oncoming traffic, which screamed their own horns at her. She swerved back into the correct lane and stepped on the accelerator.

'What rumours?' she said, keeping her eyes locked on the road ahead.

If she concentrated on driving, she didn't have to think about Hines and what that piece of shit might be doing to her right now. She looked quickly at the speedometer: sixty-five. She pressed harder on the accelerator, squeezing more power out of the already groaning engine. Slowly, the needle began to caress seventy. Next to it, a red warning sign came on. She ignored it.

'His wife apparently left him a few years ago. Just took off. Never seen again. Left him to raise their kid on their own.'

'Ian.'

'Is that the boy's name?'

Louise nodded.

'There's something odd about that kid. He kept cropping up in investigations over the past few years as well. When I last saw him, I could see there was something going on behind those dead eyes of his. I just put it down to having lost a friend.'

'Like father, like son?' Louise said nothing. 'Beth's going to be fine. She's a good detective. You both are.'

'She's... she's my friend,' Louise said. 'Jesus. I can't believe this is happening.'

'She's going to be all right,' Harris said. 'We're going to get there and bring this prick down. Turn here. It'll be the next... fuck!'

Louise stamped on the brakes. The road ahead was blocked by a crowd of people. The tyres screamed as they fought for purchase on the road. She turned the steering wheel, shifting the direction of the car just enough as it skidded to a halt, narrowly missing the crowd.

Some were fighting, some were standing either side of the throng waving placards and banners. Bottles were being thrown into the crowd. Just beyond them were a line of police vans, slowly moving forward. Behind them, police in riot gear. Pushing the crowd back. Moving them slowly on, but not putting the fighting down.

There was no way forward.

They were stuck.

CHAPTER
FIFTY-ONE

The warehouse had belonged to the Peterson family for over twenty years. It stood alone in an industrial estate that had once housed storage sheds and maintenance bays for the railways. A set of tracks, now covered with weeds and rusted, ran out from several buildings to disappear down long forgotten, and now overgrown, corridors of trees and bushes. Nearby, the river Calder snaked around the buildings, the drop down to its still surface similarly overgrown and littered with crushed cans of beer, fag packets and a hundred other items of rubbish. The jagged teeth of a broken sink stuck out at an odd angle from the wild roots, while a rusted bike clung precariously to the edge of the river, caught fast by a tangle of weeds.

This was forgotten land, relegated to the past. Discarded like all the rubbish left here to rot.

But this place hadn't been forgotten. This building with its strong foundation and proud heritage; it hadn't been forgotten. It looked like it had; its outside skin was a landscape of shattered brick and smashed glass. Crude drawings had been sprayed over its surface, crueller words daubed across the walls, their large letters weeping down the stone with red and black tears. Its roof had been broken a dozen times with thrown bricks, the prefabricated sheets tainted aqua-green with time and neglect.

But inside. Inside was so different.

Harry Peterson backed the van into a wide loading bay, the sound of the engine amplified by the wide empty canopy of the warehouse. Ian stood beside the doorway, and as soon as the van was fully within, he lowered the metal shutter, carefully letting the chain through his hands in a slow descent. The sharp metallic clack of the chain as it fed through echoed and set Ian's teeth on edge.

That could have been the excitement, though, that coursed through his body. That nervous tingle ran along every nerve, heightened every sense. He could smell the diesel of the van, the scent of old beer and cigarettes on his dad's breath. The pungent stench of body odour from them both.

Animals had got inside again. He could smell their shit and their piss. And something else. Something sweet. Something... pure.

Harry silenced the van and got out.

'Come over here,' he commanded.

Ian obeyed, coming to stand with his father by the sliding door of the van.

'We have been given a special gift. A true beauty. But we will have to work hard to find the truth within. Did you get everything like I asked?'

Ian nodded.

'Everything is ready. Is she mine?'

The slap sent the boy crashing to the ground. Dust flew up where he fell. His father towered over him, face glaring, lips spread to reveal brown teeth clamped together hard. When he spoke, the words were spat from behind.

'She doesn't belong to you. Nothing belongs to you. It can all be taken away, no matter what you believe. Like this place,' he added, sweeping his arms around to indicate the building they were in. 'This was ours. Mine, my father's. His father before him and back to the first Peterson. This was ours, even through the lean years. We thrived when others fell. But it was taken from us. Snatched from our grasp by her traitorous lies.'

Ian lay in the dirt and said nothing as his father's rage washed over him.

He had heard this before. Had learned of their history and the many wrongs cast against them. He had learned of the source of his father's hate and anger and taken it as his own.

Harry continued. 'She was the first to place the knife. To cut into the heart of our family, to slice our legacy away, a sliver at a time. She tore out the very soul of our family with her lies, her despicable stories, and then they came and took it all. Took everything from us, leaving us with nothing. Once we had ruled, and now we were mere subjects. Working at the whim of others. And all because of her ugly truth.'

Harry placed his hand on the van door, a lover's caress.

'But now. Now we reveal the inner beauty of truth, drawing it from the ugly outer layers of deception.'

He pulled the van door aside and Hines jumped out, screaming as loudly as she could as she propelled herself forward to crash into Ian and send them both tumbling to the ground.

Harry growled and grabbed for her jacket. She struggled as he lifted her off the ground, legs kicking out, boots scuffing the dusty floor of the warehouse.

'Get off me!' she yelled. 'Let me go! I'm a police officer!'

Harry spun her around and slammed her into the side of the van.

'We know very well who you are,' he said and kicked her in the stomach.

Hines fell forward and he kicked her again.

'But we're going to get to know you even better.' He bent down and grabbed her hair. Lifting her head, he stared into her eyes. 'Oh, yes. We're going to get to know you really, really well.'

Before she could reply, he punched her in the face. Letting her go, she fell face down in the dirt, unconscious.

Beyond the loading bay of the Peterson warehouse was a close series of rooms, all connected by a single corridor that led to a storage room. Here the floors were all clean, the linoleum recently mopped and free of dirt and dust. The walls were also clean, the windows that looked into each office intact. A calendar was on one wall, a naked woman staring blankly from the page, big haired and big breasted: *The Sun, Page 3 Girls 1989* in large letters. The desks were tidy and also clear of dust. Each one had an in-tray, a desk jotter and a phone.

Harry and Ian carried Hines past these offices and into the storage room. The size of two of the offices, the room had been converted for a special use. Their special use. A chest freezer lined one wall. Bookcases had been repurposed to hold a variety of instruments and tools.

In the centre of the room was a table with four leather straps fastened to it.

They carried Hines to the table and with a bit of effort lifted her on to it. Using the straps, they secured her to it; two across her legs, another two across her chest and arms. From his pocket, Ian took four small gold padlocks and fastened them to the straps.

Ian looked at his dad and grinned.

'Continue,' Harry said.

He moved to a chair beside the freezer and sat, watching his son work.

Ian moved to the head of the table. He paused, looking down on the semi-conscious Hines. Reaching out he ran his fingers through her purple hair, then leaned down to sniff her scent. She murmured something only Ian could hear and then fell silent.

He reached beneath the table and brought out another leather strap. This one he stretched across her forehead and secured it in place like the others.

'And the padlock,' his father reminded.

Ian felt in his pockets. They were empty. He looked to his dad.

'I only had four,' he said.

The slam of his father's hand on the freezer was like a gunshot in the room. Ian jumped but stayed silent. For several moments, the only sound in the room was the angry, heavy breathing of Harry as he fought his temper. Like the snort of a bull, it filled the room, a warning given.

Finally, he gained control and stood.

'No matter,' he said. 'Begin.'

Ian nodded and walked over to the bookcase. He looked along its shelves, eyes scanning the many different knives, blades and saws. All were clean. All glistened.

His gaze fell on a barber's blade. He picked it up and came and stood beside Hines. Putting the blade between his teeth, he reached down and pushed one of her jacket sleeves up, revealing the pale, pink skin of her arm.

Taking the blade, he opened it. His breathing quickened. His eyes dilated. His cock was harder than it had ever been as he placed the sharp metal against the flesh of her arm.

Ian looked at his dad.

Harry nodded.

Ian pressed the blade down. Blood pooled around it.

When he drew it across her arm, Hines' eyes snapped open and she screamed.

'That's it!' Harry shouted. 'Let out the truth!'

Hines started to twist on the table but she couldn't move. Ian moved the knife down her arm, his eyes locked on hers. He could see the fear in them. She opened her mouth to scream again so he jammed his mouth over it, silencing her as he continued to slice tiny cuts into her flesh.

. . .

Hines was crying. Her entire body burned. She had been cut in a dozen places. Her arms had criss-cross patterns. Not too deep, at least. Her shirt had been cut open, revealing her breasts. A deep cut ran down her left; the right was bruised from the boy's crushing grip. His mouth over her nipple, she had screamed when he had bitten down.

Blood coated her left side and she could hear it dripping onto the floor. She thought she had passed out for a moment when the pain had got too much, but she couldn't be sure. Her head swam, her vision was blurred.

She tried to move and found herself bound to the table.

Someone moved nearby. A shadow fell across her. She turned her eyes to see the boy… *What is his name…?* standing nearby. He still held the knife, its edge stained with blood. Her blood. *What is his name…?*

'Ian?' she said. 'That's your name isn't it? Ian.'

He said nothing. Just stared at her.

'Ian. You don't have to do this. Don't let him make you do this.'

Still nothing. His head shifted to the side. He smiled.

And started to cut again.

Harry bathed in the sound of her scream.

He was standing in one of the offices, watching through the glass as the boy worked. A proud fire burned through him. He had been alone when he released the inner beauty from his wife, working here surrounded by his family's heritage, a fitting place to begin his new journey. And the others, the ones he had saved from their torturous ways and nightmare existences; they had been hard lessons learned. Techniques mastered.

And now, with his son at his side, he could pass on what he had learned. Father to son.

And the son had done well.

Learned fast.

She screamed again.

Harry watched as his son ran his hands over the woman, his hand disappearing beneath the fold of her skirt. She was crying now, crying hard. And then he punched her and her head lolled to the side.

The sound of a car drew his gaze to the window that looked out onto the open land of the industrial estate. Four more buildings were staggered across the area, with another one, smaller than the rest, just at the entrance to the estate.

The car rolled over the gravel and came to a stop in the centre.

A police car.

Harry growled in anger and pushed the phone and in-tray off the desk to clatter to the floor.

'They can't stop this,' he mumbled. 'This is mine! They can't take this from me as well!'

With another angry yell, he tore from the office towards the storage room.

CHAPTER
FIFTY-TWO

The fighting in Savile Town had been brutal but short lived, leaving the Walton Arms burning and dozens of people injured. Even more had been arrested by the police as they had waded into the crowd. Muslim and BNP activists, both sides had been taken into custody. More had been taken to hospital with cuts and bruises. Some were more serious, having been attacked with blades or broken bottles.

The media had arrived. Local TV, newspaper reporters and photographers. Even someone from Radio Leeds. They stood around and talked into microphones, took photos and told their stories.

The fighting had pooled around the Walton Arms pub, briefly going inside as Pakistani youths rushed in with cricket bats, hitting out at everyone. The bar had been trashed and set on fire, and now two fire engines were parked outside, as water was sprayed through the main lounge window in an effort to bring the blaze under control. More were on the way.

It had taken fifteen minutes for Louise to snake the car through the crowd; going back and finding another way to the old industrial estate was out of the question. The road behind had become thick with traffic, backing up all the way into Dewsbury centre itself. No, they had had to wait, no matter how frustrating it was. No matter how scared she was for Hines.

She knew her younger companion could handle herself, whatever Peterson had in mind. Hines would hold out.

Finally, there was enough space for Louise to reach fourth gear, and the car shot forward.

Two minutes after that they were rolling onto the gravel in the centre of the deserted industrial estate.

She brought the car to a halt and turned to Harris. His eyes were already scanning across the various buildings, looking for signs of life. Of movement. Anything that would tell them which building to go to.

'Which one?' she asked.

Harris shrugged.

'Joe only said it was here. Not which one it was.'

'I bet that fucker knows exactly which one it is. Do you see anything?'

Harris shook his head. He picked up the car's radio, giving their position.

They got out of the car. The sirens of the fire engines could be heard in the distance, as could the muted shouts of those still trying to protest. It would run on for days, Louise knew. Who was to blame? Who had caused such destruction and chaos? It was another case of half a dozen of one and six of the other, but no one on either side would admit to that. And were there really sides to this? Weren't they all just one community?

Louise would have liked to think so, but knew the sad reality of it all. Differences ran deeper than skin colour, and were harder to fix. No one solution fitted all. But they had to keep trying, didn't they?

'What are you thinking?'

Louise jolted back to the present. Now was not the time to be thinking about the wider problems. They needed to find Hines.

Harris stared over the top of the car. Louise looked around frantically. They all appeared the same; shattered windows, broken masonry. Rusted metal roofs. Signs faded with time; walls overgrown with plant life. Doors hanging from frames, shutters bent and twisted.

Except that one.

'There!'

She pointed across the yard to a steel shutter that caught the light. Clean. Undamaged.

Together, they started to run towards it.

'You're going to have to work fast,' Harry said.

Below him, Hines flinched as a bright light exploded around her. He had brought a large, mirrored lamp and positioned it above her, throwing a stark light over her body.

'Open your eyes!'

Hines winced, finding herself now looking directly into her own face. Her left eye was swollen shut and her lip was split in two places. A wound in her neck wept blood and there was now a cut in her cheek, a layer of skin having been sliced away.

Harry stepped to the side and dragged a tall, wheeled tray into place. He picked up a set of wicked looking pliers and tried them. They were well oiled and clicked easily. He put them down and picked up a compact saw.

'Oh Jesus,' Hines said. 'Jesus fucking Christ. No.'

She started to thrash on the table, to try and work her bonds free. If she could just get a hand loose she might be able to release the straps.

Ian loomed beside her, his hand on her shoulder, pushing her down.

'Lie back,' he said.

'Grab her shoulders,' Harry ordered.

He waved a thin-bladed scalpel, the tip jagged and broken.

'You don't have to do this,' Hines said as Ian pushed on her shoulders.

She was talking directly to the boy again, hoping she could

get through to him, to stop him from doing this. The image of Helen, cut in two, rose in her mind, sending her into a frenzied panic. Was this how it was going to end? Was this how she was going to die, cut into pieces by this fucking lunatic and his boy?

'Jesus Christ. Let me go. Let me go!'

The tears that fell from her face almost blotted out the horrendous scene before her. Almost.

'Please. Please. Please,' she sobbed. 'Don't do this. You don't have to do this.'

'Yes I do,' Harry said, pressing the blade against the exposed skin at the top of her thigh. 'We must see your inner beauty.'

He pushed the blade into her flesh and she cried out.

Louise and Harris heard the scream and ran faster.

The shutter had a sliver of light beneath it and Harris got his fingers through the gap. Lips gritted between his teeth, he pulled upward. At first it held fast, the shutter's mechanism locked in place. Grunting, he pushed harder, his face turning red, the veins in his neck standing proud. Louise joined him, her hands cut open on the sharp edge of the metal. Ignoring the pain, she strained and the shutter moved.

With another violent heave, the shutter shook and snapped up, the noise like machine gun fire as it ratchetted up into the roof.

A van stood in the way. Louise immediately recognised it as the one outside Scruffy Pete's. Next door.

Jesus. Had Helen been in that van? Just a few feet away from her home?

They slid past the van and into the main loading bay.

'There!'

Louise pointed to a bright light coming from the corridor.

Running faster, their footsteps echoing off the linoleum, they tore down the corridor towards the light.

Another scream tore out, followed by silence.

Louise recognised the voice.

'Beth!' she called out. 'Beth! Where are you?'

'Down there!' Harris yelled, pointing.

Through the glass windows of several offices, they could see shadowy figures in what appeared to be a storeroom. Two men stood next to a table. And on that table…

'Beth!'

Crashing through the doors, they dashed into the storage room and a blood-soaked nightmare.

CHAPTER
FIFTY-THREE

Harry Peterson stood beside the table, a wicked knife in his hand. He was covered in blood; it ran down his arms and had splattered his shirt and face. It dripped from the blade.

Louise tore her eyes to Hines, who lay on the table. At first, she couldn't recognise her; Hines' face was a swollen bruise. Her chest was exposed and criss-crossed with knife wounds, but the worst injury was her leg. Through all the blood that was pouring from the wound, she could see exposed muscle and... dear God.

She looked away, focusing on the crazed man standing before her. On the opposite side of the table, Ian Peterson stood frozen. He too was covered in blood, but his eyes were blank. Distant.

Harris moved to the right, making his way towards the boy.

'Don't move!'

Harry waved the knife closer to Hines.

'Move again and I finish her.'

'You're done, Peterson. You're fucking finished.'

Harry grinned. 'I don't think so.'

'Look at me, Peterson,' Louise ordered. 'Do I look like I'm kidding?'

'You look scared,' he said, eyes trawling over her.

Harris inched towards Ian, who still stood rooted to the spot.

On the table Hines moaned in pain. Blood continued to pour from the wound in her thigh.

Louise kept Harry's eyes on her, moving closer to where he stood. He waved the blade over Hines but didn't touch her with it.

'I am scared,' she said, taking another step forward. 'I'm scared for your son. How what you've done will infect him for the rest of his life. Don't you see that? Don't you care?'

'We did this together.'

'No, Harry. You did this. This is all you. No one else.'

She stepped forward again and this time Harry brought the blade down, slicing a trench into Hines' ankle. She groaned but didn't cry out.

Harris dived forward and grabbed Ian, throwing his arms around the teenager and hugging him tight.

'Don't fucking move!' Harris said, putting one arm around the boy's neck, the other still holding him tight across the chest. 'I'll break your fucking neck if you struggle, so stand still.'

Harry's face twisted into a sneer so grotesque, Louise flinched.

'Keep him. He was always weak. Since the moment we got him, he was weak.'

'This is over, Peterson. Drop the knife.'

Harry's eyes moved from Louise to stare down at Hines on the table.

'She needs to have her inner truth revealed,' he said softly. 'They all do. All the whores.'

He looked up. Ian stared at him with tears in his eyes.

'Whores like his mum.'

He turned back to Louise.

'Not his true mum, though. We never met her. Didn't know her. She died, you know. They told us when we went to pick him up. Told us what happened. She died. Died on a road, stuck in a car all twisted and broken. Back in seventy-four. Just after he was born.'

Something cold ran down her back. Gripped her heart and squeezed. The room slipped sideways.

The trip to Edinburgh...

The country road...

The car screaming at them, crashing into them. Taking them...

'Louise?'

She turned to look at Harris. It took a moment to focus; it was like looking through a waterfall or a heat haze. She could see shapes, shapes that slowly swam into focus. Becoming faces. Becoming Harris. He still held onto the boy. Ian's eyes were now locked on her. No longer crying, his face was a mask she couldn't read.

'I knew,' Ian said. 'I've always known. Even before he told me. I knew. I found the adoption papers, but when I asked Mum about it she lied. Said I was wrong. That I didn't understand. She lied to me.'

This can't be. The room tipped again. Her entire world tipped.

Ian looked at his dad.

'But he didn't. He told me the truth. He showed me the truth. He showed me how to find the real truth. The one kept hidden. Kept secret. How to find it,' his eyes drifted to Hines, 'and bring it into the light.'

Harris tightened his grip.

'You fucking wanker. He's brainwashed you, kid.'

'It's all right, son,' Harris said. 'I have done what I needed to.'

Louise took another step closer. Harry raised the blade. She stopped.

'Harry. Don't do this.'

Sirens could be heard outside, getting louder. Getting closer.

Harry turned and gave his son a smile.

'You can continue where I stopped. Continue the Peterson legacy.'

Ian stared at his father, soaked in Hines' blood.

'Dad... what do I do?'

'Endure,' Harry said, and drew the blade across his throat.

Louise watched in horror as first a dark flow of blood soaked his neck and upper chest, and then an explosion of bright arterial blood sprayed across the prone body of Hines lying on the table.

A moment later he collapsed, blood flooding the floor. Louise fell to her knees beside him and rolled him to his back, her hand covering the wound. She knew instantly there was nothing she could do except watch him die.

Eyes locked to his, she did just that.

CHAPTER
FIFTY-FOUR

Police swarmed into the building, quickly followed by DI Manby and CS Freeman. Shouts rang out as Louise and Harris were located and then a rush of organised chaos ensued as medical teams came in.

It was a scene of horror; blood soaked the floor. The walls were sprayed with it, and nearly everyone in the room was covered, meaning it took a few tense minutes for the medical staff to determine who was actually hurt and who wasn't. Quickly establishing that Harry Peterson was gone, Hines' most dangerous wounds were treated and patched just enough that she was safe to be taken to hospital.

As she was being wheeled out, Hines reached for Louise. The straps had been removed from the table and from around her head. Her chest was a swathe of bandages, more covering her arm. Her leg had been bound and a paramedic was holding gauze against the wound. A drip had been fed into her, held aloft as they wheeled her to the ambulance waiting outside.

She didn't say anything, just let her fingers graze Louise's hand as she went by.

'I'm going with her,' Louise said.

There was no argument to be had here.

Manby nodded. 'Ben... you go too.'

'No problem.'

He had handed Ian Peterson to another officer, who hand-cuffed the boy and sat him down. No tears filled Ian's eyes; they were locked on the prone form of his father, now hidden by a sheet that had been placed over him. The lamp light had been turned off and the room swayed with shadows moving across the blood-stained walls. Only Harry's feet stuck out, the soles of his shoes filled with mud, blood and dirt.

'Jesus Christ. What a mess.'

Chief Superintendent Freeman stood in the doorway, watching Harris gently put an arm around Louise as they followed the gurney out of the warehouse.

'What a mess.'

CHAPTER
FIFTY-FIVE

Bilal and Raja Wadee stood in the line of trees that lined the cricket ground and watched the Walton Arms burn.

The night sky had darkened considerably so that the two brothers stood in the dancing shadows of the trees, their faces appearing to twist and writhe in the light thrown from the burning building.

Four engines had been needed to tackle the blaze at its height; now two remained. One had been tasked with finally putting out the blaze in the top room; the other was dampening down embers and quelling flare-ups wherever they happened. A fine mist of water was being sprayed over the remains of the building, which caused loud cracks of steam to explode into the air.

The smoke had been thick and black, almost blotting out the sun; now it was a light fog, clinging to everything it touched. Ash coated everything in the immediate vicinity; dark and grey it still floated in places like black snow.

Bilal gave a cough and spat ash onto the ground, wincing at the pain in his jaw. Raja grinned.

'Victory not to your taste, brother?'

Bilal pointed beyond the treeline, sweeping his hand along the road, littered with broken bottles, discarded signs, clothing and assorted rubbish. Several windows of adjacent houses had been smashed and a police barrier poked out of a hedge, its legs twisted.

'This is not victory,' Bilal said. 'A ruined community is not victory.'

'What they were saying was vile! What are we expected to do? Simply sit back and let them say whatever they will? Are we to let them do whatever they wish to us?'

'No, of course not.' Bilal fell silent, his anger rising. Shouting at his brother would not help him understand why this was wrong.

Across the street two men stood watching the fire brigade work. They wore the patch of the BNP group. Bilal pointed them out.

'Those two men. Would you call them your enemy?'

Raja nodded.

'They would have been in the crowd chanting for their white power over us to be enforced with violence.'

'Do you not recognise them? Look closely, brother. That one. That is Mr Howley.'

'Howley… Number sixteen, Dennison Way. We should tell the police.'

Bilal sighed.

'That is not why I pointed him out. Mr Howley comes into our store, does he not? He buys from us. He talks with us. His daughter is about to go to junior school, is she not?'

'Donna, yes she is.'

'And the other man is Edward Yates. He supplies us with milk from his farm. These people are our neighbours. They are not evil.'

'Not evil,' Raja laughed. 'They call for us to be segregated to our own schools. To leave their country. You say they are not evil; how can you do this?'

'They are not evil,' Bilal repeated, 'merely misled. Told

untruths with sincerity over and over again. Why would they not believe?'

'Then they are not evil. Just stupid. I don't know which is worse.'

'We are as bad as them if we take up violence rather than discussion.'

Another snort of derision from Raja.

'Discussion? Did they look like they wanted to discuss anything when they were pounding their fists into your face, breaking your jaw, brother? Did they look like they wanted to talk when they gouged my eye? When they gathered in the marketplace to scream vile hate against us? Did they want to talk then, or did they want to destroy us?'

Bilal laid a hand on his brother's shoulder as they began to walk back towards town.

'Destroy. Scream. Hate. These are words that hinder us. Words that stifle the healing that needs to take place.'

'What needs to take place…'

Raja's voice fell away and for a few minutes they walked together in silence.

Police officers patrolled either side of the street, some still in riot gear. As the brothers passed them, they stared at them, but didn't say anything or stop their movements.

'It's too big,' Raja finally said, his voice like that of a child. 'What we wish for is just too big and will never happen. They will never accept us.'

A car approached, slowly cruising down the road. As it drew level with them, they looked across. A man stared at them through the open window. He stuck out his hand and gave them the finger.

'Fucking Paki!' he yelled. 'Fuck off home!'

With a squeal of tyres, the car shot off. Raja turned to Bilal, who smiled ruefully.

'It is going to take time,' he laughed. 'Come on. Let us get home like he said.'

Raja stared at his brother. A moment later, his own laughter lifted into the night. They walked along Savile Road towards the centre of Dewsbury where they would be able to find a taxi, just as a light rain began to fall.

'You know,' Raja said. 'This would be better if we had a car.'

CHAPTER
FIFTY-SIX

Since being given command of the Scene of Crime forensic unit, Peter Danes had seen a lot of carnage and destruction. He had seen lives wasted and lives lost. Bedrooms trashed by angry lovers, beds ripped to shreds, pillowcases torn, the feathers scattered like confetti. Passionate crimes edged with instant regret as soon as the first sign of blood appeared.

He had also seen the remains of violent ignorance, the blood, the tissue, scattered like offal, discarded like rubbish. Bodies thrown aside as easily as last night's fish and chip paper. The marks they left were not always visible, either to science or intuition. They lay hidden, either beneath the surface, pushed down into the dark places no one went or talked about, or in plain sight, lost beneath the silent looks and cold faces.

He had seen a lot over his time, but he had never seen anything like this.

The team had set up lights around the room that had been used, at first as a storage space and then as a makeshift operating theatre. That was the only way he could describe it. Having catalogued everything that had been on the bookcase shelves and the metal wheeled tray, it was the only conclusion to reach.

What horrors had taken place here?

Some of that he could guess, just by the instruments they had recovered. Bone saws, pliers, scalpels of varying sizes. A twisted, metal speculum hinted at an agony Danes could only, briefly, imagine.

The table itself was another nightmare. Leather straps to bind the subject across the legs and chest. Another that went across the head. Underneath the table was a large metal bin. Sink might be a more appropriate word; a plug was set into the table so that any liquids above would drain directly into the bin. It could then be removed, emptied and returned. How many times had that happened?

It had been taken to the lab to be analysed. The blood inside was obviously from Beth, but there had been old stains around the rim, stains that might point to other victims who had been kept here.

There was evidence, as well, that other people *had* been here. Clothes had been found in one of the offices. Women's clothes; skirts, underwear, tights and shoes. At least four different people, judging by the variety of sizes. Those had also been bagged and taken away.

A slow examination of each of the offices had found further trace evidence of potential victims; fibres and hairs. Some jewellery. It would all be scrutinised, tested and cross-referenced with police records in the hopes that it might shed light on other cases. Other crimes.

It turned Danes' stomach.

How could this have gone on so long unnoticed? How had they not seen any of this?

And what else were they missing?

'Danes?'

He turned to see one of his technicians, whose task it had been to catalogue the contents of the freezer. It had been Danes who had opened it, breaking through the lock using a large pair of cutters. A similar pair sat on the bookcase; what it had been used for, he could only guess. That image would appear in his nightmares tonight, he knew.

Two large plastic bags had lain side by side, surrounded by a number of smaller ones. The way the packing tape had been wound tightly around each let them know exactly what was inside. The large bags had been photographed and lifted, placed on medical gurneys similar to the one that had taken Beth away.

An image of her lying there, covered in blood, her body cut and torn in dozens of places, clashed with another image of her, lying beneath him, gasping out his name. It filled his mind and he swayed in place as a sudden dizzy wave washed over him.

'Danes, are you all right?' the technician said.

It was no secret that the pair were close, the rumour that he had cheated on his wife with Elizabeth Hines no more than idle office gossip. Only he, Hines and Louise knew the truth.

'I'm fine,' Danes replied, shaking it off.

As soon as this was over, he would go to visit her in hospital. Louise was there, and Karla wouldn't be far behind. Despite everything that had happened between them, the one night they had shared together, then the scare of the baby last year, they were close. Closer than they should have been, perhaps, but she was not only a good officer, and a good detective.

She was a good friend and he would be there when she needed him.

And she would need him in the days to come. She would need them all.

'How's the freezer coming on? Any chips in there, maybe a steak?'

The technician pointed to the cluster of bags at their side. Everyone who entered a crime scene wore the same outfit, a hooded boiler suit, with mask and goggles, so Danes couldn't read the technician's face. He could see the horror in their eyes, and hear the tremor in their voice when they said, 'They are all there.'

At a quick count, Danes estimated there were a dozen or so

bags. Some small, the size he would put a steak in; others were larger. Leg of lamb size.

Or worse.

'Some of it is badly freezer burned,' the technician went on, 'but I'd say we're looking at the remains of at least seven or eight people. Arms. Legs. Internal organs.'

Danes paled. 'Jesus.'

If they hadn't got here in time, would that have been how they would have found Hines?

'Thing is; there's not enough… pieces to make up each person.' The technician paused. Took a long, deep breath. Tried to swallow and couldn't.

'What?' Danes said. A cold trickle of sweat ran down his back. 'What is it, Jimmy?'

'I know you don't like us speculating before the evidence has been analysed, but it looks like… Jesus, this is going to sound fucking crazy. It looks like… it's better if I show you.'

He moved to the row of bags and went past each one.

'We have a leg. Leg. Torso in that bigger one. Two arms there. All from different people by the looks of it, but we'll have to wait till they thaw so we can properly check. No head though. Do you see it?'

At first, he didn't, but then it clicked and his breath caught in his throat. It was a moment before he could speak, and when he did, his voice was a shocked whisper of disbelief.

'He was trying to make a new person? Is that what you're saying?'

Danes' stomach gave another flip as Jimmy continued. 'He had been finding people, and taking parts from them, discarding the rest. But that took too long and he didn't have the skills to put them together, would be my guess.'

'Fuck. And he worked at the garage,' Danes said, turning to look at the two largest bags. One held Helen Williams' torso; the other Mary King's legs. 'They started doing cut and shuts. That's where he got the idea. Faster than working on parts; just two sections.'

'Like I said, sir. It's just an idea.'

'I think you may be on to something there, Jimmy. Hopefully the search of Peterson's house will add more to it. Good work.'

He checked his watch. It was late. Probably too late to go to the hospital, but he hadn't heard anything and he was worried.

With thoughts of Hines and what she was going through filling his mind, Danes left the storage room, pulling the suit from his body and hoping he would leave the stench of death behind him.

CHAPTER
FIFTY-SEVEN

DI Manby had gone to Harry Peterson's house with three other officers, leaving Chief Superintendent Freeman to handle the fallout from the riot. His Sergeant, Tom-fucking-Bailey, wasn't one of them. That was something that would need to be dealt with, but not now. With dozens of arrests, many more injured and the property damage done to the businesses in Dewsbury marketplace as well as along Savile Road, Manby knew that the Chief Superintendent was going to be busy defending what had taken place, and his role in the decisions made.

That was a thankless task Manby was glad he didn't have to deal with, and one he couldn't see in his future anytime soon. Getting to the rank of Detective Inspector was good enough for him; he was still able to get back home to Marie at a relatively decent hour and didn't have any of the politics weighing on his mind. Most of this was down to the team he had assembled around him, a team he knew was in pain right now.

Elizabeth Hines was a good officer, one of the best he had worked with, and knowing she was in hospital, fighting for her life right at this moment, filled him with a furious anger that needed an outlet.

Most of his anger had been piled into Joe and Tommy Everad,

getting them to talk, and he knew he would have to face those consequences at a later date. Thankfully the Chief Superintendent hadn't stepped in; if he had, perhaps they wouldn't have got to Hines in time.

That thought sent a cold shiver down his back. His mouth went instantly dry and his hands began to shake. He clenched his fists, open and shut, several times, squeezing his fingertips into the palms of his hands until he couldn't picture her lying there, covered in blood. At death's door.

Harry Peterson's house was on Wesley Street and a car brought him straight there from the warehouse. The other officers had been waiting for him to arrive.

A swift kick to the front door and they had gained entrance. Stale air greeted them, the stench of old rubbish and older dust. The carpet was threadbare; torn in several places, it didn't quite reach fully across the hallway. The wooden banister that ran up the stairs had several notches in the wood, places where something thrown had taken a bite. The wallpaper was faded and, like the carpet, torn.

Manby directed two officers upstairs. The other he sent towards the kitchen.

He checked the wardrobe beside the door. An old coat, green. Waterproof. A pair of boots, thick waders, the kind a fisherman would wear to wade out into the river and cast a line. Manby had a pair just like them.

The sounds of drawers being pulled open came from upstairs, heavy feet moving from room to room.

Leaving the wardrobe, he went to the first door on the left. It creaked open on old, rusty hinges, as neglected as the rest of the house, apparently. A long cabinet was against the left wall, a tall, stacked stereo beside it. To his right was an old bureau, its lid down to reveal several small drawers. A pad of paper lay on the lid. Manby took a look, but there was nothing on it. Empty.

Under the window was a long sofa, the cushions thrown to the right in a large stack. Dust covered it and Manby wasn't surprised to see several holes in the fabric. He turned back to the long cabinet.

Kneeling in front of it, he pulled opened the twin doors. Records were lined up, about fifty in total. Manby pulled a couple out: Beethoven; the Halle Orchestra. Dvorak. Strauss. Classics all. He was about to close the doors when he spotted a book tucked between two records.

He pulled it out. It was a leather journal. No marking on the front cover. He opened it and a faded piece of paper and a photograph fell out onto the floor. Picking them up, he held his breath when he saw it was a scrap of a newspaper. ROBERTS FAMILY KILLED IN CAR CRASH. ONLY BABY SURVIVES. He didn't read it. The photo was of Harry Peterson, his wife and a baby boy about a year or two old. Turning it over, he read the scribbled mark: together at last – 1975.

What Louise had told him before going to the hospital was true. The Petersons had adopted the baby, not long after the same car crash that had taken Louise's parents. They had raised him as their own, but Harry had his demons. They warped him, and then he warped his adopted son. A sick circle of hate

He quickly leafed through the journal. Insane scribblings, rambling pages of nonsense that turned his stomach. Pictures of naked women in degrading positions taken from the stronger magazines that could only be found in backstreet specialist shops.

Manby closed it and put it aside. Standing, and shaking slightly, he turned to the stereo. It was a freestanding make, about waist high. A microphone was plugged in and resting on the case that covered the record player. Beneath that was a twin cassette deck, and below that the radio. He turned it on. The crack of electricity was quickly followed by a low hum as the machine came to life. One side of the cassette deck was full, the other empty. No label was on the cassette, but Manby recognised the make as the same as the TV advert for video tapes with the dancing skeleton.

He pressed rewind for a second or two, then switched it on.
Peterson's calm, detached voice filled the air.

*'It isn't hard to understand. The concept is quite simple. You only need
to have an open mind. To be willing to learn the truth. To seek the truth
and unearth it no matter where it may hide.'*

In the main bedroom, PC Hollins had looked under the bed, in
the bedside table and the chest of drawers and found nothing of
note. A heavy scent hung in the air. Almost sweet, it coated his
throat and stung his nostrils. Clothes were scattered around the
room, but it wasn't much messier than his own.

He now moved to the wardrobe and found the doors secured
with a padlock. When he tested it, he found the clasp hadn't been
fully punched inside the mechanism and he was able to remove
it easily enough and pull open the doors.

*'And when you find the truth, you must have the courage to act on it,
no matter what it is. This I have done, hard though it was. I did it for
her, to release her from her ugly lies, the ugly face she put on for
everyone else. Only I knew the truth of her, only I saw the shining truth
hidden within. She needed to be made whole, to be given that which she
lacked.'*

A large black bag was hidden at the back of the wardrobe. There
was no mistaking its shape.

The tape had been wound tight around the neck, the legs bent
at an awkward angle beneath to get the body to fit into the
wardrobe.

· · ·

'She is out there. The perfect woman. The one true woman. Not these whores who hide behind painted and false faces. Not this barren woman who lied her way into my life. She has started to taint the one true thing in my life and I will not have that. Her truth has been revealed. Now I will search for my true heart. And if I can't find her, I will manifest her, taking the corrupt and making them whole.'

Manby put the journal down and turned the tape off just as PC Hollins called out.

CHAPTER
FIFTY-EIGHT

Those arrested at the riot in Dewsbury had been taken to Dewsbury Police Station for charging. Everyone, that is, except for the ringleaders. Both the Everads and Colin Sanderson had been transported back to Ossett, back to the station, where they were booked in and placed into separate cells.

Their injuries treated, both Joe and Tommy had been brought into an interview room where Chief Superintendent Freeman was waiting.

Sitting at the table, he waited until their handcuffs had been removed and then gestured to the empty chairs.

'Sit, why don't you?' he said. He motioned to the officer to wait outside.

Cautiously they both pulled the chairs out and did as instructed. Joe's face was a ruined bruise, his lips swollen and one eye closed. He had a few stitches just above the eye, and a heavy plaster across his cheek. His dad didn't look much better, although he didn't have any cuts to speak of. A large bruise could clearly be seen around his neck.

'Not quite how you thought the day would end, is it?' Freeman said.

'Same for you, I'd imagine,' Tommy replied. There was menace in his voice, but if Freeman noticed, he didn't show it. Tommy didn't care. 'We got everything we wanted. You might not think so, you might even think we got our arses kicked by a bunch of brown skinned puffs, but we got everything we wanted. Our cause is out there. In the press. Did you see the number of reporters and photographers? Did you see them talking to our members? Interviewing them. Asking them all about what it is that we want. Who we are.'

Freeman's face grew cloudy.

'They saw exactly who you are,' he said. 'They saw when your members started putting bricks through windows and attacking innocent members of the community.'

Tommy laughed.

'The Pakis? Innocent. Do me a fucking favour.'

Freeman slammed his hand on the table directly between them. Tommy barely moved. Joe jumped an inch off his seat. The Chief Superintendent leaned in.

'You watch your tone when you speak to me, Tommy my lad. You need to remember your place.'

It was Tommy's turn to lean in now, his eyes locked to Freeman's.

'And you need to remember yours. When our solicitor is done with you and your lot, you'll be lucky if you're a fucking lollipop man, shooing snot nosed kids across the road to school. White ones, that is.' His voice dropped. 'Remember who you really work for.'

Freeman smiled.

'About that.'

There was a knock at the door. It opened, the officer standing to one side as a tall figure walked into the interview room.

'Mr Tallingate.'

The solicitor nodded. 'Chief Superintendent Freeman. I trust your wife is well?'

'She is. And she thanks you for the plants you sent her. They made a great addition to the garden she's creating.'

'It was my pleasure, Chief Superintendent. Now, if I could have a word with my clients in private?'

Freeman stood.

'Of course.'

He looked to Joe and Tommy. Both of their faces showed shock, but it was Tommy's expression that made Freeman beam with sickening pleasure.

Tallingate waited for the Chief Superintendent to leave, and as soon as the door shut, he sat down himself, placing his briefcase on the table and opening it.

From within he took out several folders, which he placed before Tommy Everad.

'This one,' he said, tapping a blue folder, 'is the agreement you signed that placed the Walton Arms public house under your care.'

'About that…' Tommy began, but a single glance from the solicitor silenced him.

Joe shifted in his seat, staying silent himself.

'This one is the agreement that ensures all payments for utilities, business rates and so on are paid on your behalf. As you can see it was signed six years ago. Is this your signature?'

The yellow folder was pushed towards Tommy. He didn't look down. 'Yes,' he said breathlessly. The folder was closed.

'And this one allows you to keep seventy-five percent of the profits from said Walton Arms, the remaining being paid into a funding account as directed.'

He didn't wait for a response. Just closed the folders and whisked them back into the briefcase.

'None of these facts is disputed,' Tallingate continued. You have earned a great deal of money over the last six years and yet today, the public house is nothing but a smouldering ruin, and you sit here in a police cell awaiting charges after inciting a riot over your prehistoric, and quite frankly, abhorrent, beliefs.'

Tommy had regained a little composure, some colour returning to his cheeks.

'My beliefs aside, what happened to the Walton wasn't my fault. It was those brown bastards that did it, nothing but animals, the lot of them.'

'Enough!' Tallingate roared. 'Enough of this bullshit.'

Joe took the brief sliver of silence to speak up.

'Sir, Mr Tallingate. What will happen to us? You are going to be able to get us out, aren't you?'

Tallingate turned to Joe, a look of sympathy briefly crossing his face. He took his glasses off and wiped them on the handkerchief he took from his pocket. Joe watched. Tommy was scrutinising a small spot on the table.

When he looked up again, the sympathetic look was gone.

'You and your racist father will be going to prison. Probably for a very long time.' He turned back to Tommy. 'No... don't say anything. Through your actions you have jeopardised, and brought under close scrutiny, a part of the business. This solution is generous on many different levels that you wouldn't understand, as it is apparent you don't even understand how stupid and arcane your beliefs are. We live in a changing world, Tommy. A world that is better because of its differences, not hurt by them. All that is hurt is your tiny, inconsequential ego. This is what is going to happen. You are both going to let justice have her day. You will plead guilty to any and all charges put before you, after which you will spend time locked away at Her Majesty's pleasure for the time she deems fit. And you will remain silent. For this you will be handsomely rewarded.'

Gathering everything together, Tallingate stood once more.

'Do you understand?'

Neither man said anything.

'Good. Oh, one more thing. If you see Mr Sanderson, I would stay away from him if I were you. He did not get the same deal you did. Best not to associate yourself with him during your stay as he will be leaving, quite messily, I am led to believe. Good day gentlemen.'

There was a quick, single rap on the door and it was opened.

A moment later, he was gone.

CHAPTER
FIFTY-NINE

'This is becoming a habit,' Louise said.

She sat beside Hines' bed in hospital. Owing to the nature of the incident, and her extensive injuries, a private room had been allocated, and, after getting a change of clothes, Louise had gone to Hines' home and brought several items to make it seem more welcoming, as opposed to sterile and uniform. A couple of posters she had found now graced the wall above the bed; Stevie Nicks and *Back To The Future*. A bear she always kept on her bed now lay beside Hines' sleeping head.

A book sat on the table next to an untouched glass of water. A Stephen King novel, *Misery*.

'For when she wakes up,' Louise said to Harris.

He sat in a chair opposite, still in the same clothes he had been wearing since the start of the day. His face was dirty, puffy from where he had been punched. Dried blood stained his clothes, not all his. He let out a long yawn.

'You should go home,' Louise said as softly as she could.

Beside her, the machine that monitored Hines beeped, a consistent, steady tone, reassuring despite its clinical, cold sound.

'She wouldn't be here if I hadn't suggested it,' he said.

He rubbed his hand across his chin, a finger tracing one of the cuts he'd received when he had been jumped.

'It's my fault.'

Louise looked at Hines, her heart almost stopping each time she did so.

Her friend lay sleeping, a deep healing sleep that was a coma in everything but name. She breathed unaided, which was a good sign, probably the only one. Her face still bore the scars of her trauma; her expression was pained, although the doctors said she couldn't feel anything.

But Louise knew differently. She knew Hines felt the emotional pain of what she had endured; it would be replaying itself over and over again in her mind. While she slept.

While her body healed.

'If there's something you should know about Elizabeth, it's that she never does anything she doesn't want to. She wanted to be there. She wanted to help, and if it hadn't been going under-cover with you, she'd have been on the frontlines with me. What happened wasn't your fault. That bastard Everad put this in motion, setting Peterson on her, fuelled by Joe.'

Louise let out a sigh. Joe. It always came back to Joe with Hines. Well, no more. He was going to be going away for a long time, according to Manby. He had spoken with the Chief Super-intendent, who had assured him that they would be pursuing the strongest penalty possible – a minimum of four years.

At least there was some good that had come out of all this. Helen's killer had been found; Pete could rest a little easier. She made a note to go to see him later. To let him know, though she suspected he had already heard. Manby would have made sure of it. They had found evidence that Helen had been at the Peterson house; some clothes and personal belongings, including her purse, had been found. Louise didn't think Pete needed to know that. Manby agreed.

She smiled. Manby was a good man, almost a father-figure to many. Always in their corner, fighting for them, fighting for those who were always on the receiving end. People like Hines. People like Pete and Helen.

In the bed, Hines let out a moan. Her hand moved slightly, an almost warding gesture. Louise reached out and took it, remembering how Karla did the same with her when she had bad dreams. When the nightmare of the car crash, that had taken not only her parents, but those of the baby she now knew as Ian Peterson, had tried to claim her.

Roberts had been their name. Tanya and George Roberts. He had been Ian Roberts and now he was Ian Peterson. A monster.

Could she have spotted the signs earlier?

She had told Harris he wasn't at fault, but a small part of her blamed him, just as she blamed herself. But the person she blamed most was Peterson. Harry Peterson. The true monster who had turned an innocent child into a vile creature.

The things they had done to Hines. She had seen the wounds. Her clothes had been covered in her friend's blood, clothes that now were in evidence bags to be tested and used in the trial against the boy.

Against Ian Peterson.

Louise looked over and saw that Harris had already fallen asleep, the events of the day finally catching up. Exhausted, she sat back in her own chair and pulled a blanket given to her by a kind nurse, over her knees.

The last thought that registered before she, too, fell asleep was that the monster was now caged and would never be able to hurt anyone again.

EPILOGUE

Ian Peterson had been stripped of his clothes and given a grey shirt and trousers to wear. His underwear was starchy cotton and his socks were three sizes too large and kept rolling off his feet.

After his arrest, he had been taken to Dewsbury Memorial Hospital and put into the secure wing, guarded by three police officers and never left alone for a moment, not even when he went to the toilet.

He hadn't spoken since his arrest, only nodding when asked his name.

Now he was in a cell on suicide watch. The flap in the door was opened every fifteen minutes and a bright light shone in to make sure he hadn't tried to do anything stupid. Food had been brought but he hadn't touched it. He didn't want to eat.

He didn't want to drink.

He didn't know what he wanted to do.

When he closed his eyes he saw his father, the man who had called himself Dad, open his own throat. He saw the knife. He saw the blood.

But what he saw the most, when he closed his eyes and the darkness descended, what he would always see and never forget, was the intention in his father's eyes. The focus. The absolute assuredness that what he was doing, what they *had* been doing, was right. Truly right.

When Ian closed his eyes and the blackness folded itself around him, all other sounds disappeared, everything save the last thing he father had said. His last instruction to his son:

'Endure.'

The sound of footsteps in the corridor grew louder as they approached. There came the jangle of keys and then the flap in the door opened once again. The light shone in and found Ian staring directly at the small space.

The light retreated and a face appeared. A woman's face. One he recognised.

'Hello, Ian,' she said.

The voice was golden. Light and welcoming. Ian could feel himself getting hard.

'Do you remember me? No… don't say anything. I don't expect you to,' she continued, 'but I wanted you to know that you're not alone. I'm going to help you.'

'That's enough,' the guard said.

The flap started to rise.

'Thank you, Ms Hayes,' Ian said, the first words he had spoken in nearly twenty-four hours.

Karla smiled.

'I'm going to help you. It's going to take some time, but together, we can do it. We'll speak soon.'

The flap in the door closed, plunging Ian into darkness once more.

ACKNOWLEDGMENTS

I'd like to thank Surjit Purekh and Alyson Read who both read early drafts of the book. Thanks to their insights and comments the book was enhanced in many ways.

There really was a BNP protest rally that took place in Dewsbury on June 24th, 1989, which then resulted in a riot. However, my version is a complete fiction compared to the true events. In the lead up, white parents were indeed taking their children out of school in protest at the rise in numbers of Muslim families in the region, a BNP rally was organised and a counter-protest similarly set up.

However, none of the people named in my story are real; neither are they based on anyone who was actually at the event. A pub, the Scarborough, was set on fire during the riots, but my version, the Walton Arms, only resembles it in the fact that it is a pub, and it too was burned to the ground. There is no other connection.

Until I started researching the year the book was to take place, I had no idea such a riot had happened, but it became the perfect backdrop to the story you have just read.

JONATHAN PEACE

ABOUT THE AUTHOR

Jonathan Peace is a husband, cat-dad and author of the Louise Miller novels, set in West Yorkshire during the 1980s and 1990s. Signing with Hobeck Books in January 2022, the first two books, *Dirty Little Secret* and *From Sorrow's Hold* were released in May and July 2022 to great acclaim, with this, the third in the series, *Cut and Shut* following on in January 2023.

In September 2022 he signed a new deal with Hobeck Books for the next three books in the series, with the fourth and fifth books out in 2023 and book six in 2024. He recently appeared at Bloody Scotland, the largest crime writing festival in Scotland, reading from his books, as part of the Crime In The Spotlight event.

In addition to writing the Louise Miller novels, Jonathan is working on several projects, including two new series, set in three very distinct and unique time periods: Lisbon, 1812; Yorkshire, 1972 and Derby, 2020.

He holds a first class BA (Hons) degree in Creative Writing and now writes full-time out of his home in Derbyshire, where he shares his writing office with his author wife, Lucy, and their three cats.

Jonathan is a member of the Crime Writers' Association.

Website: www.jpwritescrime.com
Newsletter: www.jpwritescrime.com/newsletter

'TIL IT BLEEDS

August, 1990

A deadly heatwave
Rising knife crime
A woman in distress

'Til It Bleeds is the fourth in the Louise Miller Series.

THE LOUISE MILLER SERIES

ONE NIGHT IN MANCHESTER

Jonathan Peace has also written a short story prequel to the Louise Miller novels which is free to subscribers to his website www.jpwritescrime.com.

WPC Louise Miller ha been pulled from her usual beat n the notorious Hulme estate into the city centre where a string of murders has led the police to believe a new serial killer is on the prowl.

As the night stretches on, what starts as a drunken dispute outside a nightclub turns into a nightmarish situation, one that will have lingering effects on Louise, and bring great change to her life.

DIRTY LITTLE SECRET

'A masterfully told thriller.' Graham Bartlett

DIRTY LITTLE SECRET

ONLY THE
DEAD STAY
SILENT

JONATHAN PEACE

March 1987

Ossett, West Yorkshire
A town of flower shows, Maypole parades and Sunday football
games. Behind all the closed doors and drawn curtains
live hidden truths and shameful lies.

A body is found
WDC Louise Miller's first case as detective in her hometown is
hampered by the sexism and misogyny of small-town
policing. Her four years on the force in Manchester have
prepared her for this. Along with ally WPC Elizabeth Hines, the
pair work the case together.

What truths lie hidden?
As their inquiries deepen, the towns secrets reveal even darker
truths that could lead to the identity of the killer. But when a
second girl goes missing, Louise realises that some secrets should
stay hidden.
Including hers.

FROM SORROW'S HOLD

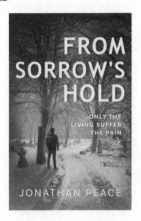

December, 1988

Christmas Beckons

What should be a time of excitement and joy is forever tainted when a teenager's body is found in the graveyard of Ossett's Holy Trinity Church.

A suspected suicide

As they respond to the devastating event, WDC's Louise Miller and Elizabeth Hines, together with psychologist Karla Hayes, each use their own experiences of suicide to help the wider community as it struggles to understand the terrible choice that was made.

Another missing teenager

Louise starts to believe there is something even more sinister behind the events...

HOBECK BOOKS – THE HOME OF GREAT STORIES

We hope you've enjoyed reading this novel by Jonathan Peace. To keep up to date on Jonathan's fiction writing please subscribe to his website: **www.jpwritescrime.com**.

Hobeck Books offers a number of short stories and novellas, free for subscribers in the compilation *Crime Bites*.

- *Echo Rock* by Robert Daws
- *Old Dogs, Old Tricks* by AB Morgan

- *The Silence of the Rabbit* by Wendy Turbin
- *Never Mind the Baubles: An Anthology of Twisted Winter Tales* by the Hobeck Team (including many of the Hobeck authors and Hobeck's two publishers)
- *The Clarice Cliff Vase* by Linda Huber
- *Here She Lies* by Kerena Swan
- *The Macnab Principle* by R.D. Nixon
- *Fatal Beginnings* by Brian Price
- *A Defining Moment* by Lin Le Versha
- *Saviour* by Jennie Ensor
- *You Can't Trust Anyone These Days* by Maureen Myant

Also please visit the Hobeck Books website for details of our other superb authors and their books, and if you would like to get in touch, we would love to hear from you.

Hobeck Books also presents a weekly podcast, the Hobcast, where founders Adrian Hobart and Rebecca Collins discuss all things book related, key issues from each week, including the ups and downs of running a creative business. Each episode includes an interview with one of the people who make Hobeck possible: the editors, the authors, the cover designers. These are the people who help Hobeck bring great stories to life. Without them, Hobeck wouldn't exist. The Hobcast can be listened to from all the usual platforms but it can also be found on the Hobeck website: **www.hobeck.net/hobcast**.